AUNT JULIA AND THE SCRIPTWRITER

Mario Vargas Llosa was born in 1936 in Peru. He has established an international reputation and is one of Latin America's most important and well known writers. His previous work includes *In Praise of the Stepmother*, *The War of the End of the World*, *The Real Life of Alejandro Mayta*, *Captain Pantoja and the Special Service*, *Who Killed Palomino Molero?*, *The Storyteller*, a study of Flaubert *The Perpetual Orgy* and *Making Waves*.

by the same author

THE TIME OF THE HERO
THE GREEN HOUSE
THE WAR OF THE END OF THE WORLD
THE REAL LIFE OF ALEJANDRO MAYTA
CAPTAIN PANTOJA AND THE SPECIAL SERVICE
WHO KILLED PALOMINO MOLERO?
THE CUBS AND OTHER STORIES
IN PRAISE OF THE STEPMOTHER
THE STORYTELLER
CONVERSATION IN THE CATHEDRAL
THE PERPETUAL ORGY
A WRITER'S REALITY
A FISH IN THE WATER
DEATH IN THE ANDES
MAKING WAVES
THE NOTEBOOKS OF DON RIGOBERTO

MARIO VARGAS LLOSA

Aunt Julia and the Scriptwriter

Translated by
Helen R Lane

faber and faber

First published in the USA in 1982 by
Farrar, Straus and Giroux, Inc., New York
First published in Great Britain in 1983
by Faber and Faber Limited
3 Queen Square London WC1N 3AU
This paperback edition first published in 1992
Reprinted with new cover 1998

Originally published in Spanish as
La tia Julia y el escribidor

Printed and bound in Great Britain by
Mackays of Chatham PLC, Chatham, Kent

A CIP record for this book
is available from the British Library

ISBN 0-571-16777-2

To Julia Urquidi Illanes
to whom this novel and I owe so much

I write. I write that I am writing. Mentally I see myself writing that I am writing and I can also see myself seeing that I am writing. I remember writing and also seeing myself writing. And I see myself remembering that I see myself writing and I remember seeing myself remembering that I was writing and I write seeing myself write that I remember having seen myself write that I saw myself writing that I was writing and that I was writing that I was writing that I was writing. I can also imagine myself writing that I had already written that I would imagine myself writing that I had written that I was imagining myself writing that I see myself writing that I am writing.

SALVADOR ELIZONDO / *The Graphographer*

One.

In those long-ago days,

I was very young and lived with my grandparents in a villa with white walls in the Calle Ocharán, in Miraflores. I was studying at the University of San Marcos, law, as I remember, resigned to earning myself a living later on by practicing a liberal profession, although deep down what I really wanted was to become a writer someday. I had a job with a pompous-sounding title, a modest salary, duties as a plagiarist, and flexible working hours: News Director of Radio Panamericana. It consisted of cutting out interesting news items that appeared in the daily papers and rewriting them slightly so that they could be read on the air during the newscasts. My editorial staff was limited to Pascual, a youngster who slicked down his hair with quantities of brilliantine and loved catastrophes. There were one-minute news bulletins every hour on the hour, except for those at noon and at 9 p.m., which were fifteen minutes long, but we were able to prepare several of the one-minute hourly ones ahead of time, so that I was often out of the office for long stretches at a time, drinking coffee in one of the cafés on La Colmena, going to class now and again, or dropping in at the offices of Radio Central, always much livelier than the ones where I worked.

The two radio stations belonged to the same owner and were next door to each other on the Calle Belén, just a few steps away from the Plaza San Martín. The two of them bore no resemblance whatsoever to each other. Or rather, like those sisters in tragic drama, one of whom has been born with every possible grace and the other with every possible defect, what was most noticeable was the contrast between them. Radio Panamericana occupied the third floor and the rooftop terrace of a brand-new building, and its personnel, its ambitions, and its programs all had about them a certain snobbish, cosmopolitan air, pretensions of being modern, youthful, aristocratic. Although its disc jockeys and m.c.'s weren't Argentines (as Pedro Camacho would have put it), they might just as well have been. The station broadcast lots of music, hours and hours of jazz and rock plus a bit of classical stuff now and again, it was always the first to put the latest hits from New York and Europe on the air in Lima, yet at the same time it did not disdain Latin American music so long as it had a modicum of sophistication; as for Peruvian selections, they were cautiously screened and allowed on the air only if they were waltzes. There were also programs calculated to appeal to intellectuals among the listening audience, such as "Portraits from the Past" or "Reports from Abroad," and even in frivolous mass-entertainment programs, such as "The Quiz Show" or "The Trampoline to Fame," there was a noticeable attempt to avoid excessive stupidity or vulgarity. One of the proofs of its cultural preoccupations was its News Section, consisting of Pascual and me, working out of a wooden shack on the rooftop terrace, from which we could see garbage dumps and the last remaining colonial windows let into the roofs of Lima. The one access to our hideaway was by way of an elevator whose doors had the disquieting habit of opening before it stopped.

Radio Central, by contrast, occupied cramped quarters in an old house with all sorts of odd corners and courtyards, and one needed only to listen to the relaxed, easygoing, slang-ridden voices of its announcers and m.c.'s to recognize its popular, plebeian, frankly parochial appeal. It broadcast very few news reports, and on its frequency Peruvian music, including popular Andean tunes, held sway, and often Indian singers from the music halls about town participated in these broadcasts, open to the public, which drew vast crowds to the doors of the studio many hours before they went on the air. It also flooded the airwaves with tropical music from Mexico and Argentina, and its programs were simple, unimaginative, attracting a wide audience: "Telephoned Requests," "Birthday

Serenades," "Gossip from the World of Entertainment," "Celluloid and Cinema." But its *plat de résistance*, served up repeatedly and in great abundance, and the feature that, according to all the surveys, attracted its vast listenership, was the serials it sent out over the airwaves.

They broadcast at least half a dozen a day, and I greatly enjoyed spying on the casts when they were in front of the microphone: hungry, shabbily dressed actors and actresses on the decline, whose tender, crystal-clear, young voices were terribly different from their old-looking faces, their bitter mouths, and their tired eyes. "The day television comes to Peru, the only way out for them will be suicide," Genaro Jr. predicted, pointing to them through the big glass panels of the studio, where, as though in an enormous aquarium, you could see them grouped around the microphone, scripts in hand, ready to begin Chapter 24 of "The Alvear Family." And what a disappointment it would have been for those housewives who grew misty-eyed on hearing the voice of Luciano Pando if they could have seen his hunchbacked body and his squinty eyes, and what a disappointment for those pensioners to whom the musical murmur of Josefina Sánchez brought back memories if they had known that she had a double chin, a mustache, ears that stuck way out, and varicose veins. But the arrival of television in Peru was still a long way off, and for the moment the modest survival of the fauna of the world of soap operas seemed assured.

I had always been curious to know who the writers were who churned out these serials that kept my grandmother entertained in the afternoon, these stories that assailed my eardrums at my Aunt Laura's, my Aunt Olga's, my Aunt Gaby's, or at my countless girl cousins' when I went to visit them (our family was a Biblical one, from the Miraflores district, and we were all very close). I suspected that the serials were imported, but it surprised me to learn that the Genaros did not buy them in Mexico or in Argentina but in Cuba. They were produced by CMQ, a sort of radio-television empire ruled over by Goar Mestre, a gentleman with silvery hair whom I had occasionally seen, on one of his visits to Lima, walking down the corridors of Radio Panamericana, solicitously escorted by the owners and the object of the reverent gaze of the entire staff. I had heard so much about the Cuban CMQ from announcers, m.c.'s, and technicians at Radio Panamericana—for whom it represented something mythical, what Hollywood represented in those days for filmmakers—that as Javier and I drank coffee in the Bransa we had often spent considerable time fantasizing about that army of polygraphic scriptwriters who, there in the distant Havana of palm trees, paradisiac beaches, gangsters, and tourists, in the air-conditioned offices of Goar Mestre's citadel, were doubtless spending eight hours a day at noiseless typewriters turning out that torrent of adulteries, suicides, passionate love affairs, unexpected encounters, inheritances, devotions, coincidences, and crimes which, from that Caribbean island, were spreading throughout Latin America, crystallized in the voices of the continent's Luciano Pandos and Josefina Sánchezes to fill with dreams the afternoons of the grandmothers, aunts, cousins, and pensioners of each country.

Genaro Jr. bought (or, rather, CMQ sold) the serials by weight and by telegram. It was he himself who had told me so one afternoon, when to his great stupefaction I had asked him if he, his brothers, or his father went over the scripts before putting them on the air. "Would *you* be capable of reading seventy kilos of paper?" he replied, looking at me with that benign condescension due the intellectual he considered me to be after he'd seen a short story of mine in the Sunday edition of *El Comercio*. "Just stop and think how much time it would take. A month, two months? Who can spend a couple of months *reading* the script of a radio serial? We just leave it to chance, and thus far, happily, the Lord of Miracles has protected us." In the best of cases, Genaro Jr. was able to find out beforehand, through ad agencies or colleagues and friends, how many countries had bought the soap operas CMQ was offering him and how many listeners had tuned in according to the surveys; in the worst of cases, he made up his mind by taking a look at the titles or simply by tossing a coin. The serials were sold by weight because that was a less tricky formula than going by the number of pages or words, since that was the only thing one could verify precisely. "Obviously, if there's not enough time to read them, there's even less time to count all those words," Javier said. He was intrigued by the idea of a novel weighing seventy-eight kilos thirty grams, the price of which, like that of beef cattle, butter, and eggs, would be determined by a scale.

But this system created problems for the Genaros. The texts

arrived full of Cuban expressions, which, a few short minutes before each broadcast, Luciano and Josefina and their colleagues translated into Peruvian themselves, as best they could (that is to say, very badly). Moreover, on the trip from Havana to Lima, in the holds of boats or the cargo bays of planes, or at customs, the typed reams of paper were sometimes damaged, entire chapters got lost, dampness made them illegible, the pages got all mixed up, or rats in the storeroom of Radio Central devoured them. Inasmuch as such disasters were noticed only at the very last moment, as Genaro Sr. was handing around the scripts, crises frequently arose. They were resolved by skipping over the lost chapter without the slightest scruple, or, in really serious cases, by having the character played by Luciano Pando or Josefina Sánchez get sick for a day, so that in the following twenty-four hours the grams or kilos that were missing could be patched together, rescued, or eliminated without excessive trauma. And since, finally, the prices that CMQ charged were high, Genaro Jr. was naturally overjoyed when he learned of the existence and prodigious gifts of Pedro Camacho.

I remember very well the day he spoke to me of this genius of the airwaves, because that very day, at lunchtime, I saw Aunt Julia for the first time. She was my Uncle Lucho's sister-in-law and had arrived from Bolivia the night before. She had just been divorced, and had come to rest and recover from the breakup of her marriage. "She's really come to look for another husband," Aunt Hortensia, the biggest backbiter of all my relatives, had said straight out at a family gathering. I ate lunch every Thursday with my Uncle Lucho and Aunt Olga, and when I arrived that noon I found the whole family still in their pajamas, eating mussels in hot sauce and drinking ice-cold beer to get over a hangover. They'd stayed up till dawn gossiping with Aunt Julia, and finished off an entire bottle of whiskey between the three of them. They all had headaches, Uncle Lucho was complaining that they'd have turned his office upside down by now, my Aunt Olga was saying that it was shameful to stay up so late except on a Saturday night, and their recently arrived guest, in a bathrobe and barefoot and with curlers in her hair, was unpacking a suitcase. It didn't bother her at all to be seen in that getup in which nobody would mistake her for a beauty queen.

"So you're Dorita's son," she said to me, planting a kiss on my cheek. "You've just gotten out of high school, haven't you?"

I hated her instantly. My slight run-ins with the family in those days were all due to the fact that everybody insisted on treating me as though I were still a child rather than a full-grown man of eighteen. Nothing irritated me as much as being called "Marito"; I had the impression that this diminutive automatically put me back in short pants.

"He's already in his first year as a law student at the university and is working as a journalist," my Uncle Lucho explained to her, handing me a glass of beer.

"Well, well. To tell you the truth, you look like a babe in arms, Marito," Aunt Julia said, giving me the *coup de grâce*.

During lunch, with that air of affectionate condescension that adults assume when addressing idiots and children, she asked me if I had a sweetheart, if I went to parties, what sport I went in for, and then, with a spitefulness that might have been either intentional or unintentional but in any case cut me to the quick, advised me to let my mustache grow *as soon as I had one*. They went well with dark hair and would help me make out with girls.

"He's not thinking about skirts or about sprees," my Uncle Lucho explained to her. "He's an intellectual. He's had a short story published in the Sunday edition of *El Comercio*."

"We'll have to watch out that Dorita's boy doesn't turn out to be a queer, in that case." Aunt Julia laughed, and I suddenly felt a wave of fellow feeling for her ex-husband. But I smiled and let her have her fun. During the rest of the lunch, she kept telling one dreadful Bolivian joke after the other and teasing me. As I was leaving, it seemed as though she wanted to make it up to me for all her nasty little digs, because she told me in a friendly tone of voice that we ought to go to the movies together some night, that she adored films.

I got back to Radio Panamericana just in time to keep Pascual from devoting the entire three o'clock bulletin to the news of a pitched battle between gravediggers and lepers in the exotic streets of Rawalpindi, a filler that had appeared in *Ultima Hora*. After I'd edited the four and five o'clock bulletins as well, I went out to have a coffee. At the door of Radio Central I ran into Genaro Jr, who was all excited. He dragged me by the arm to the Bransa. "I've got something fantastic to tell you." He'd been in La Paz for several days on business, and while there he'd seen in action that man of many parts: Pedro Camacho.

"He's not a man—he's an industry!" he corrected himself in a voice filled with amazement. "He writes all the stage plays put on in Bolivia and acts in all of them. And he also writes all the radio serials, directs them, and plays the male lead in every one of them."

But even more than his tremendous output and his versatility, it had been his popularity that had impressed Genaro Jr. In order to see him in one of his plays at the Teatro Saavedra in La Paz, Genaro had had to buy scalpers' tickets at double their original price.

"Like at bullfights, can you imagine?" he marveled. "Who is there who's ever filled an entire theater in Lima?"

He told me he'd seen, two days in a row, a huge crowd of young girls, grown women, and old ladies milling about outside the doors of Radio Illimani, waiting for their idol to come out so they could get his autograph. Moreover, the McCann Erickson office in La Paz had assured him that Pedro Camacho's radio serials attracted more listeners than any other programs broadcast over the Bolivian airwaves. Genaro Jr. was what in those days people were beginning to call a "dynamic" impresario: more interested in making profits than in honors, he was neither a member of the Club Nacional nor eager to be one, made friends with anyone and everyone, and had so much drive and energy that it was exhausting just to be around him. A man capable of lightning-quick decisions, once he'd visited Radio Illimani he immediately persuaded Pedro Camacho to come to Peru and work exclusively for Radio Central.

"It wasn't hard—he was earning starvation wages there," he explained to me. "He'll be in charge of all the serials and I'll be able to tell all those sharks from CMQ to go to hell."

I did my best to shatter his illusions. I told him that it was quite obvious that Peruvians had an antipathy toward Bolivians and that Pedro Camacho would get along very badly with all the people at Radio Central. His Bolivian accent would grate on the ears of listeners, and since he didn't know the first thing about Peru he'd make one dreadful mistake after another. But Genaro Jr. merely smiled and turned a deaf ear to all my pessimistic prophecies. Even though he'd never set foot in the country, Pedro Camacho had spoken to him of the heart and soul of the people of Lima with as much feeling and understanding as though he'd been born in Bajo el Puente, and his accent was impeccable, without a single jarring *s* or *r*; in a word, as soft and smooth as velvet.

"Between Luciano Pando and the other actors, that poor foreigner's going to be eaten up alive," Javier opined. "Or else the beauteous Josefina Sánchez will rape him."

We were in the shack talking together as I retyped news items from *El Comercio* and *La Prensa,* changing adjectives and adverbs as I went, for the Panamericana newscast at twelve. Javier was my best friend and we saw each other every day, even if only for a few minutes, to prove to each other that we were still alive and kicking. He was a creature given to short-lived, contradictory, but invariably sincere enthusiasms. He had been the star of the Department of Literature at Catholic University, where there had never before been such a hardworking student, or a more clear-sighted reader of poetry, or a more discerning interpreter of difficult texts. Everyone took it as a foregone conclusion that he would earn his degree by writing a brilliant thesis, that he would become a brilliant professor or an equally brilliant poet or critic. But one fine day, without offering any sort of explanation, he had disappointed everyone by abandoning the thesis he was working on, giving up literature and the Catholic University, and enrolling at San Marcos as a student in the Department of Economics. When someone ventured to ask him the reason for this desertion, he confessed (or remarked jokingly) that the thesis he'd been working on had opened his eyes. It was to have been entitled "Paroemias in the Works of Ricardo Palma." He had had to read Palma's *Peruvian Traditions* with a magnifying glass, searching for proverbs, and since he was a conscientious and rigorous researcher, he had managed to fill an entire file drawer with erudite index cards. And then one morning he had burned the whole drawerful of index cards in a vacant lot—he and I performed an Apache dance around the philological flames—and decided that he hated literature and that even economics was preferable to that. Javier was now a trainee at the Central Reserve Bank and could always find an excuse for dropping by Radio Panamericana every morning. One last remaining trace of his paroemiological nightmare was his habit of inflicting proverbs on me that had neither rhyme nor reason.

I was surprised to discover that, despite the fact that she was Bolivian and lived in La Paz, Aunt Julia had never heard of Pedro Camacho. But she explained that she had never listened to soap operas and hadn't set foot inside a theater since she'd interpreted the role of Twilight in the Dance of the Hours, in her last year at a school run by Irish nuns ("And don't you dare ask me how many years ago that was, Marito"). This was while we were walking from Uncle Lucho's house, at the end of the Avenida Armendáriz, to the Cine Barranco. It was she who had invited me, in the sneakiest way imaginable, at noon that day.

It was the Thursday following her arrival, and even though the prospect of being the butt of her Bolivian jokes didn't appeal to me, I didn't want to miss my weekly lunch at Uncle Lucho's and Aunt Olga's. I had hoped she wouldn't be there, since the night before—on Wednesday nights the whole family went to visit Aunt Gaby—I had heard Aunt Hortensia announce, in the tone of voice of one who is privy to the secrets of the gods: "During her first week in Lima she's gone out four times—with four different suitors, one of whom is married. There are no lengths that divorcée won't go to!"

When I arrived at Uncle Lucho's, after the noon Panamericana newscast, I found her there—with one of her suitors. I savored the sweet pleasure of vengeance on entering the living room and finding sitting next to her, gazing upon her with the eyes of a conquistador, looking absolutely ridiculous in his hopelessly old-fashioned suit, his bow tie, and his carnation boutonniere, an elderly relative of mine, Uncle Pancracio, my grandmother's first cousin. He'd been a widower for ages, he walked with his feet spread wide apart, like the hands of a clock at ten past ten, and in the family his visits set tongues to wagging maliciously because he brazenly pinched the maidservants in full view of everybody. He dyed his hair, wore a pocket watch with a silver chain, and could be seen daily at 6 p.m. hanging around the Jirón de la Unión, flirting with office girls. As I leaned over to kiss her, I whispered in the Bolivian divorcée's ear, my voice dripping with irony: "What a fine conquest, Julita." She winked an eye and nodded slyly.

During lunch, Uncle Pancracio, after holding forth on Peruvian popular music, at which he was an expert—at family celebrations he always offered a solo on the cajón, a traditional "musical instrument" that in reality was simply a wooden box or drawer on which the player drummed with his fingers or the palm of his hand—turned to her, and, licking his chops like a cat, said: "By the way, on Thursday evenings the Felipe Pinglo Association meets at the Victoria, the heart of Peruvianism. Would you like to hear a little genuine indigenous music?" Without hesitating an instant, and with an air of heartfelt regret that added insult to injury, Aunt Julia answered, pointing to me. "What a pity—Mario's already invited me to the movies." "Well then, I yield to youth," Uncle Pancracio replied, like a good sport. Later, after he'd left, I thought I was saved when Aunt Olga said to Aunt Julia: "I take it that business about the movies was just to get rid of the old lecher?" But Julia shot back immediately: "Not at all, Olga, I'm dying to see the one that's showing at the Barranco—the censors have rated it 'not suitable for minors.' " She turned to me (I was listening intently, since my fate for that evening was at stake), and to set my mind at ease added this exquisite flower: "Don't worry about the money, Marito—it's my treat."

And there we were, walking down the dark Quebrada de Armendáriz, then along the wide Avenida Grau, heading for a film that, to top everything off, was Mexican and called *Mother and Mistress*.

"The worst thing about being a divorcée isn't that all men think they're obliged to proposition you," Aunt Julia informed me. "Rather, it's the fact that because you're a divorcée they think there's no need to be romantic. They don't flirt with you, they don't whisper sweet nothings in your ear. They just come straight out with what it is they want from you, right off the bat, in the most vulgar way imaginable. That really puts me off. That's why I'd rather go to the movies with you than go out dancing with a man."

"Thanks a whole lot—I appreciate the compliment," I said.

"They're so stupid they think that every divorcée's a streetwalker," she went on, not even noticing the irony in my voice. "And what's more, all they think about is doing things with you. Even though that's not the best part—the best part's falling in love with each other, don't you think so?"

I explained to her that love didn't exist, that it was the invention of an Italian named Petrarch and the Provençal troubadours. That what people thought was a crystal-clear outpouring of emotion, a pure effusion of sentiment, was merely the instinctive desire of cats in heat hidden beneath the poetic words and myths of literature. I didn't really believe a word of what I was saying and was simply trying to impress her. My erotico-biological theory, however, left Aunt Julia quite skeptical: did I honestly believe such nonsense?

"I'm against marriage," I told her, in the most solemnly pedantic tone of voice I could muster. "I'm a believer in what's called free love, although if we were honest, we ought, quite simply, to call it free copulation."

"Does copulation mean doing things?" She laughed. But immediately a sad, disabused expression crossed her face. "In my day, boys composed acrostics, sent girls flowers, took weeks to work up enough nerve to give them a kiss. What an obscene thing love has become among kids today, Marito."

We had a slight argument at the box office as to which of us was going to pay for the tickets, and then, after sitting through an hour and a half of Dolores del Río moaning, embracing, taking her pleasure, weeping, running through the forest with her hair streaming in the wind, we headed back to Uncle Lucho's, on foot this time too, in a drizzling rain that left our hair and our clothes soaking wet. As we walked along, we talked again of Pedro Camacho. Was she absolutely certain she'd never heard of him? Because, according to Genaro Jr., he was a celebrity in Bolivia. No, she'd never even heard his name mentioned. The thought came to me that they'd put one over on Genaro, or that perhaps the supposed one-man "industry" in the world of radio and theater in Bolivia was a publicity gimmick he'd dreamed up to drum up interest in a Peruvian pen pusher he'd just hired. Three days later I met Pedro Camacho in the flesh.

I'd just had a set-to with Genaro Sr., because Pascual, with his usual irrepressible penchant for terrible catastrophes, had devoted the entire eleven o'clock bulletin to an earthquake in Isfahan.

What irritated Genaro Sr. was not so much the fact that Pascual had completely disregarded other news items to give himself time to describe, with a wealth of details, how the Persians who survived the disastrous cave-ins had been attacked by snakes that had surfaced, hissing in fury, once their subterranean refuges had been destroyed, but rather the fact that this earthquake had occurred a week previously. I had to agree that Genaro Sr. had good reason for being upset, and I let off steam by telling Pascual he was completely irresponsible. Where in the world had he come across such stale news? In an Argentine magazine. And why had he put out such an idiotic bulletin? Because there wasn't any really important hot news item to report, and this one had at least a certain entertainment value. When I explained to him that we weren't being paid to entertain the radio listeners but to give them a summary of the news of the day, Pascual, eager to make his peace with me, nodded in agreement while at the same time confronting me with his irrefutable argument: "The thing is, Don Mario, the two of us have entirely different conceptions of what news is." I was about to answer that if every time I turned my back he persisted in putting into practice his sensationalist conception of news reporting, the two of us would very soon be thrown out into the street, when a most unusual silhouette appeared in the doorway of the shack: a minuscule figure, on the very borderline between a man extremely short in stature and a dwarf, with a huge nose and unusually bright eyes with a disturbing, downright abnormal gleam in them. He was dressed in a black suit that was quite obviously old and threadbare, and a shirt and bow tie with visible stains, but at the same time he gave the impression of being extremely neat, fastidious, and proper with regard to his standard of dress, like those gentlemen in old photographs who appear to be imprisoned in their stiff frock coats and tight-fitting silk hats. He might have been anywhere between thirty and fifty, with oily black shoulder-length hair. His bearing, his movements, his expression appeared to be the absolute contrary of the natural and spontaneous, immediately mindful of an articulated doll, of puppet strings. He bowed to us politely and, with a solemnity as out of the ordinary as his person, introduced himself by saying: "I've come to steal a typewriter from you, gentlemen. I would be most grateful for your help. Which of those two machines is the best?"

His index finger pointed in turn to my typewriter and Pascual's. Despite my having become quite accustomed to the contrasts between voices and outward appearances thanks to my habit of dropping by Radio Central between Panamericana bulletins, I was amazed to hear such a firm and melodious voice, such perfect diction, come pouring out of such a tiny, unimposing figure. I had the impression that in that voice not only each letter marched past in perfect order, without a single one of them being mutilated, but also the particles and atoms of each one, the very sounds of sound. Without even noticing the surprise that his appearance, his audacity, and his voice aroused in us, he had impatiently begun to examine both typewriters carefully, to sniff them over, so to speak. He finally chose my enormous ancient Remington, a big hulk of a hearse invulnerable to the ravages of time.

Pascual was the first to react. "Are you a thief or what?" he asked him point-blank, and I realized that he was paying me back for the earthquake in Isfahan. "Do you think you're going to get away with carting off the typewriters of the News Department that way?"

"Art is more important than your News Department, you sprite," the character thundered, looking at him in lofty disdain, as though at a mere insect he had just crushed underfoot, and went on with the job at hand. As Pascual watched him, openmouthed with amazement (and doubtless trying, as I was, to figure out what he meant by "sprite"), the visitor attempted to carry off the Remington. He managed to lift the monster off the desk by dint of a superhuman effort that made the veins in his neck swell and very nearly caused his eyes to pop out of their sockets. His face turned a deeper and deeper purple and beads of sweat broke out on his forehead, but he went right on. Clenching his teeth, staggering, he managed to take a few steps in the direction of the door, but then he had to give up: in one more second his load would have come crashing to the floor, with him tumbling after. He set the Remington down on Pascual's desk and stood there panting, completely indifferent to the smiles on our two faces that this spectacle had provoked and apparently not even noticing that Pascual had tapped his forehead with his finger several times to indicate to me that we were dealing with a madman. But the moment he'd caught his breath, he reprimanded us in a stern voice: "Don't be lazy, sirs; a little human solidarity. Give me a hand."

I told him I was very sorry but that if he wanted to carry off the Remington he would first have to pass over Pascual's dead body and then, if it came to that, over mine. The little man straightened his tie, a wee bit out of place after his herculean effort. To my astonishment, with an annoyed expression on his face and showing every sign of possessing no sense of humor whatsoever, he nodded gravely and replied: "When challenged, no gentleman ever refuses to fight a duel. The place and the hour, if you please, sirs."

The providential appearance of Genaro Jr. in the shack frustrated what threatened to become formal arrangements for a duel. He came in just as the stubborn little man, turning purple, was attempting once again to lift the Remington.

"Wait a minute, Pedro, I'll help you," he said, grabbing the typewriter away from him as though it were a box of matches. Realizing then, on seeing the expression on my face and Pedro's, that he owed us some sort of explanation, he said, with a cheery, conciliatory smile: "There's no reason to look so down in the mouth—nobody's died. My father will get you another typewriter in just a few days."

"We're fifth wheels," I protested, pro forma. "You've stuck us up here in this filthy shack, you've already taken a desk away from me to give to the accountant, and now you're carrying off my Remington. And you didn't even tell me beforehand."

"We thought this gentleman was a thief," Pascual said, backing me up. "He burst in here heaping insults on us and acting as though he owned the place."

"Colleagues shouldn't quarrel," Genaro Jr. replied, playing Solomon. He'd hoisted the Remington to his shoulder and I noticed that the little man came exactly up to his lapels. "Didn't my father come up to introduce you to each other? If not, I'll do the honors, and you can stop fighting."

Immediately, with a rapid, automatic movement, the little man stretched out one of his little arms, took a couple of steps toward me, offered me a tiny child's hand, and bowing politely once again, introduced himself to me in his exquisite tenor voice: "Pedro Camacho. A Bolivian and an artist: a friend."

He repeated the gesture, the bow, and the phrase with Pascual, who was quite obviously experiencing a moment of utter confusion, unable to decide whether the little man was pulling our leg or always went through this routine. After ceremoniously shaking hands with us, Pedro Camacho turned to the entire staff of the News Department, and standing in the center of the shack in the shadow of Genaro Jr., who looked like a giant behind him and was watching him with a very serious expression on his face, raised his upper lip, screwed his face up, and bared yellowed teeth in the caricature or the specter of a smile. He waited a few seconds before favoring us with these musical words, accompanied by the gesture of a stage magician taking leave of his audience: "I don't hold it against you—I'm quite accustomed to being misunderstood. Till we meet again, gentlemen!"

He disappeared through the door of the shack, hurriedly hopping and skipping along like an elf to catch up with the dynamic impresario heading for the elevator in great long strides with the Remington on his shoulder.

Two.

On one of those sunny

spring mornings in Lima when the geraniums are an even brighter red, the roses more fragrant, and the bougainvillaeas curlier as they awaken, a famous physician of the city, Dr. Alberto de Quinteros—broad forehead, aquiline nose, penetrating gaze, the very soul of rectitude and goodness—opened his eyes in his vast mansion in San Isidro and stretched his limbs. Through the curtains he could see the sun shedding its golden light on the lawn of the carefully tended grounds enclosed by hedges of evergreen shrubs, the bright blue sky, the cheery flowers, and felt that sense of well-being that comes from eight hours of restorative sleep and a clear conscience.

It was Saturday and—providing there were not last-minute complications in the case of the woman with the triplets—he would not be obliged to go to the clinic and could devote the morning to working out at the gym and taking a sauna before Elianita's wedding. His wife and daughter were in Europe, cultivating their minds and replenishing their wardrobes, and would not be back for a month. Any other man with his considerable fortune and his looks—his hair that had turned to silver at the temples and his distinguished bearing, along with his elegant manners, awakened a gleam of desire even in the eyes of incorruptible married women—might have taken advantage of his temporary bachelorhood to have himself a little fun. But Alberto de Quinteros was a man not unduly attracted to gambling, skirt chasing, or drinking, and among his friends—who were legion—it was commonly said that "his vices are science, his family, and the gymnasium."

He ordered his breakfast sent up, and as it was being prepared he phoned the clinic. The doctor on duty informed him that the woman with the triplets had spent a quiet night and that the hemorrhaging of the woman he had operated on to remove a tumor had stopped. He gave instructions, left word that if an emergency came up he could be reached at the Remigius Gymnasium, or, if it were lunchtime, at his brother Roberto's, and said he'd drop by the clinic in any case in the late afternoon. By the time the butler brought him his papaya juice, his black coffee, and his toast with honey, Alberto de Quinteros had shaved and put on a pair of gray corduroy pants, heelless moccasins, and a green turtleneck sweater. As he ate his breakfast, he idly glanced through the usual reports of catastrophes and the gossip of the day as aired in the morning newspapers, then got out his gym bag and left the house. He stopped in the garden for a few seconds to pet Puck, the badly spoiled fox terrier, who bade him goodbye with affectionate yaps.

The Remigius Gymnasium was only a few blocks away, in the Calle Miguel Dasso, and Dr. Quinteros liked to go there on foot. He would walk along slowly, return his neighbors' greetings, peek into their gardens, which at this hour were freshly watered and the hedges neatly trimmed, and usually he dropped in at the Castro Soto Bookstore for a few minutes to pick up a couple of best sellers. Although it was early still, the inevitable gang of youngsters with open-necked shirts and unkempt hair were already outside the Davory, sitting on their motorcycles or on the bumpers of their sports cars, eating ice-cream bars, joking with each other, and planning that night's party. They greeted him respectfully, but he'd gone only a few steps past them when one dared give him one of those bits of advice that were his cross to bear at the gymnasium too, hoary jokes about his age and his profession, that he put up with day after day, patiently and good-naturedly: "Don't wear yourself out, Doctor, think of your grandchildren." He scarcely heard it because he was imagining how pretty Elianita would look in her wedding dress designed for her at Christian Dior's in Paris.

There weren't many people at the gym that morning. Just Coco, the instructor, and two weight-lifting addicts, Blacky Humilla and Polly Sarmiento, three mountains of muscles the equivalent of those of ten ordinary men. They must have arrived only a short time before, as they were still warming up.

"Well, here comes the stork," Coco said, shaking hands.

"Still up and around, after all these centuries?" Blacky Humilla called out.

Polly Sarmiento limited himself to clacking his tongue and raising two fingers, his usual greeting that he'd imported from Texas. Dr. Quinteros liked the air of breezy familiarity that his gym companions adopted toward him, as though seeing each other naked and sweating together had created an egalitarian fraternity among them, in which differences in age and social position had disappeared. He answered them by saying that if they had need of his services he was at their disposal, that at the first signs of dizziness or morning sickness they should come immediately to his office, where the rubber glove for probing their privates was ready and waiting.

"Go change clothes and come do a few warm-ups," Coco said to him, going back to jumping in place.

"If you feel a heart attack coming on, you may kick off, but so what?" Polly said encouragingly, picking up Coco's rhythm.

"The surfer's in there," he heard Blacky Humilla say as he entered the dressing room.

And indeed his nephew Richard was there, in a blue sweat suit, putting on his gym shoes. He was doing so slowly and reluctantly, as though his hands had suddenly gone as limp as a rag doll's, and he had a bitter, vacant look on his face. He sat there staring past his uncle with a completely blank expression in his blue eyes and such total indifference to his presence that Dr. Quinteros wondered whether he'd turned invisible all of a sudden.

"It's only lovers who get lost in thought like that," he said to his nephew, walking over and ruffling his hair. "Come back down to earth, my boy."

"Sorry, Uncle," Richard replied, coming to with a start and blushing furiously, as though he'd been doing something he shouldn't and been caught in the act. "I was thinking."

"Wicked thoughts, no doubt." Dr. Quinteros laughed as he opened his gym bag, chose a locker, and began to get undressed. "Things must be in an uproar at your house. Is Elianita very nervous?"

Richard glared at him with what seemed like a sudden gleam of hatred in his eyes and the doctor wondered what in the world had gotten into this youngster. But his nephew, making a visible effort to appear to be his usual self, smiled faintly. "Yes, everything's in an uproar. That's why I came down here to the gym to burn off a little fat till it's time."

The doctor thought Richard was going to add "to mount the gallows." His voice was heavy with melancholy, and his features, the clumsiness with which he was tying his shoelaces, the jerky movements of his body, betrayed how troubled, upset, and anxious he was. He was unable to keep his eyes still: he kept opening them, closing them, staring into space, looking away, staring at the same imaginary point again, looking away once more, as though searching for something impossible to find. He was a strikingly handsome boy, a young god whose body had been burnished by the elements—he went surfing even in the dead of winter and also excelled at basketball, tennis, swimming, and soccer—sports that had given him one of those physiques that Blacky Humilla claimed were "every queer's mad dream": not an ounce of fat, a smooth, muscular torso descending in a V to a wasp waist, and long, strong, supple legs that would have made the best boxer green with envy. Alberto de Quinteros had often heard his daughter Charo and her girlfriends compare Richard with Charlton Heston and conclude that Richard was even groovier-looking, that he beat Charlton all hollow. He was in his first year at the School of Architecture, and according to Roberto and Margarita, his parents, he'd always been a model child: studious, obedient, good to them and to his sister, honest, likable. Elianita and Richard were the doctor's favorite niece and nephew, and so, as he put on his jockstrap, his sweat suit, his gym shoes—Richard was standing over by the showers waiting for him, tapping his foot on the tile floor—Dr. Alberto de Quinteros was sad to see him looking so troubled.

"Problems on your mind, my boy?" he asked in a deliberately offhand way and with a kindly smile. "Anything I can do to help?"

"No, not a problem in the world, whatever gave you that idea?" Richard hastened to reply, blushing furiously once again. "I feel great and can't wait to warm up."

"Did they deliver my wedding present to your sister?" the doctor suddenly remembered to ask. "They promised me at the Casa Murguía that it would arrive yesterday."

"A super bracelet"—Richard had begun jumping up and down on the white tiles of the locker-room floor. "Sis was delighted with it."

"It's your aunt who usually takes care of things like that, but since she's still running around Europe, I had to choose it myself." A tender look came into Dr. Quinteros's eyes. "Elianita in her wedding dress—what a lovely sight that's going to be."

Because the daughter of his brother Roberto was as perfect a specimen of young womanhood as Richard was of young manhood: one of those beauties who do honor to the species and who make figures of speech comparing teeth to pearls, eyes to stars, hair to flax, and complexions to peaches and cream sound far too pedestrian. Slender, with dark hair and very white skin, her every movement graceful, even her manner of breathing, she had a tiny face with classic lineaments, and features that appeared to have been designed by an Oriental miniaturist. A year younger than Richard, she had just finished secondary school; her one defect was timidity—so excessive that the organizers of the Miss Peru contest, to their despair, had been unable to persuade her to enter—and everyone, including Dr. Quinteros, was at a loss to explain why she was getting married so soon, and above all why she was marrying Red Antúnez. There was no denying that young Antúnez had certain things going for him—his good heart and his good nature, a degree in business administration from the University of Chicago, the fertilizer company he would one day inherit, several cups he'd won bicycle racing—but among the innumerable boys of Miraflores and San Isidro who'd courted Elianita and who would have committed murder or robbed a bank to marry her, Red was beyond a doubt the least attractive and (Dr. Quinteros was ashamed of allowing himself to harbor such an opinion regarding someone who within a few hours would become his nephew by marriage) the dullest and most dim-witted.

"You take longer to change clothes than my mom, Uncle Alberto," Richard complained between leaps.

When they went into the exercise room, Coco, for whom pedagogy was not a way of earning a living but a vocation, was instructing Blacky Humilla, pointing to his stomach and preaching this axiom of philosophy to him: "When you eat, when you work, when you're at the movies, when you're humping your wife, when you're having a drink, at every moment in your life, and, if possible, even in your coffin: suck in your gut!"

"Ten minutes of warm-ups to make your carcass happy, Methuselah," the instructor ordered Dr. Quinteros.

As he jumped rope next to Richard and felt a pleasant warmth creep over his whole body, the thought came to him that, when all was said and done, it really wasn't so terrible to be fifty years old if a person was in as good shape as he was. Among his friends who were his age, was there a single one with a belly as smooth as his, such supple muscles? Without searching any farther, his brother Roberto, what with his spare tire and his potbelly and his premature hunchback, looked ten years older than he did, despite the fact that he was three years younger. Poor Roberto, he must be sad at seeing Elianita, the apple of his eye, getting married. Because, of course, he'd be losing her in a way. The doctor's daughter, Charo, would be getting married almost any day now—her fiancé, Tato Soldevilla, would soon be getting his degree in engineering—and then he, too, would feel sad and older. Dr. Quinteros went on jumping rope without getting tangled up in it or missing a step, with the agility that comes with practice, changing feet and crossing and uncrossing his hands like a consummate gymnast. He saw in the mirror, however, that his nephew was jumping too fast and recklessly tripping all over himself. His teeth were clenched, his forehead was gleaming with sweat, and he was keeping his eyes closed as though to concentrate better. Was he perhaps having woman trouble?

"That's enough rope jumping, you two lazybones." Even though he was lifting weights with Polly and Blacky, Coco had had his eye on them and was keeping track of the time. "Three sets of sit-ups. On your butts, you fossils."

Abdominals were Dr. Quinteros's strong point. He did them very fast, with his hands behind the nape of his neck, with the board raised to the second position, keeping his back raised off the floor and almost touching his knees with his forehead. Between each series of thirty he took a one-minute rest, lying stretched out flat, breathing deeply. When he'd finished the ninety, he sat down and noted, to his satisfaction, that he'd beaten Richard. After this workout, he was sweating from head to foot and could feel his heart pounding.

"I just can't understand why Elianita's marrying Red Antúnez," he suddenly heard himself say. "What does she see in him?"

It was the wrong thing to say and he immediately regretted having done so, but Richard didn't seem to be at all taken aback. Panting—he'd just finished his abdominals—he replied with a feeble joke: "They say love is blind, Uncle Alberto."

"He's a fine boy and I'm sure he'll make her very happy," Dr. Quinteros went on, feeling a bit disconcerted and trying to make up for having been so outspoken. "What I meant was that among your sister's admirers were the best matches in Lima. And what did she do but send them all packing and end up saying yes to Red Antúnez, who's a good kid, but such an, well, er, let's face it . . ."

"Such an ass, is that what you're trying to say?" Richard broke in helpfully.

"Well, I wouldn't have put it that crudely," Dr. Quinteros said, inhaling and exhaling and flinging his arms in and out. But, to tell the truth, he does seem a bit dim-witted. He'd be perfect for anyone else, but he just can't hold a candle to a girl as outstanding as Elianita. His own outspokenness made him feel uncomfortable. "Listen, you mustn't take what I said the wrong way."

"Don't worry, Uncle Alberto." Richard smiled. "Red's a good egg and if the kid's picked him she knows what she's doing."

"Three sets of side bends, you cripples!" Coco roared, with eighty kilos above his head and puffed out like a toad. "Sucking in your belly—not sticking it out!"

Dr. Quinteros thought that, with the gymnastics, Richard would forget his problems, but as he did his side bends, he saw his nephew working out with renewed fury, his face again set in an anxious, irritated expression. He remembered that in the Quinteros family there were a great many neurotics and thought that perhaps

Roberto's eldest son had inherited the tendency and was destined to carry on the tradition among the younger generation, and then he was distracted by the thought that it might have been more prudent after all to have dropped by the clinic before coming to the gym so as to have a look at the woman with the triplets and the one he'd operated on for the tumor. Then he stopped thinking altogether because the physical effort absorbed him totally, and as he raised and lowered his legs ("Leg rises, fifty times!"), flexed his trunk ("Trunk twist with bar, three sets, till your lungs burst!"), working his back, his torso, his forearms, his neck, obeying Coco's orders ("Harder, great-granddaddy! Faster, corpse!"), he was simply a pair of lungs inhaling and exhaling, skin dripping with sweat, muscles straining, tiring, aching. When Coco yelled out: "Three sets of fifteen pullovers with dumbbells!" he'd reached his limit. Out of pride, he tried nonetheless to do at least one set with twelve kilos, but he couldn't. He was exhausted. The weight slipped out of his hands on the third try and he had to put up with the jokes of the weight lifters ("Mummies to the grave and storks to the zoo!" "Call the funeral home!" "Requiescat in pace, amen!") and watch with mute envy as Richard—still in a hurry, still furious—completed his routine with no difficulty. Discipline, perseverance, balanced diets, regular habits aren't enough, Dr. Quinteros thought. Up to a certain limit they compensated for the differences; once past that limit, age created insuperable distances, unbreachable walls. Later, sitting naked in the sauna, blinded by the sweat dripping through his eyelashes, he mournfully repeated a phrase he'd read in a book: "Youth, whose memory brings despair!" As he was leaving, he saw that Richard had joined the weight lifters and was working out with them. Coco made a mocking gesture in Richard's direction and said: "This handsome lad has decided to commit suicide, Doctor."

Richard didn't even smile. He was holding the weights over his head and the expression on his beet-red face, dripping with sweat, the veins standing out, betrayed an exasperation that he appeared to be on the point of taking out on them. The idea flashed through the doctor's mind that his nephew was about to bash in the heads of all four of them with the weights he was holding in his hands. He said goodbye to the others and murmured to Richard: "I'll see you at the church in a little while."

Once he'd returned home and called the clinic, he was relieved to learn that the mother of the triplets wanted to play bridge with some friends in her room and that the woman who'd had the tumor removed had asked if she could eat some won ton in tamarind sauce today. He authorized the bridge game and the won ton, and with his mind completely at ease now, he changed into a dark blue suit, a white silk shirt, and a silver-gray tie that he fastened down with a pearl stickpin. As he was putting scent on his handkerchief, a letter from his wife arrived, with a P.S. from Charito. They had mailed it from Venice, city number 14 on the tour, and had written: "By the time you receive this letter, we'll have done at least seven more cities, all gorgeous." They were happy and Charito was very taken with Italian men: ". . . as handsome as movie stars, Papa, and you can't imagine what big flirts they are, but don't tell Tato, a thousand kisses, ciao."

He walked over to the Church of Santa María, on the Óvalo Gutiérrez. It was still early and the guests were just beginning to arrive. He sat down in one of the front rows and whiled away the time looking at the altar, decorated with lilies and white roses, and the stained-glass windows that looked like bishop's miters. Once again he realized that he didn't like this church at all: its combination of stucco and bricks was unaesthetic and its ogee arches pretentious. Every so often, he greeted an acquaintance with a smile. Naturally, since everybody he'd ever known was arriving little by little: very distant relatives, friends he hadn't seen for ages, and the crème de la crème of the city, of course, bankers, ambassadors, industrialists, politicians. Ah, that Roberto, that Margarita, such social butterflies, Dr. Quinteros thought, without acrimony, full of indulgence toward the weaknesses of his brother and sister-in-law. The wedding luncheon was bound to be a lavish affair.

He felt a rush of emotion on seeing the bride enter, just as the first bars of the Wedding March pealed out. She was really stunningly beautiful, in her filmy white dress, and her little face, in profile beneath the veil, had something extraordinarily graceful, ethereal, spiritual about it as she walked toward the altar, with lowered eyes, on Roberto's arm; corpulent and august, her father was hiding his emotion by assuming the air of a grand seigneur. Red Antúnez seemed less homely than usual in his brand-new cut-away coat, his face radiant with happiness, and even his mother—an ungainly Englishwoman who despite having lived in Peru for a quarter of a century still got her Spanish prepositions mixed up—looked attractive in her long dark dress and her hairdo two stories high. It's quite true, Dr. Quinteros thought: patience pays off. Because poor Red Antúnez had pursued Elianita ever since the two had been children, and had besieged her with thoughtful and attentive gestures that she had invariably greeted with Olympian disdain. But he had put up with all of Elianita's cutting remarks and snubs and the dreadful jokes of the youngsters in the neighborhood poking fun at his resignation. A persistent young man, Dr. Quinteros reflected, whose determination had been rewarded, and now here he was, pale with emotion, slipping the wedding band on the ring finger of the prettiest girl in Lima. The ceremony had ended, and as Dr. Quinteros was making his way toward the church reception rooms, amid a buzzing throng, nodding his head right and left, he suddenly spied Richard, standing by himself next to a column, as though he were disgustedly keeping his distance from everyone.

As he waited in line to congratulate the bride and groom, Dr. Quinteros was obliged to laugh at a dozen jokes about the government told to him by the Febre brothers, a pair of twins who looked so much alike that it was said that even their own wives couldn't tell them apart. The reception room was so jam-packed it seemed about to collapse; many of the guests were still outside in the gardens, waiting their turn to come inside. A swarm of waiters circled about, offering champagne. Laughter, jokes, toasts could be heard on every hand, and everyone agreed that the bride was absolutely beautiful. When Dr. Quinteros finally reached her, he saw that Elianita still looked serene and elegant despite the heat and the crush of people. "A thousand years of happiness, sweetheart," he said to her, embracing her, and she said in his ear: "Charito called me this morning from Rome to congratulate me, and I talked with Aunt Mercedes, too. How darling of them to have phoned me!" Red Antúnez, dripping with sweat and as red as a shrimp, was beaming with happiness. "So from now on I'll have to call you uncle, too, is that right, Don Alberto?" "Of course, nephew," Dr. Quintero answered, clapping him on the back, "and you'll have to address me in the familiar *tu* form as well."

Half asphyxiated, he left the reception room, and amid the popping of flashbulbs, the press of the crowd, greetings, he finally managed to reach the garden. There were fewer people per square centimeter there and he could at least breathe. He took a glass of champagne and soon found himself surrounded by a circle of doctor friends of his, the butt of their endless jokes about his wife's trip abroad: Mercedes wouldn't come back home, she'd stay over there with some Frenchy, you could already see tiny cuckold's horns growing out of either side of his forehead. Everybody seems bent on making fun of me today, Dr. Quinteros thought to himself, remembering the gym, as he patiently put up with their teasing. Every so often he caught a glimpse of Richard above a sea of heads, standing at the other end of the reception room, amid laughing boys and girls: glum and scowling, he was downing glasses of champagne as though they were water. Maybe he feels sad that Elianita's marrying Antúnez, Dr. Quinteros thought. Perhaps he, too, would have liked to see his sister make a more brilliant match. No, it was more likely that he was going through some sort of identity crisis. And Dr. Quinteros remembered how he himself had gone through a difficult transition period when he was Richard's age, unable to decide whether he should study medicine or aeronautical engineering. (His father had finally tipped the scales with a weighty argument: as an aeronautical engineer in Peru, he could look forward to only one career, spending the rest of his life designing kites or model airplanes.) Perhaps Roberto, who was always all wrapped up in his business affairs, was in no position to advise Richard. And Dr. Quinteros, in one of those accesses of generosity that had earned him everyone's esteem, decided that one of these days he would invite his nephew over and subtly explore the best way to help him, with precisely the delicate touch that the case required.

Roberto's and Margarita's house was on the Avenida Santa Cruz, just a few blocks from the Church of Santa María, and when the reception in the sacristy was over, the guests who had been invited to the wedding luncheon filed down the street, beneath the trees and the sun of San Isidro, to the red-brick mansion with its shingled roof, surrounded by lawn, flowers, and grillwork fence, and very prettily decorated for the wedding party. The moment Dr. Quinteros arrived at the front gate, he saw that the celebration was going to go beyond his own predictions, that he was about to attend a social event that the gossip columnists would describe as "a magnificent occasion."

Tables and umbrellas had been set up all over the garden, and at the far end of it, next to the kennels, a huge awning shaded a table with a snow-white tablecloth running the length of the wall and loaded with trays of multicolored canapés. The bar was next to the pond full of bright-gilled Japanese fish, and there were enough glasses, bottles, cocktail shakers, and pitchers of punch set out to quench the thirst of an army. Waiters in short white jackets and maids in coifs and aprons were receiving the guests and plying them, from the moment they entered the gate, with pisco sours, carob piscos, vodka and tropical fruit, glasses of whiskey or gin or flutes of champagne, and little cheese sticks, tiny potatoes with hot peppers, sour cherries stuffed with bacon, breaded shrimp, vol-au-vent, and all the tidbits dreamed up by the collective culinary genius of Lima to stimulate the appetite. Inside the house, huge baskets and bouquets of roses, gladiolas, stocks, carnations, tuberoses, standing against the walls, set out along the stairways or on the windowsills and the tables and desks and commodes and cabinets, refreshed the atmosphere. The parquet floor was newly waxed, the curtains pristine, the porcelains and silver gleaming, and Dr. Quinteros smiled at the thought that probably even the pre-Columbian figurines in their glass cases had been polished. There was also a buffet in the foyer, and in the dining room a vast assortment of desserts—marzipan, ice cream, ladyfingers, meringues, candied egg yolk, coconut sweets, walnuts in syrup—had been set out around the impressive wedding cake, a construction decorated with tulle and spun-sugar columns that set the ladies to cooing with admiration. But what aroused their curiosity most of all were the wedding presents, on display upstairs; such a long line had formed to have a look at them that Dr. Quinteros immediately decided not to queue up too, even though he would have liked to see if his bracelet looked impressive alongside all the other gifts.

After he'd wandered all over the house, more or less—shaking hands, giving and receiving friendly embraces—he went back out into the garden and sat down under an awning to sip his second glass of champagne of the day in relative peace and quiet. It was all going very well; Margarita and Roberto were really experts at the grand gesture. And even though he considered their idea of hiring a combo a touch lacking refinement—the carpets, the pedestal table, and the buffet with the ivory pieces had been removed so that there would be room to dance—he excused this inelegance as being a concession to the younger generation, since, as everybody knew, today's young people thought that a party without any dancing wasn't a party at all. They were starting to serve the turkey and the wine, and now Elianita, standing on the second step in the foyer, was tossing her bride's bouquet as dozens of her schoolmates and neighborhood girlfriends waited with outstretched arms, hoping to catch it. In a corner of the garden Dr. Quinteros spied old Venancia, Elianita's nanny since the day she'd been born, moved to tears, wiping her eyes with the corner of her apron.

His palate was unable to discern the vintage of the wine, but he knew immediately that it was an imported one, perhaps Spanish or Chilean, or for that matter—in view of all this day's mad extravagances—possibly a French one. The turkey was so tender it melted in his mouth, the puree as smooth as butter, and there was a cabbage-and-raisin salad that, despite his dietary principles, he couldn't resist the second time it came around. He was enjoying a second glass of wine, as well, and beginning to feel pleasantly drowsy, when he saw Richard making his way toward him, swaying back and forth with a glass of whiskey in his hand; his eyes were glassy and his voice quavered.

"Is there anything stupider than a wedding celebration, Uncle Alberto?" he murmured, with a scornful wave of his hand at everything around them and collapsing in the chair alongside him. His tie had come undone, there was a fresh stain on the lapel of his gray suit, and his eyes showed signs not only of all the liquor he had drunk but of a barely repressed, oceanic rage.

"Well, I grant you I'm not terribly fond of parties," Dr. Quinteros replied good-naturedly. "But the fact that at your age you don't like them very much either surprises me, Richard."

"I absolutely abhor them," his nephew muttered, looking about as though he'd like to wipe every last guest off the face of the earth. "I don't know what the hell I'm doing here."

"Just think how your sister would have felt if you hadn't come to her wedding." Dr. Quinteros pondered all the silly things that alcohol makes a person say. Hadn't he seen Richard whooping it up at many a party? Wasn't he an excellent dancer? Hadn't he often seen his nephew trooping in at the head of the gang of boys and girls coming up to Charito's rooms to have a spur-of-the-moment dance? But he didn't remind him of any of these things, and merely watched him drain his glass and ask a waiter for another whiskey.

"Be that as it may, you'd better steel yourself," he said to him. "Because when you get married, your mother and father are going to throw an even bigger party for you than this one."

Richard brought the new glass of whiskey to his lips and, half closing his eyes slowly, took a sip. Then, without raising his head, in a muffled voice that reached the doctor's ears as a slow, nearly inaudible whisper, he muttered: "I'm never going to get married, Uncle Alberto, I swear to God—never."

Before he could answer him, a slender, fair-haired girl, a blue silhouette with a determined air, planted herself in front of them, grabbed Richard by the hand, and without giving him time to react, dragged him to his feet. "Aren't you ashamed to be sitting here with the old men? Come and dance, you idiot."

Dr. Quinteros watched the two of them disappear through the door of the foyer and suddenly realized he'd lost all his appetite. He could hear those two little words, "old men"—uttered so unthinkingly and in such a sweet piping voice by the youngest daughter of his friend Aramburú, the architect—ringing in his ears like a persistent echo. After drinking his coffee, he got up and went to have a look at what was going on in the living room.

The party was in full swing now and the dancing had gradually spread beyond its original matrix in front of the fireplace, where they had installed the orchestra, into the neighboring rooms, in which couples were also dancing and singing along with the cha-cha-chas and the merengues, the cumbias, and the waltzes, at the top of their lungs. Fostered by the music, the sun, and the drinking, the wave of joy had spread from the young people to the adults and from the adults to the oldsters, and to his surprise Dr. Quinteros saw that even Don Marcelino Huapaya, an octogenarian related to the family, was waggling and shaking his creaking old bones, following the rhythm of "Nube Gris," with his sister-in-law Margarita in his arms. The atmosphere in these rooms full of smoke, noise, movement, light, and happiness suddenly made Dr. Quinteros slightly dizzy; he leaned on the banister and closed his eyes for a moment. And then, smiling and happy too, he stood there watching Elianita, still in her wedding gown but without her veil now, leading the dancing. She never once stopped for a second; at the end of each piece, twenty men surrounded her, asking for the next dance, and with flaming cheeks and shining eyes, she chose a different partner each time and returned to the maelstrom. His brother suddenly appeared at his side. Instead of the morning coat, he was now wearing a lightweight brown suit, but sweating nonetheless because he'd been dancing.

"I can't believe she's married, Alberto," he said, motioning to Elianita.

"She looks simply adorable," Dr. Quinteros said with a smile. "And you've given her a really lavish wedding, Roberto."

"The best in the world is none too good for my daughter," the brother exclaimed with a touch of sadness in his voice.

"Where are they going to spend their honeymoon?" the doctor asked.

"In Brazil and in Europe. The trip's their wedding present from Red's parents." He waved in the direction of the bar and said laughingly: "They're supposed to leave early tomorrow morning, but if he keeps on at this rate, my son-in-law's not going to be in any condition to go off on a honeymoon."

A group of Red Antúnez's pals had surrounded him and were taking turns drinking a toast with him. The groom, his face more flushed than ever, was laughing a bit anxiously and trying to cheat by merely wetting his lips in his glass each time, but his friends were protesting and making him down every last drop. Dr. Quinteros looked around for Richard, but he couldn't see him either in the bar or dancing or in the part of the garden visible from the windows.

It was at that moment that it happened. The waltz "Ídolo" was just ending, the couples were preparing to applaud, the musicians were raising their fingers from their guitars, Red was facing up to the twentieth toast, when the bride suddenly raised her right hand to her eyes as though to chase away a mosquito, staggered, and before her partner could catch her, fell to the floor. Her father and Dr. Quinteros stood there motionless, thinking perhaps that she'd slipped and would get to her feet again in a moment, laughing fit to kill, but the commotion in the living room—exclamations, people pushing and shoving to reach her, her mama's voice shouting "Elianita, Elianita, oh, my poor little darling!"—made them run to help her, too. Red Antúnez had leapt to her side and swooped her up in his arms, and with a group of friends following close behind, was now carrying her upstairs, with Señora Margarita leading the way, saying over and over: "This way, to her room, slowly, watch your step," and pleading: "A doctor, somebody call a doctor." Some of the members of the family—Uncle Fernando, Cousin Chabuca, Don Marcelino—were reassuring the guests, ordering the musicians to resume playing. Dr. Quinteros saw his brother Roberto motioning to him from the top of the stairs. How stupid of me, he thought. I'm a doctor, what am I waiting for? He bounded up the stairs two by two as people moved quickly aside to let him past.

They'd taken Elianita to her bedroom, a room decorated in pink, overlooking the garden. Roberto, Red, Venancia the nanny were standing around the bed, where the girl, still very pale, was beginning to come to and blink her eyes as her mother, sitting beside her, rubbed her forehead with a handkerchief soaked in alcohol. Red had taken one of his bride's hands in his and was looking at her with mingled rapture and anguish in his eyes.

"For the moment, you are all to go outside and leave me alone with the bride," Dr. Quinteros ordered, assuming his professional role. And as he ushered them toward the door: "Don't worry, I'm sure it isn't anything. But out you go—I want to have a look at her."

The only one who refused to leave was old Venancia; Margarita practically had to drag her out bodily. Dr. Quinteros went back over to the bed and sat down next to Elianita, who looked at him in fear and trembling from between her long black eyelashes. He kissed her on the forehead and smiled at her as he took her temperature: it wasn't anything, she mustn't be frightened. Her pulse was a bit unsteady and she was having difficulty breathing. The doctor noticed that her dress was very tight-fitting across the bosom and he helped her unbutton and take it off.

"Since you have to change clothes in any case, you'll save time this way, my girl."

When he saw the cruelly tight girdle, he realized instantly what was wrong, but kept himself from making the slightest gesture or asking a single question that might betray the fact that he'd discovered his niece's secret. Elianita's face had grown redder and redder as she took off her dress, and she was so embarrassed now that she didn't raise her eyes or say a word. Dr. Quinteros told her it wasn't necessary to remove her underclothes, just the girdle, because it was making it hard for her to breathe. Smiling the while, and assuring her, his mind seemingly elsewhere, that it was the most natural thing in the world if on her wedding day, what with all the emotion of the occasion, plus all the hustling and bustling about and all the fatigue of getting ready for the big day, and above all if she were mad enough to go on dancing for hours on end without a minute's rest, a bride happened to have a fainting spell, he palpated her breasts and her belly (which, on being freed from the powerful embrace of the girdle, had literally popped out) and deduced, with the certainty of a specialist through whose hands thousands of pregnant women had passed, that she was in her fourth month. He examined the pupils of her eyes, asked her a couple of stupid questions to put her off the track, and advised her to rest for a few minutes before going back downstairs—and above all not to go on dancing like that.

"You see, you just got a little too tired, my girl. In any event, I'm going to give you a little something to counteract all the day's excitement."

He stroked her hair, and to give her time to compose herself before her parents came back into the room, he asked her a few questions about her honeymoon trip. She answered him in a languid voice. Going on a trip like that was one of the best things that could happen to a person; with all the work he had, he could never take the time off to visit so many countries. And he hadn't even been to London, his favorite city, for almost three years now. As he spoke, he watched Elianita surreptitiously put her girdle out of sight, slip on a bathrobe, lay a skirt, a blouse with an embroidered collar and cuffs, a pair of shoes out on a chair, lie down in the bed again, and cover herself with the down quilt. He wondered whether it wouldn't have been better to have a frank talk with his niece and give her some advice as to what she should and shouldn't do on her wedding trip. No, the poor thing would have had a bad time of it, she'd have felt very embarrassed. Moreover, she'd undoubtedly been seeing a doctor in secret all this time and would know exactly what she should and shouldn't do. Nonetheless, wearing such a tight girdle was dangerous, she might have a real scare, or harm her baby if she continued to wear it. He was touched to think that Elianita, that little niece he could only think of as an innocent child, had conceived. He walked over to the door, opened it, reassured the family in a loud voice so that the bride would hear him: "She's healthier than any of the rest of us, but she's dead-tired. Send somebody out to buy her this tranquillizer and let her rest for a little while."

Venancia had rushed into the bedroom, and Dr. Quinteros saw over his shoulder that Elianita's old nanny was cooing over her and comforting her. Her father and mother entered the room, too, and Red Antúnez was about to do so as well, but the doctor discreetly took him by the arm, led him down the hall with him to the bathroom, and closed the door.

"In her condition it was imprudent of her to have danced the whole evening like that, Red," he said in an even tone of voice, as he soaped his hands. "She might have had a miscarriage. Advise her not to wear a girdle—and especially not such a tight one. How long has she been pregnant? Three months, four?"

It was at that moment that the first hint of the awful truth dawned on Dr. Quinteros, as swift and as deadly as a rattlesnake bite. In terror, sensing that the silence in the bathroom had turned electric, he looked in the mirror. Red was standing there, staring at him with incredibly wide-open eyes, his mouth contorted in a grimace that made his face look grotesque, and deathly pale.

"Three months, four?" he heard him stammer in a choked voice. "A miscarriage?"

Dr. Quinteros felt the earth sinking beneath his feet. What a stupid, ignorant fool you are, he thought. He remembered now, of course, with the terrible clarity of hindsight, that the whole thing—Elianita's getting engaged, the wedding—had taken place within just a few short weeks. He turned his eyes away from Antúnez and stood there, drying his hands too slowly, as he searched desperately in his mind for some lie, some pretext that would rescue this youngster from the hell into which he had just plunged him. He managed only to mutter something that seemed to him to be equally stupid: "Elianita mustn't find out that I know. I let her think I didn't. And above all, don't worry. She's quite all right."

He headed quickly for the door, looking at Antúnez out of the corner of his eye as he went past him. He was standing there, rooted to the spot, his eyes staring into empty space, his mouth wide open too now, and his face drenched with sweat. He heard him lock the bathroom door from inside behind him. He's going to burst into tears, he thought, pound his head against the wall and tear his hair, he's going to curse me and hate me even more than her, even more than—who? He walked slowly down the stairs, covered with guilt, full of misgivings, as he kept repeating to people, like an automaton, that Elianita was quite all right, that she'd be coming back downstairs in just a few minutes. He went out into the garden, and breathing a bit of fresh air did him good. He walked over to the bar, drank a glass of whiskey neat, and decided to go back home without waiting to witness the denouement of the drama that, out of sheer naïveté and with the very best of intentions, he had provoked. What he wanted was to shut himself up in his study, curl up in his black leather armchair, and immerse himself in Mozart.

At the front gate he came upon Richard, sitting on the grass in a lamentable state. He was sitting cross-legged like a Buddha, leaning back against the fence, his suit wrinkled and covered with dust, stains, bits of grass. But it was his face that distracted the doctor from the memory of Red and Elianita and made him pause: in Richard's bloodshot eyes, alcohol and rage seemed to have wreaked their mounting havoc in equal degrees. Two threads of spittle hung from his lips, and the expression on his face was both pitiful and grotesque.

"This can't be, Richard," he murmured, bending over and trying to make him get to his feet. "Your mother and father mustn't see you like this. Come on, let me take you home with me till you've sobered up. I never thought I'd see you in such a state, my boy."

Richard looked at him without seeing him, his head dangling, and though he obediently did his best to stand up, his legs gave way. The doctor had to take him by the arms and hoist him to his feet as though he were lifting weights. He managed to make him walk, holding him up by the shoulders. Richard teetered back and forth like a rag doll and seemed about to tumble headlong at any moment. "Let's see if we can find a taxi, because if we walk you're not even going to make it to the corner, my boy," he murmured, stopping along the curb of the Avenida Santa Cruz, and holding Richard up with one arm. Several taxis went by, but they were occupied. The doctor kept trying to flag one down. The wait, on top of the memory of Elianita and Antúnez and his anxiety as to the state his nephew was in, was beginning to make him nervous—him, Doctor Quinteros, who never lost his composure. At that moment, in the incoherent babble that was escaping Richard's lips, half under his breath, he made out the word "revolver." He couldn't help smiling, and ever cheerful in the face of adversity, said, as if to himself, without really expecting Richard to hear him or answer: "And why do you want a revolver, my boy?"

Richard's reply, as he gazed into space with rolling, murderous eyes, was slow, hoarse, perfectly clear. "To kill Red with." He had uttered each syllable with icy hatred. He paused, and then added in a voice that suddenly broke: "Or to kill myself with."

He began mumbling again, and Alberto de Quinteros could no longer make out what he was saying. Just then, a taxi stopped. The doctor shoved Richard inside, gave the driver the address, and got in himself. The moment the taxi started off, Richard burst into tears. He turned to look at him and the boy leaned over, put his head on his chest, and sobbed, his body shaking with a nervous tremor. The doctor put his arm around him, rumpled his hair just as he'd done a little while before with his sister, and reassured the taxi driver, who was looking at him through the rearview mirror, with a gesture that meant "the boy's had too much to drink." He let Richard sit there, huddled next to him, weeping and dirtying his blue suit and his silver-gray tie with his tears and spittle and mucus. He didn't blink an eye, nor did his heart skip a beat, when in his nephew's incomprehensible soliloquy, he managed to make out that phrase, repeated two or three times, that horrendous phrase that at the same time sounded beautiful and even chaste: "Because I love her as a man loves a woman and I don't give a damn about all the rest, Uncle."

In the garden of the house, Richard vomited, with wrenching spasms that frightened the fox terrier and brought disapproving looks from the butler and the maids. Dr. Quinteros took Richard by the arm and led him to the guest room, made him rinse out his mouth with water, undressed him, put him to bed, made him swallow a strong sleeping pill, and remained at his side, calming him with affectionate words and gestures—that he knew the boy could neither hear nor see—till he felt him fall into the deep sleep of the young.

Then he phoned the clinic and told the doctor on duty that he wouldn't be coming in until the next day unless some dire emergency came up, instructed the butler to say he wasn't in no matter who called or came to see him, poured himself a double whiskey, and shut himself up in the music room. He put a pile of Albinoni, Vivaldi, and Scarlatti records on the turntable, because he'd decided that a few superficial, Baroque, Venetian hours would be a good antidote for the dark shadows in his mind, and buried in his soft leather chair, with his Scotch meerschaum pipe smoking between his lips, he closed his eyes and waited for the music to wreak its inevitable miracle. The thought came to him that this was a privileged occasion for putting to the test that moral rule that he had tried to live by since his youth, that axiom that had it that it was better to understand men than to judge them. He did not feel horrified or indignant or unduly surprised. He noted in himself, rather, a hidden emotion, an invincible benevolence, mingled with tenderness and pity, as he said to himself that it was now blindingly clear why such a pretty girl had suddenly decided to marry an idiot, why the king of the Hawaiian surfboard, the handsomest youngster in the neighborhood, had never been known to have a girlfriend he was crazy about and seriously courting, and why he had always fulfilled without protest, with such laudable zeal, his duties as his younger sister's chaperone. As he savored the aroma of the tobacco and sipped the pleasantly fiery whiskey in his glass, he told himself that there was no reason to worry too much about Richard. He'd find a way to persuade Roberto to send him abroad to study, to London for instance, a city where he'd find enough new and exciting things to make him forget the past. On the other hand, he really was worried, and consumed with curiosity, as to what would happen to the two other characters in the story. As the music little by little intoxicated him, a whirlwind of unanswered questions circled around and around in his mind, growing fainter and fainter, spaced farther and farther apart: Would Red Antúnez desert his reckless, foolhardy spouse that very night? Might he have done so already? Or would he say nothing, and giving proof of what might be either exceptional nobility or exceptional stupidity, stay with that deceitful girl whom he had so persistently pursued? Would there be a great public scandal, or would a chaste veil of dissimulation and pride trampled underfoot forever hide this tragedy of San Isidro?

Three.
I saw Pedro Camacho

again a few days after the typewriter episode. It was 7:30 a.m., and after getting the first newscast of the day ready to go on the air, I was heading for the Bransa to have my morning *café con leche*. As I passed by the little window of the concierge's cubicle at Radio Central, I spied my Remington. I could hear its heavy keys hitting the platen, but I couldn't see anybody sitting behind it. I stuck my head through the window and saw that it was Pedro Camacho who was typing away. An office had been set up for him in the concierge's cubbyhole. In this tiny room, with a low ceiling and walls badly damaged by the dampness and by the ravages of time and desecrated by countless graffiti, there was now a monumental wooden desk, so dilapidated that it was about to fall apart, but nonetheless as imposing as the enormous typewriter rumbling away on it. The outsize dimensions of the desk and the Remington literally swallowed up the little runt. He had put a couple of cushions on the seat of his chair, but even so, his face came up no higher than the keyboard, so that he was typing away with his hands at eye level, thus causing him to appear to be boxing. He was so totally absorbed in his work that he didn't even notice my presence, despite the fact that I was leaning right over him. His pop-eyes were riveted on the paper as he pecked at the keys with his two forefingers, biting his tongue. He was wearing the same black suit as on the first day, and had taken off neither his suit coat nor his little bow tie. At the sight of him, with his long hair and his attire mindful of a nineteenth-century poet, sitting there rigid and dead-serious, concentrating all his attention on what he was typing so furiously, in front of that desk and that typewriter that were far too big for him, in this den that was much too small for the three of them, I couldn't quite decide whether the whole scene was pitiful or wildly funny.

"You're certainly an early riser, Señor Camacho," I greeted him, stepping halfway into the room.

Without even looking up from the paper, he merely indicated, with a peremptory jerk of his head, that I should either shut up or wait, or both. I chose the latter course, and as he finished his sentence, I noted that the desktop was littered with typed pages, and the floor strewn with discarded pages he'd wadded up into a ball and tossed there because no one had thought to provide him with a wastebasket. A few moments later his hands fell away from the keyboard, he looked up at me, rose to his feet, ceremoniously held out his right hand, and answered my greeting with a maxim: "Clock time means nothing where art is concerned. Good morning, my friend."

I didn't ask if he was suffering from claustrophobia in this tiny cubbyhole, since I was certain he would have answered me that discomfort was propitious to art. Instead, I invited him to come with me to have coffee. He consulted a prehistoric artifact clumsily sliding back and forth on his skinny wrist and murmured: "After an hour and a half of production, I deserve time out for refreshment." As we walked over to the Bransa, I asked him if he always began work that early in the morning, and he replied that in his case, unlike that of other "creators," inspiration was directly proportional to daylight.

"It dawns with the sun and gradually grows warmer along with it," he explained, musically, as a drowsy waiter swept the sawdust littered with cigarette butts and the refuse of the Bransa out from under our feet. "I begin to write at first light. By noon, my brain is a blazing torch. Then the fire dies down little by little, and around about dusk I stop, inasmuch as only embers remain. But it doesn't matter, since the actor produces more in the afternoon and at night. I have my system all carefully plotted out."

He delivered himself of this peroration in utter seriousness, and

I realized that he scarcely seemed to notice that I was still there; he was one of those men who have no need of conversational partners: all they require is listeners. Like the first time we'd met, I was taken aback by his total lack of humor, despite the puppetlike smiles—lips turning up at the corners, brow wrinkling, teeth suddenly bared—with which he embellished his monologue. His every word was uttered with extraordinary solemnity, all of which—along with his perfect diction, his dwarflike stature, his bizarre attire, and his theatrical gestures—made him appear to be an odd sort indeed. It was obvious that he took everything he said to be the gospel truth, and he thus gave the impression of being at once the most affected and the most sincere man in the world. I did my best to bring him down from the artistic heights on which he was holding forth so grandiloquently to the more earthly plane of practical matters, and asked him if he had found a place to live yet, if he had friends here, how he liked Lima. Such mundane considerations were of no interest to him whatsoever. Impatiently breaking off his flight of eloquence, he replied that he had found an "atelier" not far from Radio Central, on Quilca, and that he felt at home wherever he found himself, for wasn't the entire world the artist's homeland? Instead of coffee, he ordered a lemon verbena-and-mint herb tea, which, he informed me, not only was pleasing to the palate but also "toned up one's mind." He downed it in short, symmetrical sips, as though he had calculated the precise intervals at which to raise the cup to his lips, and the moment he'd finished it, he rose to his feet, insisted on splitting the check, and asked me to go with him to buy a map showing the streets and districts of Lima. We found what he wanted at an outdoor newsstand along the Jirón de la Unión. He unfolded the map, held it up to the light, studied it, and was pleased to note that the various districts of the city were marked off in different colors. He also asked for a receipt for the twenty *soles* the map had cost him.

"It's something I need for my work and my employers should reimburse me," he declared, as we walked back to our respective offices. His walk was also quite odd: quick, nervous strides, as though he were afraid he'd miss a train.

As we bade each other goodbye at the entrance to Radio Central, he gestured in the direction of his cramped little cubbyhole of an office as though he were proudly showing off a palace. "It's practically right out in the middle of the street," he said, pleased with himself and with things in general. "It's as if I were working out on the sidewalk."

"Won't all the noise of so many people and cars passing by distract you?" I ventured to ask.

"On the contrary," he reassured me, delighted at the chance to offer me one last edifying maxim: "I write about life, and the impact of reality is crucial to my work."

As I turned to leave, he waggled his forefinger to call me back. Pointing to the map of Lima, he asked me, in a tone of voice fraught with mystery, if I would be willing, later on that day or the day after, to provide him with further information about the city. I told him I'd be more than happy to do so.

Back in my shack at Panamericana, I found that Pascual had already written up the text of the 9 a.m. news bulletin. It began with one of those items he took such delight in. He had copied it from the morning paper, *La Crónica*, embellishing it with fancy adjectives he'd picked up in the course of his studies and made an intimate part of his cultural stock in trade: "In the tempestuous seas of the Antilles, the Panamanian freighter *Shark* sank last night, taking with it to their death its crew of eight, drowned and masticated by the sharks that infest the aforementioned sea." I changed "masticated" to "devoured" and edited out "tempestuous" and "aforementioned" before giving it my okay. Pascual didn't fly into a rage—that wasn't his way—but he nonetheless put his protest on record. "Good old Don Mario, fucking up my style as usual."

All that week I'd been trying to write a short story, based on an incident that my Uncle Pedro, who was a doctor on a big landed estate in Ancash, had passed on to me. One night a peasant had frightened another peasant half to death by disguising himself as a "pishtaco"—a devil—and leaping out at him from the middle of a canebrake. The victim of this joke had been so scared out of his wits that he'd attacked the "pishtaco" with his machete, dispatched him to the next world with a skull split in two, and taken to the hills. Shortly thereafter, a group of peasants leaving a fiesta had come upon a "pishtaco" prowling around the village and beaten him to death. The dead man turned out to be the murderer of the first "pishtaco," who was in the habit of disguising himself as a devil in order to visit his family at night. These assassins had in turn taken to the hills, and used to come down at night in the guise of devils to visit the community, where two of them had already been hacked to death with machetes by the terror-stricken villagers, who in turn, et cetera . . . What I was eager to recount in my story was not so much what had actually happened on the estate where my Uncle Pedro was employed as the ending of the story that suddenly occurred to me: at a certain moment, the Devil in person, alive and kicking and wagging his tail, slipped in among all these fake "pishtacos." I was going to entitle my story "The Qualitative Leap," and I wanted it to be as coldly objective, intellectual, terse, and ironic as one of Borges's—an author whom I had just discovered at that time. I devoted to the story all the spare moments left me by the news bulletins at Panamericana, the university, and coffee breaks at the Bransa, and I also wrote at my grandparents' house, during my lunch hours and at night. During that week, I didn't drop in at any of my uncles' houses for the midday meal, skipped my usual visits to my girl cousins', and didn't go to the movies even once. I wrote and then tore up what I wrote, or rather, the moment I'd written a sentence it struck me as absolutely dreadful and I began all over again. I was thoroughly convinced that a slip of my pen or a mistake in spelling was never a mere happenstance but rather a reminder, a warning (from my subconscious, God, or some other being) that the sentence simply wouldn't do at all and had to be rewritten. Pascual protested: "Good Lord, if the Genaros discover how much paper you've wasted, they'll take it out of our salary." Finally, one Thursday, it seemed to me that the story was finished. It was a monologue five pages long: at the very end, the reader discovered that the narrator was the Devil himself. I read "The Qualitative Leap" to Javier in my shack, after the noon Panamericana newscast.

"It's first-rate, old pal," he said approvingly, applauding. "But is it really possible to write about the Devil nowadays? Why not write a realistic story? Why not do away with the Devil altogether and make the whole thing a series of incidents involving fake "pishtacos"? Or, alternatively, an outright fantastic tale, with all the ghostly apparitions you like. But no devils, because that smacks of religion, of hypocritical piety, of all kinds of things that are terribly old hat these days."

When he left, I tore "The Qualitative Leap" to bits, tossed it into the wastebasket, decided to forget all about "pishtacos," and went to have lunch at my Uncle Lucho's. I learned there that there was apparently a budding romance between Aunt Julia and a man I'd never met but had heard a lot about: Adolfo Salcedo, the owner of a large estate and the senator from Arequipa—a distant family relation.

"Fortunately, Julia's new suitor has piles of money, a high social standing, and lots of influence, plus honest intentions toward her," my Aunt Olga commented. "He's asked for her hand in marriage."

"Unfortunately, Don Adolfo's fifty and hasn't yet done a thing to prove that that terrible thing his wife accused him of was false," Uncle Lucho retorted. "If your sister marries him, she's either going to have to live in chastity or take to adultery."

"That whole story about him and Carlota is a typical bit of slanderous Arequipa gossip," Aunt Olga argued. "Adolfo gives every appearance of being a real man."

I knew that "whole story" about the senator and Doña Carlota very well, since it had been the subject of another short story of mine that Javier's praise had caused me to consign to the wastebasket. The marriage of Don Adolfo and Doña Carlota had been the talk of the entire south of the Republic, since both of them owned huge tracts of land in Puno and the pooling of their holdings would thus create yet another enormous landed estate. The two of them had done things in the grand manner: a wedding ceremony in the splendid Church of Yanahuara attended by guests from all over Peru, followed by a Pantagruelian banquet. During the second week of their honeymoon, the bride had upped and left her spouse somewhere or other, returned all by herself to Arequipa to the scandal of everyone, and announced, to everyone's stupefaction, that she was about to appeal to Rome for a formal annulment of their marriage.

Adolfo Salcedo's mother had met Doña Carlota one Sunday after eleven o'clock Mass, and right there in the middle of the portico of the cathedral had asked her to her face, in utter fury: "Why did you abandon my poor son as you did, you shameless creature?"

With a superbly haughty wave of her hand, Doña Carlota had answered in a voice loud enough for everyone to hear: "Because, señora, the only use to which your son puts that particular piece of equipment that men are endowed with is to make peepee."

She had managed to have the religious marriage annulled, and Adolfo Salcedo had been an inexhaustible source of jokes at our family gatherings. From the day the senator had first met Aunt Julia, he had besieged her with invitations to the Bolívar Grill and the "91," showered her with gifts of perfume, and bombarded her with baskets of roses. I was happy to hear of the romance and hoped that Aunt Julia would turn up, so I could get in a few nasty digs about her new suitor. But she took the wind out of my sails when, appearing in the dining room in time to have coffee with us, with her arms loaded with parcels, she was the one who announced, laughing fit to kill: "All that gossip turned out to be perfectly true. Senator Salcedo can't get it up!"

"Julia, for heaven's sake, don't be vulgar," Aunt Olga protested. "Anybody would think that . . ."

"He told me so himself, just this morning," Aunt Julia explained, gloating over the senator's tragedy.

He'd been quite normal up until the age of twenty-five. And then, in the course of an ill-starred trip to the U.S. on vacation, the terrible mishap had occurred. In Chicago, San Francisco, or Miami—Aunt Julia didn't remember which exactly—young Adolfo had met a woman in a night club and made a conquest (or so he thought). She had taken him to a hotel, and he was going at it hot and heavy with her, when suddenly he felt the point of a knife blade in his back, turned around, and saw a one-eyed man a good six feet six inches tall. They didn't use the knife on him or beat him; they merely robbed him of his watch, a gold religious medal, his dollars. That was how it all began. Simple as that. Ever since then, the minute he was with a woman and about to get down to some serious action, he would feel the touch of cold metal on his spinal column, see the ravaged face of the one-eyed man, start to sweat, and find himself with all desire gone and his spirits drooping. He had consulted an endless number of doctors and psychologists, and even a quack healer in Arequipa, who had him bury himself up to the neck at the foot of volcanoes on moonlit nights.

"Don't be mean, don't make fun of the poor man, Julia," Aunt Olga said, shaking with laughter.

"If I were certain he'd stay that way, I'd marry him for his dough," Aunt Julia said crassly. "But what if I cured him? Can't you just see that old gaffer trying to make up for lost time with me?"

I thought how happy the adventure of the senator from Arequipa would have made Pascual, how enthusiastically he would have devoted an entire newscast to him. Uncle Lucho warned Aunt Julia that if she was going to be so demanding, she'd never find a Peruvian husband. And she in turn complained that here too, as in Bolivia, the good-looking men were poor and the rich ones ugly, and when a good-looking rich man came along, he inevitably turned out to be married. Suddenly she looked me straight in the eye and asked me if I hadn't shown up all that week because I was afraid she'd drag me off to the movies again. I said that wasn't the reason, made up a story about exams I had coming up, and proposed that we go see a film that night.

"Great, we'll go to the one that's showing at the Leuro," she decided dictatorially. "It's a real tearjerker."

On the way back to Radio Panamericana in the jitney, I mulled over the possibility of trying my hand at another short story, one based this time on the misadventures of Adolfo Salcedo; something light and entertaining, in the manner of Somerset Maugham, or perversely erotic, as in Maupassant. At the radio station, Nelly, Genaro Jr.'s secretary, was giggling to herself at her desk. "What's so funny?" I asked her.

"There's been a terrible row over at Radio Central between Pedro Camacho and Genaro Sr.," she informed me. "The Bolivian insisted he didn't want any Argentine actors playing roles in his serials, and if they did, he was leaving. He managed to get Luciano Pando and Josefina Sánchez to back him up, and finally got his way. They're going to cancel the Argentines' contracts—isn't that great news?"

There was a fierce rivalry between the native announcers, m.c.'s, and actors and the Argentine ones—wave after wave of the latter kept arriving in Peru, many of them expelled from their own country for political reasons—and I surmised that the Bolivian scriptwriter had taken this stand so as to get on the good side of his Peruvian co-workers. But I soon discovered that he was incapable of this sort of calculated maneuver. His hatred of Argentines in general, and of Argentine actors and actresses in particular, appeared to be entirely disinterested. I went to see him after the seven o'clock news broadcast, to tell him I had a little spare time and could help him with the data he'd said he needed. He invited me into his lair and with a munificent gesture offered me the only seat possible, outside of his own chair: a corner of the table that served him as a desk. He still had his suit coat and his little bow tie on, and before him were countless typed sheets of paper, which he had assembled in a neat pile alongside the Remington. The map of Lima, pinned down with thumbtacks, covered part of the wall. It now had more colored patches, a number of strange symbols drawn in red pencil, and different initials labeling each district of the city. I asked him what these marks and letters stood for.

He nodded, with one of his little mechanical smiles that always bore traces of a sense of self-satisfaction and a sort of kindly condescension. Settling back comfortably in his chair, he delivered himself of one of his perorations: "I work from life; my writings are firmly rooted in reality, as the grapevine is rooted in the vinestock. That's why I need this. I want to know whether that world there is or is not as I have represented it."

He was pointing to the map, and I leaned closer to see if I could figure out what he was trying to get across to me. The initials were hermetic; as far as I could tell, they referred to no recognizable institution or person. The only thing that was quite clear was that he had singled out the altogether dissimilar districts of Miraflores and San Isidro, La Victoria and El Callao, by drawing red circles around them. I told him I didn't understand at all, and asked him to explain.

"It's very simple," he replied impatiently, in the tone of a parish priest. "What is most important is the truth, which is always art, as lies, on the other hand, never are, or only very rarely. I need to know if Lima is really the way I've shown it on the map. Do the two capital A's, for example, fit San Isidro? Is it in fact a district where one finds Ancient Ancestry, Affluent Aristocracy?"

He stressed the initial A's of these words, with an intonation meant to suggest that "It is only the blind who cannot see the bright light of day." He had classified the districts of Lima according to their social status. But the curious thing was the type of descriptive adjectives he had used, the nature of his nomenclature. In certain cases he had hit the nail squarely on the head, and in others his labels were completely arbitrary. I granted, for instance, that the initials MCLPH (Middle Classes Liberal Professions Housewives) fitted the Jesús María section of Lima, but cautioned him that it was rather unfair to sum up the districts of La Victoria and El Porvenir under the dreadful label BFHH (Bums Fairies Hoodlums Hetaerae), and extremely questionable to reduce El Callao to SFS (Sailors Fishermen Sambos) or El Cercado and El Agustino to FDFWFI (Female Domestics Factory Workers Farmhands Indians).

"It's not a scientific classification but an artistic one," he informed me, making magic passes with his tiny pygmy hands. "It's not *all* the people who live in each district, but only the flashiest, the most immediately noticeable, those who give each section of the city its particular flavor and color. If a person is a gynecologist, he should live in the part of town where he belongs, and the same goes for a police sergeant."

He subjected me to a lengthy and amusing interrogation (amusing to me, that is to say, since he for his part remained dead-serious throughout) on the human topography of the city, and I noted that the things that interested him most had to do with extremes: millionaires and beggars, blacks and whites, saints and criminals. Depending on my answers, he added, changed, or erased initials on the map with a swift gesture, not hesitating a second, thus leading me to think that he had invented this system of classification some time ago and had been using it regularly since. Why, I asked him, were Miraflores, San Isidro, La Victoria, and El Callao the only districts he'd circled in red?

"Because, beyond question, they'll be the principal settings of my scripts," he said, his pop-eyes surveying those four sections of the city with Napoleonic self-importance. "I'm a man who can't abide halftones, murky waters, weak coffee. I like a straightforward yes or no, masculine men and feminine women, night or day.

In my works there are always blue bloods or the hoi polloi, prostitutes or madonnas. The bourgeoisie doesn't inspire me or interest me—or my public, either."

"You're like Romantic writers," I unfortunately remarked.

"In point of fact, *they're* like *me*," he shot back in a resentful tone of voice, bouncing up and down on his chair. "I've never plagiarized anybody. I'm quite willing to put up with every sort of carping criticism of my work, save that infamous libel. On the other hand, there are people who have stolen from me in the most nefarious way imaginable."

I endeavored to explain to him that my remark about his resembling the Romantics had not been made with any intention of offending him, that it had been a mere feeble pleasantry, but he didn't hear me, because all of a sudden he had fallen into a seething rage, and gesticulating as though he were before an audience hanging on his every word, he raved in his magnificent voice: "All of Argentina is flooded with works of mine that have been debased by hack penny-a-liners from that country. Have you had many dealings with Argentines in your life? When you see one, cross the street and walk on the other side, because the Argentine national character is like measles: a contagious disease."

He had turned pale and his nose was quivering. He clenched his teeth and grimaced in disgust. I was disconcerted by this new facet of his personality and stammered something in the way of a vague general remark about its being most regrettable that there were no strict copyright laws in Latin America, no legal protection for intellectual property. I had put my foot in my mouth again.

"That's not the point at all. I couldn't care less if I'm plagiarized," he replied, more furious still. "We artists don't create out of a desire for fame and glory, but rather out of love of humanity. What better could I ask for than to see my work becoming more and more widely disseminated throughout the world, even if it bears other people's names? But what I can't forgive those Argentine cacographers is the fact that they make changes in my scripts, that they cheapen them. Do you know what they do to them? I mean, of course, in addition to changing the titles of them and the names of the characters? They add typical Argentine ingredients to spice them up—"

"Arrogance," I broke in, certain this time that I was saying exactly the right thing. "Vulgarity."

He shook his head contemptuously, and with tragic solemnity, pronouncing each syllable slowly, in a cavernous voice that bounced off the walls of that tiny den, he uttered the only two dirty expressions I ever heard cross his lips: "Chasing after cunt and assholing with queers."

I was tempted to draw him out, to find out why his hatred of Argentines was more vehement than was the case with normal people, but on seeing how overwrought he was, I didn't dare to. A bitter look came over his face and he rubbed a hand over his eyes, as though to blot out certain phantoms of things past. Then, with a doleful expression, he closed the windows of his cubbyhole, centered the platen of the Remington and put its cover over it, straightened his little bow tie, took a weighty tome out of his desk, tucked it under his arm, and motioned toward the door as a sign to me that we were leaving. He turned the light out and, once outside, locked up his cave after him. I asked him what the book was. He stroked the spine of it affectionately, as he might have petted a beloved cat.

"An old traveling companion who's been through thick and thin with me," he murmured in a voice tinged with emotion, as he handed the volume to me. "A faithful friend and an invaluable help in my work."

The book, published in prehistoric times by Espasa Calpe—its thick worn covers had all sorts of stains and scratches on them and its pages were yellow with age—was by an author nobody had ever heard of, despite his pompous compendium of credentials (Adalberto Castejón de la Reguera, M.A. in Classical Literature, Grammar, and Rhetoric), and the title was nothing if not vast in scope: *Ten Thousand Literary Quotations Drawn from the Hundred Best Writers in the World,* with the subtitle: "What Cervantes, Shakespeare, Molière, etc., have had to say about God, Life, Death, Love, Suffering, etc. . . ."

We had already walked as far as the Calle Belén. As I shook hands with him to bid him goodbye, I happened to glance at my watch. I panicked: it was 10 p.m. I had the impression that I'd spent half an hour at most with him, but in fact the sociological-analysis-cum-gossipy-chitchat about the city and the abominable character of Argentines had gone on for three. I headed for Panamericana as fast as my legs could carry me, convinced that Pascual had no doubt devoted the entire fifteen minutes of the nine o'clock newscast to some pyromaniac in Turkey or an infanticide in El Porvenir. But things couldn't have gone as badly as all that, since I ran into the Genaros, Jr. and Sr., in the elevator, and they gave no sign of being beside themselves with rage. They told me that they had signed a contract that afternoon with Lucho Gatica, hiring him to come to Lima for a week of broadcasts to be transmitted exclusively by Panamericana. Up in my rooftop shack, I had a look at the news bulletins that had gone out over the air and found them more or less acceptable. With my mind thus set at ease, I then sauntered down to the Plaza San Martín to catch the jitney.

I arrived at my grandparents' house at 11 p.m. to find everyone fast asleep. They were in the habit of leaving my dinner ready in the oven for me, but this time, in addition to the breaded steak with rice and a fried egg—my invariable evening meal—there was a message written in a shaky hand: "Your Uncle Lucho called to say that you stood up Julia, who was waiting to go to the movies with you, that you're an ill-mannered monster, and that you must call her to apologize. Grandfather."

The thought occurred to me that forgetting all about newscasts and a date with a lady on account of the Bolivian scriptwriter was going too far. I went to bed ill at ease and out of sorts for having been so impolite without intending to be. I mulled all this over in my mind interminably before I finally dropped off to sleep, trying to persuade myself that it was Aunt Julia's fault for having insisted on going to the movies with me, for being so terribly overbearing, and searching my mind for some possible excuse to give her when I phoned her the next day. Nothing plausible occurred to me, and I didn't dare tell her the unvarnished truth. I resorted instead to an epic gesture. After the 8 a.m. newscast, I went to a downtown florist's and sent her a bouquet of roses that cost me ten *soles*, along with a card on which, after much hesitation, I wrote what impressed me as a miracle of laconic elegance: "Humblest apologies."

That afternoon, between one news broadcast and the next, I

drafted several outlines of my erotico-picaresque short story based on the tragedy of the senator from Arequipa. I had every intention of working hard on it that night, but Javier dropped by after he was through work at Panamericana to take me to a spiritualist séance in Barrios Altos. The medium was a clerk I'd been introduced to in the offices of the State Reserve Bank. Javier had often talked to me about this medium, since the latter frequently told him all about his contacts with departed souls, who hastened to communicate with him not only when he convoked them in official séances but also spontaneously, in the most unexpected circumstances. It was their habit to play tricks on him, such as causing his telephone to ring at dawn: when he picked up the receiver, he could hear at the other end the unmistakable laugh of his great-grandmother, who'd been dead for half a century and had been dwelling since her demise (as she herself informed him) in Purgatory. The souls of those who had passed on appeared to him in public buses, in jitneys, or as he was walking down the street. They whispered in his ear and he was obliged to remain mute and impassive ("to snub them," were the words he reportedly used), so that people wouldn't think he was crazy. I was intrigued, and had asked Javier to organize a séance with this bank-clerk medium. The latter had agreed, but kept putting the séance off from week to week, for what he claimed were meteorological reasons. It was imperative to wait for certain phases of the moon, the shifting of tides, and other conditions that were even more special, since it appeared that departed souls were sensitive to the degree of humidity, the position of constellations, the direction of the wind. But the right day had finally arrived.

It was no easy matter to find the place where the bank-clerk medium lived, a squalid apartment squeezed into the back of a block of town houses on the Jirón Cangallo. The man proved to be a much less interesting character in person than in Javier's stories about him. A widower in his sixties, balding and smelling of liniment, he had a bovine gaze, and his conversation was so doggedly banal that no one would ever have suspected him of being in close touch with spirits. He received us in a grubby, dilapidated little front room, and offered us crackers with thin little slices of fresh cheese and a few niggardly drops of pisco. He sat there till the clock struck twelve, telling us, in a tedious, matter-of-fact way, of his experiences of the beyond. They had begun when his wife died, twenty years before. Her passing on had plunged him into a state of inconsolable despair, until one day a friend had saved him by putting him on the path of spiritualism. It was the most important thing that had happened to him in his whole life.

"Not only because one has the opportunity of continuing to see and hear one's loved ones," he said to us in the tone of someone commenting on a christening party, "but also because it's a wonderful distraction. The hours go by without one's even noticing."

Listening to him, one had the impression that speaking with the dead was something more or less comparable to seeing a movie or watching a soccer match (though, doubtless, less entertaining). His version of life in the beyond was terribly pedestrian and disheartening. There was no difference whatsoever in "quality" between this world and that, to judge from what the spirits told him: they suffered from illnesses, fell in love, got married, reproduced, traveled—the one and only difference was that they never died. I was bored to tears and casting murderous glances in Javier's direction when the clock struck twelve. The bank clerk had us sit around the table (which was not round but rectangular), turned the lights out, and ordered us to hold hands. There were a few seconds of silence, and as I sat there in tense anticipation, I had the (mistaken) impression that matters were about to take a more interesting turn. But then the spirits began to appear to the clerk, who began asking them the most tedious questions in the world, in the same bland, banal tone of voice as before: "Well, hello there, Zoilita, how are things with you? I'm delighted to hear your voice; I'm sitting here with two friends, very fine persons both of them, interested in communicating with your world, Zoilita. What's that you say? Tell them you send them your regards? Of course I will, Zoilita. She says she sends you her most affectionate regards and asks you to pray for her from time to time, if you can, so she can get out of Purgatory sooner." After Zoilita, a series of relatives and friends made their appearance, and the bank clerk had similar conversations with each of them. They were all in Purgatory, they all sent us their regards, they all asked for our prayers. Javier insisted that someone who was in Hell be summoned, so as to put an end to our doubts, but without a second's hesitation the medium explained to us that that was out of the question: the ones from *there* could be *contacted* only on the first three days of an odd-numbered month and their voices were barely audible. Javier then asked to be put in touch with the nursemaid who had brought up his mother and himself and his brothers. Doña Gumercinda duly appeared, sent her regards, said that she had the fondest of memories of Javier, and that at the moment she was getting her belongings together to leave Purgatory and go meet Our Lord. I asked the bank clerk to summon my brother Juan, and surprisingly (since I'd never had any brothers), he came and told me, by way of the kindly voice of the medium, not to worry about him, because he was with God, and that he prayed continually for me. Reassured by this bit of news, I lost interest in the séance and occupied myself mentally writing my story about the senator. An enigmatic title popped into my mind: "The Incomplete Face." While Javier tirelessly went on pressing the clerk to conjure up an angel, or at the very least, some historical figure such as Manco Cápac, I decided that the senator would eventually solve his problem thanks to a Freudian fantasy: when he made love to his wife, he would make her wear a pirate's eye patch.

The séance ended around two in the morning. As we walked through the streets of Barrios Altos in search of a taxi that would take us to the Plaza San Martín, where we could catch the jitney, I infuriated Javier by telling him that it was all his fault that the beyond had lost its poetry and mystery for me, that it was all his fault that I had had incontrovertible proof that dead people became stupid idiots, that it was all his fault that I could no longer be an agnostic and would henceforth have to live with the certainty that in the next life, *which beyond a doubt existed*, an eternity of imbecility and boredom awaited me. We found a taxi and as punishment Javier paid for it.

Back home, alongside the breaded steak, the egg, and the rice, I found another message: "Julia phoned you: she received your roses, they're very pretty, they pleased her a lot. But you're not to get the idea that you'll get out of taking her to the movies one of these days by sending roses. Grandfather."

The next day was Uncle Lucho's birthday. I bought a tie to give him and was getting ready to leave for his house at noon, when Genaro Jr. turned up in my shack at just the wrong moment and dragged me off to the Raimondi to have lunch with him. He wanted me to help him draft the text of the advertisements that were going to be published in the Sunday papers, announcing Pedro Camacho's serials, which were to start on Monday. "But wouldn't it have been more logical for the author himself to have had a hand in writing these announcements?" I asked.

"The hitch is that he's refused to have anything to do with them," Genaro Jr. explained, smoking like a chimney. "He claims his scripts don't need paid publicity, that they command attention by themselves, and all sorts of other nonsense. The guy's turning out to be a tough one to figure out; he's got all sorts of manias. You heard about that whole hassle over the Argentines, didn't you? He forced us to cancel contracts, to pay indemnities. I just hope his programs justify all his high-handedness."

As we wrote the ads, downed two sea bass, drank ice-cold beer, and watched little gray mice scamper across the overhead beams of the Raimondi every so often, as though they'd been put there on purpose as proof of how old the place was, Genaro Jr. told me of another run-in he'd had with Pedro Camacho. The reason behind this one: the protagonists of the four serials that represented his debut in Lima. In all four of them, the male lead was a man in his fifties "who had miraculously retained his youth."

"We explained to him that all the surveys have proved the public wants leading men between thirty and thirty-five, but he's as stubborn as a mule," Genaro Jr. said in a doleful voice, exhaling cigarette smoke through his mouth and his nose. "What if I've made a terrible mistake and the Bolivian is a colossal failure?"

I remembered that at one point in our conversation the evening before, in his cubbyhole at Radio Central, Camacho had held forth, dogmatically and eloquently, on the subject of the man in his fifties. The age at which his intellectual powers and his sensuality are at their peak, he had said, the age at which he has assimilated all his experiences. That age at which one is most desired by women and most feared by men. And he had insisted, in a highly suspect way, that old age was an "optative" phenomenon. I had deduced that the Bolivian scriptwriter was fifty himself and terrified at the prospect of old age: a tiny crack of human frailty in that spirit as solid as marble.

When we finished writing the ads, it was too late in the afternoon to drop by Miraflores, so I phoned Uncle Lucho to tell him that I'd come by that evening to give him a birthday hug. I had presumed that I'd find a whole bunch of relatives gathered together to celebrate the occasion, but no one was there except Aunt Olga and Aunt Julia. The relatives had trooped in and out of the house during the day. The two of them were drinking whiskey and they poured me a glass, too. Aunt Julia thanked me again for the roses—I saw them on the sideboard, so few of them as scarcely to make a decent bouquet—and she began to poke fun at me, as usual, pressing me to confess what sort of "program" I'd gotten involved with on the night I'd stood her up: a dusky-skinned little chick from the university, a crisis at Radio Central? She was wearing a blue dress and white shoes, and had a salon makeup job and hairdo; her laugh was hearty and spontaneous, her voice throaty, and the look in her eyes downright provocative. I discovered, somewhat belatedly, that she was an attractive woman. In a sudden burst of enthusiasm, Uncle Lucho said that a person celebrated his fiftieth birthday only once in his life and that he was inviting all of us to the Bolívar Grill. The thought crossed my mind that for the second day in a row I would be obliged to postpone writing my story about the perverted eunuch senator (what if I used that phrase as the title?). But I didn't regret having to put it aside, and was more than happy to find myself included in the gala supper party. After looking me over, Aunt Olga decreed that my attire wasn't exactly suitable for the Bolívar Grill and had Uncle Lucho lend me a clean shirt and a flashy tie that would somewhat compensate for my threadbare, badly wrinkled suit. The shirt was miles too big for me, and I was concerned about the way I looked with my neck waggling back and forth inside the collar (thereby causing Aunt Julia to begin calling me Popeye).

I'd never been to the Bolívar Grill and it seemed to me the most chic and elegant place in the world, and the supper we had the most exquisite meal I'd ever tasted. An orchestra played boleros, paso dobles, and blues, and the star of the show was a French girl, as white as snow, who caressed each syllable of her songs while seemingly masturbating the microphone with her hands, and Uncle Lucho, with a euphoria heightened by each drink he downed, cheered her on in a gibberish that he took to be French: "Vravooooo! Vravooooooo, mamuasel cherí!" I was the first one to venture out onto the dance floor, dragging Aunt Olga with me, to my own vast surprise, since I didn't know how to dance (at the time, I was firmly convinced that a literary vocation was incompatible with dancing and sports), but happily the floor was crowded, and in the crush and the darkness no one noticed. Aunt Julia, in turn, gave Uncle Lucho a hard time of it for a while, making him dance apart from her and do fancy twists and turns. She was a good dancer and many of the women watched her every move.

I took Aunt Julia out onto the floor for the next piece and cautioned her that I didn't know how to dance, but as they were playing a very slow blues number, I turned out to be a fairly decent partner. We danced the next few pieces, too, and gradually got farther and farther away from Uncle Lucho's and Aunt Olga's table. Just as the orchestra stopped playing and Aunt Julia started to step away from me, I held her back and planted a kiss on her cheek, very close to her lips. She looked at me in astonishment, as though she'd witnessed a miracle. There was a break as another orchestra took over, and we were obliged to return to the table. The minute we sat down, Aunt Julia began to joke with Uncle Lucho about being fifty, the age at which males reached their second youth and started to become dirty old men. Every so often she darted a quick glance in my direction, as though to make sure I was really there, and from the look in her eyes, it was plain that she couldn't get over the fact that I'd kissed her. Aunt Olga was tired now and wanted us to leave, but I insisted on having one more dance. "Our intellectual's becoming perverted," Uncle Lucho remarked, and dragged Aunt Olga out for one last turn around the dance floor. I followed with Aunt Julia, and as we danced, there wasn't a peep out of her—for the first time. When Uncle Lucho and Aunt Olga were out of sight amid the crowd of couples on the dance floor, I held her tighter and snuggled up cheek-to-cheek with her. "Listen, Marito," I heard her murmur disconcertedly, but I interrupted her by whispering in her ear: "I forbid you to call me Marito ever again—I'm not a little kid any more." She drew her face away to look at me and tried to force herself to smile, and at that point, almost automatically, I leaned over and kissed her on the mouth. Our lips barely touched, but she was not expecting any such thing, and this time she was so surprised she stopped dancing for a moment. She was absolutely dumfounded now: standing there wide-eyed and openmouthed. When the piece ended, Uncle Lucho paid the check and we left. As we drove back to Miraflores—Aunt Julia and I were sitting in the back seat—I took her hand, gave it an affectionate squeeze, and held it in mine. She didn't draw it away, but she was obviously still bowled over and didn't once open her mouth. As I got out of the car at my grandfather's, I suddenly wondered how many years older she was than me.

Four.
In the El Callao night,

damp and dark as a wolf's mouth, Sergeant Lituma turned up the collar of his greatcoat, rubbed his hands together, and prepared to do his duty. He was a man in the prime of life, his fifties, whom the entire Civil Guard respected; he had served in commissariats in the roughest districts without complaining, and his body still bore scars of the battles he had waged against crime. The prisons of Peru were full of malefactors whom he had clapped in handcuffs. He had been cited as an exemplary model in orders of the day, praised in official speeches, and twice decorated: but these honors had not altered his modesty, no less great than his courage and his honesty. He had been working out of the Fourth Commissariat of El Callao for a year now, and for the past three months he had been assigned the toughest duty that can fall to the lot of a sergeant in the port district: night patrol.

The distant bells of the church of Nuestra Señora del Carmen de la Legua struck midnight, and punctual as always, Sergeant Lituma—broad forehead, aquiline nose, penetrating gaze, the very soul of rectitude and goodness—began his rounds, leaving behind him the old wooden headquarters building of the Fourth Commissariat, a blaze of light amid the darkness. He imagined the scene inside in his mind's eye: Lieutenant Jaime Concha would be reading Donald Duck, officers Snotnose Camacho and Apple Dumpling Arévalo would be sugaring their freshly made coffee, and the only prisoner of the day—a pickpocket caught in flagrante in the Chucuito–La Parada bus and brought to the commissariat, with bruises from head to foot, by half a dozen irate passengers—would be curled up in a ball, sleeping on the floor of his cell.

He began his rounds in the Puerto Nuevo district, where the guard on duty was Shorty Soldevilla, a young man from Túmbez who sang *tonderos* in an inspired voice. Puerto Nuevo was the terror of the guards and detectives of El Callao, because in its labyrinth of shanties made of wood, galvanized iron, corrugated tin, bricks, only an infinitesimal proportion of the inhabitants earned their living as dockers or fishermen. The majority were bums, thieves, drunks, pickpockets, pimps, and queers (not to mention the countless whores), who went at each other with knives on the slightest provocation and sometimes shot each other. This district, without water or sewers, without electricity or paved streets, had more than once run red with the blood of officers of the law. But things were exceptionally quiet that night. As he made his way along the meanders of the neighborhood in search of Shorty, stumbling over invisible stones, wrinkling up his nose at the stench of excrement and rotten garbage rising to his nostrils, Sergeant Lituma thought: The cold has sent the night birds to bed early. For it was mid-August, the dead of winter, and a heavy fog that blurred and distorted everything, along with a steady drizzle that saturated the air, had turned this night into a dreary and inhospitable one. Where could Shorty Soldevilla be? Chilled to the bone or scared of the thugs, that chicken from Túmbez might very well have gone off to one of the bars along the Avenida Huáscar to get warm and have himself a drink. No, he wouldn't dare, Sergeant Lituma thought. He knows that I'm making my rounds and if I find he's abandoned his post his goose is cooked.

He finally came across him on the corner opposite the national slaughterhouse and cold-storage plant, standing under a lamppost. He was rubbing his hands together furiously and his face had disappeared behind a spectral scarf that left only his eyes visible. On catching sight of him, Shorty gave a start and raised his hand to his gun belt. Then, recognizing him, he clicked his heels.

"You scared me, sergeant," he said, laughing. "Seeing you at a distance, looming up out of the dark like that, I took you for a ghost."

"A ghost, my ass," Lituma said, shaking hands. "You thought I was a thug."

"No such luck. There aren't any thugs abroad, what with this cold," Shorty said, rubbing his hands together again. "The only madmen out tonight in weather like this are you and me. And those critters."

He pointed to the roof of the slaughterhouse, and the sergeant, squinting, managed to make out a half-dozen turkey buzzards, huddled up with their beaks tucked underneath their wings, sitting in a straight line on the peak of the roof. How hungry they must be, he thought. Even though they're freezing, they're sitting there smelling death. Shorty Soldevilla signed his report in the dim light of the streetlamp, with the chewed stub of a pencil that kept slipping out of his fingers. There was nothing to report: no accidents, no crimes, no drunken brawls.

"A quiet night, sergeant," he said, as he walked a few blocks with him to the Avenida Manco Cápac. "I hope it stays that way till my relief takes over. After that, the world can come to an end as far as I'm concerned."

He laughed as though he'd just said something very funny, and Sergeant Lituma thought: The mentality of certain guards beggars belief. As though he'd guessed what the sergeant was thinking, Shorty Soldevilla added, in a grave tone of voice: "Because I'm not like you are, sergeant. I don't like this whole bit. The only reason I wear the uniform is that it keeps food in my belly."

"If it were up to me, you wouldn't be wearing it," the sergeant muttered. "The only ones I'd allow to stay in the corps would be the ones that believed in it a hundred percent."

"That would just about empty out the Guardia Civil," Shorty retorted.

"It's better to be alone than in bad company," said the sergeant, laughing.

Shorty laughed, too. They were walking along in the dark, through the vacant lot around the Guadalupe Commission Merchants' depot, where the street urchins kept shooting out the bulbs of the lampposts with their slingshots. The sound of the sea could be heard in the distance, and from time to time the engine of a taxi going down the Avenida Argentina.

"You'd like all of us to be heroes," Shorty burst out all of a sudden. "To give our hearts and our souls and our lives to defend all these shits." He pointed toward El Callao, Lima, the world in general. "And do you think the bastards are grateful? Haven't you heard the things they yell after us in the streets? Is there anybody who respects us? People have nothing but contempt for us, sergeant."

"This is where we part company," Lituma said, as they reached the Avenida Manco Cápac. "Don't leave your sector. And don't let things get you down so. You can't wait to leave the corps, but the day they hand you your discharge, you're going to suffer like a dog. That's how it was with Tits Antezana. He used to come round to the commissariat to see us and his eyes would fill with tears. 'I've lost my family,' he used to say."

From behind his back, he heard Shorty's voice mutter: "A family without any women—what kind of a family is that?"

Maybe Shorty was right, Sergeant Lituma thought, as he walked down the deserted avenue in the middle of the night. It was true: people didn't like the police, and never gave them a second thought, unless they were afraid of something all of a sudden. But so what? He didn't knock himself out so that people would like him or respect him. I couldn't care less about people, he thought. Why was it, then, that he didn't have the same attitude toward the Guardia Civil as his buddies, just doing his job without killing himself, making the best of things, goofing off at every opportunity or pocketing a bribe, a few dirty coins here and there, if there weren't any of his higher-ups around to see? Why, Lituma? He thought: Because you like being in the Guardia Civil. Because you like your work—the way other people like soccer or horse racing. The idea came to him that the next time some soccer nut asked him: "What team do you root for, Lituma, the Sports Boys or Chalaco?" he'd answer: "I root for the Guardia Civil." He laughed in the fog, the mist, the dark, pleased with his little joke, and at that point he heard the noise. He gave a start, raised his hand to his gun belt, and stopped dead in his tracks. He'd been so taken by surprise by the noise that he'd almost been frightened. But only *almost*, he thought, because you didn't feel afraid and you never will, you don't even know what fear is, Lituma. On his left was the vacant lot, and on his right, the dock of the first of the warehouses in the port district. It had come from there: a very loud noise, crates and drums falling down and bringing others crashing down with them. But now everything was quiet again, and the only sound was the slapping of the waves in the distance and the wind whistling as it hit the tin roofs and caught in the barbed-wire fences of the port terminal. A cat that was chasing a rat and knocked over a crate, which knocked over another one, and then everything came tumbling down, he thought. He thought of the poor cat, crushed to death along with the rat, beneath a mountain of boxes and barrels. He was now in Corny Román's sector. But of course Corny wasn't anywhere around; Lituma knew very well that he was at the other end of his patrol area, in the Happy Land, or the Blue Star, or in one of the many other cheap bars and sailors' brothels at the opposite end of the avenue, lining that little narrow street that the foul-mouthed residents of El Callao called Chancre Street. He'd be down there at one of the battered bar counters, downing a free beer he'd sponged off the proprietress. And as he walked down the avenue toward these dens of iniquity, Lituma imagined the frightened look on Román's face if he were suddenly to appear behind him: "So you're drinking on duty, are you, Corny? You're through."

He'd gone about two hundred yards when suddenly he stopped short. He turned and looked back: there, in the shadow, with one of its walls dimly lighted by the feeble glow of a streetlamp miraculously spared from the urchins' slingshots, lay the warehouse, silent now. It wasn't a cat, he thought, it wasn't a rat. It was a thief. His heart began to pound and he could feel his forehead and the palms of his hands break out in a cold sweat. It was a thief, a thief. He stood there motionless for a few seconds, though he already knew he'd go back there. He was sure: he'd had presentiments like this before. He drew his pistol from its holster, released the safety catch, and gripped his flashlight in his left hand. He strode back in the direction of the warehouse, with his heart in his mouth. Yes, no doubt about it, it was a thief. On reaching the building, he stopped again, panting. What if it wasn't just one thief, but several? Wouldn't it be better to hunt up Shorty, Corny before he went inside? He shook his head: he didn't need anybody, he could handle the situation by himself. If there were several of them, so much the worse for them and so much the better for him. He put his ear to the wall and listened: complete silence. The only sound to be heard, somewhere off in the distance, was the lapping of the waves and an occasional car going by. A thief, my ass, he thought. You're imagining things, Lituma. It was a cat, a rat. He was no longer cold; he felt warm and tired. He walked around the outside of the warehouse, looking for the door. When he found it, he could see by the light of his flashlight that the lock hadn't been broken open. He was about to leave, telling himself, What a fool you are, Lituma, your nose isn't as sharp as it used to be, when, with a last mechanical sweep of his flashlight, he discovered in its yellow beam the hole in the wall a few yards from the door. They'd done a crude job of breaking in, simply chopping an opening in the wooden wall with an ax, or kicking a few planks in. The hole was just big enough for a man to crawl through on all fours.

He felt his heart pounding wildly, madly, now. He turned his flashlight off, made sure the safety catch of his pistol was off, looked round about him: nothing but pitch-black shadows and, in the distance, like match flames, the streetlights of the Avenida Huáscar. He took a deep breath and roared, in as loud a voice as he could muster: "Have your men surround this warehouse, corporal. If anybody tries to escape, fire at will. Get a move on, all of you!"

And to make the whole thing more believable, he began running back and forth, stamping his feet loudly. Then he glued his face to the wall of the warehouse and shouted at the top of his lungs: "Hey, you in there! The jig is up: you've had it. You're surrounded. Come on out the way you came in, one at a time. We'll give you just thirty seconds!"

He heard the echo of his shouts fade away in the darkness, and then nothing but the sound of the sea and a few dogs barking. He counted off the seconds: not thirty but sixty. He thought: You're making an ass of yourself, Lituma.

He felt a mounting wave of anger, and shouted: "Keep your eyes open, boys. At the first false move, mow 'em all down, corporal!"

And screwing up his courage, agile despite his years and his heavy greatcoat, he got down on all fours and crawled through the opening. Once inside, he got quickly to his feet, ran on tiptoe to one side, and leaned his back against the wall. He couldn't see a thing, but didn't want to turn his flashlight on. He couldn't hear a sound, but again he was absolutely certain. There was somebody there, hiding in the dark as he was, listening and trying to see. He thought he could make out the sound of someone breathing, a panting noise. He had his finger on the trigger, holding the pistol at chest height. He counted to three and turned the flashlight on. The cry that followed came as such a surprise that in his fear the flashlight slipped out of his hand and rolled to the floor, revealing big bulky shapes that appeared to be bales of cotton, barrels, planks, and (fleeting, totally unexpected, beggaring belief) the figure of the black, hunched over and stark-naked, trying to cover his face with his hands, yet at the same time peeking through his fingers with panic-stricken eyes, staring at the flashlight as though the one danger confronting him was light.

"Stay right where you are or I'll shoot! Freeze, sambo, or you're a dead man!" Lituma roared, in such a loud voice it made his throat hurt, as he crouched down and fumbled about for the flashlight. And then, with savage satisfaction: "You've had it, sambo! You fucked up, sambo!"

He was yelling so hard he felt dizzy. He'd recovered the flashlight and the beam of light swept about, searching for the black. He hadn't escaped, he was still right there, and Lituma stared at him in open-eyed amazement, unable to believe what he was seeing. It wasn't his imagination, it wasn't a dream. He was really stark-naked, as naked as the day he was born: no shoes, no underpants, no shirt, no nothing. And he didn't seem to be embarrassed or even realize that he was naked, since he made no move to cover his privates, swinging gaily back and forth in the beam of the flashlight. He simply crouched there, his face half hidden behind his fingers, not moving, hypnotized by the little round beam of light.

"Hands on top of your head, sambo," the sergeant ordered, without stepping any closer to him. "Just cool it if you don't want to get pumped full of lead. You're under arrest for breaking into private property and for going around with your nuts dangling in the air."

And at the same time—his ears alert for the least little sound that would reveal the presence of an accomplice in the pitch-black darkness of the warehouse—the sergeant said to himself: This guy's not a thief. He's a madman. Not only because he was bare-ass naked in the middle of winter, but because of the cry he'd given on being discovered. Not the cry of a normal man, the sergeant thought. It had been a really strange sound, something between a howl, a bray, a burst of laughter, and a bark. A sound that didn't seem to have come only from his throat, but from his belly, his heart, his soul as well.

"Hands on your head, I said, damn it," the sergeant bellowed, taking a step toward the man. The latter didn't obey, didn't move a muscle. He was very dark and so thin that in the dim light Lituma could make out the ridges of his ribs distending the black skin and his pipestem legs, but he had a huge belly that drooped down over his pubis, and Lituma was immediately reminded of the skeleton-like children of the slums with bellies swollen with parasites. The black just stood there, not moving, hiding his face, and the sergeant took two more steps toward him, watching him closely, certain that at any moment he'd start running. Madmen don't respect revolvers, he thought, and took two more steps. He was now only a few feet away from the black, and it was at that moment that he first caught sight of the scars crisscrossing his shoulders, his arms, his back. Good Christ! Lituma thought. Were they from some sort of sickness? Injuries, or burns?

He spoke in a quiet voice so as not to frighten him. "Let's keep it nice and cool and easy, sambo. Hands on your head, walking over to the hole you came in through. If you behave yourself, I'll give you some coffee at the commissariat. You must be half frozen to death, running around bare-naked like that in weather like this."

He was about to take one step more toward the black when all of a sudden the man moved his hands away from his face—Lituma stood there dumfounded on seeing, beneath the mass of kinky matted hair, those terror-stricken eyes, those horrible scars, that enormous thick-lipped mouth with a single, long, filed tooth sticking out of it—and gave that same hybrid, incomprehensible, inhuman cry once again, looked all about, anxious, skittish, nervous, like an animal searching for a way to escape, and finally chose precisely the one he shouldn't have, the path the sergeant's body was blocking. Because he didn't try to knock him over but to run straight through him. The move was so unexpected that Lituma couldn't stop him and felt him crash into him. The sergeant had steady nerves: his finger didn't squeeze the trigger; he didn't fire a single shot. As his body collided with the sergeant's, the black snorted like an animal, and then Lituma gave him a shove and saw him fall to the floor like a rag doll. To keep him quiet, he kicked him a few times.

"Stand up," he ordered. "You're not only a madman, but a stupid idiot as well. And how you stink!"

He had an indefinable smell, of tar, acetone, cat piss. He'd rolled over onto his back and lay there looking up at Lituma with terror in his eyes.

"Where in the world can you have come from?" the sergeant muttered. He brought his flashlight a little closer and in utter bewilderment examined for a moment that incredible face crisscrossed with rectilinear incisions, a network of little fine slashes running across his cheeks, his nose, his forehead, his chin, and down into the folds of his neck. How had a guy with a mug like that, with his nuts dangling in the air, been able to walk through the streets of El Callao without anybody notifying the police?

"Stand up, I said, or else I'll really work you over," Lituma said. "Madman or not, I've had enough of you."

The guy didn't budge. He'd begun making noises with his mouth, an indecipherable mutter, a purr, a murmur, a sound that seemed to have more to do with birds, insects, or wild beasts than with human speech. And he kept staring at the flashlight in utter terror.

"Get up, don't be afraid," the sergeant said, reaching down with one hand and grabbing the black by the arm. The sambo made no move to resist, but at the same time not the slightest effort to get to his feet. How thin you are, Lituma thought, amused almost at the meowing, gurgling, babbling sound that poured out of the man's mouth in a steady stream. And how afraid of me you are. He jerked him to his feet and couldn't believe how little the man weighed; he had no sooner given him a slight push in the direction of the opening in the wall when he felt him stumble and fall to the floor. But this time he got up all by himself, with great effort, hanging on to a barrel of oil for support.

"Are you sick?" the sergeant asked. "You're hardly able to walk, sambo. Where in hell can a jaybird like you have come from, anyway?"

He dragged him over to the opening, made him crouch down and crawl through it in front of him to the street. The sambo went on making noises, not letting up for a second, as though he had a piece of iron in his mouth and was trying to spit it out. Yes, the sergeant thought, he's a madman. The drizzle had stopped, but now a strong wind was sweeping down the streets, howling round about them as Lituma, giving the sambo little pushes and shoves to hurry him up, headed toward the commissariat. Even bundled up as he was in his thick greatcoat, he could feel the cold.

"You must be frozen, old boy," Lituma said. "Bare-ass naked in this weather, at this hour. If you don't catch pneumonia, it'll be a miracle."

The black's teeth were chattering and he was walking along with his arms crossed over his chest, rubbing his sides with his huge bony hands, as though it were his ribs that felt the cold most. He was still snorting or roaring or croaking, but to himself now, and obeying docilely whenever the sergeant motioned to him to turn. As they threaded their way through the streets, they met neither cars nor dogs nor drunks. As they reached the commissariat—the light from its windows, with its oily glow, made Lituma as happy as a shipwreck victim sighting the beach—the booming bell in the tower of the church of Nuestra Señora del Carmen de la Legua was just striking two.

On seeing the sergeant appear with the naked black, handsome young Lieutenant Jaime Concha didn't drop his Uncle Donald comic book—his fourth one that night, not to mention the three Supermans and the two Mandrakes he'd read as well—but his mouth opened so wide in surprise that he nearly dislocated his jaw. Guards Camacho and Arévalo, who were having themselves a little game of Chinese checkers, also stared in wide-eyed amazement.

"Where in the world did you get *this* scarecrow?" the lieutenant finally asked.

"Is it a man, an animal, or a thing?" Apple Dumpling Arévalo said, getting to his feet and sniffing at the black. The latter hadn't uttered a sound since setting foot inside the commissariat but simply stood there, moving his head in all directions with a terrified look on his face, as though he were seeing electric lights, typewriters, civil guards for the first time in his life. But on seeing Arévalo approaching him, he again let out his hair-raising howl—Lituma noted that Lieutenant Concha was so taken aback he almost fell to the floor, chair and all, and that Snotnose Camacho tipped over the Chinese-checker board—and tried to go back outside. The sergeant held him back with one hand and gave him a little shake. "Quiet, sambo, don't panic on me."

"I found him in the new warehouse down at the harbor terminal, lieutenant," he said. "He got in by kicking a hole in the wall. Should I make out an arrest report for robbery, for breaking and entering, for indecent exposure, or for all three?"

The black had hunched over again as the lieutenant, Camacho, and Arévalo scrutinized him from head to foot.

"Those aren't smallpox scars, lieutenant," Apple Dumpling said, pointing to the slash marks on his face and body. "They were made with a knife, incredible as that may seem."

"He's the skinniest man I've ever seen in my life," Snotnose said, looking at the naked black's bones. "And the ugliest. Good lord, what kinky hair! And what enormous hands!"

"We're curious," the lieutenant said. "Tell us your life story, black boy."

Sergeant Lituma had taken off his kepi and unbuttoned his greatcoat. Sitting at the typewriter, he was beginning to write up his report. He shouted over: "He doesn't know how to talk, lieutenant. He just makes noises you can't understand."

"Are you one of those guys who pretends to be nuts?" the lieutenant went on, more curious than ever. "We're too old to fall for a trick like that, you know. Tell us who you are, where you come from, who your mama was."

"Or else we'll teach you to talk all over again with a few good punches in the snout," Apple Dumpling added. "To sing like a canary, Little Black Sambo."

"But if those are really knife scars, they must have cut him a good thousand times," Snotnose said in amazement, taking another good look at the tiny slash marks crisscrossing the black's face. "How is it possible for a man to get himself marked up like that?"

"He's freezing to death," Apple Dumpling said. "His teeth are chattering like maracas."

"You mean his molars," Snotnose corrected him, examining the man from very close up, as though he were an ant. "Can't you see that he's only got one front tooth, this elephant tusk here? Man, what a hideous-looking character: straight out of a nightmare."

"I think he's got bats in his belfry," Lituma said, without looking up from the typewriter. "Nobody in his right mind would go around like that in this cold, isn't that so, lieutenant?"

And at that moment the commotion made him look up: suddenly electrified by something, the black had pushed the lieutenant aside and darted like an arrow between Camacho and Arévalo. Not toward the street, however, but toward the Chinese-checkers table, and Lituma saw him grab up a half-eaten sandwich, stuff it into his mouth, and swallow it in a single ravenous, bestial gulp. As Arévalo and Camacho went for him and began cuffing him over the head, the black was downing the remains of the other sandwich on the table with the same ravenous haste.

"Don't hit him you guys," the sergeant said. "Be charitable—offer him some coffee instead."

"This isn't a welfare institution," the lieutenant said. "I don't know what the devil I'm going to do with this character." He stood there looking at the black, who after wolfing down the sandwiches had taken his lumps from Snotnose and Apple Dumpling without batting an eye and was now lying quietly on the floor, panting softly. The lieutenant finally took pity on him and growled: "All right, then. Give him a little coffee and put him in the detention cell."

Snotnose handed him half a cup of coffee from the thermos. The black drank slowly, closing his eyes, and when he'd finished licked the aluminum cup, searching for the last few drops in the bottom, till it shone. Then he went along with them, quietly and peacefully, as they led him to the cell.

Lituma reread his report: attempted robbery, breaking and entering, indecent exposure. Lieutenant Jaime Concha had come back to his desk, and as his eyes wandered about the room, he suddenly said to Lituma with a happy smile, pointing to the pile of multicolored magazines: "Aha! Now I know who it is he reminds me of! The blacks in the Tarzan stories, the ones in Africa."

Camacho and Arévalo had gone back to their Chinese checkers, and Lituma put his kepi back on and buttoned up his greatcoat. As he was going out the door, he heard the shrill cries of the pickpocket, who had just woken up and was protesting against his new cellmate: "Help! Save me! He's going to rape me!"

"Shut your trap or we'll be the ones who'll rape you," the lieutenant threatened. "Let me read my comic books in peace."

From the street, Lituma could see that the black had stretched out on the floor, indifferent to the outcries from the pickpocket, a very thin Chinese who was scared to death. Imagine waking up and finding yourself face to face with a bogeyman like that, Lituma thought and laughed to himself, his massive bulk again turned to the wind, the drizzle, the darkness. With his hands in his pockets, the collar of his greatcoat turned up, his head lowered, he continued unhurriedly on his rounds. He went first to Chancre Street, where he found Corny Román leaning on the counter of the Happy Land, laughing at the jokes of Mourning Dove, the old fairy with dyed hair and false teeth tending bar there. He noted in his report that patrolman Román "gave signs of having drunk alcoholic beverages while on duty," even though he knew full well that Lieutenant Concha, a man extremely tolerant of his own weaknesses and those of others, would look the other way. He left the port district then and strode up the Avenida Sáenz Peña, deader than a cemetery at this hour of the night. He had a terrible time finding Humberto Quispe, whose patrol area was the market district. The stalls were closed and there were fewer bums than usual sleeping curled up on sacks or newspapers underneath stairways and trucks. After several useless searches from one end of the area to the other, blowing the recognition signal countless times on his whistle, he finally located Quispe on the corner of Colón and Cochrane, helping a taxi driver whose skull had been cracked open by two thugs who had then robbed him. They took him to the public hospital to get his head sewed up and then went to have a bowl of fish-head soup at the first stall in the market to open up, that of Señora Gualberta, a fishwife. A cruising patrol car picked Lituma up on Sáenz Peña and gave him a lift to the fortress of Real Felipe, where Little Hands Rodríguez, the youngest Guardia Civil assigned to the Fourth Commissariat, was on patrol duty at the foot of the walls. He surprised him playing hopscotch, all by himself, in the darkness.

He was hopping gravely and intently from square to square, on one foot, on two, and on seeing the sergeant he immediately stood at attention. "Exercise helps keep you warm," he said to him, pointing to the squares marked off in chalk on the sidewalk. "Didn't you ever play hopscotch when you were a kid, sergeant?"

"I went in more for top spinning, and I was pretty good at kite flying," Lituma replied.

Little Hands Rodríguez told him of an incident that, he said, had made his shift that night an amusing one. He'd been patrolling along the Calle Paz Soldán, around midnight, when he'd spied a guy climbing through a window. Revolver in hand, he'd ordered the man to halt, but the guy had burst into tears, swearing he wasn't a thief but a man whose wife insisted that he come in the house that way, in the dark and through the window. And why not through the door, like everybody else? "Because she's half crazy," the man whimpered. "It makes her more affectionate if she sees me entering the house like a thief—can you imagine? And other times she makes me threaten her with a knife to scare her, and even disguise myself as the Devil. And if I don't do what she wants, she won't give me so much as a kiss, sir."

"He saw that you were an inexperienced kid and handed you a real cock-and-bull story." Lituma smiled.

"It's the absolute truth," Little Hands insisted. "I knocked at the door, we went in, and the wife, an uppity little samba, said it was true and why shouldn't she and her husband have the right to play their little game of robbers? The things you see in this job, eh, sergeant?"

"You said it, kid," Lituma agreed, thinking of the black.

"On the other hand, a man would never get bored with a woman like that, sergeant," Little Hands said, smacking his lips.

He accompanied Lituma to the Avenida Buenos Aires, where the two of them separated. As the sergeant headed toward the boundary line of the Bellavista precinct—the Calle Vigil, the Plaza de la Guardia Chalaca—a long trek, usually the stretch where he first began to feel tired and sleepy, the sergeant remembered the black. Could he have escaped from the insane asylum? But Larco Herrera Asylum was such a long way away that some Guardia Civil or patrol car would have seen him and arrested him. And those scars? Could they really be from knife cuts? Damn, that would really hurt, like being slowly burned to death. How hideous—making one little tiny cut after another till the guy's face was covered with them. Or could he have been born like that? It was still pitch-dark, but already there were signs of approaching dawn: cars, an occasional truck, silhouettes of early risers. You who've seen so many real oddballs—

why are you so concerned about that guy you found stark-naked, the sergeant wondered. He shrugged: mere curiosity, a way of keeping his mind occupied till it was time to go off duty.

He had no difficulty finding Zárate, a Guardia Civil who'd served with him in Ayacucho. He found him with his report already made out and signed: one traffic accident, nobody hurt, nothing important. Lituma told him about the black, and the only part that Zárate thought was funny was the bit about the sandwiches. He was a demon stamp collector and, as he accompanied the sergeant for a few blocks, began telling him how he'd managed, just that morning, to come by some triangular stamps from Ethiopia, with lions and snakes, in green, red, and blue, a very rare issue, for which he'd swapped five Argentine stamps not worth anything at all.

"But which they'll doubtless think are worth a whole lot," Lituma interrupted.

Zárate's mania, which ordinarily he put up with good-naturedly, irritated him tonight and he was happy when they separated. A faint blue light was dawning in the sky and the buildings of El Callao, ghostly, grayish, rusty, teeming, loomed up out of the darkness. Hurrying along almost at a trot, the sergeant counted the blocks he still had to go before reaching the commissariat. But this time, he admitted to himself, he was hurrying not so much because he was tired after the long night and all the walking he'd done but because he was eager to see the black again. It's almost as if you believed the whole thing was a dream and the darky doesn't really exist, Lituma.

But he did indeed exist: he was there, sleeping curled up in a ball on the floor of the cell. The pickpocket had fallen asleep at the other end, with a fearful expression on his face still. The others were asleep, too: Lieutenant Concha with his head resting on a pile of comic books, and Camacho and Arévalo shoulder to shoulder on the bench in the entryway. Lituma stood staring at the black for a long time: his ribs sticking out, his kinky hair, his mouth with the thick lips, his thousand scars, his body shivering from head to foot. Where in the world have you come from, darky? he thought.

He finally went to hand in his report to the lieutenant, who opened red, puffy eyes. "Another damned shift that's just about over," he said, his mouth as dry as dust. "One day less to serve in the corps, Lituma."

And one day less to live, too, the sergeant thought. He clicked his heels together smartly and left. It was six in the morning and he was free. As usual, he went to the market to Doña Gualberta's to have a bowl of steaming-hot soup, meat pies, beans with rice, and a custard, and then to the little room where he lived, in the Calle Colón. He had trouble getting to sleep, and the minute he finally did, he began dreaming about the black man. He saw him surrounded by red, green, and blue lions and snakes, in the heart of Abyssinia, with a top hat, boots, and an animal tamer's whip. The wild beasts did tricks to the rhythm of his cracking whip, and a crowd sitting amid the jungle vines, the tree trunks, and the thick foliage enlivened by the songs of birds and the screams of monkeys applauded him madly. But instead of bowing to the audience, the black got down on his knees, stretched out his hands in a gesture of supplication, tears welled up in his eyes, and his big thick-lipped mouth opened and from it there came pouring out, in an anguished, tumultuous rush, his gibberish, his absurd music.

Lituma woke up around three in the afternoon, in a bad humor and very tired, despite having slept seven hours. They must have taken him to Lima by now, he thought. As he washed his face like a cat and got dressed, he followed the black's trajectory in his mind's eye: the nine o'clock patrol car would have come to pick him up, they'd have given him a rag to cover himself with, they'd have taken him to the prefecture and opened a file on him, they'd have put him in the cell for prisoners awaiting trial, and there he'd be this minute, in that dark hole, among bums, sneak thieves, muggers, and troublemakers picked up in the last twenty-four hours, shivering from the cold and dying of hunger, scratching his lice.

It was a gray, humid day; people were moving about in the fog like fish in dirty water, and Lituma walked, slowly and pensively, over to Doña Gualberta's to eat lunch: two rolls with cream cheese and a coffee.

"You're in a strange mood today, Lituma," Doña Gualberta, a little old woman who knew a thing or two about life, said. "Money troubles or love troubles?"

"I'm thinking about a darky I found last night," the sergeant said, testing his coffee with the tip of his tongue. "He'd broken into a warehouse down at the harbor terminal."

"And what's so strange about that?" Doña Gualberta asked.

"He was stark-naked, full of scars, with a head of hair as matted as a jungle, and doesn't know how to talk," Lituma explained. "Where can a character like that be from anyway?"

"From Hell." The old woman laughed as he paid the bill.

Lituma walked down to the Plaza Grau to meet Pedralbes, a petty officer in the navy. They'd known each other for years, ever since the days when the sergeant was just a private in the Guardia Civil and Pedralbes an able-bodied seaman and both of them were stationed in Pisco. After that, their respective careers had separated them for almost ten years, and then, in the last two years, brought them back together again. They were in the habit of spending their days off-duty together, and Lituma felt like one of the family at the Pedralbes house. They went off today to La Punta, to the club for seamen and petty officers, to have a beer and play toad-in-the-hole. The sergeant told him straightway the story of the black, and Pedralbes immediately came up with an explanation. "He's a savage from Africa who got here as a stowaway on a boat. He hid aboard all during the crossing and when the ship docked at El Callao he slipped into the water in the dark of night and entered Peru illegally."

It was as though the sun had just come out: suddenly everything was plain as day to Lituma.

"You're right, that's exactly how it was," he said, clacking his tongue and clapping his hands. "He's come from Africa. Of course: it all fits. Once the ship docked here in El Callao, they made him get off for some reason. So as not to pay for his passage, because they discovered him in the hold, to get rid of him."

"They didn't hand him over to the authorities because they knew they wouldn't let him into the country," Pedralbes said, filling in the details of the story. "They forced him to get off the ship: shift for yourself, you jungle savage."

"In other words, that darky doesn't even know where he is," Lituma said. "And those strange sounds he keeps making aren't those of a madman but of a savage; that is to say, the sounds of his own language."

"It's as though they put you on a plane and you landed on Mars, old pal," Pedralbes said helpfully.

"How clever we are," Lituma said. "We've just discovered that darky's whole life story."

"You mean how clever *I* am," Pedralbes protested. "And what will they do with the guy now?"

Who knows? Lituma thought. They played six games of toad-in-the-hole and the sergeant won four, so Pedralbes had to pay for their beers. Then they walked over to the Calle Chanchamayo, where Pedralbes lived, in a little house with bars over the windows. Domitila, Pedralbes's wife, was just finishing feeding the three children, and the minute she saw the two of them come in, she put the littlest one to bed and ordered the other two not to even peek so much as their noses through the door. She fixed her hair a little, linked arms with the two of them, and they went out to see an Italian movie at the Cine Porteño, on Sáenz Peña. Lituma and Pedralbes didn't like the movie at all, but she said she'd even go back and see it again. They walked back to the Calle Chanchamayo —the kids had all gone to sleep—and Domitila warmed up some *olluquitos con charqui*—potatoes and dried salt meat—for their supper. It was ten-thirty when Lituma left. He arrived at the Fourth Commissariat exactly at the hour he was to go on duty: eleven on the dot.

Lieutenant Jaime Concha didn't even give him time to catch his breath; he called him aside and, out of the blue, gave him specific orders, in a couple of Spartan sentences that left Lituma dizzy and made his ears ring. "The higher-ups know what they're doing," the lieutenant assured him, clapping him on the back encouragingly. "They have their reasons, and we just have to go along with them. Our superiors are never wrong, isn't that so, Lituma?"

"Yes, of course," the sergeant stammered.

Apple Dumpling and Snotnose were pretending to be terribly busy. Out of the corner of his eye, Lituma saw Apple Dumpling carefully inspecting traffic tickets as though they were photographs of naked women, and Snotnose was arranging, disarranging, and then rearranging things on his desk.

"Can I ask you a question, lieutenant?" Lituma said.

"Go ahead. I don't know if I can answer it, though."

"How come the higher-ups have chosen *me* for this little job?"

"That I can tell you," the lieutenant replied. "For two reasons. Because you were the one who captured him and it's only right that the one who begins a caper should be the one who ends it. And secondly, because you're the best Guardia Civil in this commissariat and perhaps in all of El Callao."

"I'm honored by your compliment," Lituma murmured, not pleased in the slightest.

"Our superiors know very well that this is a tough job, and that's why they've entrusted it to you," the lieutenant said. "You should feel proud that it's you they've chosen from among the hundreds of Guardias stationed in Lima."

"In other words, on top of everything else, I ought to thank them," Lituma said, shaking his head in stupefaction. He thought the whole thing over for a moment, and then added in a low voice: "Does it have to be done right away?"

"This very instant," the lieutenant answered in a fake-jovial tone of voice. "Don't put off till tomorrow what you can do today."

Now you know why you couldn't get that black's face out of your mind, Lituma thought.

"You want to take one of these guys with you to give you a hand?" he heard the lieutenant saying.

Lituma could feel Camacho and Arévalo sitting there petrified. A polar silence descended on the commissariat as the sergeant looked at the two Guardias and deliberately took his time choosing between them so as to make them squirm a little. Apple Dumpling, his fingers shaking, continued to look through the pile of traffic tickets, and Snotnose had bent over his desk to hide his face.

"I'll take him," Lituma said, pointing to Arévalo. He heard Camacho let out a deep breath and saw a sudden gleam of utter hatred appear in Apple Dumpling's eyes that immediately told him the latter was mentally cursing his sergeant's whore of a mother.

"I've got a terrible cold and I was just about to ask permission to stay inside tonight, lieutenant," Arévalo stammered, trying to play dumb.

"Stop acting like an idiot and get your coat on," Lituma broke in, walking past him without looking at him. "We're leaving this minute."

He went to the cell and unlocked the door. For the first time that day, he took a look at the black. They'd dressed him in a ragged pair of pants that just barely reached his knees, and covered his chest and back with a burlap bag with a hole cut out of it for his head. He was barefoot and calm; he looked Lituma in the eye, with neither fear nor joy. He was sitting on the floor, chewing something; instead of handcuffs, he had a rope tied around his wrists, long enough for him to be able to scratch himself or to eat. The sergeant made signs to him to stand up, but the black didn't seem to understand. Lituma walked over to him, took him by the arm, and the man obediently got to his feet. He walked down the corridor ahead of Lituma, with the same indifference. Apple Dumpling Arévalo already had his greatcoat on and his scarf wound around his neck. Lieutenant Concha didn't even turn around to watch them leave: he had his face buried in a Donald Duck (But he doesn't realize he's holding it upside down, Lituma thought). Camacho, on the other hand, gave them a smile of commiseration.

Once out on the street, the sergeant placed himself on the curb side, leaving the wall to Arévalo. The black walked along between the two of them, at the same pace, in long steady strides, still chewing.

"He's been gnawing on that hunk of bread for almost two hours now," Arévalo said. "When they brought him back from Lima tonight, we gave him all the stale rolls in the pantry, the ones that had gotten as hard as rocks. And he's eaten every last one of them. Chewing like a grinder. He must be half starved to death, don't you imagine?"

Duty first and sentiments later, Lituma was thinking. He mapped out the itinerary in his mind: up the Calle Carlos Concha to Contralmirante Mora and then down the avenue to the banks of the Rímac and along the river to the ocean. He calculated: three quarters of an hour to get there and back, an hour at most.

"It's all your fault, sergeant," Arévalo grumbled. "Who asked you to capture him anyway? When you realized he wasn't a thief, you should have let him go. And now look at all the trouble you've gotten us into. Tell me something: do you go along with what the brass hats think? That this guy came here as a stowaway on a boat?"

"That's what Pedralbes thinks, too," Lituma said. "It's possible. Otherwise, how the devil do you explain how an outlandish-looking character like this, with that hair and those scars and naked as a jaybird and talking that gibberish of his, happens to pop up all of a sudden in the port of El Callao? They must be right."

The echo of the Guardias' two pair of boots resounded in the dark street; the sambo's bare feet made no sound at all.

"If it were up to me, I'd have left him in prison," Arévalo went on. "Because a savage from Africa isn't to blame if he's a savage from Africa, sergeant."

"But it's for that very reason that he can't stay in prison," Lituma murmured. "You heard the lieutenant: prison is for thieves, murderers, bandits. What legal grounds would the state have for keeping him in prison?"

"Well, they ought to send him back to his own country, then," Arévalo growled.

"And how the devil do you find out what country he's from?" Lituma said, raising his voice. "You heard the lieutenant. They tried at headquarters in Lima to talk to him in all languages: English, French, Italian even. But he doesn't talk languages: he's a savage."

"In other words, you approve of our having to take him out someplace and shoot him because he's a savage," Apple Dumpling Arévalo muttered angrily.

"I'm not saying I approve," Lituma murmured. "I'm just repeating what the lieutenant said the higher-ups said. Don't be an ass."

They started down the Avenida Contralmirante Mora just as the bells of Nuestra Señora del Carmen de la Legua struck twelve, a lugubrious tolling to Lituma's ear. He strode along resolutely, looking straight ahead, but every so often, despite himself, his head turned to his left and he stole a quick glance at the black. He saw him, for the space of a second, walking through the feeble cone of light at the foot of a lamppost, and each time he looked exactly the same: still stolidly moving his jaw up and down, striding along in step with the two of them, without the slightest sign of anxiety. The only thing in this world that seems to matter to him is chewing, Lituma thought. And a moment later: He's a man condemned to death who doesn't know he is. And almost immediately thereafter: There's no doubt about it, he's a savage.

And at that point he heard Arévalo say: "Even so, why don't our superiors just let him go free to get along as best he can?" he groused. "Just let him be another bum, along with all the others there are in Lima. One more, one less—what the hell would it matter?"

"You heard the lieutenant," Lituma answered. "The Guardia Civil can't encourage the breaking of the law. And if you let this character loose in the middle of the city, the only way he can survive is to steal. Or else he'll just die like a dog. We're really doing him a favor. He'll kick off in a second if we shoot him. That's better than dying slowly, inch by inch, from hunger, cold, loneliness, sadness."

But Lituma could feel that what he was saying wasn't at all convincing, and on hearing his own voice he had the sensation that he was listening to another person speaking.

"Be that as it may, let me say just one thing," he heard Apple Dumpling protest. "I don't like this job at all, and you played a dirty trick on me when you picked me."

"Listen, do you think *I* like it?" Lituma murmured. "And don't you think my superiors played a dirty trick on *me* by picking me?"

They walked past the Naval Arsenal just as a siren blew, and as they crossed the vacant lot along the dry dock, a dog came out of the shadows and barked at them. They walked along in silence, hearing their boots clatter on the sidewalk, the sound of the sea only a short distance away, feeling in their nostrils the damp salty air.

"Gypsies camped out on this vacant lot last year," Apple Dumpling burst out all of a sudden, his voice breaking. "They put up tents and gave a circus show. They told fortunes and did magic tricks. But the mayor made us chase them out because they didn't have a city license."

Lituma didn't answer. He suddenly felt sorry, not only for the black, but for Apple Dumpling and the gypsies as well.

"And are we going to leave his dead body lying there on the beach for the pelicans to peck to bits?" Apple Dumpling almost sobbed.

"We're going to leave it at the garbage dump so the city sanitation trucks will find it, take it to the morgue, and give it to the med school for students to autopsy," Lituma said angrily. "You heard the instructions, Arévalo; don't make me repeat them."

"I heard them, but I can't get used to the idea that we have to kill him like this, in cold blood," Apple Dumpling said a few moments later. "And you can't get used to it either, no matter how hard you try. I can tell by your voice that you don't approve of this order either."

"Our duty isn't to approve of the order but to carry it out," the sergeant said in a faint voice. And then, after a pause, speaking even more slowly: "You're right, of course. I don't approve of it either. I'm obeying because it's necessary to obey."

At that moment they came to the end of the pavement, the avenue, the streetlights, and began to walk through the pitch-black shadows on soft ground. A thick, almost solid stench enveloped them. They were in the garbage dump along the banks of the Rímac, very close to the sea, in the rectangular area between the beach, the riverbed, and the avenue, where every morning, beginning at seven, the Sanitation Department trucks came to dump the refuse from Bellavista, La Perla, and El Callao and where, beginning around about the same hour, a horde of kids, grown men and women, and oldsters began to paw through the piles of filth in search of objects of value, and to fight with the seabirds, the buzzards, the stray dogs for the edible remains of food mixed in with the garbage. They were very close to that wasteland now, heading toward Ventanilla, toward Ancón, and the long line of El Callao fish-meal factories.

"This is the best place," Lituma said. "All the garbage trucks pass this way."

The sound of the sea was very loud now. Manzanita stopped and the black stopped too. The Guardias had turned their flashlights on and were examining, in the flickering light, the face crisscrossed with tiny scars, imperturbably chewing.

"The worst of it is that he doesn't have any reflexes or intuitions about things," Lituma murmured. "Anybody else would realize what's about to happen and be terrified, try to escape. What gets me is how calm he is, how much he trusts us."

"I've got an idea, sergeant." Arévalo's teeth were chattering as though he were freezing. "Let's allow him to escape. We'll say we killed him and then, well, think up some sort of story to explain how come there's no corpse . . ."

Lituma had drawn his revolver and was removing the safety catch.

"Are you daring to suggest to me that I disobey my superior's orders and then lie to them on top of it?" the sergeant boomed, his voice shaking. His right hand pointed the gun barrel at the black's temple.

But two, three, several seconds went by and he didn't shoot. Would he do so? Would he obey? Would the shot ring out? Would the dead body of the mysterious immigrant roll over onto the heap of unidentifiable rotting garbage? Or would his life be spared, would he flee, blindly, wildly, along the beaches beyond the city, as an irreproachable sergeant stood there, amid the putrid stench and the surge of the waves, confused and sad at heart at having failed to do his duty? How would this tragedy of El Callao end?

Five.

Lucho Gatica's visit to

Lima was described by Pascual in our news bulletins as "an unforgettable artistic occasion and a four-star event in the history of Peruvian radio broadcasting." His appearance on the airwaves of Panamericana cost me a story and an almost new shirt and tie, and caused me to stand Aunt Julia up for the second time. Before the Chilean bolero singer arrived in town, I'd seen countless photographs and laudatory articles about him in the papers ("Unpaid publicity, the very best kind," Genaro Jr. said), but I didn't really realize how famous he was till I noticed the huge crowd of women lined up in the Calle Belén hoping to get passes to the broadcast. Since the auditorium of the station was small—a hundred seats or so—only a few lucky women managed to get the precious passes. On the night of the broadcast there was such a big crowd outside the doors of Panamericana that Pascual and I had to get up to our shack by way of the building next door, which opened onto the same rooftop terrace as our building. We prepared the seven o'clock bulletin, but there was no way of getting it down to the second floor.

"There's a whole shitload of women blocking the stairway, the door, and the elevator," Pascual told me. "I tried to get through, but they took me for a gate crasher."

I phoned Genaro Jr., who was beside himself with joy.

"There's still an hour to go before Lucho's broadcast, and the crowd outside has already stopped traffic along the Calle Belén. All Peru is tuned in to Radio Panamericana at this moment."

I asked him whether, given the circumstances, we should skip the seven and eight o'clock bulletins, but resourceful as ever, he came up with the idea of having us dictate them over the phone to the announcers downstairs. We did so, and in the hour between the two, Pascual listened, enraptured, to Lucho Gatica's voice on the radio and I reread the fourth version of my story about the eunuch-senator, which I'd finally ended up calling, in the manner of a Gothic horror tale, "The Ruined Face." At nine on the dot we heard the end of the program, the voice of Martínez Morosini bidding Lucho Gatica goodbye and the applause from the audience that this time wasn't canned but real.

Ten seconds later the telephone rang and I heard Genaro Jr.'s voice say in alarm: "Get down here, any way you can. Things are getting out of hand."

We had a terrible time making a hole in the solid wall of women jammed together on the stairway, whom Jesusito, the corpulent doorman stationed at the entrance to the auditorium, was holding back. Pascual kept shouting: "Ambulance corps! Ambulance corps! We're coming to get somebody who's been hurt!" The women, young ones for the most part, looked at us indifferently or smiled, but didn't move aside and we had to push them out of the way. Once inside, we were greeted by a disconcerting spectacle: the celebrated artist was demanding police protection. He was a short little man, livid and filled with hatred toward his female admirers. The dynamic impresario was trying to calm him down, telling him that calling in the police would make a very bad impression, that this horde of girls was a tribute to his talent. But the celebrity was not at all swayed by that line of argument. "I know their kind all too well," he said, half terrified and half enraged. "They begin by asking for an autograph and end up scratching and biting."

We laughed, but reality bore out his predictions. Genaro Jr. decided that we should wait half an hour, thinking that Lucho's admirers would eventually get bored and go away. At ten-fifteen (I had a date with Aunt Julia to go to the movies), we'd gotten tired of waiting for them to get tired and made up our minds to leave. Genaro Jr., Pascual, Jesusito, Martínez Morosini and I linked arms and formed a circle round the celebrity, whose already pale face positively blanched the moment we opened the door. We managed to get down the first steps with no great damage done, by pushing and shoving with our elbows, knees, heads, and chests against the sea of females, who for the moment were content to applaud, sigh, and stretch out their hands to touch their idol—who, with a fixed smile on his marble-white face, kept muttering under his breath: "Careful, fellows, don't let go of each others' arms." But we fell victim to an all-out attack. They grabbed us by our clothes and tugged, and screaming at the top of their lungs reached for their idol with their fingernails to tear off pieces of his shirt and suit. When, after ten minutes of nearly being smothered or crushed to death, we finally fought our way to the exit, I thought we were about to let go of each other and had a vision: the little bolero singer was snatched away from us and torn limb from limb by his admirers before our very eyes. This didn't happen, but when we put him in Genaro Sr.'s car—he'd been waiting at the wheel for an hour and a half—Lucho Gatica and his iron guard had been transformed into survivors of a catastrophe. They had yanked my tie off and my shirt was in shreds; they had torn Jesusito's uniform and stolen his cap; and Genaro Jr. had a big purple bruise on his forehead where he'd been clouted with a handbag. The star was unhurt, but the only items of his attire that had remained intact were his shoes and his undershorts. The next morning, as we were taking our ten o'clock break at the Bransa, I told Pedro Camacho about the amazing feats of Lucho Gatica's horde of admirers. He wasn't at all surprised. "My dear young friend," he said to me philosophically, with a faraway look in his eyes, "music *too* touches the soul of the multitude."

As I had been struggling to defend the physical integrity of Lucho Gatica, Señora Agradecida, the charwoman, had cleaned the shack upstairs and thrown in the trash the fourth version of my story about the senator. Instead of being upset, I felt as though I'd been freed of a weight and took the whole thing as having been a warning from the gods. When I told Javier that I wasn't going to rewrite it yet again, he congratulated me for having come to that decision rather than trying to persuade me to change my mind.

Aunt Julia found my story of my experience as a bodyguard terribly amusing. Since the night of the furtive kisses in the

Bolívar Grill, we'd been seeing each other almost every day. The day after Uncle Lucho's birthday, I'd dropped by the house unexpectedly, and luckily Aunt Julia was there alone.

"They've gone to visit your Aunt Hortensia," she said, showing me into the living room. "I didn't go with them because I know very well that that gossip spends all her time making up nasty stories about me."

I took her by the waist, drew her to me, and tried to kiss her. She didn't push me away, but she didn't kiss me either: all I felt was her cold mouth against mine. As we stepped apart, I saw that she was looking at me without smiling: not in surprise, as on the night before, but rather with a certain curiosity and a faintly mocking gleam in her eyes.

"Look, Marito"—her voice was calm, affectionate—"I've done all sorts of really crazy things in my life. But *this* is one I'm not going to do." She burst into laughter. "Me, seducing a kid? Never!"

We sat down and chatted for nearly two hours. I told her the whole story of my life—not my past life, but the one I was going to have in the future, when I lived in Paris and was a writer. I told her I'd wanted to write ever since I'd first read Alexandre Dumas, that since that moment I'd dreamed of going off to France and living in a garret, in the artists' *quartier*, dedicating my heart and soul to literature, the most marvelous thing in the world. I told her I was studying law to please my family, but that being a lawyer struck me as the dullest and most stupid of professions, one I had no intention of ever practicing. I realized at one point that I was speaking in the most heartfelt tones, and told her that this was the very first time I'd ever confessed such intimate things not to a buddy but to a woman.

"I seem like your mama to you, and that's the reason you're confiding in me," Aunt Julia psychoanalyzed. "So Dorita's boy has turned out to be a bohemian—who would ever have thought it? The trouble is, my son, that you're going to starve to death."

She told me she hadn't slept a wink the night before, thinking of those furtive kisses in the Bolívar Grill. She couldn't get over the idea that Dorita's boy, the youngster that only yesterday she and his mama had taken off to Cochabamba to put in the La Salle school, the kid she thought of as still wearing short pants, the baby she let escort her to the movies so as not to have to go alone, had all of a sudden kissed her square on the mouth like a full-grown, experienced man.

"But I am a full-grown, experienced man," I assured her, taking her hand and kissing it. "I'm eighteen years old. And I lost my virginity five whole years ago."

"Well, what does that make me then, if I'm thirty-two and lost mine fifteen years ago?" she laughed. "A decrepit old lady!"

She had a loud, hearty laugh, spontaneous and joyous, that made her large, full-lipped mouth open wide and her eyes crinkle. She gave me an ironic, mischievous look that told me I was not yet a full-grown, experienced man in her eyes, but no longer a kid either. She got up to pour me a whiskey.

"After the liberties you took last night, I can't offer you Cokes any more," she said, pretending to be embarrassed. "I'm going to have to treat you like one of my suitors."

I told her the difference in age between us wasn't all that tremendous.

"Not all that tremendous, no," she answered. "But almost—I'm very nearly old enough for you to be my son."

She told me the story of her marriage. Everything had gone very well the first few years. Her husband had a ranch in the interior and she'd become so accustomed to living in the country that she rarely went to La Paz. The ranch house was very comfortable and she loved the peace and quiet of the place, the healthy, simple life: riding horseback, going on outings in the countryside, attending Indian fiestas. The first dark clouds had appeared when she couldn't get pregnant: her husband suffered at the thought of not having children. He'd begun to drink then, and from that time on the marriage had gone downhill, by way of quarrels, separations, and reconciliations, till finally they had broken up for good. They had remained good friends after the divorce.

"If I should ever happen to get married, I'd never have children," I announced. "Children and literature are incompatible."

"Does that mean that I can present myself as a candidate and line up with the others?" Aunt Julia teased me.

She was very good at clever repartee, told risqué stories charmingly, and (like all the women I'd ever known thus far in my life) was terribly aliterary. I had the impression that during her many long, idle hours on her Bolivian hacienda the only things she'd ever read were Argentine magazines, some of Delly's trashy books, and no more than a couple of novels at most that she considered memorable: *The Sheik* and *Son of the Sheik,* by a certain E. M. Hull. As I said goodbye to her that evening, I asked her if we could go to the movies together, and she had replied: "Yes, *that's* possible." So we went to the movies almost every night, and besides sitting through a good many Mexican and Argentine melodramas, we'd given each other a good many kisses. The movies gradually became a pretext; we chose theaters (the Montecarlo, the Colina, the Marsano) that were the farthest away from the house on Armendáriz so as to be able to be together longer. After the movies let out, we took long strolls, "making *empanaditas*" (she told me that that was how you said "holding hands" in Bolivia), wandering through all the empty streets of Miraflores (we let go of each other's hand every time a passerby or a car appeared), talking about all sorts of things as—it was that dreary season known in Lima as winter—the continual drizzle soaked us to the skin. Aunt Julia went out every day to have lunch or tea with one or another of her many suitors, but she saved her evenings for me. We spent them at the movies, as a matter of fact, sitting in one of the very last rows at the back, where (especially if it was a terrible film) we could kiss without bothering the other spectators and without running the risk of somebody recognizing us. Our relationship had soon stabilized at some amorphous stage; it was situated at some indefinable point between the opposed categories of being sweethearts and being lovers. This was a subject that cropped up constantly in our conversations. We shared certain of the classic traits of lovers—secretiveness, the fear of being discovered, the feeling we were taking great risks—but we were lovers spiritually, not materially, since we didn't make love (and, as Javier was later shocked to learn, we didn't even "feel each other up"). At the same time we shared with sweethearts a respect for certain classic rites observed by adolescent couples of Miraflores in those days (going to the movies, kissing during the film, walking down the street hand in hand), and our behavior was equally chaste (in that Stone Age the girls of Miraflores were almost always still virgins on their wedding day and would allow their breasts and their pudenda to be touched only after their sweetheart had been officially promoted to the status of fiancé and their engagement been formally announced, but how could that ever happen to us, given the difference in age between us and the fact that we were relatives?). Realizing how ambiguous and offbeat our relationship was, we made a game of thinking up amusing names for it and called it our English engagement, our Swedish romance, our Turkish drama.

"The love affair of a baby and an old lady who's also more or less your aunt," Julia said to me one night as we were crossing the Parque Central. "A perfect subject for one of Pedro Camacho's serials."

I reminded her that she was only my aunt by marriage, and she replied that on the three o'clock serial a boy from San Isidro, terrifically handsome and an expert surfer, had had relations with his sister, no less, and, horror of horrors, had gotten her pregnant.

"Since when have you been listening to radio serials?" I asked.

"It's a contagious vice I caught from my sister," she answered. "The ones on Radio Central are fantastic, I must say, tremendous dramas that break your heart."

And she confessed to me that sometimes she and Aunt Olga sat there listening with tears in their eyes. This was the first indication I had of the impact that Pedro Camacho's pen was having in the households of Lima. I had others during the next few days, in the households of several relatives. I happened to drop by Aunt Laura's, and the minute she spied me in the doorway of the living room she put her finger to her lips to signal me to be quiet, as she sat there leaning over her radio as though trying not only to hear but also to smell, to touch the (tremulous or harsh or ardent or crystalline) voice of the Bolivian artist. I appeared at Aunt Gaby's and found her and Aunt Hortensia mechanically unwinding a ball of yarn as they followed a dialogue, full of proparoxytones and gerunds, between Luciano Pando and Josefina Sánchez. And in my own house, my grandparents, who had always "had a liking for little novels," as my Grandmother Carmen put it, had now conceived a genuine passion for radio serials. I woke up in the morning nowadays to the strains of Radio Central's theme song—in their compulsive eagerness not to miss the day's first serial, the one at 10 a.m., they'd turned in far ahead of time; I ate my lunch listening to the one at two in the afternoon; and no matter what hour of the day I came home, I found my two little old grandparents and the cook curled up in the downstairs parlor, concentrating all their attention on the radio, a great heavy monster the size of a buffet that, to top everything else off, they always kept turned up to full volume.

"Why is it you like radio serials so much?" I asked my granny one day. "What do they have to offer that books don't, for example?"

"It's more lifelike, hearing the characters talk, it's more real," she explained, after thinking about it. "And what's more, when you're my age, your hearing is better than your eyesight."

I made a similar survey among some of my other relatives, and the results were inconclusive. Aunt Gaby, Laura, Olga, and Hortensia liked radio serials because they were entertaining, sad, or dramatic, because they were diverting and set a person to dreaming, to living things that were impossible in real life, because there were truths to be learned from them, or because every woman remains more or less of a romantic at heart. When I asked them why they liked soap operas more than books, they protested: what nonsense, there was no comparison, books were culture and radio serials mere claptrap to help pass the time. But the truth of the matter was that they lived with their ears glued to the radio and that I'd never seen a one of them open a book. During our nocturnal rambles. Aunt Julia sometimes gave me a résumé of certain episodes that had impressed her, and I in turn gave her a rundown of my conversations with the scriptwriter, and thus, little by little, Pedro Camacho became a constituent element in our romance.

It was Genaro Jr. himself who brought me solid proof of the success of the new serials, on the very same day that I finally managed, after a thousand protests, to get my typewriter back.

He turned up in our shack with a folder in his hand and a radiant expression on his face. "It's exceeded our most optimistic calculations," he told us. "The number of listeners tuned in to the serials has gone up twenty percent in two weeks. Do you realize what that means? A twenty percent increase in the ad rates we charge sponsors!"

"And does it mean that we'll get a twenty percent raise in salary, Don Genaro?" Pascual said, bouncing up and down on his chair.

"You don't work at Radio Central but at Panamericana," Genaro Jr. reminded us. "We're a station with good taste—we don't broadcast serials."

The entertainment sections in the newspapers soon came up with feature stories on the large audience that the new serials had attracted and began singing the praises of Pedro Camacho. And Guido Monteverde, in his column in *Última Hora,* pulled out all the stops, calling him "an expert scriptwriter with a tropical imagination and a romantic gift for words, an intrepid symphony conductor of radio serials, and himself a versatile actor with a mellifluous voice." But the object of these laudatory adjectives took no notice of the wave of enthusiasm surrounding him. As I dropped by his cubicle one morning on my way to the Bransa to pick him up for our usual coffee break together, I found a sign pasted on the window with the crudely lettered inscription: "No journalists admitted and no autographs given. The artist is working! Respect him!"

"Do you mean that, or is it a joke?" I asked him, as I sat sipping my *café con leche* and Pedro Camacho his cerebral cocktail of verbena-and-mint tea.

"I mean it in all seriousness," he answered. "The local press has begun to hound me, and if I don't put a stop to them there'll soon be a bunch of listeners lined up over there—he gestured in the direction of the Plaza San Martín as though such an eventuality were the most natural thing in the world—asking for autographs and photos. My time is as precious as gold to me and I don't want to waste it on foolish trifles."

There wasn't an ounce of conceit in what he was saying, only sincere anxiety. He was wearing his usual black suit and little bow tie and smoking awful-smelling cigarettes, a brand called Aviación. As always, he was in an utterly serious mood. I thought I'd please him by telling him that all my aunts had become fanatic listeners of his and that Genaro Jr. was overjoyed at the results of the surveys showing how many new listeners his serials had attracted. But he was merely bored and shut me up—as though these things were inevitable and he'd always known all about them—and instead went on talking about how indignant he was at the lack of sensitivity on the part of "the merchants" (an expression that from then on he always used when referring to the Genaros).

"There's a weak spot that's ruining the serials and it's my duty to remedy it and their duty to help me," he announced, frowning. "But obviously art and money are mortal enemies, like pigs and daisies."

"A weak spot that's ruining the serials?" I said in amazement. "But they're a complete success."

"The merchants don't want to fire Pablito, even though I've insisted that he has to go," he explained to me. "They say they have to keep him on for sentimental reasons, because he's worked at Radio Central for I don't know how many years, and other such nonsense. As though art had anything to do with charity! That sick man's incompetence is absolutely sabotaging my work!"

Big Pablito was one of those indefinable, picturesque characters that the world of radio broadcasting attracts or produces. The diminutive suggested that he was just a kid, whereas in reality he was a mestizo in his fifties, who dragged his feet when he walked and had attacks of asthma that filled the air about him with clouds of effluvia. He was always somewhere about Radio Central and Panamericana, from morning to night, doing a little bit of everything, from giving the janitors a hand and going out to buy tickets for the movies and bullfights for the Genaros to distributing passes for broadcasts. His most permanent job was doing the sound effects for the serials.

"Those people think sound effects are dumb little things that any idiot can do. But in fact they're art too, and what does a half-moribund brachycephalic like Pablito know about art?" Pedro Camacho raved, with icy hauteur.

He assured me that, "if need be," he would not hesitate to eliminate, with his own hands, any obstacle to the "perfection of his work" (and he said it in such a way that I believed every word he said). He added that to his vast regret he had not had time to train a sound-effects technician, teaching him everything from A to Z, but that after rapidly reconnoitering the "Peruvian radio dial," he had found what he was looking for.

He lowered his voice, glanced stealthily all around, and concluded, with a Mephistophelean air: "The individual we ought to have for the serials is on Radio Victoria."

Javier and I analyzed how good the chances were that Pedro Camacho would carry out his homicidal intentions with regard to Big Pablito, and we agreed that the latter's fate depended entirely on the surveys: if the number of listeners tuning in to the serials kept going up, he'd be ruthlessly sacrificed. As a matter of fact, before the week was out, Genaro Jr. suddenly appeared in the shack, surprising me in the midst of writing another story—he must have noticed my confusion and the haste with which I ripped the page out of the typewriter and slipped it in among the news bulletins, but he was tactful enough not to say anything—and, addressing both Pascual and me, announced with the sweeping gesture of a great Maecenas: "All your griping has finally gotten you the new editor you've been wanting, you two lazybones. Big Pablito is going to be working with you from now on. Don't rest on your laurels!"

The reinforcement thus received by the News Service turned out to be more moral than material, inasmuch as when Big Pablito appeared in the office the next morning, very punctually, at seven on the dot, and asked me what he should do and I gave him the job of making a brief summary of a parliamentary report, a look of terror came over him, he had a coughing fit that left him purple in the face, and finally managed to stammer that that was impossible. "The thing is, sir, I don't know how to read or write."

I took the fact that Genaro Jr. had sent us an illiterate to be our new editor as a choice sample of his playful sense of humor. Pascual, who'd been a bit upset when he learned that he and Pablito were to be co-editors, positively gloated on hearing the latter confess that he was illiterate. He upbraided his brand-new colleague in my presence for his apathetic attitude, for not having been capable of educating himself as he, Pascual, had done, at an adult age, by going to free night-school classes. Big Pablito, scared to death, kept nodding in agreement, repeating like an automaton: "That's true, I hadn't thought of that, that's so, you're absolutely right," looking at me as though he expected to be fired on the spot. I immediately set his mind at rest, telling him that his job would be to take the news bulletins downstairs to the announcers. In actual fact, he soon became Pascual's slave, obliged to trot all day long from the shack to the street and vice versa to fetch Pascual cigarettes or stuffed potatoes from a street vendor on the Calle Carabaya, or simply to go see if it was raining outside. Big Pablito endured his slavery in an exemplary spirit of sacrifice, and in fact his attitude toward his torturer was even more respectful and friendly than his attitude toward me. When he wasn't running errands for Pascual, he would curl up in a corner of the office, and leaning his head against the wall, fall asleep instantly, snoring in steady, sibilant wheezes, like a rusty overhead fan. He was a generous-spirited man. He didn't feel the slightest ill will toward Pedro Camacho for having brought in an outsider from Radio Victoria to replace him. He had nothing but praise for the Bolivian scriptwriter, for whom he felt the most sincere admiration. He often asked my permission to go downstairs to sit in on rehearsals of the serials, returning each time more enthusiastic than ever. "That man is a genius," he would say, his voice choking with emotion. "The ideas that pop into his head are simply miraculous."

He always brought back very amusing stories of Pedro Camacho's inspired talents as an artist. One day he swore to us that Pedro had advised Luciano Pando to masturbate before delivering a love dialogue, claiming that by so doing he'd weaken his voice and produce a very romantic pant. Luciano Pando had flatly refused.

"I understand now why it is that every time there's a love scene coming up Don Pedro makes a visit to the downstairs bathroom, Don Mario," Big Pablito said, crossing himself and kissing his fingers. "To jerk off—that's why. And that's how come his voice sounds so soft and gentle afterwards."

Javier and I had a long discussion as to whether this could be true or was just a story that our new editor had made up, and we arrived at the conclusion that, all things considered, there was sufficient reason not to regard it as absolutely impossible.

"It's things like that you should be writing a story about, not about Doroteo Martí," Javier admonished me. "Radio Central is a literary gold mine."

The story I was trying my best to write at the time was based on an incident that Aunt Julia had told me about, one she herself had witnessed at the Teatro Saavedra in La Paz. Doroteo Martí was a Spanish actor who was touring Latin America, causing overflow audiences to shed floods of tears over *La Malquerida* and *Todo un Hombre* or other even more heartrending melodramas. Even in Lima, where theater was a mere curious relic, having died out the century before, the Doroteo Martí Company had drawn a full house at the Teatro Municipal for a performance of what, according to legend, was the *ne plus ultra* of its repertory: the Life, Passion, and Death of Our Lord. The actor had a strong sense of practicality, and malicious gossip had it that on occasion Christ broke off his sobbing soliloquy during his night of sorrows in the Garden of Olives to announce to the audience, in an affable tone of voice, that the following day the company would give a special performance to which ladies accompanied by an escort would be admitted free (whereupon Christ's Passion continued). It was in fact a performance of the Life, Passion, and Death that Aunt Julia had seen at the Teatro Saavedra. At the supreme instant, as Jesus Christ was dying on the heights of Golgotha, the audience noted that the wooden cross to which he was tied, surrounded by clouds of incense, was beginning to collapse. Was it an accident or a deliberately planned effect? Prudently, exchanging stealthy glances, the Virgin, the Apostles, the Roman soldiers, the populace in general began backing away from the teetering cross on which, his head still bowed upon his chest, Jesus-Martí had begun to murmur in a low voice that was nonetheless audible in the first rows of the orchestra: "I'm falling, I'm falling." Paralyzed, doubtless, with horror at the thought of committing sacrilege, none of the invisible occupants of the wings ran onstage to hold the cross upright, and it was now pivoting back and forth, defying numerous physical laws, amid cries of alarm that had replaced prayers on the actors' lips. Seconds later the spectators of La Paz saw Martí of Galilee come tumbling down, falling flat on his face on the stage of his great triumph, beneath the weight of the sacred rood, and heard the tremendous crash that shook the theater. Aunt Julia swore to me that Christ had managed to roar out in a savage voice, seconds before coming a cropper on the boards: "Damn it to hell, I'm falling!" It was, above all, this very last scene that I wanted to re-create; my story, too, would end up with a bang, with Jesus cursing like a trooper. I I wanted it to be a funny story, and to learn the techniques of writing humor, I read—on jitneys, express buses, and in bed before falling asleep—all the witty authors I could get my hands on, from

Mark Twain and Bernard Shaw to Jardiel Poncela and Fernández Flórez. But as usual I couldn't get the story to turn out right, and Pascual and Big Pablito kept count of the number of sheets of paper I consigned to the wastebasket. Luckily, as far as paper was concerned, the Genaros were more than generous with the News Service.

Two or three weeks went by before I met the man from Radio Victoria who had replaced Big Pablito. In the days before Pedro Camacho's arrival at the station, anyone who wanted to could attend the recording sessions of serials, but the new star director had forbidden everyone except the actors and technicians to enter the recording studio, and to prevent anyone else from doing so he had ordered the doors to be closed and stationed Jesusito's intimidating bulk in front of them. Not even Genaro Jr. himself was exempt from this iron rule.

I remember the afternoon when, as always happened whenever he had problems and needed a shoulder to cry on, he appeared in the shack, his nostrils quivering with indignation, to tell me his complaints. "I tried to enter the studio and he immediately stopped the program and refused to record it till I cleared out," he said in a furious voice. "And he gave me to understand that the next time I interrupted a rehearsal he'd throw the microphone at my head. What shall I do? Kick him out on his ass, or swallow the insult?"

I told him what he wanted to hear: that in view of the success of the serials ("for the greater glory of the entire Peruvian radio broadcasting industry," etc.) he should swallow the insult and not set foot in the artist's territory again. He took my advice, but I for my part was still dying of curiosity and wanted desperately to attend a recording session of one of the scriptwriter's programs.

One morning as we were having our usual break at the Bransa, after feeling out the ground very cautiously I ventured to broach the subject to Pedro Camacho. I told him I was eager to see the new sound-effects man in action and find out whether he was as good as he said he was.

"I didn't say he was good; I said he was average," he immediately corrected me. "But I'm training him and he might be good someday."

He drank a sip of his herb tea and scrutinized me with his little cold, punctilious eyes, assailed by inner doubts. Finally he gave in, and reluctantly agreed. "All right then. Come tomorrow, to the one at three. But I can't allow you to come again, I regret to say. I don't like the actors to be distracted, any alien presence disturbs them, I lose control of them, and it's goodbye catharsis. The recording of an episode is a Mass, my friend."

In fact, it was something even more solemn. Among all the Masses I remembered (I hadn't been to church in years), I never witnessed such a moving ceremony, such a deeply lived rite, as that recording of chapter 17 of "The Adventures and Misadventures of Don Alberto de Quinteros" to which I was admitted. The session couldn't have lasted more than thirty minutes—ten to rehearse and twenty to record—but it seemed to me that it lasted for hours. I was immediately impressed by the reverent religious atmosphere that reigned in the little room with a glass panel and dusty green carpeting that went by the name of Radio Central Recording Studio Number One. Big Pablito and I were the only spectators present; the others were active participants. On entering the studio, Pedro Camacho had informed us with a martial look in his eye, we must remain as motionless as statues of salt throughout the session. The author-director seemed transformed: taller, stronger, a general issuing orders to disciplined troops. Disciplined? Enraptured, rather; bewitched, brainwashed fanatics. I could scarcely recognize Josefina Sánchez, with her mustache and her varicose veins, whom I had so often seen recording her lines while chewing gum and knitting, with her mind somewhere else entirely and giving the impression that she hadn't the least idea what she was saying, as being the same person as this utterly serious creature before me who, when not absorbed in going over the script word for word, like someone praying, kept her eyes trained, respectfully and obediently, on the artist, trembling like an innocent little girl gazing at the altar on the day of her First Communion. And the same was true of Luciano Pando and the other three actors (two women and a very young man). They didn't exchange a single word or so much as look at each other: as though magnetized, their eyes went from their scripts to Pedro Camacho. And on the other side of the glass panel even that popinjay, the sound engineer Ochoa, was enraptured: carefully monitoring the controls, pressing buttons, turning lights on and off, following with a grave and attentive frown everything that was happening in the studio.

The five members of the cast were standing in a circle around Pedro Camacho, who—dressed as usual in his black suit and little bow tie and with his hair flying every which way—was delivering a sermon on the chapter that they were about to record. It was not instructions that he was giving them, at least not in the prosaic sense of concrete indications as to how they were to speak their lines—in measured tones or exaggeratedly, slowly or rapidly—but rather, as was his habit, noble, olympian, pontifical pronouncements having to do with profound aesthetic and philosophical truths. And naturally it was the words "art" and "artistic" that were repeated most frequently in this feverish discourse, like some sort of magic formula that revealed and explained everything. But even more surprising than the Bolivian scriptwriter's words was the fervor with which he uttered them, and perhaps more surprising still, the effect that they caused. Gesturing furiously and standing on tiptoe as he talked, he spoke in the fanatical voice of a man in possession of an urgent truth that he must disseminate, share, drive home. He succeeded completely in doing so: the five actors and actresses listened to him in stupefaction, hanging on his every word, opening their eyes wide as though the better to absorb these maxims concerning their work ("their mission," as the author-director put it). I was sorry Aunt Julia wasn't there, because she'd never believe me when I told her how I had seen, with my own eyes, this handful of practitioners of the most miserable profession in Lima totally transformed, transfixed, spiritualized, for the space of an eternal half hour, beneath the sway of Pedro Camacho's effervescent rhetoric. Big Pablito and I were sitting on the floor in one corner of the studio; in front of us, surrounded by all sorts of strange paraphernalia, was the brand-new acquisition, the defector from Radio Victoria. He too had listened to the artist's harangue with mystical rapture; the moment the recording of the chapter began, he became the center of the spectacle for me.

He was a stocky, copper-colored man, with stiff straight hair, dressed almost like a beggar: worn overalls, a much-mended shirt, big clodhoppers without laces. (Later I found out that he was called by the mysterious nickname of Puddler.) His work tools consisted of a wooden plank, a door, a washtub full of water, a whistle, a sheet of tinfoil, a fan, and other such ordinary-looking everyday articles. Puddler then proceeded to put on an extraordinary one-man show involving ventriloquism, acrobatic feats, multiple simultaneous impersonations, the creation of imaginary physical effects. At a given signal from the director-actor—a magisterial waggling of his index finger in the air filled with dialogue, tender sighs, and lamentations—Puddler, walking across his plank at a pace whose crescendo or diminuendo was carefully calculated, made the footsteps of the characters approach or retreat in the distance, and at another signal, turning the fan to blow at different speeds across the sheet of tinfoil, he produced the sound of rain falling or the wind howling, or at yet another, putting three fingers in his mouth and whistling, he filled the studio with the chirping of birds waking up the heroine in her country house on a spring morning. It was especially impressive when he created the sounds of a city street. It was Ochoa who provided, by means of a prerecorded tape, the sound of motors and horns honking, but all the other effects were produced by Puddler, by clacking his tongue, clucking, uttering, whispering (he seemed to be doing all these things at once), and all you needed to do was close your eyes to hear, reconstructed in the little Radio Central studio, the voices, the scattered words, the laughter, the exclamations that a person distractedly hears on walking down a crowded street. But as though this were not enough, at the same time that he was producing dozens of human voices, Puddler was also walking or leaping on the plank, manufacturing the footfalls of the pedestrians on the sidewalks and the sound of their bodies brushing against each other. He "walked" both with his feet and with his hands (thrust into a pair of shoes), squatting on his haunches, his arms dangling like a monkey's, slapping his thighs with his elbows and his forearms. After having been (acoustically speaking) the Plaza de Armas at noon, it was a relatively trivial feat for him to re-create the chamber music, so to speak, of a tea offered by a Lima society matron to a group of her lady friends in her mansion and the tinkling of the porcelain cups by hitting two little iron bars together, scratching on a sheet of glass, and rubbing little pieces of wood on his behind to imitate the gliding of chairs and ladies' feet over the thick, soft carpets; or, by roaring, croaking, grunting, screaming, to incarnate phonetically (and enrich with a number of species not to be found there) the Barranco zoo. By the time the recording session was over, he looked as though he'd run the

Olympic marathon: he was panting, his eyes had big dark circles under them, and he was sweating like a horse.

Pedro Camacho had contrived to imbue his collaborators with his own sepulchral seriousness. It was an enormous change. The serials from the CMQ in Cuba had most often been recorded in a circus atmosphere, and as the actors read their lines they would make faces or obscene gestures at each other, making fun of themselves and of what they were saying. But nowadays one had the impression that if someone had cracked the least little joke, the others would have flung themselves on him to punish him for his sacrilege. I thought for a time that they might perhaps be pretending so as to curry favor with their boss, so as not to be thrown out like the Argentines, that in their heart of hearts they weren't as certain as he was that they were "priests of art," but I was wrong. On my way back to Panamericana, I walked a few blocks along the Calle Belén with Josefina Sánchez, who was going home between serials to have herself a nice cup of tea, and I asked her whether the Bolivian scriptwriter always delivered a sermon before they recorded or whether the one I'd heard had been exceptional in any way. She gave me such a scornful look it made her double chin quiver.

"He said very little today and he wasn't inspired. Sometimes it breaks your heart to think that his ideas won't be preserved for posterity."

Since she was someone "who'd had so much experience," as I put it, I asked her if she really thought that Pedro Camacho was a person possessed of great talent. It took her a few seconds to find words adequate to express her feelings on the subject: "That man sanctifies the acting profession."

Six.

One bright summer morning,

tidily dressed and punctual as usual, Dr. Don Pedro Barreda y Zaldívar, examining magistrate, First Criminal Division, Superior Court of Lima, entered his chambers. He was a man who had reached the prime of life, his fifties, and in his person—broad forehead, aquiline nose, a penetrating gaze, the very soul of rectitude and goodness—and in his bearing his spotless moral virtue was so apparent as to earn him people's immediate respect. He dressed with the modesty that befits a magistrate with a meager salary who is constitutionally incapable of accepting a bribe, but with such impeccable neatness that it gave the impression of elegance. The Palace of Justice was beginning to awaken from its nocturnal slumber, and the massive building was commencing to swarm with a crowd of attorneys, petty clerks, bailiffs, plaintiffs, notaries, executors of estates, law students, and idle spectators. In the heart of this beehive, Dr. Don Barreda y Zaldívar opened his briefcase, took out two dossiers, seated himself at his desk, and prepared to begin his day. A few seconds later, his secretary appeared in his chambers, as rapidly and silently as a meteorite hurtling through space: Dr. Zelaya, a short little man with glasses and a minuscule mustache that moved rhythmically up and down as he spoke.

"A very good day to you, Your Honor," he greeted the magistrate, bowing deeply from the waist.

"The same to you, Zelaya." Dr. Don Barreda y Zaldívar smiled affably. "And what does the day have in store for us?"

"Rape of a minor with mental violence as an aggravating circumstance," the secretary replied, depositing a voluminous folder on the magistrate's desk. "The accused, who lives in the Victoria district and has typical Lombrosian criminal features, denies the allegations against him. The principal witnesses are waiting outside in the corridor."

"Before hearing them, I need to reread the police report and the plaintiff's deposition," the magistrate reminded him.

"They'll wait as long as necessary," the secretary replied, and left the room.

Beneath his solid juridical cuirass, Dr. Don Barreda y Zaldívar had the soul of a poet. One reading of cold legal documents was all he required to remove the rhetorical crust of wherefores and whereases and Latin phrases and arrive at the facts themselves by way of his powers of imagination. Thus, reading the police report drawn up in La Victoria, he was able to reconstruct, in vivid detail, the events that had led to formal charges being brought against the accused. He saw the thirteen-year-old girl named Sarita Huanca Salaverría, a pupil at the Mercedes Cabello de Carbonera public-school complex, enter, on Monday last, the commissariat of this motley, parti-colored district. She arrived in tears and with bruises on her face, arms, and legs, accompanied by her parents, Don Casimiro Huanca Padrón and Doña Catalina Salaverría Melgar. This minor had been dishonored the evening before, in room H of the tenement located at Number 12, Avenida Luna Pizarro, by the accused, Gumercindo Tello, a tenant in the same building (room J). On overcoming her embarrassment, Sarita had revealed to the guardians of law and order, in a quavering voice, that her defloration had been the tragic end result of a long and secret pursuit to which she had been subjected by the rapist. For the past eight months, in fact—that is to say, ever since the day that he had come to install himself at Number 12, like some strange bird of ill omen—the latter had plagued Sarita Huanca by waylaying her where her parents or the other tenants couldn't see and paying her indecent compliments or making bold advances (such as telling her: "I'd love to squeeze the lemons of your orchard" or: "One of these days I'm going to milk you"). From prophecies, Gumercindo Tello had gone on to overt acts, succeeding in his attempts, on a number of occasions, to fondle and kiss the pubescent girl, in the courtyard of the building at Number 12 or in nearby streets, as she was coming home from school or when she went out to run errands. Out of understandable timidity and a natural sense of modesty, the victim had not told her parents of this harassment.

On Sunday evening, ten minutes after her parents had gone off to the Cine Metropolitán, Sarita Huanca heard a knock at the door as she was doing her homework. She went to see who it was and found herself face to face with Gumercindo Tello. "What is it you want?" she asked him politely. Assuming the most innocent air imaginable, the rapist claimed that his portable stove had run out of fuel: it was too late to go out to buy more and he'd come to borrow just enough kerosene to prepare his evening meal (and promised to return what he'd borrowed the following day). Generous-hearted and naïve, little Sarita Huanca Salaverría invited the man in and showed him the can of kerosene sitting between the stove and the bucket that served as a toilet

(Dr. Don Barreda y Zaldívar smiled at this slip of the pen on the part of the officer of the law who had drawn up the complaint and thus inadvertently attributed to the Huanca Salaverrías the habit, so common among inhabitants of Buenos Aires, of attending to their calls of nature in a bucket located in the same room in which they eat and sleep.)

Once he had contrived, by means of this stratagem, to get inside room H, the accused locked the door. He then got down on his knees and, joining his hands, began to murmur words of love to Sarita Huanca Salaverría, who only then began to be alarmed as to the outcome of this visit from her neighbor. In language that the young girl described as romantic, Gumercindo Tello urged her to accede to his desires. And what were these desires? That she remove all her clothes and allow herself to be fondled, kissed, and robbed of her maidenhead. Pulling herself together, Sarita Huanca emphatically rejected his propositions, reprimanded Gumercindo Tello, and threatened to call the neighbors. On hearing these words, the accused, abandoning his supplicating attitude, drew a knife from his clothes and threatened to stab the girl if she made the slightest outcry. Rising to his feet, he advanced toward Sarita, saying: "Come, come, off with all your clothes, my love," and when, despite everything, she did not obey him, he gave her a hail of blows and kicks until she fell to the floor. And then as she lay there, so frightened that, according to the victim, her teeth chattered, the rapist tore all her clothes off, proceeded to unbutton his own as well, and fell upon her, perpetrating there on the floor the carnal act, which, due to the resistance offered by the girl, was accompanied by further blows, of which she still bore the traces in the form of bumps and bruises. Once his desires had been satisfied, Gumercindo Tello left room H, after advising Sarita Huanca Salaverría not to say a word about what had happened if she wanted to live to a ripe old age (and brandishing the knife to show that he meant what he said). On returning from the Metropolitán, the girl's parents found their daughter with tears streaming down her face and her body ravaged. After caring for her injuries, they pleaded with her to tell them what had happened, but out of shame she refused to do so. And thus the entire night went by. The following morning, however, having somewhat recovered from the emotional shock of losing her maidenhead, the girl told her parents everything, and they immediately presented themselves at the commissariat of La Victoria to bring a complaint.

Dr. Don Barreda y Zaldívar closed his eyes for a moment. He felt great pity for what had happened to the girl (despite his daily contact with crime, he had not grown callous), but he said to himself that, to all appearances, this was a case involving a prototypical crime, with nothing bizarre or mysterious about it, one minutely dealt with in the Penal Code, under the sections having to do with rape and abuse of a minor, along with the classic aggravating circumstances of premeditation, verbal and physical violence, and mental cruelty.

The next document that he reread was the report of the officers of the law who had placed Gumercindo Tello under arrest.

In accordance with instructions from their superior, Captain G. C. Enrique Soto, Guardias Civiles Alberto Cusicanqui Apéstegui and Huasi Tito Parinacocha had appeared at Number 12, Avenida Luna Pizarro, with a warrant for the arrest of the aforementioned Tello, but the individual in question was not at home. They learned from the neighbors that he was an automobile mechanic who worked at the "El Inti" Garage and Welding Shop, at the opposite end of the district, almost in the foothills of El Pino. The two officers of the law proceeded there immediately. At the garage, they were surprised to discover that Gumercindo Tello had just left, and were informed by the owner of the garage, Señor Carlos Príncipe, that he had asked for the day off to attend a baptism. When the Guardias questioned the other mechanics as to what church he might be found in, the latter exchanged sly glances and smiles. Señor Príncipe explained that Gumercindo Tello was not a Catholic, but a Jehovah's Witness, and that in this religious sect the rite of baptism was not celebrated in church with a priest, but by giving the candidate for baptism a good ducking somewhere out of doors.

Suspecting (as has proved to be the case) that the aforesaid sect was a brotherhood of perverts, Cusicanqui Apéstegui and Tito Parinacocha demanded that they be taken to the site where the accused might be found. After considerable hesitation and discussion, the owner of "El Inti" personally took them to the spot where, he said, Tello might possibly be, since once, some time ago now, when the latter had been trying to convert him and his fellow mechanics at the garage, he had invited him to attend a ceremony there (an experience that had left the aforementioned Señor Príncipe entirely unmoved).

The latter had driven the two officers of the law to the area bounded by the Calle Maynas on one side and the Parque Martinetti on the other, a vacant lot where people who live in that neighborhood burn their garbage and where there is a little branch of the Rímac. And that, in fact, was where the Jehovah's Witnesses were. Cusicanqui Apéstegui and Tito Parinacocha spied a dozen persons of various ages, male and female, standing waist-deep in the muddy waters, not in bathing suits but all dressed up: a number of the men were wearing ties, and one of them was even wearing a hat. Indifferent to the jokes, the gibes, the garbage tossed at them, and the other childish pranks of the people living nearby who had congregated on the riverbank to watch them, they were devoutly going on with a ceremony that to the two officers of the law appeared at first glance to be nothing less than an attempted murder by drowning. This is what they saw: as they fervently chanted strange hymns, the Witnesses, keeping a tight grip on the arms of an old man in a poncho and a wool cap, plunged him again and again into the filthy waters—as an intended sacrifice to their God? But when the two officers of the law, drawing their revolvers and getting their leggings all muddy, ordered them to cease their criminal act, the old man was the first to become thoroughly incensed, demanding that they withdraw and calling them strange names (such as "Romans" and "papists."). The guardians of law and order were forced to resign themselves to waiting until the baptism was over to arrest Gumercindo Tello, whom they had managed to identify thanks to Señor Príncipe. The ceremony went on for a few minutes more, in the course of which the Witnesses continued to pray and immerse the old man being baptized until the latter began to roll his eyes, swallow water, and choke, whereupon the Witnesses decided to drag him back to shore, where they began congratulating him on the new life that, they said, had just begun for him.

It was at this juncture that the officers of the law arrested Gumercindo Tello. The mechanic did not offer the slightest resistance, made no attempt to escape, and gave no sign of being surprised at having been taken into custody, limiting himself to saying to the others as the Guardias put him in handcuffs: "Brothers, I'll never forget you." The Witnesses immediately began singing more hymns, gazing heavenward and turning up the whites of their eyes, and accompanied them in this fashion to Señor Príncipe's car. The latter then drove the Guardias and their prisoner back to the commissariat of La Victoria, where the two officers bade him goodbye and thanked him for his services.

Inside the commissariat, Captain G. C. Enrique Soto asked the prisoner if he would like to dry his shoes and pants in the courtyard, and Gumercindo Tello replied that he was quite accustomed to going around in wet clothes because of the great number of conversions to the true faith that had taken place recently in Lima. The captain then proceeded forthwith to interrogate him, receiving the willing cooperation of the accused. Questioned as to his identity, he replied that his name was Gumercindo Tello, the son of Doña Gumercindo Tello, a native of Moquegua and now deceased, and of an unknown father, and that he too had probably been born in Moquegua, some twenty-five to twenty-eight years ago. With respect to this doubt as to his exact age, he explained that soon after he had been born his mother had handed him over to an orphans' home for boys run in the aforementioned city by the papist sect, in whose aberrations, he said, he had been educated and from which he had happily freed himself at the age of fifteen or eighteen. He indicated that he had remained at the orphanage until that age, at which time the institution burned to the ground in a huge fire, in which all the records were destroyed as well; it was for this reason that he was not at all certain exactly how old he was. He explained that the fire had been a providential event in his life, since it had been on that occasion that he had met a pair of wise men journeying on foot from Chile to Lima, opening the eyes of the blind and the ears of the deaf to the truths of philosophy. He said further that he had come to Lima with this pair of wise men, whose names he declined to reveal, claiming that it was enough to know that they existed and there was no need to label them. He then stated that from then on he had divided his time between working as a mechanic (a trade that he had learned in the orphanage) and spreading knowledge of the truth. He said he had lived in Breña, in Vitarte, in Los Barrios Altos, and had moved to La Victoria eight months before because he had found employment in the "El Inti" Garage and Welding Shop, which was located a fair distance from his former domicile.

The accused admitted that during this period he had lived in the building at Number 12, Avenida Luna Pizarro, as a tenant. He also admitted that he was acquainted with the Huanca Salaverría family, to whom, he said, he had proposed enlightening discussions and excellent reading matter on several occasions, to no avail however since they, like the other tenants of the building, were badly intoxicated by Roman heresies. Confronted with the name of his alleged victim, little Sarita Huanca Salaverría, he said he remembered her and intimated that, given the tender age of the person in question, he had not lost hope of setting her on the right path some day. Apprised at that point of the details of the charge that had been brought against him, Gumercindo Tello manifested great surprise, emphatically denying the accusation and then a moment later (feigning a mental disturbance with an eye to establishing the grounds for his future defense?) bursting into joyous laughter and saying that this was God's way of putting him to the test in order to measure his faith and his spirit of sacrifice. He added that now he understood why he had not been called up for military service, an occasion that he had been awaiting impatiently so as to preach by example, refusing to wear a uniform and swear allegiance to the flag, these being attributes of Satan. Captain G. C. Enrique Soto then asked him if that meant he was against Peru, to which the accused replied that that wasn't what he was talking about at all, that he was referring only to matters having to do with religion. And he thereupon proceeded to explain to Captain Soto and the guards, in fervent tones, that Christ was not God but His Witness and that the papists were lying when they maintained that he had been crucified since what had really happened was that he'd been nailed to a tree and that the Bible proved it. In this regard he counseled them to read *The Watchtower*, a bimonthly that for the price of two *soles* shed light on this subject and other aspects of culture and provided wholesome entertainment. Captain Soto shut him up, pointing out to him that it was forbidden to advertise commercial products within the commissariat. And he adjured him to reveal where he had been and what he had been doing the evening before during the hours when Sarita Huanca Salaverría swore that she had been raped and assaulted by him. Gumercindo Tello stated that he had spent the entire evening, as was his habit every night, alone in his room, absorbed in meditation on the Trunk and the fact that, contrary to what certain people maintained, it was not true that all men would be brought back to life on the day of the Last Judgment, a fact that proved the mortality of the soul. On being reprimanded a second time, the accused apologized and said he wasn't deliberately disobeying the captain's orders, but that he couldn't keep himself from trying at every moment to bring a little light to others, inasmuch as it made him despair to see the utter darkness amid which other people lived. And he stated that he did not remember having seen Sarita Huanca Salaverría at any time that evening or later that night, and asked that the record show that despite his having been slandered by the girl he bore her no ill will and was even grateful to her because he suspected that, through her, God had been testing the strength of his faith. Seeing that it was not going to be possible to obtain from Gumercindo Tello any more precise details concerning the charges brought against him, Captain G. C. Enrique Soto brought his interrogation of him to an end and transferred the accused to the detention cell in the Palace of Justice, in order that the examining magistrate might proceed with his investigation of the case in due and proper form.

Dr. Don Barreda y Zaldívar closed the folder containing the dossier of the accused and, amid the morning din of justice being done, reflected. Jehovah's Witnesses? He knew their kind only too well. Not many years before, a man making his way about the world on a bicycle had knocked at the door of his house and offered him a copy of *The Watchtower*, which, in a moment of weakness, he had accepted. From that moment on, with astral punctuality, the Witness had laid siege to his house, at all hours of the day and night, insisting on enlightening him, inundating him with pamphlets, books, magazines of all sizes and descriptions having to do with any number of subjects, until, finding himself incapable of putting a stop to the Witness's unwelcome visits by virtue of such civilized methods as persuasion, earnest entreaties, and stern lectures, the magistrate had finally called the police. So the rapist was one of these irrepressible proselytizers. This case was beginning to be an interesting one, Dr. Don Barreda y Zaldívar said to himself.

It was only midmorning and the magistrate, distractedly fingering the long, sharp letter opener with the Tiahuanaco handle on his desk, a token of the affection of his superiors, colleagues, and subordinates (who had presented him with it on the day of his twenty-fifth anniversary in the legal profession), called his secretary into his chambers and told him to show in the deponents in the case.

The two Guardias Civiles, Cusicanqui Apéstegui and Tito Parinacocha, entered first, and in respectful tones confirmed the circumstances under which they had arrested Gumercindo Tello, noting also for the record that the latter, despite having denied the charges brought against him, had been altogether cooperative, though a bit tiresome due to his religious mania. Dr. Zelaya, his glasses sliding up and down the bridge of his nose, took down their testimony word for word as they spoke.

The parents of the minor entered next, a couple whose advanced age surprised the magistrate: how could this pair of doddering oldsters have engendered a daughter only thirteen years before? Toothless and rheumy-eyed, the father, Don Isaías Huanca, immediately confirmed the statements concerning him as set down in the police report and then inquired, in an urgent tone of voice, whether Señor Tello was going to marry Sarita. He had barely put this question to the magistrate when Señora Salaverría de Huanca, a little woman with a wizened face, approached Dr. Don Barreda y Zaldívar, kissed his hand, and in a pleading voice implored him to be kind enough to force Señor Tello to take Sarita to the altar. The magistrate had great difficulty explaining to this elderly couple that the duties and powers conferred upon him by virtue of his high office did not include those of matchmaker. To all appearances, the girl's parents were far more interested in marrying their daughter off than in seeing the man who had deflowered her brought to justice, scarcely mentioning the rape and then only when urged to do so, and wasting a great deal of time enumerating Sarita's virtues, as though offering her for sale.

As he smiled to himself, the thought occurred to the magistrate that these humble peasants—it was obvious that they were from the Andes and had lived close to the soil—made him feel like an acrimonious father refusing to give his son his permission to marry. He did his best to make them think the matter through clearly: how could they possibly want to marry their daughter off to a man capable of raping a helpless girl? But they kept interrupting, insisting Sarita would be a model wife, even though she was scarcely more than a child she already knew how to cook and sew and all the rest, the two of them were far along in years and didn't want to leave her a defenseless orphan when they died, Señor Tello seemed to be a responsible, hardworking man, he had admittedly gone too far with Sarita the other night, but on the other hand they had never seen him drunk, he was very respectful, he left for work very early every morning with his toolbox and his bundle of little magazines that he peddled from house to house. Wasn't a young man who worked that hard to make a living a good match for Sarita? And with outstretched hands the two oldsters implored the magistrate: "Have pity on us and help us, Your Honor."

Like a little black cloud heavy with rain, a hypothesis drifted through Dr. Don Barreda y Zaldívar's mind: what if all this were merely a plot hatched by this couple to marry off their daughter? But the medical report stated categorically: the girl had been raped. Not without difficulty, he dismissed the two witnesses, and had the victim brought in.

Sarita Huanca Salaverría's entrance seemed to light up the austere chambers of the examining magistrate. A man who had seen everything, before whose eyes every conceivable bizarre human type and weird psychological case had passed in review, as perpetrators of crime and as victims of crime, Dr. Don Barreda y

Zaldívar nonetheless told himself that confronting him was a genuinely unusual specimen. Was Sarita Huanca Salaverría a little girl? No doubt, judging from her chronological age, her little body with the full rounded curves of femininity timidly beginning to make their appearance, her hair done up in braids, and the schoolgirl's blouse and skirt that she was wearing. On the other hand, however, her markedly feline way of moving, her way of standing, legs apart, one hip thrust out, shoulders thrown back, her two little hands resting provocatively on her waist, and above all the look in her velvety, worldly eyes and her way of biting her lower lip with little mouse teeth, made Sarita Huanca Salaverría appear to possess vast experience, a wisdom as old as time itself.

Dr. Don Barreda y Zaldívar's interrogations of minors were always extraordinarily tactful. He knew how to gain their confidence, use circumlocutions so as not to hurt their feelings, and by being gentle and patient it was easy for him to lead them around to talking about the most scandalous subjects. But this time his experience was of little use to him. The moment he asked the minor, euphemistically, whether it was true that Gumercindo Tello had bothered her for some time by making indecent remarks, Sarita Huanca began to talk in a steady stream. Yes, ever since he'd come to La Victoria to live; everywhere; at all hours of the day. He would be waiting at the bus stop and walk home with her, saying things like "I'd love to suck your honey," "You've got two little oranges and I've got a little banana," and "I'm dripping with love for you." But it was not these risqué figures of speech, so out of place in the mouth of a little girl, that made the magistrate's cheeks flush and froze Dr. Zelaya's fingers on his typewriter keys, but, rather, the gestures whereby Sarita began to illustrate the harassment of which she had been the object. The mechanic was always trying to touch her, here: and her two little hands rose to cup her tender little breasts and lovingly stroke them to warm them. And here too: and her little hands descended to her knees and fondled them, then crept up and up, wrinkling her skirt, along her little thighs (until very recently those of a pre-adolescent child). Blinking his eyes, coughing, exchanging a rapid glance with the secretary, Dr. Don Barreda y Zaldívar paternally explained to the girl that it was not necessary to be that explicit, that she could limit herself to generalities. And he'd also pinch her here, Sarita interrupted him, turning halfway round and thrusting toward him a buttock that suddenly seemed to grow bigger and bigger, to inflate like a balloon. The magistrate had the dizzying presentiment that his chambers might well turn into a strip-tease parlor at any moment.

Making an effort to overcome his nervousness, the magistrate urged the minor, in a calm voice, to skip the preliminaries and concentrate on the act of rape itself. He explained to her that although she should do her best to give an objective account of what had happened, it was not absolutely necessary to dwell on the details, and she could omit—Dr. Don Barreda y Zaldívar, feeling slightly embarrassed, cleared his throat—those that might offend her modesty. The magistrate wanted, for one thing, to end the interview as soon as possible, and for another, to keep it within the bounds of decency, and he thought that the girl, who would quite naturally be upset on recounting the erotic assault, would be brief and synoptic, circumspect and superficial.

But on hearing the judge's suggestion, Sarita Huanca Salaverría, like a fighting cock smelling blood, grew bolder, cast all decency to the winds, and launched into a salacious soliloquy and a mimetico-seminal representation that took Dr. Don Barreda y Zaldívar's breath away and plunged Dr. Zelaya into a state of frankly indecorous (and perhaps masturbatory?) corporeal agitation. The mechanic had knocked at the door like this, and when she'd opened it he'd looked at her like this, and then spoken these words to her, and after that knelt down like so, touching his heart this way, declared his passion for her in phrases such as these, swearing that he loved her thus and so. Stunned, hypnotized, the judge and the secretary watched the child-woman flutter like a bird, stand on tiptoe like a ballerina, crouch down and draw herself up to her full height, smile and become angry, speak in two different voices, imitate herself and Gumercindo Tello both, and finally fall on (his, her) knees and confess (his) love for (her). Dr. Don Barreda y Zaldívar stretched out one hand, stammered that that was enough, but the loquacious victim was already explaining that the mechanic had threatened her with a knife like this, had flung himself upon her like this, causing her to fall to the floor like this and then lying down on top of her like this and pulling up her skirt like this, and at that moment the judge—a pale, noble, majestic, wrathful Biblical prophet—leapt from his chair and roared: "Enough! Enough! That will do!" It was the first time in his life that he had ever raised his voice.

From the floor, where she had stretched out full-length on reaching the neuralgic point of her graphic deposition, Sarita Huanca Salaverría looked up in panic at the index finger that appeared to be about to send a lightning bolt through her.

"I don't need to know any more," the magistrate repeated in a gentler voice. "Get up, straighten your skirt, and go rejoin your parents."

The victim obediently rose to her feet, her little face devoid now of even the slightest trace of histrionics or indecency, a child once again, visibly distressed. Humbly bowing, she backed away to the door and left. The judge then turned to his secretary, and in an even, not at all sarcastic tone of voice suggested that he stop typing: had he perchance failed to notice that the sheet of paper had slid to the floor and that he was typing on the empty platen? His face crimson, Dr. Zelaya stammered that what had just happened had gotten him all flustered.

Dr. Don Barreda y Zaldívar smiled at him. "We have been privileged to witness a most unusual spectacle," the magistrate philosophized. "That youngster has the devil in the flesh, and what's worse, she probably doesn't even know it."

"Is that what Yankees call a Lolita?" the secretary asked in an attempt to further his knowledge.

"I'm certain of it—a typical Lolita," was the judge's verdict. And in an effort to put the best possible face on things, an impenitent sea wolf who draws optimistic lessons even from typhoons, he added: "We can at least feel pleased to have discovered that the colossus of the North doesn't enjoy a monopoly in this field. That little home-grown product could steal any gringa Lolita's man away from her."

"I take it she drove that mechanic out of his mind and he deflowered her," the secretary mused. "But after seeing and hearing her you'd swear that she was the one who raped him."

"Stop right there. I forbid you to assume any such thing," the judge said sternly, and the secretary paled. "Let's have none of these suspect oracular pronouncements. Have them bring in Gumercindo Tello."

Ten minutes later, on seeing the man enter his chambers escorted by two guards, Dr. Don Barreda y Zaldívar realized immediately that he did not fit the neat pigeonhole that the secretary had too hastily assigned him. This was not a classic Lombrosian criminal type, but in a certain sense a far more dangerous type: a believer. With a mnemonic shiver that made the hair on the back of his neck stand on end, the judge, on seeing Gumercindo Tello's face, remembered the implacable gaze of the man with the bicycle and the copies of *The Watchtower* who had given him so many nightmares, that serenely stubborn gaze of a man who knows, who has no doubts, who has solved all his problems. Rather short in stature, he was a young man, doubtless not yet thirty, whose frail physique, nothing but skin and bones, proclaimed to the four winds his scorn for bodily nourishment and the material world, with hair cropped so short his skull was nearly bare, and a swarthy complexion. He was dressed in a gray suit the color of ashes, the costume neither of a dandy nor of a beggar but something in between, which was dry now but very wrinkled from the baptismal rites, a white shirt, and ankle boots with cleats. Just one glance sufficed for the judge—a man with a flair for anthropology—to discern immediately his distinctive personality traits: circumspection, moderation, fixed ideas, imperturbability, a spiritual vocation. Obviously well-mannered, the moment he entered the room he bade the judge and the secretary good morning in a polite, friendly tone of voice.

Dr. Don Barreda y Zaldívar ordered the guards to remove the man's handcuffs and leave his chambers. This was a habit he had adopted from the very beginning of his career as a magistrate: he had always interrogated even the most depraved criminals without officers of the law being present, without coercion, paternally, and in the course of these tête-à-têtes, even the most hard-bitten of them usually opened their hearts to him, like penitents to a confessor. He had never had cause to regret this risky practice. Gumercindo Tello rubbed his wrists and thanked the judge for this proof of his trust. The latter pointed to a chair and the mechanic sat down on the very edge of it, his spine rigid, like a man who feels uncomfortable at the very idea of comfort. The magistrate composed in his mind the motto that no doubt governed the Witness's life: get up out of bed though still sleepy, get up from the table though still hungry, and (if he ever went) leave the movie before the end. He tried to imagine him lured, set on fire by the thirteen-year-old femme fatale of La Victoria, but immediately abandoned this mental exercise as being detrimental to the rights of the defendant. Gumercindo Tello had begun talking.

"It's true that we don't swear to obey governments, parties, armies, and other visible institutions, all of which are stepdaughters of Satan," he said quietly, "that we don't pledge allegiance to any bit of colored cloth, that we refuse to wear uniforms, because we are not taken in by fripperies or disguises, and that we don't accept skin grafts or blood transfusions, because science cannot undo what God hath wrought. But none of this means that we do not fulfill our obligations. Your Honor, I place myself at your entire disposal and would pay you all due respect even if I had good reason not to."

He spoke slowly and deliberately, as though to make the secretary's task easier as the latter provided a musical accompaniment for his peroration on his typewriter. The judge thanked him for his kind words, informed him that he respected every person's ideas and beliefs, particularly those having to do with religion, and permitted himself to remind him that he was not under arrest for those he professed but because he had been charged with having assaulted and raped a minor.

An otherworldly smile crossed the face of the young man from Moquegua. "A witness is one who testifies, who offers testimony, who attests," he said, revealing his familiarity with semantics and looking the magistrate straight in the eye. "One who, knowing that God exists, makes His existence known, one who, knowing the truth, makes the truth known. I am a Witness and you two may become Witnesses as well with a little effort of will."

"Thank you, perhaps some other time," the judge interrupted him, picking up the thick dossier and setting it before him as though it were a dish of food. "Time is pressing and this is what is important. Let's get straight to the point. And first off, a word of advice: I strongly urge you, in your own best interests, to tell the truth, the whole truth, and nothing but the truth."

The accused, moved by some secret memory, heaved a deep sigh. "The truth, the truth," he murmured sadly. "Which truth, Your Honor? Isn't what you're after, rather, the product of those calumnies, those fabrications, those Vatican tricks that, by taking advantage of the naïveté of the masses, they try to foist off on us as the truth? With all due modesty, I believe I know the truth, but, with no offense meant, may I ask you: do you know it?"

"It's my intention to discover it," the judge replied shrewdly, tapping the folder.

"The truth about the fiction of the cross, the farce of Peter and the rock, the miters, the papal immortality-of-the-soul hoax?" Gumercindo Tello asked sarcastically.

"The truth about the crime you committed by abusing the minor Sarita Huanca Salaverría," the magistrate counterattacked. "The truth about your assaulting an innocent thirteen-year-old girl. The truth about the beating you gave her, the threats that terrified her, the rape that humiliated her and perhaps left her pregnant." The magistrate's voice had risen, accusing, Olympian.

Gumercindo Tello looked at him gravely, as rigid as the chair he was perched on, showing no sign of either shame or repentance. But finally he nodded like a docile cow. "I am prepared for any test to which Jehovah wishes to put me," he assured him.

"It's not a question of God but of you," the magistrate said, bringing him back down to earth. "Of your appetites, your lust, your libido."

"It's always a question of God, Your Honor," Gumercindo Tello stubbornly insisted. "Never of you, or me, or anyone else. Of Him, and Him only."

"Be responsible," the judge exhorted him. "Keep to the facts. Admit your guilt and Justice may take your confession into account. Act like the religious man you're trying to make me believe you are."

"I repent of all my sins, which are infinite," Gumercindo Tello said gloomily. "I know very well that I am a sinner, Your Honor."

"Well then, the concrete facts," Dr. Don Barreda y Zaldívar pressed him. "Describe to me, with neither morbid delectation nor jeremiads, how you raped her."

But the Witness had burst into sobs, covering his face with his hands. The magistrate remained unmoved. He was accustomed to the sudden cyclothymic shifts of mood of accused criminals he was interrogating and knew how to take advantage of them to ascertain the facts. Seeing Gumercindo Tello sitting there with his head bowed, shaking from head to foot, his hands wet with tears, Dr. Don Barreda y Zaldívar said to himself, with the solemn pride of the professional noting the effectiveness of his technique, that the accused had reached that climactic emotional state in which, no longer capable of dissimulating, he would eagerly, spontaneously, abundantly confess to the truth.

"Facts, facts," he insisted. "Facts, positions, words spoken, acts performed. Come on, be brave and tell all!"

"The trouble is, I don't know how to lie, Your Honor," Gumercindo Tello stammered between hiccups. "I'm prepared to suffer the consequences, whatever they may be—insults, prison, dishonor. But I can't lie! I never learned how, I'm incapable of it!"

"There, there, that very fact does you honor," the judge exclaimed with an encouraging gesture. "Prove it to me. Come on, tell me, how did you rape her?"

"That's the whole problem," the Witness said in a desperate tone of voice, swallowing hard. "I didn't rape her!"

"I'm going to tell you something, Señor Tello," the magistrate said, pronouncing each word slowly and distinctly, in the deceptively bland voice of a sly, contemptuous serpent. "You're a false Jehovah's Witness! An impostor!"

"I didn't touch her, I never talked to her alone, I didn't even see her yesterday," Gumercindo Tello bleated like a lamb.

"A cynic, a fake, a spiritual prevaricator," the judge declared in a stern, cold voice. "If Justice and Morality don't matter to you, at least respect that God whose name is so often on your lips. Think of how He is watching you at this very moment, how revolted He must be to hear you lie."

"I have never offended that child—neither by my thought nor by my gaze," Gumercindo Tello repeated in heartrending accents.

"You threatened her, beat her, raped her," the magistrate thundered. "With your filthy lust, Señor Tello."

"With-my-fil-thy-lust?" the Witness repeated, like a man hit over the head with a hammer.

"That's right, with your filthy lust," the magistrate reiterated, and then, after a deliberately dramatic pause: "With your sinful penis!"

"With-my-sin-ful-pe-nis?" the accused stammered in a faltering voice, staring at him in utter astonishment. "My-sin-ful-pe-nis-did-you-say?"

Looking frantically about him in wild-eyed amazement, his gaze darted from the secretary to the judge, from the floor to the ceiling, from the chair to the desk, lingering on the papers, dossiers, blotters lying on top of it. Then suddenly his eyes lit up, caught by the artistic pre-Hispanic glint of the Tiahuanaco letter opener, and before the judge or the secretary could stop him, Gumercindo Tello made a lunge for it and grabbed it by the handle. He did not make a single threatening gesture with it: quite to the contrary, he clasped it to his breast like a mother cradling her child and stood looking at the two petrified men with a reassuring, kindly, sad expression in his eyes.

"You offend me by thinking I might harm you," he said in the tone of voice of a penitent.

"You won't be able to escape, you fool," the judge warned him, collecting himself. "The Palace of Justice is full of guards; they'll kill you."

"Me, try to escape?" the mechanic asked sarcastically. "How little you know me, Your Honor."

"Can't you see that you're giving yourself away?" the magistrate persisted. "Give me back the letter opener."

"I borrowed it from you to prove my innocence," Gumercindo Tello calmly explained.

The judge and the secretary looked at each other. The accused had risen to his feet. There was a Nazarene expression on his face, and the knife in his right hand gave off a terrible premonitory gleam. His left hand slid down unhurriedly toward his trousers fly concealing the zipper, as he said in a pained voice: "I am pure, Your Honor, I have never known a woman. What other men use to sin with, I only use to pee with . . ."

"Stop right there," Dr. Don Barreda y Zaldívar interrupted him as a terrible suspicion dawned on him. "What are you going to do?"

"Cut it off and throw it in the trash to prove to you how little it means to me," the accused replied, pointing toward the wastebasket with his chin.

He spoke without false pride, with quiet determination. Their mouths gaping open in surprise, struck dumb, the judge and the secretary were unable to raise any sort of outcry. Gumercindo Tello was now holding the corpus delicti in his left hand and, an executioner brandishing the ax and mentally measuring its trajectory to the victim's neck, raising the knife and preparing to let it fall to consummate the inconceivable proof.

Would he go through with it? Would he thus deprive himself, in one stroke, of his integrity? Would he sacrifice his body, his youth, his honor, as an ethico-abstract demonstration? Would Gumercindo Tello turn the most respectable judge's chambers in Lima into a sacrificial altar? How would this forensic drama end?

Seven.

My romance with Aunt Julia

was going along swimmingly, except that things were getting complicated because it was becoming more and more difficult to keep it a secret. By common agreement, in order not to arouse suspicion in the family, I had drastically cut down my visits to Uncle Lucho's. I continued, however, to appear regularly at the house for lunch on Thursdays. In order to go to the movies together at night, we invented various ruses. Aunt Julia would go out early in the evening, telephone Aunt Olga to tell her she'd be having dinner with a girlfriend, and wait for me at a place we'd agreed on beforehand. This modus operandi was rather inconvenient, however, in that Aunt Julia was obliged to while away several hours on the streets till I got off work, and most of the time she also had to go without dinner. At other times I went to pick her up in a taxi without getting out; she'd wait in the house, keeping an eye peeled, and the minute she saw the cab stop she'd come running out. But this was a risky operation: if anybody in the family spied me, they'd know immediately that there was something going on between Aunt Julia and me; and in any event her mysterious gentleman friend who invited her out for the evening but kept himself hidden in the back seat of a taxi was bound sooner or later to arouse curiosity, malicious gossip, a great many questions . . .

We had decided therefore to see each other less often at night and more often in the daytime, during the hours when I had nothing to do at the radio station. Aunt Julia would take a jitney downtown around eleven in the morning, or five in the afternoon, and wait for me in a coffee shop on Camaná or in the Cream Rica on the Jirón de la Unión. I'd leave a couple of bulletins all edited and ready to go on the air and we could spend two hours together. We avoided the Bransa on La Colmena because it was a favorite hangout of all the people from Panamericana and Radio Central. From time to time (to be more precise, on paydays), I would invite her to lunch and we'd have as many as three hours together. But my meager salary didn't really permit such extravagances. After making an elaborate speech, I'd managed to persuade Genaro Jr. to raise my salary, one morning when I'd found him in a euphoric mood because of Pedro Camacho's successes, to exactly five thousand *soles*. I gave two thousand of it to my grandparents to help out with household expenses. The remaining three thousand had previously been more than enough for my vices: cigarettes, movies, and books. But since my romance with Aunt Julia, my spending money seemed to vanish into thin air immediately and I was always broke, so that I often had to touch my friends for loans and even had to resort to taking some of my belongings to the National Pawnshop, in the Plaza de Armas. Since, moreover, I had deep-rooted Spanish prejudices with regard to the relations between men and women and never allowed Aunt Julia to pick up a check, my financial situation became dramatic. To remedy it, I began to do something that Javier reprovingly called "prostituting my pen," that is to say, writing book reviews and articles for literary supplements and periodicals published in Lima. I wrote under a pseudonym so as to feel less ashamed at how bad they were. But the two or three hundred extra *soles* they brought me each month were a big help in making ends meet.

These secret meetings in downtown cafés of Lima were really quite innocent: long, romantic conversations, holding hands, gazing into each other's eyes, and if the topography of the establishment permitted it, rubbing knees. We kissed each other only when nobody could see us, something that rarely happened, since at these hours the cafés were always full of cheeky, nosy office clerks. We talked about ourselves, naturally, about the risks we were running of being surprised by some member of the family, about ways of getting around this danger; we told each other in minute detail everything we had done since the last time we'd been together (a few hours before, that is to say, or the previous day), but on the other hand we never made any sort of plans for the future. This was a subject that by tacit agreement was banished from our conversations, no doubt because both of us were equally convinced that our relationship was destined not to have a future. Nonetheless, I think that what had begun as a game little by little became serious in the course of these chaste meetings in the smoke-filled cafés of downtown Lima. It was in such places that, without our realizing it, we gradually fell in love.

We talked a great deal about literature as well; or rather, Aunt Julia listened and I talked, about the Paris garret (an indispensable ingredient in my vocation) and about all the novels, plays, essays I'd write once I'd become a writer. The afternoon that Javier discovered us together in the Cream Rica on the Jirón de la Unión, I was reading my story on Doroteo Martí aloud to Aunt Julia. I had given it the medieval-sounding title of "The Humiliation of the Cross," and it was five pages long. It was the first story of mine that I'd ever read her, and I did so very slowly so as to conceal my anxiety as to what her verdict would be. The experience had a devastating effect on the susceptibility of the future writer.

As I read on, Aunt Julia kept interrupting me. "But it wasn't like that at all, you've turned the whole thing topsy-turvy, that wasn't what I told you, that's not what happened at all . . ." she kept saying, surprised and even angry.

I couldn't have been more upset, and broke off my reading to inform her that what she was listening to was not a faithful, word-for-word recounting of the incident she'd told me about, but *a story, a story,* and that all the things that I'd either added or left out were ways of achieving certain effects: "*Comic* effects," I emphasized, hoping she'd see what I was getting at. She smiled at me, if only out of pity for my misery.

"But that's precisely the point," she protested vehemently, not giving an inch. "With all the changes you've made, it's not a funny story at all any more. What reader is going to believe that such a long time goes by between the moment the cross begins to teeter and the moment it comes crashing down? The way you've told it, what's there to laugh at?"

Even though I'd already decided—feeling utterly crushed and secretly humiliated—to toss the story about Doroteo Martí in the wastebasket, I'd nonetheless launched into a passionate, pained defense of the rights of literary imagination to transgress reality, when I suddenly felt a tap on the shoulder.

"If I'm interrupting, please tell me and I'll clear out immediately, because I hate being a nuisance," Javier said, drawing up a chair, sitting down, and asking the waiter to bring him a cup of coffee. He smiled at Aunt Julia. "I'm delighted to meet you, I'm Javier, the best friend of this prose writer here. You certainly have kept her well hidden, old pal."

"This is Julia, my Aunt Olga's sister," I explained.

"What! The famous woman from Bolivia?" He'd more or less had the wind taken out of his sails: when he came across us we'd been holding hands and hadn't let go when he sat down with us, and now he was staring intently at our intertwined fingers and had lost his air of worldly self-assurance of a few moments before. "Well, well, Varguitas!" he murmured.

"The famous woman from Bolivia, you say? May I ask what I'm famous for?" Aunt Julia asked.

"For being so disagreeable, for those spiteful jokes of yours when you first arrived," I explained to her. "Javier knows only the first part of the story."

"You kept the best part a secret, you bad narrator and worse friend," Javier said, recovering his aplomb and pointing to our clasped hands. "Come on, tell me the rest, you two."

He was really charming that afternoon, talking a blue streak and making all sorts of jokes and witty remarks. Aunt Julia found him delightful, and I was happy that he'd discovered us; I hadn't planned to tell him about her, because I detested sharing confidences about my love life (especially in this case, since the whole thing was so complicated), but now that he had chanced to discover my secret, I was glad that I was going to be able to talk with him about the ins and outs of this affair of the heart with Aunt Julia.

As he left us that day, he kissed her on the cheek, bowed, and said: "I'm a first-rate pander. If I can be of help in any way, you can count on me."

"How come you didn't tell us you'd even tuck us in bed?" I said testily the moment he appeared later that afternoon in my shack at Radio Panamericana, eager to hear all the details.

"She's more or less an aunt of yours right?" he replied, clapping me on the back. "In any case, I'm really impressed. A mistress who's old, rich, and divorced: you get an A in the course!"

"She's not my aunt; she's my uncle's wife's sister," I said, explaining again what he already knew as I edited a news item in *La Prensa* on the Korean War for an upcoming bulletin. "She's not my mistress, she's not old, and she doesn't have money. The only part of your description that's true is that she's divorced."

"What I meant by old was older than you, and the part about her being rich wasn't intended as criticism but as a way of extending my congratulations, since I'm all in favor of marrying for money." Javier laughed. "And am I to take it that she's not your mistress? If not, what is she exactly? Your girlfriend?"

"Something between the two," I told him, knowing that that would irritate him.

"Ah, I get it, you want to keep your deep dark secrets to yourself. Well, the hell with you, then. What's more, you're a bastard: I tell you everything about what's going on between me and Nancy and you won't tell me one thing about the catch you've made."

So I told him the whole story from the very beginning, the complicated schemes we had to resort to just to see each other alone, and he realized why I'd hit him for a loan two or three times during the last few weeks. He was intrigued by our story, asked me one question after another, and after hearing me out swore he'd be my fairy godmother. But as he was leaving he said in a solemn tone of voice: "I take it that this whole thing is only a game. But even so, don't forget that you and I are still just kids," he admonished me, looking me straight in the eye like a stern but kindly father.

"If I get pregnant, I swear to you I'll get an abortion," I reassured him.

Once he left, and as Pascual was telling Big Pablito all about an amusing nose-to-tail chain collision in Germany involving some twenty cars that had crashed into each other when an unthinking Belgian tourist had suddenly braked to a halt right in the middle of the Autobahn to rescue a little dog, I thought over what he'd said. Was it certain that Aunt Julia and I weren't getting seriously involved with each other? Yes, certain. It was simply a different experience, a bit more mature and daring than the ones I'd had before, but if I was to have pleasant memories of our affair, it shouldn't last very long. I had thought things through that far when Genaro Jr. appeared to invite me to lunch. He took me to Magdalena, to a restaurant with an outdoor patio that specialized in Peruvian cuisine, insisted that I order the rice with duck and the fritters with honey, and then, as we were having coffee, handed me the check, so to speak. "You're the only friend he's got, talk to him, he's getting us into terrible trouble. I don't dare say a word to him, he calls me an ignoramus, and yesterday he called my father a mesocrat. I don't want to have any more run-ins with him. I'd have to fire him and that would be a disaster for the corporation."

The problem was a letter from the Argentine ambassador to Radio Central, couched in poisonous language, protesting the "slanderous, perverse, and psychotic" references to the fatherland of Sarmiento and San Martín that cropped up everywhere in the serials (which the diplomat called "sensationalist stories presented in episodic form"). The ambassador offered a number of examples which, he assured his addressees, had not been sought *ex professo* but collected at random by the personnel of the legation "with a penchant for this sort of broadcast." In one of them it had been suggested, no less, that the proverbial virility of Argentine men residing in the capital was a myth since nearly all of them practiced homosexuality (and, preferably, the passive form); in another, that in Buenos Aires families, noted for living together in teeming hordes, it was customary to allow useless members—the oldsters and the invalids—to die of hunger so as to lighten the budget; on another, that beef cattle were raised for export only because in Argentine homes the meat that was most highly prized was horseflesh; in another, that the widespread participation in the sport of soccer had damaged the national genes, above all because of the players' practice of butting the ball with their heads, thus explaining the ever-increasing numbers of oligophrenics, acromegalics, and other subvarieties of cretins on the shores of the tawny-colored Río de la Plata; that in the homes of Buenos Aires—"a similar cosmopolis," as the letter put it—it was a common custom to attend to one's biological necessities in a simple bucket, in the same room where one ate and slept . . .

"You're laughing. We laughed too, but today we had a visit from a lawyer and suddenly the whole thing doesn't seem the least bit funny," Genaro Jr. said, biting his fingernails. "If the embassy formally protests to the government, they can make us stop broadcasting serials, fine us, close down the station. Plead with him, threaten him, anything, so long as he drops the subject of Argentines."

I promised to do what I could, but without much hope of getting anywhere, since the scriptwriter was a man of unshakable convictions. I had come to feel genuine friendship for him; above and beyond the entomological curiosity he aroused in me, I truly respected him. But was the feeling mutual? Pedro Camacho didn't seem to me to be capable of wasting his time, his energy, on friendship or on anything else that would distract him from "his art"; that is to say, his work or his vice, that urgent necessity that swept aside men, things, appetites. It was true, however, that he was more tolerant of me than of others. We had coffee together (or, rather, I had coffee and he had his verbena-and-mint tea), and I dropped by his cubbyhole every so often to spend a few minutes with him, thus giving him a brief respite between one page and another. I listened to him very attentively and perhaps he found this flattering; he may have considered me a disciple, or I might simply have been for him what a lapdog is to an old maid and crossword puzzles to the pensioner: something, someone to help while away the empty hours.

Three things about Pedro Camacho fascinated me: what he said; the austerity of his life, entirely devoted to an obsession; and his capacity for work. This latter especially. I had read about Napoleon's tremendous endurance in Emil Ludwig's biography of him, how his secretaries would collapse in utter exhaustion and he would go on dictating, and I often pictured the Emperor of the French as having the same face with the prominent nose as the scriptwriter, and for some time Javier and I called Pedro Camacho the Napoleon of the Altiplano (or, alternatively, the Balzac of Peru). Out of curiosity, I managed to calculate the number of hours of work he put in every day, and even though I often had proof that my calculations were correct, his schedule always seemed to beggar belief.

In the beginning, he turned out four serials a day, but in view of their great success, their number gradually increased to ten, which were broadcast from Monday through Saturday, with each chapter of each serial lasting half an hour (or, more precisely, twenty-three minutes, since commercials took up seven minutes of each half hour). Since he directed all of them as well as playing a role in each, he must have spent around seven hours a day at the studio, if one takes into account the fact that rehearsing and recording each program took approximately forty minutes (between ten and fifteen minutes being required at each of these sessions for his initial sermon and the run-through). He wrote the serials as needed for each day's broadcasts; I noted that each chapter took him barely twice the time required to act it out on the air: one hour. In any event, this meant spending around ten hours a day at his typewriter. He was able to cut this down a bit thanks to his labors on Sunday, his day off, which he naturally spent in his tiny little office, getting a head start on his scripts for the week coming up. His work day was thus fifteen to seventeen hours long from Monday to Saturday and eight to ten hours long on Sunday. And all of them demonstrably productive hours, an amazing "artistic" output.

He arrived at Radio Central at eight in the morning and left around midnight; the only times he went out for a break were with me, to the Bransa, to have a cup of cerebrally stimulating herb tea. He ate his lunch in his lair, a sandwich and a soft drink that Jesusito, Big Pablito, or one of his actor-disciples devotedly went out to get for him. He never accepted invitations, I never heard him say he'd gone to a movie, a theatrical performance, a soccer match, or a party. I never saw him read a book, a magazine, or a newspaper, outside of the big bulky volume of quotations and the city maps that were his "work tools." No, I am mistaken: one day I discovered him poring over a yearbook listing the members of the Club Nacional.

"I slipped the concierge a few coins so as to have a look at it," he explained when I asked him about it. "How else could I get the right names for my aristocrats? My ears suffice for the others: I pick plebeian names up out of the gutter."

The way in which he produced his serials, the single hour it took him to grind out each script, without ever once stopping, never ceased to amaze me. I often watched him as he composed these chapters. Unlike the recording sessions, where he kept what transpired a closely guarded secret, he didn't care in the least if there were people around when he was writing. As he sat typing away at his (my) Remington, he was often interrupted by his actors, Puddler, or the sound engineer. He would raise his eyes, answer their questions, give a baroque instruction, send the visitor on his way with his epidermic little smile, as different from a laugh as anything I've ever witnessed, and go on writing. I often used to come down to his lair on the pretext that I needed a place to study, that I had to put up with too much noise and too many people in my pigeon coop upstairs (I was studying for my year-end exams in my law courses and forgot everything the minute I'd taken them: the fact that I never flunked one didn't so much speak well of me as it spoke badly of the university). Pedro Camacho didn't object to my studying there, and in fact gave every appearance of being not at all displeased by this human presence feeling him "create."

I would sit myself down on the windowsill and bury my nose in one law code or another. What I was really doing was spying on him. He wrote very quickly, typing with just his index fingers. I watched and couldn't believe my eyes: he never stopped to search for a word or ponder an idea, not the slightest shadow of a doubt ever appeared in his fanatic, bulging little eyes. He gave the impression that he was writing out a fair copy of a text that he knew by heart, typing something that was being dictated to him. How was it possible, at the speed with which his little fingers flew over the keys, for him to be *inventing* the situations, the incidents, the dialogue of so many different stories for nine, ten hours a day? And yet it was possible: the scripts came pouring out of that tenacious head of his and those indefatigable hands one after the other, each of them exactly the right length, like strings of sausages out of a machine. Once a chapter was finished, he never made corrections in it or even read it over; he handed it to the secretary to have copies run off and immediately started in on the next one. I once told him that when I watched him work I was reminded of the theory of the French Surrealists with regard to automatic writing, which according to them flowed directly from the subconscious, bypassing the censorship of reason.

I was greeted with a chauvinist reply: "Our mestizo Latin American brains can give birth to better things than those Frogs. Let's not have any inferiority complexes, my friend."

Why was it that he didn't use the scripts he'd written in Bolivia as a basis for his stories about Lima? I put this question to him, and he answered in generalities that fell far short of being a concrete explanation. In order to reach the public, stories, like fruits and vegetables, ought to be fresh, since art would not tolerate canned ones, much less those food products that were so old they'd turned rotten. Moreover, they had to be "stories of the same provenance as the listeners." Since the latter were from Lima, how could they be expected to be interested in episodes that took place in La Paz? But he offered these reasons because his need to theorize, to turn everything into an impersonal truth, an eternal axiom, was as compulsive as his need to write. Doubtless, his real reason for not using his old scripts was far simpler: the fact that he didn't have the slightest interest in saving himself work. For him, to live was to write. Whether or not his works would endure didn't matter in the least to him. Once his scripts had been broadcast, he forgot about them. He assured me he didn't have a single copy of any of his serials. They had been composed with the tacit conviction that they would cease to exist as such once they had been digested by the public.

I once asked him whether he had ever considered publishing them. "My writings are preserved in a more indelible form than the printed page," he replied immediately. "They are engraved upon the memory of my radio listeners."

I brought up the subject of the Argentine protest on the very same day that I had had lunch with Genaro Jr. I dropped by Pedro's lair around 6 p.m. and invited him to the Bransa. Fearing his reaction, I announced this piece of news in a roundabout way: there were certain people whose sensibilities were all too easily wounded, who were incapable of tolerating the slightest hint of irony, and furthermore, libel laws in Peru were extremely strict and a radio station could be closed down for the most trivial reason. Giving ample demonstration of their total lack of sophistication, the

Argentine embassy had taken offense at certain allusions and was threatening to lodge an official protest with the Foreign Office . . .

"In Bolivia they even threatened to break off diplomatic relations," he interrupted me. "A scandal sheet went so far as to intimate that they were massing troops on the border."

He said this in a resigned tone of voice, as though he were thinking: by its very nature the sun is obliged to shine, and what recourse is there if its rays start a fire?

"The only thing the Genaros ask is that you try your best to refrain from speaking ill of Argentines in your serials," I finally worked up my nerve to tell him straight out, coming up at the same time with an argument I hoped would win him over: "In a word, it's better if you don't say anything at all about them. When you come right down to it, are they worth bothering about?"

"Yes, they are, because *they* inspire me," he explained, thus putting an end to the discussion.

As we were walking back to the radio station, he informed me, in a mischievous voice, that the international incident he'd set off in La Paz had come about because of a play he'd written and staged on the subject of "the bestial habits of gauchos," which according to him had "hit home." Once back at Panamericana, I told Genaro Jr. he ought not to labor under any illusions as to how effective a mediator I'd be.

Two or three days later I got a chance to see Pedro Camacho's living quarters. Aunt Julia had come down to the station to meet me after the last evening newscast because she wanted to see a movie that was showing at the Metro, starring one of Hollywood's great romantic couples: Greer Garson and Walter Pidgeon. As we were crossing the Plaza San Martín around midnight to catch a jitney, I spied Pedro Camacho coming out of Radio Central. The moment I pointed him out to her, Aunt Julia wanted to meet him. We walked over to him, and on learning that Aunt Julia was a compatriot of his, he warmed to her immediately.

"I'm a great admirer of yours," Aunt Julia said to him, and to flatter him even more, she lied: "I first began listening to your serials in Bolivia, and I never miss one."

We walked along with him, almost without realizing it, to the Jirón Quilca, and on the way Pedro Camacho and Aunt Julia had a patriotic conversation from which I was excluded, in which there passed in review the mines of Potosí and Taquiña beer, the corn soup called *lagua,* stewed corn with cream cheese, the climate of Cochabamba, the beauty of the women of Santa Cruz, and other national glories of Bolivia. The scriptwriter seemed to enjoy talking of the marvels of his native land. On arriving at the door of a building with balconies and jalousies, he stopped but didn't bid us goodnight.

"Come on upstairs with me," he proposed. "I'm having a simple dinner but we can share it."

The La Tapada rooming house was one of those old three-story residences in downtown Lima, built in the last century, that were often spacious and comfortable and sometimes even sumptuous, but later on, as people who were well-off gradually deserted the center of the city and moved to resorts on the seashore, old Lima gradually became unfashionable, these houses gradually began to fall into ruin, grew more and more crowded as they were subdivided, and eventually turned into veritable hives thanks to the installation of partitions that doubled or quadrupled the number of rooms and the haphazard creation of minuscule living quarters in all sorts of odd corners in the entry halls, on the roof terraces, and even on the balconies and stairways. The La Tapada rooming house appeared to be about to collapse at any moment; the steps of the stairs we climbed to get to Pedro Camacho's room swayed beneath our weight, and our feet stirred up little clouds of dust that made Aunt Julia sneeze. A thick film of dirt covered everything, walls and floors, and it was plain to see that the place had never been swept or mopped. Pedro Camacho's room was like a cell. It was very small and almost empty. There was a cot without a headboard, covered with a faded blanket and on it a pillow without a pillowcase, a small table covered with an oilcloth, a chair with a straw seat, a suitcase, and a line strung between two walls with undershorts and socks drying on it. The fact that the scriptwriter washed his own clothes didn't surprise me, but it did surprise me that he did his own cooking. There was a Primus stove on the windowsill, a bottle of kerosene, a couple of tin plates and eating utensils, a few glasses.

He offered Aunt Julia the chair and me the bed with a grand

gesture. "Please be seated. My dwelling is humble but my welcome to you is from the heart."

It took him two minutes to prepare dinner. He had the ingredients in a plastic sack, stored on the windowsill to keep cool. The menu consisted of fried eggs and boiled sausages, bread with butter and cheese, and yogurt with honey. We watched him prepare it with no wasted motions, like someone accustomed to doing so every day, and I was certain that this must be what he always had for dinner.

As we ate, he was at once courtly and chatty, condescending to deal with subjects such as the recipe for cup custard (that Aunt Julia asked him for) and the most economical laundry soap for doing white clothes. He didn't clean up his plate; as he pushed it aside, he pointed to what was left on it, and allowed himself to venture a little joke. "For the artist, eating is a vice, my friends."

Seeing what a good mood he was in, I dared to come right out and ask him a number of questions about his work habits. I told him I was envious of his stamina, of the fact that despite his galley-slave schedule he never seemed tired.

"I have my stratagems to make my day interesting," he confessed to us.

Lowering his voice, as though to keep imaginary rivals from discovering his secret, he told us that he never worked for more than sixty minutes at a time on the same story and that changing from one subject to another was refreshing, since at the beginning of each hour he thus had the sensation that he was just starting to work.

"Pleasure stems from variety, my friends," he repeated, with an excited gleam in his eye and the facial contortions of an evil gnome.

Hence, when writing stories, it was important that contrast, not continuity, be the ruling principle of composition: the complete change of place, milieu, mood, subject, and characters reinforced the exhilarating sensation that one was starting afresh. Moreover, cups of mint-and-verbena tea were helpful: they cleared one's synapses, and one's imagination was grateful. And leaving the typewriter every so often to go over to the studio, turning from writing to directing and acting, was also relaxing, a transition that had a tonic effect. But, in addition to all this, he had made an important discovery over the years, something that to the ignorant and insensitive might perhaps appear absolutely childish. But then, did it matter what that breed thought?

We saw him hesitate; he fell silent and a sad look came over his little cartoon-character face. "Unfortunately I can't put it into practice here," he said dejectedly. "Only on Sundays, when I'm alone. There are too many busybodies around on weekdays, and they wouldn't understand."

Since when had he, who looked upon mortals with Olympian detachment, had such scruples? I noted that Aunt Julia, too, was hanging on his every word. "You can't leave us in suspense like this," she said pleadingly. "What is this secret you've discovered, Señor Camacho?"

He observed us for some time, in silence, like the conjurer who contemplates, with evident satisfaction, the attention that he has contrived to arouse. Then, with sacerdotal slowness, he rose to his feet (he had been sitting on the windowsill, next to the Primus stove), went over to his suitcase, opened it, and began to pull out of the depths of it, like a prestidigitator pulling rabbits or flags out of a top hat, an incredible collection of objects: an English magistrate's court wig, false mustaches of various sizes, a fireman's hat, military badges, masks of a fat woman, an old man, an idiot child, a traffic policeman's stick, a sea dog's cap and pipe, a surgeon's white smock, false ears and noses, cotton beards . . . Like a little electric robot, he showed us these props, and—the better to demonstrate their effect to us? out of some intimate inner need?—he began putting them on and taking them off, with an agility that betrayed a long-standing habit, constant practice. As Aunt Julia and I watch in openmouthed amazement, by changing props and costumes Pedro Camacho transformed himself, before our very eyes, into a doctor, a sailor, a judge, an old lady, a beggar, a bigot, a cardinal . . . And all during this series of lightning-quick changes he kept talking, in a fervent tone of voice.

"And why shouldn't I have the right to become one with characters of my own creation, to resemble them? Who is there to stop me from having their noses, their hair, their frock coats as I describe them?" he said, exchanging a biretta for a meerschaum, the meerschaum for a duster, and the duster for a crutch. What does it matter to anyone if I lubricate my imagination with a few bits of cloth? What is realism, ladies and gentlemen—that famous realism we hear so much about? What better way is there of creating realistic art than by materially identifying oneself with reality? And doesn't the day's work thereby become more tolerable, more pleasant, more varied, more dynamic?"

But naturally—and his voice became first furious, then disconsolate—through stupidity and lack of understanding, people were bound to get the wrong idea. If he were seen at Radio Central wearing disguises as he wrote, tongues would immediately begin to wag, the rumor would spread that he was a transvestite, his office would become a magnet attracting the morbid curiosity of the vulgar. He finished putting away the masks and other objects, closed the valise, and returned to the windowsill. He was in a melancholy mood now. He murmured that in Bolivia, where he always worked in his own atelier, he'd never had any problem "with his props and his bits of cloth." Here, however, it was only on Sundays that he could write in the way that had long been his habit.

"Do you acquire disguises to fit your characters, or do you invent your characters on the basis of disguises you already have?" I asked, just to be saying something, still overcome with astonishment.

He looked at me as though I were a newborn babe.

"It's plain from your question that you're still very young," he chided me gently. "Don't you know that in the beginning is the Word—always?"

When, after thanking him effusively for his invitation, we went back down to the street, I said to Aunt Julia that Pedro Camacho had given us an exceptional proof of his confidence by letting us in on his secret, and that I'd been touched by his doing so. She was happy: she'd never imagined that intellectuals could be such amusing characters.

"Well, they're not all like that." I laughed. "Pedro Camacho is an 'intellectual' in quotation marks. Did you notice that there wasn't a single book in his room? He once explained to me that he doesn't read, because other writers might influence his style."

Holding hands, we walked back through the silent downtown streets to the jitney stop and I told her that some Sunday I'd come down to Radio Central by myself just to see the scriptwriter become one with his creatures by way of his disguises.

"He lives like a beggar—there's no justice," Aunt Julia expostulated. "Since his serials are so famous, I thought he must earn piles of money."

She couldn't help remembering that she hadn't seen a bathtub or a shower in the La Tapada rooming house, just a toilet and a washstand green with mold on the first landing. Did I think Pedro Camacho never bathed? I told her that the scriptwriter couldn't care less about such trivial details. She confessed to me that it had turned her stomach when she'd seen how filthy the *pensión* was, that she'd had to make a superhuman effort to get the sausage and the egg down.

Once we'd gotten in the jitney, an old rattletrap that kept stopping at every corner all along the Avenida Arequipa, as I was slowly kissing her on the ear, in the neck, I heard her say in alarm: "In other words, if you're a writer you're poverty-stricken. That means you're going to be down-and-out all your life, Varguitas."

Ever since she'd heard Javier calling me that, she too now addressed me as Varguitas.

Eight.

Don Federico Téllez Unzátegui

looked at his watch, saw that it was noon, told the half-dozen employees of Rodent Exterminators, Inc., that they could go out to lunch, and did not remind them to be back by three on the dot, not one minute later, since all of them knew full well that, in this company, lack of punctuality was sacrilege: those who were late were fined or even fired on the spot. Once they had left, Don Federico, as was his habit, double-locked the office himself, put on his mouse-gray hat, and headed down the crowded sidewalks of the Jirón Huancavelica to the parking lot where he kept his car (a Dodge sedan).

He was a man who aroused fear and dismal thoughts in the minds of others; a person had only to see him passing by on the street to note immediately that he was different from his fellows. He was in the prime of life, his fifties, and his distinguishing traits—a broad forehead, an aquiline nose, a penetrating gaze, the very soul of rectitude and goodness—might have made him a Don Juan had he been interested in women. But Don Federico Téllez Unzátegui had devoted his entire existence to a crusade and allowed nothing and no one—with the exception of those hours that had necessarily to be set aside for sleeping, eating, and family life—to distract him from it. He had been waging this war for forty years now, his ultimate goal being the extermination of every last rodent in the land.

His acquaintances and even his wife and their four children did not know the reason behind this chimerical campaign. Don Federico Téllez Unzátegui kept it a secret but never forgot it: it haunted his memory day and night, a persistent nightmare from which he drew new strength, renewed hatred enabling him to persevere in this combat that some people considered preposterous, others repellent, and the rest commercial. At this very moment, as he entered the parking lot, checked with the eye of a condor whether the Dodge had been washed, started it, and waited precisely two minutes by his watch for the engine to warm up, his thoughts, moths hovering about flames in which they would burn their wings, went back yet again in time and space to the remote village of his childhood and the terror that had forged his destiny.

It had happened in the first decade of the century, when Tingo María was just a tiny dot on the map, a few cabins in a clearing surrounded by dense jungle. Adventurers abandoning the soft life of the capital with the dream of conquering virgin forest ended up there from time to time, after countless hardships. That was how the engineer Hildebrando Téllez had happened to come to the region, along with his young wife (in whose veins, as her name, Mayte, and surname, Unzátegui, proclaimed, Basque blood flowed) and their young son: Federico. The engineer had grandiose plans: cutting down trees, exporting precious woods for building mansions and making furniture for the affluent, growing pineapples, avocados, watermelon, custard apples, and eggfruit for the world's exotic palates, and in time, steamboat service up and down the rivers of the Amazon basin. But the gods and men reduced these fires to ashes. Natural catastrophes—rains, plagues, floods—and human limitations—the shortage of workers, the indolence and stupidity of the few he did have, alcohol, the scarcity of credit—wiped out all the pioneer's vast projects, one after the other, so that, two years after his arrival in Tingo María, he was obliged to earn his living in a very modest, humble way, by growing sweet potatoes on a small farm up the Pendencia River. It was there, in a cabin built of logs and palm fronds, that on a stifling hot night rats ate alive María Téllez Unzátegui, the couple's newborn daughter, as she lay in her crib without a mosquito netting.

The way the tragedy happened was both simple and horrible. The father and the mother were to stand as godparents at a baptism and would be spending the night on the other side of the river, attending the usual festivities in honor of such an occasion. They had left the farm in charge of the foreman, who lived, along with the two farmhands, in a lean-to a long distance away from the boss's cabin. The cabin was where Federico and his sister were to sleep. But when the weather was very hot, the little boy would often take his straw pallet down to the banks of the Pendencia, where the sound of the water lulled him to sleep. That was what he had done that night (and all the rest of his life was to reproach himself for having done so). He bathed himself in the river in the moonlight, lay down on his pallet, and fell asleep. In his dreams he seemed to hear a baby crying. But the sound was not loud enough or did not last a long enough time to awaken him. At dawn he felt sharp little teeth biting his foot. He opened his eyes and thought he would die, or rather, that he had died and was in Hell: he was surrounded by dozens of rats, writhing, twisting, stumbling over each other, jostling each other, and above all devouring everything within their reach. He leapt up from the pallet, grabbed a stick, and managed to alert the foreman and the farmhands by shouting at the top of his lungs. Among all of them, they were able to drive the colony of invaders off with torches, clubs, kicks. But when they entered the cabin all that was left of the baby (the pièce de résistance of the famished rodents' feast) was a little pile of bones.

The two minutes were up and Don Federico Téllez Unzátegui started off. In a serpentine of cars, he slowly made his way along the Avenida Tacna, intending to head off down Wilson and Arequipa to the Barranco district, where lunch was waiting for him. As he stopped for the red lights, he closed his eyes and felt, as he always did whenever he remembered that terrifying dawn, a burning, effervescent sensation, like acid bubbling inside him. Because, as folk wisdom has it, "misfortunes never come one at a time." As a result of the tragedy, his mother, the young woman of Basque descent, contracted chronic hiccups, which brought on spasms, kept her from being able to eat, and struck other people as hilariously funny. She never again uttered a single word: only croaks and gurgles. She went about like that, with terror-stricken eyes, hiccuping constantly, wasting away, until she finally died of exhaustion a few months later. His father let himself go, lost all his ambition, all his energy, the habit of washing. When, out of sheer negligence, he lost the farm and it was sold at auction to pay off his creditors, he earned his living for a while as a raftsman, ferrying human passengers, goods, and animals from one shore of the Huallaga to the other. But one day when the river was in flood the current drove the raft into a clump of trees, completely destroying it, and he lost all interest in building another one. He took to the slopes of that pornographic mountain with maternal breasts and eager hips they call the Sleeping Beauty, built himself a refuge of leaves and stalks, let his hair and beard grow, and remained there for years, eating wild herbs and smoking leaves that make your head swim. When Federico, by then an adolescent, left the jungle, the ex-engineer was known in Tingo María as the Sorcerer and lived near the grotto of Las Pavas, cohabiting with three Indian women from Huánuco, who had borne him several half-wild children with round bellies.

Only Federico was able to confront the catastrophe creatively. That very morning, after having been whipped for leaving his sister alone in the cabin, the boy (who had become a man in the space of a few hours) had knelt beside the little mound of earth that was María's tomb and swore to devote his life, to his last breath, to the annihilation of the murderous species. To seal his vow, he sprinkled the earth covering the little girl with drops of blood from the gashes left by the whip.

Forty years later, Don Federico Téllez Unzátegui, the very exemplar of the single-mindedness of men of honor that moves mountains, could tell himself, as his sedan rolled down the avenues toward his frugal daily lunch, that he had proved that he was a man of his word. For in all those years it was probable that, thanks to his labors and his inspiration, the number of rodents that had perished in Peru exceeded the number of Peruvians born. Difficult work, involving many sacrifices and no rewards, that had made him a dour, inflexible, friendless man with odd habits. In the beginning, when he was still a child, the hardest part had been overcoming his feelings of repugnance toward the nasty gray creatures. His initial technique had been primitive: setting traps for them. With his pocket money he bought (at the Deep Sleep Mattress Shop and General Store on the Avenida Raimondi) one that he used as a model for making many others. He cut wood and wire to the proper size, assembled his traps, and set them out twice a day all over the farm. Sometimes the little creatures caught in them were still alive. Trembling with emotion, he would kill them by slowly burning them to death or torture them by stabbing them, mutilating them, putting their eyes out before doing them in.

But young as he was, his intelligence told him that if he gave in to such inclinations he would fail in the task he had set himself: his goal was quantitative, not qualitative. It was not a question of inflicting the greatest possible suffering on each individual enemy but of destroying the greatest possible number of enemies at one and the same time. With a clearheadedness and a strength of will remarkable at his tender years, he rooted out every last remaining trace of sentimentality within him and thereafter pursued his genocidal goal in accordance with impeccably objective criteria, coldly, statistically, scientifically. Stealing time from his studies at the Canadian Brothers' School and from sleep (though not from recreation, since after the tragedy he no longer ever played), he perfected the traps, adding a blade to them that chopped the victims' bodies to bits so that they never remained alive after being caught (not in order to spare them pain but in order not to have to waste time killing them off). He then built multifamily traps, with a broad base, in which a fork with curved tines could simultaneously crush the father, the mother, and four little ones. Everyone in the region soon heard about his skills at rat killing, and little by little it ceased to be merely a penitence, a personal vendetta, and became a service to the community, for which he was paid very little, but a mere pittance was better than nothing. The boy was summoned to farms both near and far the moment there were signs of an invasion, and with the diligence of an omnipotent ant, he would rid them of every last rodent in a matter of a few days. They began to call upon his services in Tingo María as well, to clean out cabins, houses, offices, and the youngster had his moment of glory when the captain of the Guardia Civil gave him the job of ridding the commissariat of the rats that had overrun the building. He spent all the money he received building more traps in order to expand what naïve souls took to be his business—or his perversion. When the ex-engineer buried himself in the sexualoid tangle of jungle growth of the Sleeping Beauty, Federico, who had dropped out of school, began to complement his clean weapon, traps, with another, more cunning one: poisons.

This work allowed him to earn his own living at an age when other boys are still spinning tops. But it also turned him into an outcast. People would call him in to get rid of their hordes of scampering rodents, but they never invited him to sit down at table with them and never had a kind word to say to him. If this hurt his feelings, he did not let it show; on the contrary, it almost seemed to please him that his fellows found him repellent. He was an unsociable, taciturn adolescent; no one could boast of ever having made him laugh, or even seen him laugh, and his one passion seemed to be killing the filthy creatures that were his enemy. He charged people only a modest fee for his work, and moreover waged campaigns *ad honorem*, in the dwellings of poor folk, appearing on their doorstep with his gunnysack full of traps and his vials of poison the moment he learned that the enemy had set up camp there. In addition to killing the lead-colored vermin, a technique that the lad kept tirelessly perfecting, there was the problem of getting rid of the dead bodies, the part of the whole business that families, housewives, or maidservants found most repugnant. Federico expanded his commercial enterprise by hiring the village idiot, a cross-eyed hunchback who lived at the convent of the Sisters of Saint Joseph, who for a pittance collected the remains of the victims and took them off to burn them behind the Coliseo Abad or offer them as a feast to the dogs, cats, pigs, and vultures of Tingo María.

What a long time had gone by since then! As he stopped at the red light on the corner of the Avenida Javier Prado, Don Federico Téllez Unzátegui said to himself that he had undoubtedly come up in the world since the days when, a raw youth still, he went up and down the muddy streets of Tingo María from sunup to sundown, followed by the idiot, waging his war against the murderers of his little sister María with his craftsmanship and skill as his only weapon. He was scarcely past childhood then, had nothing but the clothes on his back, and one helper at most. Thirty-five years later, he was the head of a vast technico-commercial enterprise, with branches in every city in Peru, with fifteen trucks in its motor pool and seventy-eight experts in the fumigation of rat-holes, the compounding of poisons, and the installation of traps. The latter operated on the front lines—the streets, houses, and fields of the entire country—wholeheartedly devoted to searching out, surrounding, and annihilating the enemy, and receiving orders, advice, and logistic support from the headquarters staff over which he presided (the six technocrats who had just gone out to lunch). But in addition to this constellation, Don Federico had enlisted the aid of two laboratories in his crusade, by signing contracts with them (that were practically subsidies) for constant experimentation with new poisons, a crucial tactic in view of the enemy's prodigious capacity for acquiring immunity: after two or three campaigns, the toxics became obsolete, simply a source of food for the creatures they were intended to kill. Moreover, Don Federico—who at this moment shifted into first as the light turned green, and continued on his way toward the residential districts along the seashore—had set up a scholarship whereby Rodent Exterminators, Incorporated sent a newly graduated chemist to the University of Baton Rouge each year to do advanced research on rat poisons.

It had been precisely this concern—placing science at the service of his religion—that, twenty years before, had impelled Don Federico Téllez Unzátegui to marry. Being only human after all, he had one day begun to conceive the idea of a dense phalanx of males, scions of his very own blood and spirit, in whom he would inculcate, from their earliest days at their mother's breast, his fury toward the disgusting rodent breed, and who, having received an exceptional upbringing and education, would continue his mission, perhaps even beyond the borders of their native land. The image of six, seven Téllezes with doctorates from top-ranking institutions who would repeat and perpetuate *in aeternum* the vow that he had sworn, impelled him, a man who was marital inappetency incarnate, to have recourse to a matrimonial agency, which, in return for a somewhat excessive fee, supplied him with a twenty-five-year-old spouse, perhaps not a raving beauty—she had several teeth missing and, like those little ladies from the region irrigated by that supposedly silvery stream that goes by the (hyperbolic) name of the Río de la Plata, great rolls of fat around her waist and at the backs of her knees—but nonetheless possessed of the three qualities he had demanded: perfect health, an intact hymen, and high fertility.

Doña Zoila Saravia Durán was a girl from Huánuco whose family, by one of those turns of the wheel of fortune that are life's favorite game, had come down in the world from the provincial aristocracy to the subproletariat of the capital. She had received her education at the free school run by the Salesian Mothers—for reasons of conscience or as publicity?—next door to their school for paying pupils, and like all her schoolmates had come to suffer from an Argentine complex as she grew up; in her case it took the form of meekness, silence, and gluttony. She had spent her life working as a classroom monitor for the Salesian Mothers, and her vague, undefined status as such—was she a servant? a worker? a salaried employee?—aggravated the servile insecurity that caused her to acquiesce and nod her head like a docile cow in any and every situation. When she was left an orphan at the age of twenty-four, she finally worked up the courage to visit, after much hesitation and painful soul-searching, the matrimonial agency that put her in touch with the man who was to be her lord and master. Due to the lack of erotic experience of both spouses, the consummation of the marriage was an extremely slow process, a serial in which, between false starts and impulses gone astray, fiascos due to faulty aim or precocious emission or the wrong position, the chapters followed one upon the other, the suspense mounted, and the stubborn hymen remained unperforated. Paradoxically, in view of the fact that they were an extremely virtuous couple, Doña Zoila first lost her virginity (not out of vice but due, rather, to mere blind chance and the newlyweds' lack of practice) heterodoxically; that is to say, sodomitically.

Apart from this fortuitous abomination, the couple's life had been a model of moral rectitude. Doña Zoila was a conscientious, hardworking, thrifty wife, and doggedly determined to respect her husband's principles (which certain people chose to call eccentricities). She had never objected, for instance, to Don Federico's strict injunction against the use of hot water (since, according to him, it sapped one's will and caused head colds), despite the fact that even after twenty years she still turned purple from the cold on entering the shower. She had never failed to comply with the clause of the family code (unwritten but engraved upon the memory of each of its members) decreeing that no one was to sleep more than five hours a night so as not to encourage indolence, even though their crocodile yawns made the windowpanes quiver when the alarm clock went off every morning at 5 a.m. She had accepted with resignation her husband's ukase that movies, dancing, theater, radio were to be excluded as permissible forms of family entertainment, on the grounds that they were immoral, and that meals in restaurants, travel, and any sort of fanciful caprice with regard to bodily attire or household furnishings was likewise forbidden as being too great a strain on the budget. It was only with respect to her one sin, gluttony, that she had been incapable of obeying the master of the house. Meat, fish, and rich desserts with whipped cream had very often appeared on the menu. This was the one and only area in his conjugal life in which Don Federico had been unable to impose his will: a strictly vegetarian diet.

But Doña Zoila had never made any attempt to indulge in her vice in secret, behind her husband's back, and as the latter's sedan entered the coquettish Miraflores district, he told himself that his wife's forthrightness in this respect, while it might not have redeemed her sin, made it at most a venial one. When her irrepressible appetites were more powerful than her spirit of obedience, she devoured her beefsteak with onions, or her sole with hot peppers, or her apple pie with whipped cream before his very eyes, her cheeks beet-red with shame, and resigned beforehand to the punishment that would be meted out to her for that particular transgression. She had never objected to the sanctions he imposed. If (on account of a grilled steak or a chocolate bar) Don Federico forbade her to speak for three days, she herself stuffed a gag in her mouth so as not to disobey even in her sleep, and if the penalty was twenty spanks on her bare bottom, she hastened to undo her skirt and get the arnica out.

No, Don Federico Téllez Unzátegui said to himself as he cast an absentminded glance at the gray (a color he detested) Pacific Ocean beyond the seawall of Miraflores that his sedan had just started across, when everything was said and done, Doña Zoila hadn't disappointed him. His great failure in life was his children. What an enormous difference between the bold vanguard of princes of extermination that he had dreamed of and the four offspring that God and his gluttonous wife had inflicted upon him.

Their first two children had both been boys. But then came a rude blow. The thought had never even crossed his mind that Doña Zoila might give birth to girls. The first one had been a disappointment, something that might be attributed to mere chance. But when his wife's fourth pregnancy also produced a creature without a visible penis or testicles, Don Federico, terrified at the prospect of continuing to engender incomplete beings, drastically eliminated the possibility that a momentary whim might lead to his begetting more offspring (by replacing the big double bed in their room by twin beds). He didn't hate females; but, quite simply, since he was neither an erotomaniac nor a gourmand, what possible use did he have for persons whose greatest aptitudes were for fornicating and cooking? His one reason for reproducing had been to perpetuate his crusade. This hope had gone up in smoke with the arrival of Teresa and Laura, since Don Federico was not one of those modernists who stoutly maintain that a female, in addition to a clitoris, also has brains and can work side by side with males as their equal. Furthermore, he was deeply distressed by the possibility that his family name might be trampled in the mud. Didn't statistics prove, *ad nauseam,* that ninety-five percent of women have been, are, or will be whores? In order to make certain that his daughters would end up among the five percent of virtuous females, Don Federico had organized their lives in rigorous detail: no low necklines at any time, dark stockings and long-sleeved smocks and sweaters both winter and summer, no nail polish, lipstick, rouge, eye makeup, no bangs, braids, ponytails, or any of the other bait that girls use to hook boys; no sports or diversions that might bring them into proximity with males, such as going to the beach or attending birthday parties. Infractions of these rules always met with corporal punishment.

But it was not only the intrusion of females among his descendants that had discouraged him. His sons—Ricardo and Federico Jr.—had not inherited their father's virtues. They were weak-willed and lazy, given to useless activities (such as chewing gum and playing soccer), and they had not shown the slightest signs of enthusiasm when Don Federico explained what a glorious future lay in store for them. When, during vacations, he sent them out to work with the first-line combatants in order to train them, they proved to be slackers and took their places on the battlefield with obvious repugnance. And once he even overheard them muttering obscenities about his life's work and confessing quite frankly that they were ashamed of their father. He had immediately shaved their heads like convicts, naturally, yet this did not in any way relieve the feeling of betrayal aroused in him by this conspiratorial conversation. Don Federico no longer entertained any illusions. He knew that, once he was dead or had grown feeble with age, Ricardo and Federico Jr. would stray from the path he had traced for them, would change professions (choosing some other with greater chrematistic attractions), and knew that his work—like a certain famous symphony—would remain unfinished.

It was at that precise moment that Don Federico Téllez Unzátegui, to his physical and psychical misfortune, spied the magazine that a news vendor was thrusting through the windows of the sedan, its lurid cover gleaming in the bright morning sun. His face contorted in a grimace of disgust on noting that the cover photo showed a beach with two female bathers clad only in that mere simulacrum of swimsuits that certain hetaerae dared to parade about in, when, with a sort of painful rending of his optic nerve and his mouth gaping open like a wolf's howling at the moon, Don Federico recognized the two half-naked bathers with obscene smiles on their faces. He felt a sudden horror rivaling that which he had felt, in that early Amazon dawn on the banks of the Pendencia, on seeing, in a cradle black with rat dung, the scattered bones of his sister's corpse. The traffic light had turned green; the cars behind him were honking. With fumbling fingers, he took out his wallet, paid for the licentious publication, shifted into first, and took off, and sensing that he was about to have a collision—the steering wheel was slipping out of his hands and the car was lurching violently—he braked and drew to a stop along the curb.

Sitting there trembling with indignation, he stared for several long minutes at the terrible evidence. There was no possible doubt: it was his daughters. Photographed, no doubt, without their being aware of it by a brazen paparazzo hidden among the other bathers, the girls were not looking at the camera; they appeared to be chatting together as they lay on the sands of a voluptuous beach that might be Agua Dulce or La Herradura. Little by little Don

Federico recovered his breath; despite being absolutely crushed, he managed to think of the incredible series of happenstances: that a roving photographer should chance to snap a picture of Laura and Teresa, that an ignoble magazine should expose them to the view of this rotten world, that he should happen to see them . . . And so, by the workings of blind chance, there the awful truth was, spread out before his eyes in lurid color. So his daughters obeyed him, then, only when he was present; so, the minute he turned his back, with the collusion, doubtless, of their brothers and, alas—Don Federico felt a sudden stab of pain in his heart—of his own wife, they defied his orders and went to the beach, they took their clothes off and exhibited themselves. Tears streamed down his face. He took a closer look at their bathing suits: two minuscule bits of cloth whose function was not to hide anything but simply to catapult the imagination to the most perverted extremes. There they were, within full view of anyone and everyone: the legs, arms, bellies, shoulders, necks of Laura and Teresa. He felt indescribably ridiculous as the thought crossed his mind that he himself had never seen these extremities and members that were now displayed before the entire universe.

He dried his eyes and started the engine up again. He had calmed down on the surface, but a blazing fire was burning deep within him. As the sedan proceeded very slowly toward his little house on the Avenida Pedro de Osma, he told himself that since they went to the beach naked it was only natural to presume that in his absence they also went to parties, wore pants, hung around with men, sold their bodies—did they perhaps receive the men they lured into their beds under his very own roof? was it Doña Zoila who set the prices and collected the money? Ricardo and Federico Jr. probably were in charge of the unspeakable task of hustling up customers for their sisters. Gasping for breath, Don Federico Téllez Unzátegui saw the whole horrifying cast assembled before his very eyes: your daughters, the whores; your sons, the pimps; and your wife, the madam.

His daily contact with violence—after all, he had killed off thousands upon thousands of living beings—had made Don Federico a man who could not be provoked without grave risk. One day an agronomist with pretensions to being an expert in nutrition had dared to state in his presence that, in view of the lack of beef cattle in Peru, it was necessary to intensify the raising of guinea pigs as a source of food for the nation. Don Federico Téllez Unzátegui politely reminded the bold planner that guinea pigs were first cousins to rats. The expert, not giving an inch, cited statistics, spoke of their great nutritive value and the agreeable taste of their flesh. Don Federico then proceeded to slap him and, as the nutrition expert fell to the floor, rubbing his face, called him names he roundly deserved: a shameless wretch and a public-relations man for murderers. Now, as he got out of the car, locked it, and walked unhurriedly toward the door of his house, frowning and very pale, the man from Tingo María felt a volcanic lava boiling up within him, as on the day that he had taught the nutrition expert a lesson. He was carrying the infernal magazine, like a red-hot iron bar, in his right hand and felt an intense itching sensation in his eyes.

He was so upset he was unable to imagine a punishment that would fit the heinous crime. His mind felt hazy, he realized he was so angry he couldn't think straight, and this made him more bitter still, for Don Federico was a man whose conduct was ruled by reason, and who despised that uncouth breed that acted, like animals, out of instinct and sheer gut feeling rather than out of conviction. But this time, as he took out his key, fumblingly inserted it in the keyhole, his fingers trembling with rage, and finally managed to get the door unlocked and push it open, he realized that he was not going to be able to act calmly and deliberately, but rather as his wrath dictated, following the inspiration of the moment. As he closed the door behind him, he took a deep breath, trying to get hold of himself. He was ashamed to think that those ingrates would doubtless see how profoundly they had humiliated him.

On the downstairs floor of his house were a little entry hall, a small living room, the dining room, and the kitchen; the bedrooms were on the upstairs floor. Don Federico spied his wife from the doorway of the living room. She was standing next to the buffet, ecstatically munching some disgusting sticky sweet—a caramel, a chocolate, Don Federico thought, Turkish delight, toffee—holding the part she hadn't yet eaten in her fingers. On seeing him, she smiled at him with an intimidated look in her eyes, pointing to what she was eating with self-deprecating resignation.

Don Federico walked unhurriedly toward her, unfolding the magazine and holding it out between his two hands so that his wife could contemplate the cover in all its baseness. He thrust it under her nose without saying a word and enjoyed watching her turn deathly pale, her eyes nearly pop out of their sockets, her mouth gape open, and a little thread of saliva full of biscuit crumbs begin running out of it. The man from Tingo María raised his right hand and slapped the trembling woman as hard as he could across the face. She gave a moan, staggered, and fell on her knees, continuing to contemplate the cover photo with an expression of rapturous devotion, mystical illumination. Towering over her, rigid and stern-faced, Don Federico gazed down at her accusingly.

Then he curtly called upstairs to summon the two guilty parties: "Laura! Teresa!"

A noise made him turn his head. There they were, at the foot of the stairs. He hadn't heard them come down. Teresa, the older one, was wearing a smock, as though she'd been cleaning the house, and Laura had on her school uniform. In bewilderment, the girls looked at their mother on her knees on the floor, at their father walking slowly, hieratically toward them, a high priest approaching the sacrificial stone where the knife and the vestal await, and, finally, at the magazine that Don Federico, having reached them, thrust accusingly before their eyes. His daughters' reaction was not what he had expected. Instead of turning pale, falling on their knees, and stammering explanations, the precocious creatures blushed and exchanged a swift glance that could only be one of complicity, and Don Federico said to himself, in the depths of his despair and rage, that he had not yet drained the bitter cup of that morning to the dregs: Laura and Teresa *knew* that they had been photographed, that the photograph was going to be published, and were even delighted—what else could that gleam in their eyes mean?—that it had been. The revelation that he had incubated, in his very own home, which he had believed to be pristinely innocent, not only the municipal vice of nudism on the beach but also exhibitionism (and, why not?, nymphomania), made his muscles sag, gave him a chalky taste in his mouth, and caused him to ponder whether life was worth living. And also—all that took no more than a second—to ask himself whether the only proper punishment for such an abomination was not death. The idea of committing filicide tormented him less than the knowledge that thousands of human beings had feasted (merely with their eyes?) on the physical intimacies of his daughters.

Then he went into action. He let the magazine fall to the floor to give himself more freedom of movement, grabbed Laura by her uniform jacket with his left hand, pulled her an inch or so closer to him to have her within better range, raised his right hand high enough to ensure that the slap he was about to give her would be as powerful as possible, and let fly with the full force of his rancor. He thereupon experienced the second unbelievable surprise of that extraordinary day, one perhaps even more breathtaking than that of the pornographic cover photo. Ridiculously, frustratingly, instead of Laura's soft cheek, his hand met empty air and his arm was painfully wrenched as the blow missed its target altogether. And that was not all: the worst was yet to come. For the girl was not content to have dodged the hard slap in the face—something that, in his immense bitterness, Don Federico suddenly remembered that no member of his family had ever done before. On the contrary, after stepping back, her little fourteen-year-old countenance contorted with hatred, she flung herself upon him—*him*, her own father—and began to pommel him with her fists, scratch him, push him, and kick him.

He had the sensation that his blood ceased flowing in his veins out of sheer stupefaction. It was as though the stars had suddenly escaped from their orbits and were racing toward each other, colliding, shattering each other to bits, hurtling hysterically through space. Unable to react, he reeled back, his eyes gaping, pursued by the girl, who, growing bolder, beside herself with rage, was not only lashing out at him with all her might now but also shouting: "You brute, you bastard, I hate you, kick off, die, go to hell, damn you!" He was thinking he'd gone mad when—everything was happening so fast that the moment he realized what was going on the entire situation abruptly changed—he saw Teresa run toward him, but instead of holding her sister back she was helping her. His elder daughter was now attacking him too, screaming the most abominable insults—"Tightwad, cretin, maniac, filthy beast, tyrant, madman, rat killer"—and between the two of them the adolescent furies little by little were backing him into a corner against the wall. He had begun to defend himself, overcoming at last his paralyzing stupefaction, and was trying to shield his face when he felt a sudden sharp pain in his back. He turned around: Doña Zoila had risen to her feet and was biting him.

Even at this point he was capable of feeling utter amazement on seeing that his wife had undergone an even greater transformation than his daughters. Was Doña Zoila, the woman who had never let a murmur of complaint cross her lips, never once raised her voice, never shown the slightest ill temper, the same person with blazing eyes and brutal hands who was pounding him with her fists, hitting him over the head, spitting on him, ripping his shirt, and screaming like a madwoman: "Let's kill him, let's avenge ourselves, let's make him swallow his manias, let's tear his eyes out"? The three of them were yelling at the top of their lungs and Don Federico thought that their screams had ruptured his eardrums. He was defending himself with all his strength, trying to return their blows, but found himself unable to do so because—putting into practice a technique they had treacherously perfected in secret?—two of them took turns holding his arms while the third went at him hammer and tongs. He felt burning sensations, swellings, shooting pains, he saw stars, and little stains that suddenly appeared on the hands of his assailants revealed to him that he was bleeding.

He had no illusions when he saw Ricardo and Federico Jr. appear at the foot of the stairway. Having been converted to wholehearted skepticism in a matter of seconds, he was certain that they were coming to join the others, to participate in the mayhem, to give him the *coup de grâce*. Terrified, with no dignity or honor left, he had only one thought: to make his way to the front door, to flee. But it was not easy. He managed to run two or three steps, but then one of them tripped him and sent him sprawling. Lying there on the floor, curled up in a ball to protect his manhood, he saw his heirs attack his humanity with ferocious kicks as his wife and daughters armed themselves with brooms, feather dusters, the fireplace poker, in order to go on working him over. Before telling himself that he had no idea what was going on except that the whole world had gone mad, he managed to hear his sons' voices, too, calling him a maniac, a tightwad, a filthy beast, a rat killer, rhythmically punctuating each insult with another kick. As everything began to go black, a tiny gray intruder suddenly popped out of an invisible little hole in one corner of the dining room, a mouse with white canines that contemplated the man lying on the floor with a mocking gleam in its bright eyes . . .

Was Don Federico Téllez Unzátegui, the indefatigable executioner of the rodents of Peru, dead? Had parricide, epithalamicide, been committed? Or was he merely stunned—this husband and father who lay, amid a disorder without precedent, beneath the dining-room table as his family, having swiftly packed their personal belongings, abandoned their home and fireside in exultation? How would this unfortunate affair in the Barranco district end?

Nine.
The failure of my story

about Doroteo Martí left me discouraged for several days. But the morning I heard Pascual tell Big Pablito of his discovery at the airport, I felt my vocation come to life again and began to plan another story. Pascual had surprised a bunch of ragamuffins practicing a risky and exciting sport. As darkness was falling, they would lie down on the end of the runway at Limatambo airport, and Pascual swore that each time a plane took off the kid lying on the ground would be lifted up a few centimeters or so because of the pressure of the air thus displaced, and levitate, as in a magic show, for a few seconds, and then, once the lift effect had disappeared, would suddenly come down to earth again. At about that same time I had just seen a Mexican film, *Los Olvidados*, that I was all excited about (it was not until years later that I found out it was a Buñuel film, and who Buñuel was). I decided to write a story in the same spirit: a tale of men-children, young wolf cubs toughened by the harsh conditions of life in the suburbs. Javier was skeptical and assured me that Pascual's anecdote couldn't possibly be true, that the change in air pressure caused by a plane taking off wouldn't be sufficient to lift even a newborn babe off the ground. We argued back and forth, and I finally told him that the characters in my story would levitate yet at the same time it would be a realistic story ("No, fantastic!" he shouted), and we finally agreed to go with Pascual to the vacant lots of Córpac some night to see with our own eyes what was true and what was false in his account of these dangerous games (that was the title I'd chosen for the story).

I hadn't seen Aunt Julia that day but was expecting to see her on the following day, Thursday, at Uncle Lucho's. But when I arrived at the house on Armendáriz at noon for the usual Thursday lunch, I discovered she wasn't there. Aunt Olga told me she'd been invited out to lunch by "a good match": Dr. Guillermo Osores, a physician who was some sort of distant family relation, a very presentable man in his fifties with quite a bit of money, whose wife had died fairly recently.

"A good match," Aunt Olga repeated, winking at me. "Rich, responsible, good-looking, and with only two sons, who are already almost grown up. Isn't he exactly the husband my sister needs?"

"She's been mooning about and wasting her time these last few weeks," Uncle Lucho commented, also pleased at this new development. "She didn't want to go out with anybody and was living the life of an old maid. But the endocrinologist has taken her fancy."

I felt such pangs of jealousy that I lost my appetite, and sat there in a foul, bitter mood. It seemed to me that my aunt and uncle, on seeing how upset I was, would surely guess why I was in such a state. There was no need for me to fish for more details about Aunt Julia and Dr. Osores because that was all they talked about. She'd met him some ten days before, at a cocktail party at the Bolivian embassy, and on learning where she was staying, Dr. Osores had come by to visit her. He had sent her flowers, phoned her, invited her to have tea with him at the Bolívar and now to lunch with him at the Club de la Unión. The endocrinologist had said jokingly to Uncle Lucho: "Your sister-in-law is super, Luis. Isn't it possible that she's the candidate I've been looking for so as to commit matrisuicide a second time?"

I tried my best to appear totally disinterested in the subject, but I did a very bad job of concealing how distraught I was, and Uncle Lucho asked me, at one point when the two of us were alone, what was troubling me: had I gone poking around in places I shouldn't have and caught myself a good dose of the clap? Luckily, Aunt Olga began talking about the radio serials, and that gave me a breathing spell. As she went on to say that Pedro Camacho sometimes laid it on too thick and that all her friends thought he'd gone too far with his story of the minister who "wounded himself" with a letter opener in front of the judge to prove that he hadn't raped a thirteen-year-old girl, I silently went from rage to disillusionment and from disillusionment to rage. Why hadn't Aunt Julia said a single word to me about the doctor? We'd seen each other several times during the last ten days and she'd never once mentioned him. Could it really be true, as Aunt Olga claimed, that she'd finally "gotten interested" in someone?

In the jitney, as I was going back to Radio Panamericana, my mood suddenly shifted from humiliation to pride. Our innocent love affair had lasted a long time, after all; we were bound to be found out at any moment now, and that would provoke scandal and unkind laughter in the family. Moreover, what was I doing, wasting my time with a woman who, as she herself said, was almost old enough to be my mother? As an experience, what we'd already had together was quite enough. Osores's appearance on the scene was providential; it saved me the trouble of having to get rid of her. I felt restless and upset, full of unusual impulses such as wanting to get drunk or punch somebody in the nose, and on arriving back at the radio station I had a run-in with Pascual, who, faithful to his nature, had devoted half the three o'clock news bulletin to a fire in Hamburg that had burned a dozen Turkish immigrants to death. I told him that in the future he was strictly forbidden to include any news item about dead people in the bulletins without getting my okay first, and I was curt and unfriendly to a pal from San Marcos who called me up to remind me that Law School still existed and to warn me that there was an exam in criminal law awaiting me the next day. Almost the moment I hung up, the phone rang again. It was Aunt Julia.

"I stood you up for an endocrinologist, Varguitas. I presume you missed me," she said, cool as a cucumber. "You're not angry?"

"Angry? Why should I be?" I replied. "Aren't you free to do as you please?"

"Ah, so you *are* angry," I heard her say in a more serious tone of voice. "Don't be an idiot. When can we see each other, so that I can explain?"

"I can't see you today," I replied curtly. "I'll phone you later."

I hung up, more furious with myself than with her, and feeling that I'd made a fool of myself. Pascual and Big Pablito were looking at me in amusement, and the lover of catastrophes subtly got back at me for having bawled him out. "Well, well, our Don Mario is certainly high-handed with the ladies, I must say."

"He's right to treat 'em that way," Big Pablito said, backing me up. "There's nothing that pleases 'em as much as being kept on a tight leash."

I told my two editors to go to hell, wrote up the four o'clock bulletin, and went to see Pedro Camacho. He was recording a script and I waited for him in his cubicle, idly leafing through the papers on his desk without understanding what I was reading because my mind was entirely occupied with the question of whether the phone conversation I'd just had with Aunt Julia meant that we'd broken up. In the space of just a few seconds I went from hating her with all my heart to missing her with all my soul.

"Come with me to buy some poison," Pedro Camacho said in a somber voice from the doorway, shaking his lion's mane. "We'll have time to go have something to drink afterwards."

As we wandered up and down the side streets off the Jirón de la Unión hunting for the poison, the artist explained that the mice at La Tapada rooming house had become intolerable.

"If they were content simply to scamper around underneath my bed, I wouldn't mind, they're not children, and as far as animals are concerned, I don't have any phobias," he said a few moments later as he sniffed with his prominent nose at some yellow powder that according to the shopkeeper could kill a cow. "But those mustached critters eat my food; every night they nibble on the provisions I leave on the windowsill to keep cool. There's no way round it—I'm obliged to exterminate them."

He haggled over the price of the poison, with arguments that left the shopkeeper nonplussed, paid for it, had them wrap up the little envelopes full of yellow powder, and the two of us went to a café on La Colmena. He ordered his usual herb concoction and I ordered coffee.

"I've got love troubles, my friend Camacho," I said to him straight out, surprised at hearing myself use a soap-opera cliché; but it seemed to me that by speaking in this way I distanced myself from my own story and at the same time managed to vent my feelings. "The woman I love is cheating on me with another man."

He gave me a searching look, his little pop-eyes colder and more humorless than ever. His black suit had been washed, ironed, and worn so threadbare that it was as shiny as an onion peel.

"In these countries whose manners and morals have become so vulgar and plebeian, dueling has become a crime punished by imprisonment," he reminded me, very seriously, making jerky motions with his hands. "As for suicide, it's a gesture no one appreciates nowadays. A person kills himself, and rather than remorse, cold shivers, admiration, it's laughter that he provokes. The best thing is practical recipes, my friend."

I was happy that I had taken him into my confidence. I knew very well that, inasmuch as no one outside himself existed for Pedro Camacho, my problem was the farthest thing from his mind; it had simply been a device to set his mechanism for churning out systematic theories in motion. Hearing the one he'd come up with would console me more (and have lesser consequences) than going out and getting drunk.

After giving me a faint smile, Pedro Camacho spelled out his recipe in detail. "A hard, cutting, lapidary letter to the adulteress," he said to me, wielding his adjectives with aplomb. "A letter that will make her feel like a miserable snake in the grass, a filthy hyena. Proving to her that you're not stupid, that you know how she's betrayed you, a letter dripping with contempt, that will show her what it means to be an adulteress." He fell silent, thought for a moment, and then, in a slightly different tone of voice, offered me the greatest proof of his friendship that I could possibly expect from him: "If you like, I'll write it for you."

I thanked him effusively, but said that, knowing as I did what long hours he put in working like a galley slave, I could never accept burdening him with my personal affairs in addition. (I later regretted having had such scruples, which kept me from having a holograph text of the scriptwriter's.)

"As for the seducer," Pedro Camacho went on immediately, with an evil gleam in his eye, "the best thing is an anonymous letter, with all the necessary malicious slander. Why should the victim sit with folded hands as he's being cuckolded? Why should he allow the adulterous couple to take their pleasure and fornicate in peace? It's necessary to ruin their love, to hit them where it hurts, to poison them with doubts. Let them begin to mistrust each other, to be suspicious of each other, to hate each other. Isn't vengeance sweet?"

I hinted that perhaps it was not gentlemanly to resort to anonymous letters, but he reassured me immediately: one should behave like a gentleman when dealing with gentlemen and like a bastard when dealing with bastards. This was "honor rightly understood": all the rest of it was errant nonsense.

"With the letter to her and the anonymous letters to him, the lovers get the punishment they deserve," I said. "But what about my problem? Who's going to relieve me of my resentment, my frustration, my heartache?"

"There's nothing like milk of magnesia for all that," he replied, but I was feeling too depressed even to laugh. "I know," he went on, "that strikes you as far too materialistic an answer. But, believe me, I've had a great deal of experience in life. Most of the time, so-called heartaches et cetera are simply indigestion—tough beans that won't dissolve in the stomach, fish that's not as fresh as it should be, constipation. A good laxative blasts the folly of love to bits."

There was no doubt this time, he was a subtle humorist, he was making fun of me the way he made fun of his listeners, he didn't believe one word of what he was saying, he was practicing the aristocratic sport of proving to himself that we mortals were hopeless imbeciles.

"Have you had a great many love affairs, an extremely rich love life?" I asked him.

"Yes, extremely rich," he avowed, looking me straight in the eye over the cup of verbena-and-mint-tea he had raised to his lips. "But I have never loved a flesh-and-blood woman."

He paused dramatically, as though he were sizing up exactly how innocent or stupid I was. "Do you think it would be possible to do what I do if women sapped my energy?" he said reprovingly, with disgust in his voice. "Do you think that it's possible to produce offspring and stories at the same time? That one can invent, imagine, if one lives under the threat of syphilis? Women and art are mutually exclusive, my friend. In every vagina an artist is buried. What pleasure is there in reproducing? Isn't that what dogs, spiders, cats do? We must be original, my friend."

Before the last word had died away, he suddenly leapt to his feet, announcing that he had just time enough to get back to the studio for the five o'clock serial. I was disappointed; I would willingly have spent the rest of the afternoon listening to him, and I had the impression that I had inadvertently touched a sore point of his personality.

When I got back to my office at Panamericana, Aunt Julia was there waiting for me. Seated at my desk like a queen, she was receiving the homage of Pascual and Big Pablito, who were bustling about solicitously, showing her the bulletins and explaining to her how the News Department functioned. She was smiling and seemed not to have a care in the world; but as I walked into the room a serious look came over her face and she paled slightly.

"Well, what a surprise," I said, just to say something.

But Aunt Julia was in no mood for polite chitchat. "I came to tell you that nobody hangs up on me," she said in a resolute voice. "Much less a brat like you. Would you kindly explain what's gotten into you?"

Pascual and Big Pablito just stood there, turning their heads to look at her and then at me and vice versa, bursting with curiosity as to how this dramatic scene just beginning would end. When I asked them to leave us alone for a moment, they were furious, but didn't dare to refuse. They left the room exchanging dark looks with Aunt Julia to show where their sympathies lay.

"I hung up on you, but what I really wanted to do was wring your neck," I said to her once we were alone.

"I've never known you to have fits of rage like this," she said, looking me straight in the eye. "May I ask what in the world is wrong with you?"

"You know very well what's wrong with me, so don't play dumb," I said.

"Are you jealous because I went out to lunch with Dr. Osores?" she asked me in a slightly mocking tone of voice. "How easy it is to see you're still just a kid, Marito."

"I've forbidden you to call me Marito," I reminded her. I could feel that my anger was getting the better of me, that my voice was trembling and I no longer had any idea what I was saying. "And I now forbid you to call me a kid."

I sat down on the corner of my desk, and as though to counterbalance me, Aunt Julia rose to her feet and walked a few steps over to the window. With her arms crossed over her chest, she stood there looking out at the gray, damp, vaguely ghostly morning, not really seeing it, because she was searching for words to tell me something. She was wearing a blue tailored suit and white shoes, and all of a sudden I wanted to kiss her.

"Let's get things straight," she finally said, her back still turned to me. "You can't forbid me to do anything, even as a joke, for the pure and simple reason that you're nothing to me. You're not my husband, you're not my fiancé, you're not my lover. That little game of holding hands, of kissing at the movies isn't really serious, and above all, it doesn't give you any hold over me. You have to get that through your head, my boy."

"The truth of the matter is that you're talking to me as though you were my mama," I said to her.

"The fact is, I *could* be your mama," Aunt Julia said, and a sad look came over her face. It was as though she'd gotten over being angry, and the only thing left in its place was a feeling of irritation that went far back in time, a profound bitterness. She turned around, walked back toward the desk, and stopped very close to me. She looked at me sorrowfully. "You make me feel old, Varguitas, even though I'm not. And I don't like that. What there is between us has no reason for being, much less a future."

I put my arms around her waist and drew her to me. She did not resist, but as I kissed her, very tenderly, on the cheek, on the neck, on the ear—her warm skin palpitated beneath my lips, and feeling the secret life coursing through her veins made me tremendously happy—she went on talking in the same tone of voice:

"I've been doing a lot of thinking and I don't like this situation, Varguitas. Don't you realize it's absurd? I'm thirty-two years old, I'm a divorcée—can you tell me what I'm doing with a kid eighteen years old? That's a typical perversion of women in their fifties, and I'm not old enough yet for that."

I felt so excited and so much in love as I kissed her neck, her hands, slowly nibbled her ear, ran my lips across her nose, her eyes, or wound locks of her hair around my fingers, that every so often I lost track of what she was saying. Moreover, she kept alternately raising and lowering her voice, and at times it faded to a mere whisper.

"At the beginning it was amusing, on account of having to meet in secret and all," she said, allowing herself to be kissed, but making no move to reciprocate, "and above all because it made me feel as though I were a young girl again."

"Where does that leave us, then, may I ask?" I murmured in her ear. "Do I make you feel like a perverted fifty-year-old woman or a young girl?"

"This whole business of being with a kid who never has a cent to his name, not doing anything but holding hands and going to the movies and giving each other tender little kisses, takes me back to when I was fifteen," Aunt Julia went on. "It's true that it's nice to fall for a shy youngster who respects you, who doesn't paw you, who doesn't dare go to bed with you, who treats you like a little girl who's just made her First Communion. But it's a dangerous game, Varguitas, it's based on a lie . . ."

"That reminds me—I'm writing a story that's going to be called 'Dangerous Games,' " I whispered in her ear. "It's about a bunch of little street urchins who levitate at the airport, thanks to the lift effect from planes that are taking off."

I heard her laugh. A moment later she threw her arms around my neck and put her cheek to mine. "Okay, I've gotten over being angry," she said. "Because I came here determined to tear your eyes out. But it'll be too bad for you the next time you hang up on me."

"And it'll be too bad for you the next time you go out with that endocrinologist," I told her, searching for her mouth. "Promise me you'll never go out with him again."

She drew away and looked at me with a belligerent gleam in her eye. "Don't forget that I came to Lima looking for a husband," she answered, half jokingly. "And I think that this time I've found just the right one for me. Good-looking, cultivated, well-off financially, graying at the temples."

"Are you certain that this marvel is going to marry you?" I asked her, enraged and jealous all over again.

Placing her hands on her hips in a provocative pose, she replied: "I have ways of getting him to marry me."

But, on seeing the expression on my face, she laughed, threw her arms around my neck again, and there we were, kissing each other lovingly and passionately, when we heard Javier's voice: "You're going to be arrested for indecent and pornographic conduct in public."

He was in a happy mood, and embracing the two of us, he announced: "Little Nancy has accepted my invitation to a bullfight, and that calls for a celebration."

"We've just had our first big fight and you caught us right in the middle of our big reconciliation scene," I explained to him.

"It's plain to see you don't know me very well," Aunt Julia informed me. "When I have a really big fight I break dishes, I scratch, I'm out to kill."

"The best part about having fights is making up afterwards," Javier, an expert on the subject, opined. "But, damn it all, I come bouncing in here all set to commemorate my glorious victory and you start raining on my parade. What kind of friends are you, anyway? Come on, you two, I'm inviting you to lunch to fete this grand occasion."

They waited for me while I wrote up a couple of news bulletins and then we headed for a little café on the Calle Belén that delighted Javier, since, despite its being filthy and little more than a hole in the wall, they served the best chitlings in all of Lima there. I ran into Pascual and Big Pablito standing downstairs in the doorway of Panamericana, flirting with girls passing by, and sent them back upstairs to the News Department. Despite the fact that it was broad daylight and right in the middle of the downtown area, within full view of countless pairs of eyes of relatives and friends of the family, Aunt Julia and I walked along holding hands and I kept kissing her almost every step of the way. Her cheeks were as bright red as a mountain girl's, and she looked as happy as could be.

"That's enough of your pornography, you selfish creatures, think about me for a minute," Javier protested. "Let's talk about Nancy a little."

Nancy was a pretty young cousin of mine, a terrible flirt, whom Javier had been in love with ever since he'd reached the age of reason and whom he pursued with the persistence of a bloodhound. She had never taken him seriously, yet always managed to keep him on the string and lead him to think that maybe . . . that very soon . . . that the next time . . . This pre-romance had been going on since we were in high school, and I, as Javier's confidant, bosom buddy, and go-between, had been in on every detail. Nancy had stood him up countless times, left him waiting for her countless times at the door of the Leuro while she went to the Colina or to the Metro for the Sunday matinee, appeared countless times at parties on Saturday nights with another escort. The first time in my life I ever got drunk, I was keeping Javier company, helping him drown his troubles in wine and beer in a little bar in Surquillo the day he found out that Nancy had given herself to an agronomy student named Eduardo Tiravanti (a boy who was very popular in Miraflores because he could put a lighted cigarette in his mouth and then take it out and go on smoking it as though that were the most natural thing in the world). Javier was weeping and sniveling, and in addition to serving as a shoulder to cry on, I'd been assigned the mission of taking him back to his *pension* and putting him to bed once he'd reached a comatose state ("I'm going to get plastered to the gills," he'd warned me, imitating Jorge Negrete). But I was the one who succumbed, with spectacular fits of vomiting and an attack of the d.t.'s in the course of which—according to Javier's vulgar version of events—I had climbed up onto the bar counter and harangued the topers, night owls, and rowdies who constituted the clientele of El Triunfo: "Lower your pants, all of you: you're in the presence of a poet."

He had never quite forgiven me for the fact that instead of taking care of him and consoling him on that sad night, I'd obliged him to drag me through the streets of Miraflores to my grandparents' villa in Ocharán, so far gone that he'd handed my remains over to my terrified grandmother with the imprudent comment: "Señora Carmencita, I think Varguitas is about to die on us."

Since that time, little Nancy had by turns taken up with and thrown over half a dozen boys from Miraflores, and Javier, too, had had several steady girlfriends. But instead of making him forget his great love for my cousin, they made it all the more intense, and he continued to phone her, visit her, invite her out, declare his feelings, taking no note of the refusals, insults, affronts, broken dates he suffered at her hands. Javier was one of those men who are able to put passion before vanity and it didn't really matter to him in the slightest that he was the laughingstock of all his friends in Miraflores, among whom his tireless chasing after my cousin was a constant source of jokes. (One of the boys in our neighborhood swore that he'd seen Javier approach little Nancy one Sunday after Mass and make her the following proposal: "Hi there, Nancyta, nice morning, shall we go have a drink together? a Coke, a sip of champagne?") Nancy sometimes went out with him—usually when she was between boyfriends—to the movies or a party, and Javier would then have great hopes and go around in a state of euphoria. That was the mood he was in now, talking a blue streak as we ate our chitling sandwiches and drank our coffee in the little café on the Calle Belén called El Palmero. Aunt Julia and I rubbed knees underneath the table and sat there holding hands and gazing into each other's eyes as we vaguely listened to Javier babbling on and on, like background music, about little Nancy.

"She was impressed by my invitation," he was telling us. "Because which of those guys in Miraflores, who are always flat broke, ever invites a girl to a bullfight, can you tell me that?"

"And how did you manage to scrape up the money?" I asked him. "Did you have a winning lottery ticket?"

"I sold the boardinghouse radio," he told us, without the slightest regret. "They think it was the cook and they've fired her for stealing."

He explained to us that he'd worked out a foolproof plan. In the middle of the corrida he'd surprise Nancy by offering her a gift that would melt her heart: a Spanish mantilla. Javier was a great admirer of the Mother Country and everything connected with it: bullfights, flamenco music, Sarita Montiel. He dreamed of going to Spain (as I dreamed of going to France) and the idea of giving Nancy a mantilla had occurred to him when he'd seen an ad in the paper. It had cost him a month's salary from the Reserve Bank, but he was certain that the investment would pay off. He explained how he planned to go about it. He would take the mantilla to the bullfight, discreetly wrapped in plain paper, and would wait for an especially stirring moment, whereupon he would open the package, unfold the shawl, and place it about my cousin's delicate shoulders. What did we think? What would Nancy's reaction be? I advised him to really do things up brown by giving her a Sevillian ornamental comb and a pair of castanets as well and singing her a fandango, but Aunt Julia seconded him enthusiastically and told him that his whole plan was wonderful and that if Nancy had any feelings at all, she'd be moved to tears. And she assured him that if a boy were to offer *her* such touching demonstrations of his affection, she'd be won over instantly.

"It's just like I keep telling you—can't you see that?" she said to me, as though scolding me for something or other. "Javier's a real romantic, he woos his beloved the way she ought to be wooed."

Javier, absolutely charmed by her, proposed that the four of us go out together, any day we liked the following week, to the movies, to tea, to dance.

"And what would my little cousin Nancy say if she saw the two of us going out on a date together?" I said, to bring him back down to earth.

But he floored us by answering: "Don't be silly, Varguitas, she knows everything and thinks it's great. I told her all about it the other day." And, on seeing how dumfounded we were, he added with a mischievous twinkle in his eye: "The truth of the matter is that I don't keep anything a secret from your cousin, since sooner or later, come hell or high water, she's going to end up marrying me."

It worried me to hear that Javier had told her all about our romance. Nancy and I were very close, and I was quite certain she wouldn't give us away deliberately, but she might let a word or two slip out inadvertently, and the news would spread like wildfire in the family forest. Aunt Julia had been left speechless for a moment, but now she was doing her best to conceal her surprise by encouraging Javier to proceed with his taurino-sentimental plan. He walked back with us to Panamericana and said goodbye to me at the downstairs door, and Aunt Julia and I arranged to see each other again that evening, on the usual pretext that we were just going out to take in a flick together. As I kissed her goodbye, I said in her ear: "Thanks to the endocrinologist, I've realized I'm in love with you." "So I see, Varguitas," she agreed.

I watched her walk off with Javier toward the bus stop, and it was only then that I noticed the crowd that had gathered outside the doors of Radio Central, young women for the most part, although there were a few men as well. They had formed a double line, but as more people arrived, everyone started shoving and pushing and the lines broke up. I walked over to see what was going on, presuming that whatever it was, it undoubtedly had something to do with

Pedro Camacho. And in fact they turned out to be autograph hunters. I then caught sight of the scriptwriter standing at the window of his lair, with Jesusito on one side of him and Genaro Sr. on the other, scrawling a signature with fancy flourishes on the pages of autograph books, notebooks, loose sheets of paper, the margins of newspapers, and dismissing his admirers with an Olympian gesture. They were gazing at him in rapture, approaching him timidly and respectfully, stammering a few heartfelt words of appreciation.

"He causes us headaches, but there's no doubt that he's the king of the Peruvian airwaves," Genaro Jr. said to me, putting a hand on my shoulder and pointing to the mob. "What do you think of that?"

I asked how long these autographing sessions had been going on.

"For a week now, half an hour a day, from six to six-thirty. You're not very observant, are you?" the progressive-minded impresario answered. "Haven't you seen the ads we're publishing, don't you listen to the radio network you work for? I was skeptical, but you can see how wrong I was. I thought people would only show up for a couple of days, and I realize now that this may go on for a month."

He invited me to have a drink with him at the Bolívar bar. I ordered a Coke, but he insisted that I have a whiskey with him.

"Do you have any idea what those lines mean? They're a public demonstration of what a great hit Pedro's serials are with radio listeners," he explained to me.

I said I didn't have any doubts as to how popular he was, and he made me blush by suggesting that, since I too had "literary inclinations," I should follow the Bolivian's example and learn his tricks for winning a mass audience. "You mustn't shut yourself up in an ivory tower," he advised me. He'd had five thousand photographs of Pedro Camacho printed, and beginning the following Monday, they'd be given out free to autograph hunters. I asked him if the scriptwriter had toned down his diatribes against Argentines.

"It doesn't matter any more. He can run down anybody he pleases," he said, assuming an air of mystery. "Haven't you heard the big news? The General never misses one of Pedro's serials."

He went into details to convince me. Since affairs of state didn't allow him time to hear them during the day, the General had tape recordings made and listened to them, one after another, each night before he went to sleep. The President's wife herself had personally reported this to a great many ladies in Lima.

"It would appear that the General is a sensitive man, despite what people say to the contrary," Genaro Jr. concluded. "So, if the supreme authority in the nation is on our side, what does it matter if Pedro rants and raves against the Argentines to his heart's content? They deserve it, don't they?"

The conversation with Genaro Jr. and the reconciliation with Aunt Julia had given me a tremendous lift, and I rushed back to the shack in a mood of white-hot inspiration to dash off my story about the gang of levitators, as Pascual cranked out the news bulletins. I already knew how I'd end it: during one of these games, one of the urchins levitated much higher than the others, suddenly lost altitude, came crashing down, broke his neck, and died. The last sentence would describe the surprised, frightened faces of his little pals as they contemplated him beneath a roar of airplane engines. It would be a Spartan story, as precise as a chronometer, in the manner of Hemingway.

A few days later I went to visit my cousin Nancy to find out how she'd taken the story of my romance with Aunt Julia. I found her still under the effect of Operation Mantilla.

"Do you realize what a fool that idiot made of me?" she said as she ran from one end of the house to the other, looking for Lasky. "All of a sudden, right there in the middle of the Plaza de Acho, he undid a package, took out a bullfighter's cape, and draped it over my shoulders. Everybody was looking at me, and even the bull was dying of laughter. He made me keep it on during the entire corrida. And he even wanted me to walk down the street in that thing, can you imagine! I've never been so humiliated in my life!"

We found Lasky under the butler's bed—in addition to being an ugly-looking, shaggy-haired dog, he was forever trying to bite me—and took him back out to his kennel. Then Nancy dragged me to her bedroom to see the corpus delicti. It was a fashion artist's creation that brought to mind exotic gardens, gypsy tents, de luxe brothels: every imaginable shade of red, from bloody crimson to blushing tea-rose pink, was visible in its iridescent folds, it had a long knotted black fringe, and its rhinestones and spangles sparkled so garishly they left one feeling slightly nauseated. My cousin made bullfight passes with it or wrapped it around herself, roaring with laughter. I told her I wouldn't allow her to make fun of my friend and asked her if she was ever going to take him seriously as a suitor.

"I'm thinking about it," she replied, as usual. "But as a friend I find him simply delightful."

I told her she was a heartless tease, that Javier had gone so far as to commit robbery in order to get the money to buy her that present.

"And what about you?" she said to me, folding the mantilla and putting it away in the armoire. "Is it true you're running around with Julita? Aren't you ashamed of yourself? Getting serious with Aunt Olga's sister?"

I told her it was true, that I wasn't at all ashamed, though I could feel my face burning. Nancy was a little embarrassed too, but being a girl from Miraflores, her curiosity got the better of her and she said, aiming straight for my heart: "If you marry her, in twenty years you'll still be young and she'll be a little old lady." She took me by the arm and dragged me downstairs to the living room. "Come on, we're going to listen to music and you can tell me all about your love affair, from A to Z."

She selected a pile of records—Nat King Cole, Harry Belafonte, Frank Sinatra, Xavier Cugat—as she confessed to me that ever since Javier had told her about us, her hair had stood on end every time she thought about what would happen if the family found out. Surely I realized that our relatives were such busybodies that every time she went out with a different boy ten uncles, eight aunts, and five cousins phoned her mama to tell her? Me in love with Aunt Julia! What a scandal, Marito! And she reminded me that the family had great expectations for me, that I was the hope of the tribe. It was true: that cancerous family of mine had every expectation that I'd be a millionaire someday, or at the very least President of the Republic. (I have never understood how they had come to have such a high opinion of me. It certainly couldn't have been on account of my grades in school, which had never been outstanding. Maybe it was because ever since I'd been a little boy I'd written poems to all my aunts, or because apparently I'd been a precocious child who had definite opinions about everything.) I made Nancy swear she'd be as silent as the grave about us. She was dying to know the details of our romance. "Do you just like Julita a lot, or are you mad about her?"

I'd sometimes shared secrets about my affairs of the heart with her, and since she already knew about us, I did so now, too. It had all been just a game in the beginning, but all of a sudden, on the very day I'd had a fit of jealousy because of an endocrinologist, I realized that I'd fallen in love. However, the more I thought about it, the more convinced I was that the romance was going to turn out to be a real headache. Not only because of the difference in age. I still had three years to go before I got my law degree, and what was more, I suspected I'd never practice that profession, since the only thing I really liked was writing. But writers starved to death. For the moment, I earned just enough to buy myself cigarettes and a few books and go to the movies. Was Aunt Julia going to wait for me until I was financially solvent, if in fact I ever reached that point?

My cousin Nancy was such a good confidante that instead of offering counter-arguments, she agreed with me. "It's a problem, all right—not to mention the fact that when that day comes you may not like Julita any more and you'll leave her," she said realistically. "And the poor thing will have wasted years of her life, and all for nothing. But tell me, is she really in love with you, or is it just a game with her?"

I told her that Aunt Julia wasn't a frivolous weather vane like her (the expression pleased her immensely). But I'd asked myself the same question a number of times, and it was one I also asked Aunt Julia a few days later. We'd gone down to sit by the sea, in a lovely little park with an unpronounceable name (Domodossola or something like that), and it was there, in each other's arms, exchanging endless kisses, that we had our first conversation about the future.

"I know what it's like, down to the very last detail, I saw it in a crystal ball," Aunt Julia said to me, without the least trace of bitterness. "In the best of cases, our love affair will last three, maybe four years or so; that is to say, till you meet up with a little chick who'll be the mother of your children. Then you'll throw me over and I'll have to seduce another gentleman friend. And at that point the words THE END appear."

As I kissed her hands, I told her she'd been listening to too many serials for her own good.

"It's quite obvious that *you* never listen to them," she retorted. "In Pedro Camacho's soap operas there are hardly ever any love affairs or anything like that. Right now, for example, Olga and I are all caught up in the one that comes on at three o'clock. The tragedy of a young man who can't sleep because the minute he closes his eyes he starts reliving how he ran over a poor little girl and crushed her to death."

Returning to the subject we'd been discussing, I told her that I was more optimistic. In ardent tones, to convince myself as well as her, I assured her that, whatever the difference in age might be, love based on the purely physical lasted only a short time. Once the novelty had disappeared, as routine set in, sexual attraction gradually diminished and finally died (in the case of the man especially), and the couple could then survive only if there were other attractions between them: spiritual, intellectual, moral. And for this sort of love the question of age was of no importance.

"It all sounds fine the way you tell it, and I only wish it were true," Aunt Julia said, rubbing her nose, which as usual was ice-cold, against my cheek. "But it's all false, from beginning to end. The physical something secondary? It's what matters most for two people to be able to put up with each other, Varguitas."

Had she gone out with the endocrinologist again?

"He's phoned me several times," she said to me, keeping me in suspense. Then, kissing me, she dispelled my doubts. "I told him I wouldn't go out with him any more."

Beside myself with joy, I talked to her at length about my levitation story: I'd written ten pages, it was coming along nicely, and I was going to try to get it published in the literary supplement of *El Comercio* with a cryptic dedication: "To the feminine of Julio."

Ten.
The tragedy of Lucho

Abril Marroquín, a young pharmaceutical detail man with every sign of a bright future before him, began on a sunny summer morning on the outskirts of a historic locale: Pisco. He had just finished making the rounds that, ever since he had first accepted employment in this itinerant profession ten years before, had taken him around the cities and towns of Peru, visiting doctors' offices and pharmacies to give out samples and literature from the Bayer Laboratories, and now he was on his way back to Lima. His visit to the various physicians and druggists of the town had taken him about three hours. And even though he had a former classmate who was now a captain in the Ninth Air Squadron at San Andrés, at whose home he ordinarily had lunch when he came to Pisco, this time he had decided to head straight back for the capital. He was a married man, with a little wife with white skin and a French name, and his young blood and passionate heart urged him to return as soon as possible to the arms of his spouse.

It was just past noon. His brand-new Volkswagen, bought on credit at the same time he had entered into matrimony—three months before—was parked under the shade of a leafy eucalyptus in the main square. Lucho Abril Marroquín put his case with the samples and the brochures inside it, removed his suit coat and tie (which, in accordance with the strict Helvetian standards of the Laboratory, were always to be worn by its representatives when visiting clients, to give an impression of reliability and professionalism), decided again that he would not drop in on his aviator friend, and instead of a proper lunch would simply have a snack, knowing that a full meal would make him feel even sleepier during the three-hour drive across the desert.

He crossed the square to the Piave ice-cream parlor, ordered a Coke and a dish of peach ice cream from the Italian, and as he downed this Spartan repast he did not think of the past of this southern port, the colorful disembarkation of the hesitant hero San Martín and his Liberation Army, but rather (egoism and sensuality of men with ardent temperaments) of his warm, cuddly little wife —almost a child, really—with her snow-white complexion, her blue eyes, her curly golden locks, and of how, in the romantic darkness of night, she brought him to extremes of Neronian fever by singing in his ear, with the moans of a languorous little cat, in the erotic language par excellence (a French all the more exciting in that it was incomprehensible to him), a song entitled "Les feuilles mortes." Noting that these marital reminiscences were beginning to have their effect on him, he put such thoughts out of his mind, paid, and left.

In a nearby service station he filled the tank with gas and the radiator with water and took off. Despite the fact that at this hour, when the sun was at its hottest, the streets of Pisco were empty, he drove slowly and carefully, thinking not so much of the safety of pedestrians as of his yellow Volkswagen, which, after his little blond French wife, was the apple of his eye. As he made his way through the streets of the town, he thought about his life. He was twenty-eight years old. After finishing high school, he'd decided to go to work, for he was too impatient to go all the way through the university before getting himself a job. He'd been hired by the Bayer Laboratories after taking an exam. In these ten years his salary had gone up steadily, he'd had several promotions, and his work wasn't boring. He preferred a job that took him outside the office rather than vegetating behind a desk. Except that now it was out of the question for him to go on spending all his time traveling, leaving the delicate flower of France in Lima, a city that, as everyone knows, is full of sharks lying in wait for mermaids. Lucho Abril Marroquín had already spoken with his superiors. They had great regard for him, and had reassured him: he would remain on the road for only a few months more, and at the beginning of the following year they would give him a post in the provinces. And Dr. Schwalb, a laconic Swiss, had added: "A post that will be a promotion." Lucho Abril Marroquín couldn't help thinking that perhaps they would offer him the job of managing director of the branch office in Trujillo, Arequipa, or Chiclayo. And what more could he ask?

He was leaving the city now, heading off down the main highway to Lima. He had made the trip back and forth along this route so many times—on interurban buses, in jitneys, being driven or driving himself—that he knew it by heart. The ribbon of black asphalt disappeared in the distance, amid dunes and bare hills, without the least quicksilver gleam that would reveal the presence of other vehicles on the road up ahead. In front of him was an old rattletrap of a truck, and he was just about to pass it when he spied the bridge and the intersection where the Southern Highway branches off in a cloverleaf from the road he was on, which continues on up the sierra in the direction of the metallic mountains of Castrovirreina. He therefore decided (prudence of the man who loves his car and fears the law) to wait until after the turnoff. The truck was lumbering along at no more than thirty miles an hour and Lucho Abril Marroquín resignedly slowed down and trailed along after it, keeping a good ten yards' distance. Up ahead he could see the bridge, the intersection, flimsy buildings—roadside stands selling cold drinks and cigarettes, the Southern Highway toll booth—and silhouettes whose faces he could not make out—the sun behind them was shining directly in his eyes—walking back and forth alongside the buildings.

The little girl loomed up all of a sudden, as though she had emerged from underneath the truck, just as he reached the end of the bridge. That tiny figure suddenly appearing directly in his path would remain engraved on his memory forever, her little face frozen in terror and her hands in the air, hitting the front of the Volkswagen like a stone. It all happened so fast that he had no time either to brake or to swerve aside till after the catastrophe (the beginning of the catastrophe). In utter horror, and with the weird sensation that none of this had anything to do with him, he felt the dull thud of the body against the front bumper, and saw it rise in the air, trace a parabolic curve, and fall to the ground eight or ten yards farther on.

He managed to brake then, so abruptly that the steering wheel hit him in the chest, and with his mind a blank and his ears ringing, he got out of the car immediately, and tripping over his own feet, thinking: "I'm an Argentine, I kill children," he ran over to the little girl and picked her up in his arms. She looked to be about five or six years old, and was barefoot and poorly dressed, with crusts of dirt and filth on her face, hands, and knees. There were no visible signs of blood, but her eyes were closed and she didn't seem to be breathing. Staggering like a drunk, Lucho Abril Marroquín looked all about and shouted to the sand dunes, to the wind, to the distant waves: "An ambulance, a doctor!" As though in a dream, he could hear a truck coming down the mountainside and perhaps he noted that its speed was excessive for a vehicle approaching an intersection. But if in fact he noticed this, his attention was immediately diverted on seeing a Guardia Civil come running out of one of the buildings, headed his way. Panting, perspiring, a custodian of law and order out to do his job properly, he looked at the little girl and asked: "Is she knocked unconscious, or is she dead?"

For all the rest of his life Lucho Abril Marroquín would ask himself what the right answer would have been at that moment. Was she just badly hurt, or had she been killed? He never did answer the panting Guardia Civil because the latter had no sooner asked that question than suddenly such a horrified expression came over his face that Lucho Abril Marroquín turned his head just in time to realize that the truck that was coming down the mountainside was hurtling straight toward them, its horn blaring madly. He closed his eyes; a tremendous roar tore the little girl from his arms and plunged him in a darkness full of tiny stars. He could still hear a terrible din, screams and cries, as he fell into an almost-mystical stupor.

Much later he was to learn that he had been knocked down, not because there was such a thing as immanent justice, charged with fulfilling the equitable proverb: "An eye for an eye, a tooth for a tooth," but because the brakes of the truck from the mines had failed. And he was also to learn that the Guardia Civil had died instantly from a broken neck and that the poor little girl—a true daughter of Sophocles—had not only been killed in this second accident (if in fact the first one had not been fatal), but her body crushed spectacularly flat (a joyous devils' carnival) as the double rear wheel of the truck ran over her.

But with the passage of the years Lucho Abril Marroquín was to tell himself that of all the instructive experiences of that morning, the most unforgettable had not been either the first or the second accident but what happened afterwards. Because, curiously enough, despite the violence of the impact (which was to keep him for many weeks in the Social Security Clinic as they mended his body, which had suffered countless broken bones, dislocations, cuts, and contusions), the medical detail man had not lost consciousness, or at most had been unconscious for only a few seconds. When he opened his eyes, he realized that the accident had happened only instants before, because he could see—though the sun was still shining directly in his eyes—ten, twelve, perhaps fifteen skirts and pairs of pants come running toward him from the flimsy roadside buildings. He couldn't move, but he felt no pain, only relief and a calm reassurance. The thought came to him that he didn't have to think any more; he thought of the ambulance, doctors, devoted nurses. They were there, they'd already arrived. He tried to smile at the faces bending down toward him. But then, feeling fingers tickling him, poking him, prying at him, he realized that the newcomers were not helping him: they were yanking his watch off, putting their hands in his pockets, snatching his wallet, jerking off the medal of El Señor de Limpias that he'd worn around his neck ever since his First Communion. And it was at that moment that Lucho Abril Marroquín, overcome with amazement at human nature, was plunged into darkest night.

That night, practically speaking, lasted an entire year. In the beginning, the consequences of the catastrophe had seemed to be merely physical. When Lucho Abril Marroquín recovered consciousness, he was in Lima, in a small hospital room, bandaged from head to foot, and at his bedside (Guardian Angels bringing peace of mind to a soul in agitation), keeping anxious watch over him, were the blond compatriot of Juliette Greco and Dr. Schwalb of Bayer Laboratories. Amid his tipsiness brought on by the smell of chloroform, he was suddenly overcome with happiness, and tears streamed down his cheeks, as he felt his wife's lips brush the gauze bandages covering his forehead.

The knitting of bones, the return of muscles and tendons to their proper place, and the closing and healing of his wounds—in other words, the mending of the animal half of his person—took a number of weeks, which were relatively tolerable thanks to the superb skills of his doctors, the attentiveness of the nurses, the Magdalene-like devotion of his wife, and the solicitude of the Laboratories, whose behavior toward him was impeccable both from the point of view of sentiment and of cash on the line for his every need. And in the Social Security Clinic, in the middle of his convalescence, Lucho Abril Marroquín learned a gratifying piece of news: his little French wife had conceived and in seven months would give birth to his child.

It was only after he was let out of the hospital and went back to his little house in San Miguel and his job that the secret, complicated wounds that his mind had suffered in the two accidents came to light. Of the many ills that now befell him, insomnia was the most benign. Unable to sleep, he spent his nights wandering all about the house in the dark, chain-smoking in a state of extreme agitation, and muttering disjointed phrases in which, to his wife's vast surprise, the word "Herod" kept recurring. When his insomnia was overcome chemically through the use of sleeping pills, the result was even worse: Abril Marroquín's sleep was haunted by nightmares in which he saw himself hacking his own as yet unborn daughter to pieces. His wild shrieks terrified his wife in the beginning and eventually caused her to have a miscarriage: the fetus was probably of the female sex. "My dreams have come true, I've killed my own daughter, the only thing left to do is go live in Buenos Aires," the oneiric filicide lugubriously repeated night and day.

But even this was not the worst of it. The nights when he didn't sleep at all, or had terrible nightmares, were followed by awful days. Ever since the accident, Lucho Abril Marroquín had suffered from a visceral phobia toward any wheeled vehicle, to the point where he could not get in one, either as the driver or as a passenger, without feeling dizzy, having vomiting spells, sweating profusely, and bursting into screams. His every attempt to overcome this taboo proved completely fruitless, with the result that he was obliged to resign himself to living, in the middle of the twentieth century, as though he were back in the days of the Inca empire (a society in which the wheel was unknown). If the distances that he had to cover were merely a question of the five kilometers between his house and the Bayer Laboratories, this would not have been such a serious matter; for a tormented spirit, the two-hour walk morning and evening might have had a sedative effect. But for a medical detail man whose area of operations was the vast territory of Peru, this phobia toward all wheeled vehicles was tragic. Since there was not the slightest possibility of reviving the athletic era of Indian couriers, the professional future of Lucho Abril Marroquín was seriously threatened. The Laboratory agreed to give him a sedentary job in the Lima office, and even though they did not reduce his salary, from the moral and psychological point of view, the change (he was now in charge of inventorying samples) represented a demotion. And as a crowning misfortune, his little French wife, who, a worthy emulator of the Maid of Orleans, had courageously borne up under the strain of her husband's nervous afflictions, eventually also succumbed to hysteria, especially after her miscarriage. The couple decided to separate until better days came along, and the young woman (pale cheeks mindful of dawn and Antarctic nights) went off to France to seek consolation in her parents' château.

Such was the situation of Lucho Abril Marroquín a year after the accident: abandoned by his young spouse, condemned (*stricto sensu*) to a pedestrian life, with no other friend save anguish. (The yellow Volkswagen became overgrown with ivy and covered with spiderwebs before being sold to pay for his blond wife's passage to France.) His colleagues and acquaintances were whispering behind his back that he had no choice left him save going quietly off to the insane asylum or dramatically committing suicide, when the young man learned (manna that falls from heaven, rain on thirsty desert sands) of the existence of someone who was neither a priest nor a sorcerer yet nonetheless cured souls: Dr. Lucía Acémila.

A superior woman, without complexes, who had reached what science agrees is the ideal age—her fifties—Dr. Acémila—broad forehead, aquiline nose, penetrating gaze, rectitude and goodness itself—was the living negation of her surname (literally, a pack mule; figuratively, a stupid ass) (which she was proud of and paraded like a glorious victory banner before the eyes of mortals on her visiting cards or the plaques outside her office), a person in whom intelligence was a physical attribute, something that her patients (she preferred to call them her "friends") could see, hear, smell. She had earned countless diplomas and academic honors in the world's great centers of learning—Teutonic Berlin, phlegmatic London, sinful Paris—but the principal university in which she had acquired her extensive knowledge of human misery and its remedies had been (naturally) life. Like every individual who has risen above the average, she was talked about, criticized, and derided by her colleagues, those psychiatrists and psychologists who, unlike her, were incapable of working miracles. But to Dr. Acémila it did not matter in the least that they called her a witch, a satanist, a corruptress of the corrupted, a madwoman, and other vile names. As proof that she was the one who was right, she needed only to remember the gratitude of her "friends," that legion of schizophrenics, parricides, paranoiacs, arsonists, manic-depressives, onanists, catatonics, hardened criminals, mystics, and stutterers who, once they had passed through her hands and undergone her treatment (she herself would have preferred calling it "sharing her advice"), had returned to everyday life as unusually loving fathers, obedient sons, virtuous wives, honest and hard-working jobholders, fluent conversationalists, and pathologically law-abiding citizens.

It was Dr. Schwalb who advised Lucho Abril Marroquín to consult Dr. Acémila, and he himself who (Swiss promptitude that has given the world its most precise timepieces) arranged an appointment. More resigned than confident, the insomniac presented himself at the hour agreed upon at the mansion with pink walls, surrounded by a garden full of fragrant floripondios, in the San Felipe residential section in which Lucía Acémila's office (temple, confessional, laboratory of the spirit) was located. A neatly groomed nurse took down certain details of his personal and medical history and showed him into the doctor's office, a high-ceilinged room with shelves full of leather-bound volumes, a mahogany desk, thick carpets, and a couch upholstered in mint-green velvet.

"Get rid of the prejudices you've brought with you, and your suit coat and tie as well," Dr. Lucía Acémila greeted him with the disarming straightforwardness of those possessed of genuine wisdom, pointing to the couch. "And stretch out there, face up or face down as you prefer, not because I believe in Freudian sanctimony, but because I want you to feel comfortable. And now don't tell me your dreams or confess to me that you're in love with your mother—just tell me, as precisely as you possibly can, how that stomach of yours is behaving."

Presuming that the doctor had confused him with another patient, the medical detail man, already stretched out on the comfortable couch, timidly mumbled that he hadn't come to consult her about his stomach but about his mind.

"They are indissociable," the lady practitioner informed him. "A stomach that empties itself promptly and totally is the twin of a clear mind and an upright soul. A sluggish, lazy, avaricious stomach, on the other hand, engenders bad thoughts, sours the character, fosters complexes and perverted sexual appetites, and gives rise to criminal tendencies, a need to take out on others one's own excremental tortures."

Thus enlightened, Lucho Abril Marroquín confessed that he sometimes suffered from attacks of indigestion, constipation, and even avowed that his stools, in addition to being irregular, also varied in color, volume, and no doubt—though he did not recall having palpated them in recent weeks—consistency and temperature. The lady doctor nodded approvingly, murmuring, "I knew it." And she ordered the young man to eat without fail, until further advice to the contrary, a half-dozen prunes each morning on an empty stomach.

"Now that that basic question has been resolved, let's go on to others," the lady philosopher added. "You may tell me what's troubling you. But I warn you beforehand that I shall not castrate you of your problem. I shall teach you to love it, to feel as proud of it as Cervantes of his useless arm or Beethoven of his deafness. Speak."

With a fluency learned in ten years of professional dialogues with disciples of Hippocrates and apothecaries, Lucho Abril Marroquín frankly summed up his history, from the disastrous accident outside Pisco to his most recent nightmares and the apocalyptic consequences that this drama had had for his marital life. Overcome with self-pity, he burst into tears as he recounted the final chapters and finished his story with an outburst that to anyone else but Lucía Acémila would have been heartbreaking: "Doctor, help me!"

"Your story doesn't sadden me. On the contrary, it's so banal and stupid it bores me," this engineer of souls comforted him affectionately. "Wipe your nose and persuade yourself that in the geography of the mind your illness is the equivalent of an ingrown toenail in the geography of the body. And now listen to me."

With the manners and turns of speech of a woman who frequents high-society salons, she explained to him that what led men astray was the fear of the truth and the spirit of contradiction. With regard to the former, she enlightened the insomniac by explaining to him that chance, so-called *accidents*, did not exist; they were merely subterfuges invented by men to hide from themselves how evil they were.

"In a word, you *wanted* to kill that little girl, and so you killed her," the doctor said, dramatically summing up her thoughts on the matter. "And then, since you were ashamed of what you'd done and afraid of the police or of Hell, you *wanted* to be hit by the truck, as punishment for what you'd done or as an alibi for the murder."

"But, but . . ." he stammered, his bulging eyes and his forehead drenched with perspiration, betraying his abject despair. "What about the Guardia Civil? Did I kill him, too?"

"Who hasn't killed a Guardia Civil at some time or other?" the lady scientist reflected. "Perhaps you killed him, perhaps it was the truck driver, perhaps it was a suicide. But this isn't a special performance, where two people get in for the price of one. Let's concentrate on you."

She explained to him that, on frustrating their natural impulses, people aroused unconscious feelings of resentment in their mind, which thereupon took its vengeance by engendering nightmares, phobias, complexes, anxiety, depression.

"One can't fight with oneself, for this battle has only one loser," the lady apostle pontificated. "Don't be ashamed of what you are; take consolation in the thought that all men are hyenas, and that being a good person simply means knowing how to dissimulate. Look at yourself in the mirror and tell yourself: I'm an infanticide and a cowardly speed demon. Let's have no more of these euphemisms of yours: don't talk to me about accidents or wheel syndromes."

And going on to cite examples, she told him that the emaciated onanists who came to her on their knees begging her to cure them, she treated by giving them pornographic magazines, and that patients who were drug addicts, dregs of humanity crawling on the floor and tearing their hair as they spoke of the hand of fate, she treated by offering them marijuana cigarettes and handfuls of coca leaves.

"Are you going to recommend that I go on killing children?" the medical detail man roared, a lamb suddenly turned into a tiger.

"If that's what gives you pleasure, why not?" the lady psychologist answered coldly. "And I warn you: no more of this shouting at me. I'm not one of those shopkeepers who believe that the customer is always right."

Lucho Abril Marroquín burst into tears once again. Paying no attention whatsoever to him, Dr. Lucía Acémila spent the next ten minutes covering several sheets of paper with her elegant penmanship, labeling them "Exercise for learning how to live sincerely." She handed them to him and made an appointment with him for eight weeks later. As she bade him goodbye with a cordial handshake, she reminded him not to forget to eat his prunes every morning.

Like the majority of Dr. Acémila's patients, Lucho Abril Marroquín left her office feeling as though he'd been the victim of a psychic ambush, and certain that he had fallen in the toils of an absolute madwoman who would only make his ailments worse if he were to be foolish enough to follow her recommendations. He made up his mind to flush the "Exercises" down the toilet without even looking at them. But that very same night (debilitating insomnia that drives the sufferer to excesses), he read them. They struck him as pathologically absurd and he laughed so hard he got the hiccups (he rid himself of them by drinking a glass of water from the far edge, as his mother had taught him); but then he felt a burning curiosity. As a distraction, to while away the long sleepless hours, with no faith in their therapeutic effectiveness, he decided to try them.

Visiting the toy section of Sears, he had no difficulty finding the car, the truck number 1 and the truck number 2 that he needed, as well as the figurines that were to represent the little girl, the Guardia Civil, the thieves, and himself. Following the doctor's instructions, he painted the vehicles the same colors he remembered them as being, and the clothes of the figurines as well. (He had an aptitude for painting, and so the guard's uniform and the little girl's humble garments and crusts of filth turned out very well.) To imitate the sand dunes of Pisco, he used a sheet of wrapping paper, on one edge of which, in his obsessive desire for verisimilitude, he painted the Pacific Ocean: a blue strip with a border of sea foam. The first day it took him nearly an hour, kneeling on the floor of the living room/dining room of his house, to reproduce the story, and when he came to the end, that is to say when the thieves flung themselves on the medical detail man to rob him, he was almost as terrified and heartsick as on the day it had actually happened. He lay on his back on the floor, in a cold sweat and racked with sobs. But on the following days the nervous shock became less intense, and the operation became a sort of sport, an exercise that took him back to his childhood and filled the hours he would not have otherwise known how to occupy, now that his wife was gone, since he'd never prided himself on being a voracious reader or a great music lover. It was like playing with a Meccano set, putting a jigsaw puzzle together, or doing crosswords. Sometimes, as he was handing out samples to the detail men in the warehouse of the Bayer Laboratories, he surprised himself by digging down in his memory in search of a detail, a gesture, a motive for what had happened that would allow him to introduce a variation, to prolong his re-creations of events when he got home that evening. On seeing little wooden figurines and little plastic toy cars all over the living room/dining room floor, the cleaning woman asked him if he was thinking of adopting a child, warning him that, if so, she would charge more. In accordance with the progression outlined in the "Exercises," he was now staging sixteen reconstructions of the—accident?—on a Lilliputian scale each night.

The section of the "Exercises for learning how to live sincerely" having to do with children seemed even more preposterous to him than the business with the figurines, but (the inertia that leads to vice or the curiosity that is responsible for scientific progress?) he faithfully followed it as well. It was subdivided into two parts:

"Theoretical Exercises" and "Practical Exercises"; and Dr. Acémila pointed out that it was imperative that the former precede the latter, for wasn't man a rational being whose ideas preceded his acts? The theoretical part left ample scope for the pharmaceutical representative's gift for observation and speculative turn of mind. All it prescribed was: "Reflect daily on the disasters to humanity caused by children." He was to do so systematically, at all hours, and wherever he might be.

"What harm did innocent little children do humanity? Were they not grace, purity, happiness, life itself?" Lucho Abril Marroquín asked himself on the morning of the first theoretical exercise as he walked the five kilometers to his office. But, more out of a desire to make this exercise assigned him as interesting as possible than out of heartfelt conviction, he admitted to himself that at times they could be very noisy. As a matter of fact, they cried a lot, at all hours, for all sorts of reasons, and since they were not yet rational creatures, they did not realize the harm caused by this propensity, nor could they be *persuaded* of the virtues of silence. He then remembered the case of that worker who, after his exhausting day's work in the mine, returned home and was unable to sleep because of the frantic wailing of his newborn baby, whom he had finally—murdered? How many millions of similar cases occurred around the globe? How many manual laborers, peasants, shopkeepers, office clerks, who—the high cost of living, low salaries, lack of adequate housing—lived in tiny apartments and shared their cramped quarters with their offspring, were prevented from enjoying a well-deserved night's sleep by the howls of a baby incapable of telling its progenitors whether its bawling meant it had diarrhea or wanted to be nursed again?

Thoroughly searching his mind that evening as he walked the five kilometers home, Lucho Abril Marroquín discovered that they could be held responsible for causing a great deal of havoc. Unlike any animal, it took them much too long before they could manage on their own without being watched every minute, and how much damage resulted from this shortcoming! They broke everything, from artistic bibelots to rock-crystal vases, they pulled down curtains that the mistress of the house had strained her eyes sewing, and without the slightest embarrassment placed their hands smeared with number two on the starched tablecloth or the lace mantilla purchased with love and privation. Not to mention the fact that they were in the habit of sticking their fingers in light sockets and causing short circuits, or stupidly electrocuting themselves, with all that that implied for the family: a little white coffin, a grave, a wake, a death announcement in *El Comercio*, mourning dress, bereavement.

He acquired the habit of devoting himself to these mental gymnastics as he walked to and from the Laboratories and San Miguel. In order not to repeat himself, he began by making a rapid summary of the charges leveled at *them* in the previous reflection and then proceeded to explore another one. One theme led quite naturally to another, and he never found himself short of arguments.

Their economic misdeeds, for example, furnished enough material to occupy his mind for thirty kilometers. Wasn't it distressing how *they* ruined the family budget? They ate up the paternal income in inverse proportion to their size, not only because of their persistent gluttony and their delicate stomachs which required special foods, but also because of the countless institutions *they* had given rise to, midwives, day nurseries, child-care centers, kindergartens, nannies, circuses, children's matinees, toy stores, juvenile courts, reformatories, not to mention the specialists in the treatment of children who (arborescent parasites that asphyxiate the host plant) had sprouted in medicine, psychology, odontology, and other sciences, an army, in a word, that had to be dressed, fed, and pensioned off at the expense of the poor *fathers*.

Lucho Abril Marroquín found himself about to burst into tears one day just thinking about those young mothers who, zealously fulfilling their moral responsibilities and ever mindful of what people might say, bury themselves alive in order to care for their offspring, giving up parties, movies, vacation trips, and by so doing end up being abandoned by their spouses, who, on being obliged to go out so often by themselves, inevitably stray from the path of virtue. And how do these children repay all these sleepless nights, all this suffering? By growing up, by moving away from home and founding their own family, by forsaking their mothers in the lonely orphanhood of their old age.

And thus, by imperceptible degrees, he finally destroyed the myth of *their* innocence and goodness. Taking advantage of the well-known pretext that they lacked the powers of reason, did they not tear the wings off butterflies, roast live baby chicks in the oven, flip tortoises onto their backs and leave them to die, pluck squirrels' eyes out? Was a slingshot for killing little birds an adult weapon? And were they not totally without pity for children weaker than themselves? Moreover, how could one possibly apply the word "intelligent" to beings who, at an age when any little kitten can already hunt its own food, are still clumsily toddling about, bumping into walls, and getting black and blue all over?

Lucho Abril Marroquín was possessed of acute aesthetic sensibilities, and they provided him with food for thought for many a walk between home and office. He would have liked all women to stay lithe and supple until the menopause, and it pained him to inventory the ravages undergone by mothers as a result of childbirth: their wasp waists that would fit in one hand all went to fat, and likewise their breasts and buttocks and smooth bellies, expanses of flesh as hard as metal that lips did not dent, went soft, swelled, sagged, wrinkled, and certain women, as a consequence of all the pushing and contractions of difficult births, waddled like ducks afterwards. Remembering the statuesque body of the little Frenchwoman who bore his name, Lucho Abril Marroquín was happy and relieved to think that she had given birth not to a chubby creature that had utterly destroyed her beauty but to little more than a blob of human detritus. Another day, as he was sitting on the toilet—the prunes had made his bowels as punctual as an English train—he realized that it no longer made him tremble with fear to think of Herod. And one morning he found himself giving a little beggar boy a clout on the head.

He knew then that, without any conscious intent on his part, he had gone on (as stars naturally journey on from night to day) to the "Practical Exercises." Dr. Acémila had subtitled these instructions "Direct Action," and Lucho Abril Marroquín had the impression that he was hearing her scientist's voice speaking as he reread them. Unlike the instructions for the theoretical exercises, these were quite precise. Once he had become clearly aware of the disasters *they* caused, it was now a matter of engaging in minor acts of reprisal, on an individual level. It was necessary to do so in a discreet manner, in view of the tyrannical demagoguery underlying such sentiments as "Children are defenseless creatures,"

"Never hit a child, not even with a rose," and "Whippings cause complexes."

These instructions admittedly proved difficult to follow in the beginning, and when he passed one of *them* on the street, neither the latter nor he himself knew whether that hand laid on the little one's childish head was meant as a chastisement or as a clumsy pat. But with the self-assurance that comes with practice, he little by little overcame his timidity and ancestral inhibitions, growing bolder, bettering his score, taking the initiative, and after a few weeks, as the "Exercises" predicted, he noted that the cuffs on the head that he dealt out on street corners, the pinches that left bruises, the kicks that caused the recipients to howl in pain, were no longer a duty he took upon himself for moral and theoretical reasons, but a sort of pleasure. He enjoyed seeing little boys who went around selling lottery tickets burst into tears when they walked up to him to offer him a lucky number and to their surprise got their ears soundly boxed, and it excited him as much as watching a bullfight when the boy guide of a blind woman, who had approached him with his tin alms saucer tinkling in the morning air, fell to the ground rubbing the shin on which a good swift kick had just landed. The "Practical Exercises" were risky, but realizing that at heart he was fearless and foolhardy, this spurred him on rather than dissuading him. Not even on the day that he stamped on a soccer ball till it burst and was pursued with sticks and stones by a pack of pygmies did his determination falter.

Thus, during the weeks that the treatment lasted, he committed a great many of those acts that (mental laziness that turns people into idiots) are ordinarily referred to as evil deeds. He decapitated the dolls with which, in public parks, nursemaids entertained *them;* he snatched lollipops, toffee, caramels that little girls were about to put in their mouths and trampled them underfoot or threw them to dogs; he hung about circuses, children's matinees, and puppet theaters, and pulled braids and ears, pinched little arms and legs and behinds till his fingers turned numb, and, naturally, made use of the age-old stratagem of sticking his tongue out at them and making faces, and talked to them at length, till his voice grew hoarse or gave out altogether, of the Bogeyman, the Big Bad Wolf, the Policeman, the Skeleton, the Witch, the Vampire, and other characters created by the imagination of adults to frighten *them.*

But (a snowball that on rolling down the mountainside turns into an avalanche) one day Lucho Abril Marroquín gave himself such a scare that he rushed to Dr. Acémila's office, taking a taxi so as to get there sooner. The moment he entered her austere consultation room, in a cold sweat, his voice trembling, he exclaimed: "I very nearly pushed a little girl under the wheels of the San Miguel streetcar. At the very last instant I restrained myself because I saw a policeman." And sobbing like one of *them*, he cried: "I was just on the point of becoming a criminal, Doctor!"

"You've already been a criminal, young man, have you forgotten?" the lady psychologist reminded him, stressing each syllable. And after looking him up and down, she announced, in a satisfied tone of voice: "You're cured."

Lucho Abril Marroquín suddenly remembered then (a blinding flash of light in the darkness, a shower of shooting stars falling into the sea) that he had arrived in—a taxi! He was about to fall on his knees but the lady savant stopped him. "No one licks my hands except my Great Dane. Enough of these effusions! You may go now, for new *friends* are awaiting me. You will be receiving my bill shortly."

"It's true: I'm cured!" the medical detail man kept joyously repeating to himself: during the last week he had slept seven hours a night, and instead of nightmares he had had pleasant dreams in which he was lying on exotic beaches, tanning himself beneath a glorious sun as round as a soccer ball, watching giant tortoises slowly lumbering along amid tall palms with tapering fronds and the roguish fornications of dolphins in the blue waves. This time (determination and foolhardiness of the man who has undergone baptism under fire) he took another taxi to the Laboratories and during the trip there he wept on perceiving that the only effect that *riding* through life was having on him was not the deathly fear, the cosmic anxiety of days gone by, but merely a slight dizzy feeling. He ran to kiss the Amazonian hands of Don Federico Téllez Unzátegui, calling him "my wise counselor, my savior, my new father," a gesture and words that his superior accepted with the deference that every self-respecting master owes his slaves, while at the same time (Calvinist possessed of a heart impervious to sentiment) pointing out that, cured or not of his homicidal complexes, he was to show up for work on time at Rodent Exterminators, Incorporated or be fined.

It was thus that Lucho Abril Marroquín emerged from the tunnel that, following the accident amid the dust of Pisco, his life had been. From that time on, things began to straighten out. The sweet daughter of France, recovered from her trials and tribulations thanks to pampering by her family and invigorated by a Norman diet of runny Camemberts and slimy snails, returned to the land of the Incas with glowing cheeks and a heart full of love. The couple's reunion turned out to be a prolonged honeymoon—intoxicating kisses, compulsive embraces, and other emotional dissipations that brought the amorous spouses to the very edge of anemia. The medical detail man (serpent with redoubled energies after shedding its skin) promptly regained the preeminent position he had formerly held in the Laboratories. At his own request, wishing to prove to himself that he was the same capable man as before, he was again entrusted by Dr. Schwalb with the responsibility of visiting the cities and towns of Peru, by air, land, river, and sea, to acquaint doctors and pharmacists with the virtues of Bayer products. Thanks to his wife's thrifty habits, the couple were soon able to pay off all the debts they had contracted during the crisis and buy a new Volkswagen on credit—a yellow one, naturally.

To all appearances (but doesn't popular wisdom recommend "not trusting in appearances?"), there was not a single cloud on the horizon threatening to darken the life that the Abril Marroquíns were leading. The Bayer representative rarely remembered the accident, and when he did, he felt proud rather than remorseful, a fact which (being a mesocrat who respected social conventions) he was careful to keep to himself. But within the privacy of his own home (a nest of turtledoves, a fire blazing on the hearth to the accompaniment of Vivaldi violins), something had survived (light that continues to shine in space when the star that emitted it has ceased to exist, fingernails and hair of the dead man that continue to grow) from Professor Acémila's therapy. On the one hand, an inordinate penchant, at Lucho Abril Marroquín's age, for playing with wooden figurines, Meccano sets, toy trains, tin soldiers. Little by little the apartment became cluttered with toys that annoyed the maids and bewildered the neighbors, and the first shadows cast upon the conjugal harmony of the couple made their appearance the day the little French wife began to complain that her husband spent all his Sundays and holidays sailing little paper boats in the bathtub or flying kites from the roof terrace. But even more serious than this exaggerated fondness for toys, and obviously incompatible with it, was the phobia toward children that had continued to linger in Lucho Abril Marroquín's mind ever since the days of the "Practical Exercises." It was not possible for him to meet one of *them* on the street, in a park, or in a public square, without inflicting what the vulgar would call cruelty on him, and in conversations with his wife he was in the habit of using such scornful expressions as "the weanies" or "the limbomanes" when he spoke of *them*. This hostility turned into acute anxiety the day the blonde became pregnant again. The couple (heels that fear transforms into propellers) flew to Dr. Acémila's office to seek her moral and scientific advice.

She heard them out without being in the least alarmed. "You are suffering from infantilism, and at the same time you are a potential infanticidal recidivist" was her skillful, telegraphic diagnosis. "Two bits of foolishness that don't deserve being taken seriously and that I cure as easily as I spit. Have no fear: you'll recover before the fetus grows eyes."

Would she cure him? Would she free Lucho Abril Marroquín of these specters? Would the treatment for infantophobia and herodism be as risky as that which had emancipated him from his wheel complex and his obsession with crime? How would this psychodrama of San Miguel end?

Eleven.

Midyear exams at the

university were approaching, and because I had attended classes less since my romance with Aunt Julia and written more (Pyrrhic) stories, I was ill-prepared for this critical moment. One of my fellow students, a boy from Camaná whose name was Guillermo Velando, was my salvation. He lived in a boardinghouse downtown, just off the Plaza Dos de Mayo, and was a model student who never cut class, took exhaustive lecture notes that even indicated where and how long the professors paused for breath, and learned the articles of the Code by heart, the way I learned poems. He was always talking about his home town, where he'd left a fiancée, and he could hardly wait to get his law degree so as to be able to leave Lima, a city he detested, and set himself up in practice in Camaná, where he would do battle to bring progress to the region where he'd been born. He lent me his notes, whispered answers to me when we had tests, and whenever exams were coming up, I would go to his boardinghouse in the hope that he could give me some miraculous synthesis of what had gone on in class.

I was on my way home from there that Sunday, after spending three hours in Guillermo's room, with my brain reeling with legal terms, terrified by the thought of how much jargon in Latin I had to memorize, when, arriving at the Plaza San Martín, I spied in the distance the little window of Pedro Camacho's lair, standing open in the dull gray façade of Radio Central. I naturally decided to go say hello to him. The more time I spent with him—even though our relationship was still limited to very brief conversations over a café table—the more fascinated I was by his personality, his physical appearance, his rhetoric. As I headed across the plaza toward his office, I thought once more of the iron will that was responsible for this little man's tremendous capacity for work, his ability to produce, from dawn to dark, from morning to night, stories full of tempestuous passions. At whatever hour of the day I happened to think of him, I would say to myself: "He's busy writing," and I could see him, as I had so many times, pecking away at the keys of the Remington with two lightning-quick index fingers and gazing at the platen with delirious eyes, whereupon I would feel a curious admixture of pity and envy.

The window of his little cubicle was halfway open—I could hear the typewriter keys pounding away rhythmically inside—and as I pushed it open all the way, I called out: "Hello there, hardworking sir." But I had the impression that I'd poked my nose into the wrong place or was addressing some unknown person, and it took me several seconds to recognize the Bolivian scriptwriter beneath his disguise consisting of a white smock, a surgeon's skullcap, and a long rabbinical black beard. He went on writing impassively, without even looking at me, his back slightly hunched over his desk. After a moment, as though he were pausing between one thought and the next, but without turning his head in my direction, I heard him say in his perfectly placed, tender voice: "The gynecologist Alberto de Quinteros is delivering his niece's triplets, and one of the little runts is going to be a breech birth. Can you wait five minutes for me? I'll do a Caesarean on the girl and then I'll go have a verbena-and-mint tea with you."

I sat on the windowsill smoking a cigarette as I waited for him to finish the breech delivery of the triplets, an operation that as a matter of fact took him no more than a few minutes. Then, as he removed his costume, carefully folded it up, and put it away in a plastic sack along with the patriarchal false beard, I said to him: "It only takes you five minutes to deliver triplets, Caesarean and all. I'm amazed: I struggled for three weeks over a story of three little kids who levitate by taking advantage of the lift effect of planes taking off."

As we were walking over to the Bransa, I told him that after having turned out a whole bunch of stories that were miserable failures, the one about the levitating kids struck me as passable and that I'd taken it to the Sunday supplement of *El Comercio*, in fear and trembling. The editor-in-chief had read it in front of me and given me a mysterious answer: "Leave it, and we'll see what we can do with it." Two Sundays had gone by since then; I'd rushed out each weekend to buy the paper, and thus far, there'd been no sign of its appearing.

But Pedro Camacho was not one to waste his time on other people's problems. "Let's skip our pick-me-up and walk instead," he said, taking me by the arm just as I was about to sit down, and leading me back to La Colmena. "I have pins and needles in my calves, a sure sign I'll soon be having cramps in them. It's the sedentary life I live. I need exercise."

It was only because I knew what his answer was going to be that I suggested that he follow the example of Victor Hugo and Hemingway and write standing up.

But this time I was wrong. "Interesting things are happening at La Tapada," he said without even answering me, as he led me round and round the monument to San Martín, almost at a trot. "There's a young man staying there who weeps on moonlit nights."

I rarely came downtown on Sundays and I was surprised to see how different the people who were there on weekdays were from the ones I saw now. Instead of middle-class office workers, the square was full of maids on their day off, mountain boys with ruddy cheeks and big clumsy clodhoppers, girls with braids and bare feet, and itinerant photographers and women selling food wandering amid the motley crowd. I made the scribe stop in front of the female figure in a tunic in the center section of the monument who represents the Motherland, and to see whether I could get a laugh out of him, I told him why an Auchenia was bizarrely perched on her head: when the bronze was cast, here in Lima, the foundry workers had not understood the sculptor's instructions to crown her with a votive flame—a *llama votiva*—and instead had topped the statue off with the animal of the same name.

Naturally, he didn't even smile. He took me by the arm again, and as he hurried me along, bumping into people out for a leisurely stroll, he went on with his monologue, indifferent to everything around him, beginning with me. "Nobody's seen his face, but there is reason to believe he's some sort of monster—the bastard son of the owner of the *pensión* perhaps?—suffering from all sorts of hereditary defects, dwarfism, bicephalism, a hunchback, whom Doña Atanasia hides during the day so as not to frighten us and lets out only at night to get a breath of fresh air."

He said all this without the slightest emotion, like a recording machine, and to pump him for more information, I said his hypothesis sounded farfetched to me: couldn't he be a young man who was weeping over his love troubles?

"If he were a love-smitten young man, he'd have a guitar, or a violin, or sing," he replied with scorn tinged with compassion. "But all this one does is weep."

I tried to get him to explain the whole thing to me from the beginning, but he was vaguer and more self-absorbed than usual. The only thing I could get out of him was that someone, for several nights now, had been crying in some corner of the rooming-house or other and that the lodgers at La Tapada were complaining. The owner of the place, Doña Atanasia, claimed she knew nothing about it, and according to the scriptwriter, used "the ghost alibi."

"It's also possible that he's weeping over a crime," Pedro Camacho speculated, in the tone of voice of an accountant adding up figures aloud, still holding me by the arm and steering me toward Radio Central after a dozen turns around the monument. "A family crime? A parricide who's tearing his hair and gouging his flesh in remorse? A son of the rat man?"

He wasn't the least bit agitated, though I noted that he was more distant than usual, more incapable than ever of listening, of conversing, of remembering that there was someone with him. I was certain that he didn't even see me. I tried to get him to go on with his monologue, for it was like seeing his imagination working at top speed, but as abruptly as he'd begun speaking of the invisible weeper, he suddenly fell silent. I watched him settle down to work again in his lair, taking off his black suit coat and his little bow tie, tucking his wild mane into a hairnet, and putting on a woman's wig with a bun that he took out of another plastic sack.

I was unable to contain myself and let out a roar of laughter. "And who is this lady in whose company I have the pleasure of finding myself?" I asked him, still laughing.

"I must give some advice to a Francophile laboratory assistant who's killed his son," he explained to me in a sarcastic tone of voice, gluing a coquettish beauty mark on his face this time instead of the patriarchal beard he'd worn before, and putting on a pair of colored earrings. "Goodbye, *friend.*"

The moment I turned around to leave, I heard—coming back to life, steady, self-assured, compulsive, eternal—the Remington pounding away. Riding back to Miraflores in a jitney, I thought about Pedro Camacho's life. What social milieu, what concatenation of circumstances, persons, relations, problems, events, happenstances had produced this literary vocation (literary? if not that, what should it be called, then?) that had somehow come to fruition, found expression in an *oeuvre,* and secured an audience? How could he be, at one and the same time, a parody of the writer and the only person in Peru who, by virtue of the time he devoted to his craft and the works he produced, was worthy of that name? Were all those politicians, attorneys, professors who went by the name of poets, novelists, dramatists really *writers,* simply because, during brief parentheses in lives in which four fifths of their time was spent at activities having nothing to do with literature, they had produced one slim volume of verses or one niggardly collection of stories? Why should those persons who used literature as an ornament or a pretext have any more right to be considered real writers than Pedro Camacho, who lived *only* to write? Because they had read (or at least knew that they should have read) Proust, Faulkner, Joyce, while Pedro Camacho was very nearly illiterate? When I thought about such things, I felt sad and upset. It was becoming clearer and clearer to me each day that the only thing I wanted to be in life was a writer, and I was also becoming more and more convinced each day that the only way to be one was to devote oneself heart and soul to literature. I didn't want in the least to be a hack writer or a part-time one, but a real one, like—who? The person I'd met who came closest to being this full-time writer, obsessed and impassioned by his vocation, was the Bolivian author of radio serials: that was why he fascinated me so.

Javier was waiting for me at my grandparents', brimming over with happiness, with a program for the rest of that Sunday that would have been enough to raise the dead. He'd just received the money order that his parents sent him every month from Piura, along with a good bit extra for the national holidays, and he had decided that the four of us would spend this unexpected windfall together.

"In your honor, I've drawn up a cosmopolitan, intellectual program," he said to me, with a hearty clap on the back. "Francisco Petrone's Argentine theatrical company, a German repast at the Rincón Toni, and winding up the festivities French-style at the Negro-Negro, dancing boleros in the dark."

Just as Pedro Camacho was the closest thing to a writer that I'd ever seen in my short life, among all my acquaintances Javier was the one whose generosity and exuberance made him most resemble a Renaissance prince. Moreover, he was a very efficient planner: he'd already informed Aunt Julia and Nancy of what was awaiting us that night, and he already had the theater tickets in his pocket. His program couldn't have been more enticing, and it immediately dispelled my gloomy reflections on the vocation and the miserable fate that awaited the man of letters in Peru. Javier was also very happy: he'd been going out with Nancy for a month now, and their keeping company together was taking on the proportions of a real romance. My having confessed my feelings toward Aunt Julia to my cousin had been very useful to him because, on the pretext of helping us hide our secret and making it easier for us to go out together by double-dating, he'd been managing to see Nancy several times a week. My cousin and Aunt Julia were inseparable now: they went out shopping and to the movies together and exchanged confidences. My cousin had become an enthusiastic fairy godmother of our romance, and one afternoon she raised my morale by remarking to me: "Julita has a way about her that cancels out any difference in age, Marito."

The grandiose program for that Sunday (a day on which, I firmly believe, a large part of my future was determined by the stars) got off to an excellent start. In Lima in the fifties we had very few chances to see first-rate theater, and the Argentine company of Francisco Petrone brought us a series of modern works that had never been performed before in Peru. Nancy went by Aunt Olga's to get Aunt Julia and the two of them came downtown in a taxi. Javier and I were waiting for them at the door of the Teatro Segura. Javier, who was a great believer in the grand gesture, had rented an entire box, which turned out to be the only one occupied, so that there were almost as many eyes focused on us as on the stage. My guilty conscience made me quite certain that any number of relatives and acquaintances would see us and immediately suspect the truth. But the moment the performance began, my fears evaporated. They were doing *Death of a Salesman,* by Arthur Miller, the first nontraditional play, violating the conventions of time and space, that I'd ever seen. I was so excited and so enthused that during the intermission I began to talk a blue streak, praising the work to the skies, commenting on its characters, its technique, its ideas, and later, as we were eating sausages and drinking dark beer in the Rincón Toni on La Colmena, I went on raving about it and got so absorbed in what I was saying that Javier later told me: "You would have thought you were a parrot that had been slipped a dose of Spanish fly." My cousin Nancy, who had always thought my literary inclinations were as peculiar as the odd hobby that fascinated our Uncle Eduardo—a little old man, my grandfather's brother, now a retired judge, whose life was centered on the unusual pastime of collecting spiders—after hearing my interminable peroration on the work we had just seen, suspected that my literary bent might lead me off the deep end. "You're going off your rocker, my boy," she warned me.

Javier had chosen the Negro-Negro to end the evening because it had a certain intellectual-bohemian atmosphere—on Thursdays they gave little shows, one-act plays, monologues, recitals, and it was a favorite gathering place for painters, musicians, and writers—but besides that, it was also the darkest *boîte* in Lima, a basement in the arcades of the Plaza San Martín that had twenty tables at most, with a decor we thought was "existentialist." It was a night spot that, the few times I had been there, gave me the illusion that I was in a *cave* in Saint-Germain-des-Prés. They seated us at a little table on the edge of the dance floor, and Javier, more princely than ever, ordered four whiskies. He and Nancy immediately got up to dance, and there in that tiny, crowded basement, I went on talking to Julia about theater and Arthur Miller. We were sitting almost on top of each other, holding hands, she was patiently listening to me, and I went on and on about how that night I had discovered the theater: it could be something as complex and profound as the novel, and because it was something living, requiring the participation of flesh-and-blood beings in order to take on material form, and other arts, painting, music, it was perhaps even superior.

"I've decided all of a sudden that I'm going to change genres and start writing plays instead of stories," I told her, all excited. "What do you say to that?"

"There's no reason you shouldn't, as far as I'm concerned," Aunt Julia answered, rising to her feet. "But now, Varguitas, come dance with me and whisper sweet nothings in my ear. Between pieces, if you like, you have my permission to talk to me about literature."

I followed her instructions to the letter. We held each other very tightly and kissed as we danced, I told her that I was in love with her, and she answered that she was in love with me, and aided by the intimate, exciting, sensuous atmosphere and Javier's whiskies, for the very first time I made no effort to hide the desire that she aroused in me; as we danced, my lips nuzzled her neck, my tongue stole into her mouth and sipped her saliva, I held her very close so as to feel her breasts, her belly, and her thighs, and then, back at the table, under cover of the darkness, I fondled her legs and breasts. That's what we were doing, so happy we were giddy, when Nancy came back to the table, during a break between two boleros, and made our blood run cold by blurting out: "Good Lord, just look who's here: Uncle Jorge."

It was a danger we ought to have thought of. Uncle Jorge, our youngest uncle, daringly combined, in a superfrenetic life, all sorts of business affairs and commercial ventures and an intense night life filled with wine, women, and song. A tragicomic story about him had made the rounds, the scene of which was another *boîte*: the Embassy. The show had just begun, the girl who was singing couldn't go on because a drunk sitting at one of the tables kept interrupting her by shouting insults. Uncle Jorge had risen to his feet in the middle of the crowded nightclub, roaring like a Don Quixote: "Shut your mouth, you wretch, I'm going to teach you to respect a lady," and with his fists raised like a boxer had started to move in on the idiot, only to discover a moment later that he was making a fool of himself since the pseudo-customer's interruption of the chanteuse was part of the show. And there he was, sitting just two tables away from us, looking very elegant, his face just barely visible in the light of the matches being struck by the smokers in the place and the waiters' flashlights. I recognized his wife, my Aunt Gaby, sitting next to him, and despite the fact that they were only a few feet away from us, both of them were deliberately avoiding looking in our direction. It was all quite obvious: they'd seen me kissing Aunt Julia, they'd immediately guessed everything, and had opted for a diplomatic blindness. Javier asked for the check, we left the Negro-Negro almost at once, and Uncle Jorge and Aunt Gaby carefully looked the other way even when we rubbed elbows as we passed their table on the way out. In the taxi on the way back to Miraflores, the four of us just sat there with long faces, not saying a word, till Nancy finally summed up what all of us were thinking: "All that scheming for nothing; the fat's in the fire now."

But, as in a good suspense film, nothing at all happened during the next few days. There was not the slightest sign that the family clan had been alerted by Uncle Jorge and Aunt Gaby. Uncle Lucho and Aunt Olga didn't say one word to Aunt Julia that would lead her to think that they knew, and that Thursday, when I screwed up my courage and turned up for lunch at their house as usual, they were as outgoing and affectionate with me as always. Nor was Cousin Nancy the object of a single captious question on the part of Aunt Laura and Uncle Juan. And at my house, my grandparents seemed to be lost in daydreams and kept asking me, with the most angelic innocence imaginable, whether I was still taking Aunt Julia to the movies ("So nice of you—Julita's such a film fan"). Those were anxious days, during which, taking extra precautions, Aunt Julia and I decided not to see each other, even in secret, for at least a week. We nonetheless talked to each other on the telephone. Aunt Julia would go out to the grocery store on the corner to phone me at least three times a day, and we would exchange our respective observations regarding the dreaded family reaction and entertain all sorts of hypotheses. Could Uncle Jorge possibly have decided to keep our secret to himself? I knew that this was unthinkable, in view of the family's usual habits. So what in the world was happening? Javier advanced the thesis that Aunt Gaby and Uncle Jorge had downed so many whiskies that night that they hadn't really realized what was going on, that the only thing that lingered in their memory was a vague suspicion, and that they hadn't wanted to unleash a scandal over something that was not absolute proven fact. More or less out of curiosity, but also out of masochism, I made the rounds and dropped in at the homes of the entire clan that week so as to know what to expect. I noted nothing out of the ordinary, save for an omission that intrigued me and set off a pyrotechnical explosion of speculation on my part. Aunt Hortensia, who had invited me to come have tea and biscuits with her, didn't mention Aunt Julia once in the course of a two-hour conversation. "They know everything and have plans afoot," I assured Javier, who was sick and tired of hearing me talk of nothing else. "When you come right down to it, you're dying to get your whole family up in arms so as to have something to write about," he commented.

During that eventful week I also found myself unexpectedly involved in a street fight and playing the part of Pedro Camacho's bodyguard, so to speak. I had gone one day to San Marcos University, where the results of an exam in criminal law had just been posted, and was full of remorse at having discovered that I had received a higher grade than my friend Velando, who was the one who had had everything down pat. As I was crossing the Parque Universitario, I ran into Genaro Sr., the patriarch of the phalanx that owned Radio Panamericana and Radio Central, and the two of us walked as far as the Calle Belén together, talking as we strolled along. He was a gentleman who always dressed in black and was always very solemn, and the Bolivian scriptwriter sometimes referred to him—for reasons not at all difficult to guess—as The Slave Driver.

"Your friend the genius is still giving me headaches," Genaro Sr. said to me. "I've had it up to here with him. If he weren't so productive, I'd have booted him out long before this."

"Another protest from the Argentine embassy?" I asked.

"I don't know what sort of a hopeless mess he's cooking up," he complained. "He's taken to pulling people's leg, shifting characters from one serial to an entirely different one or changing their names all of a sudden so as to get our listeners all confused. My wife had already told me what was going on, and now we're starting to get phone calls, and we've even received two letters. It seems that the priest from Mendocita now has the name of the Jehovah's Witness and vice versa. I'm far too busy to listen to serials. Do *you* ever listen to them?"

We had reached La Colmena and were heading toward the Plaza

San Martín, past buses leaving for the provinces and little Chinese cafés, and I remembered that Aunt Julia, speaking of Pedro Camacho a few days before, had made me laugh and confirmed my suspicions that the scriptwriter was secretly a humorist at heart. "Something really weird has happened. The young wife had her kid, but it died at birth, and they buried it with all the rites of the Church. So how do you explain the fact that in this afternoon's chapter they took the baby to the Cathedral to be baptized?"

I told Genaro Sr. that I didn't have time to listen to them either and that perhaps these interchangeable characters and mixed-up plots were Pedro Camacho's highly original way of telling a story.

"We aren't paying him to be original; we're paying him to entertain our listeners," Genaro Sr. informed me, making it quite plain that he for his part was not a progressive-minded impresario but a thoroughgoing traditionalist. "If he keeps on with jokes like that, he's going to make us lose our listeners, and sponsors will withdraw their commercials. You're his friend: pass the word on to him to cut out these modernist gimmicks, or else he's liable to end up without a job."

I suggested that he tell him so himself: since he was the boss, the threat would carry more weight.

But Genaro Sr. shook his head, with an air of compunction that Genaro Jr. had inherited. "He won't even let me speak to him. Success has gone to his head, and every time I try to have a word with him, he's disrespectful."

Genaro Sr. had gone to his cubicle to tell him, as politely as possible, that the station had been receiving phone calls, and show him the letters of complaint. Without saying a single word in reply, Pedro Camacho had taken the two letters, torn them to pieces without opening them, and tossed them in the wastebasket. He then began typing, as though there were no one present, and as Genaro Sr., on the edge of apoplexy, was leaving that hostile lair, he heard him mutter: "Let the cobbler stick to his last."

"I can't put up with any more insults like that; I'd have to kick him out, and that wouldn't be realistic either," he concluded with a weary gesture. "But you don't have anything to lose. He's not going to insult you—you're more or less a writer too, aren't you? Give us a hand, do it for the corporation, talk to him."

I promised him I would, and in fact, to my misfortune, I went down after the twelve o'clock Panamericana newscast to invite Pedro Camacho to come have a cup of verbena-and-mint. We were leaving Radio Central when two big strapping young men blocked our path. I recognized them immediately: the barbecue cooks, two brothers with big bushy mustaches, from the Argentina Grill, a restaurant located on the same street, across from the school run by the Little Sisters of Bethlehem; dressed in white aprons and tall chef's toques, they were the ones who prepared the rare steaks and grilled tripe that were the specialty of the restaurant.

The two of them surrounded him, looking as though they were out for trouble, and the older and fatter one said to him in a threatening tone of voice: "So we're child-killers, are we, Camacho, you bastard? Did you think there was nobody in this country who could teach you a little respect, you bum?"

He grew more and more excited as he spoke, turning bright red and stumbling over his words. The younger brother kept nodding in agreement, and as his elder paused for a moment, choking with rage, he too put in his two cents' worth. "And what about the lice? So you think, do you, that women where we come from eat the vermin they pull out of their kids' hair as a special treat, you fucking son of a bitch? Do you think I'm going to let you get away with insulting my mother?"

The Bolivian scriptwriter hadn't backed away an inch and stood there listening to them with a magisterial air, his exophthalmic eyes slowly shifting from one to the other. Then, with a characteristic little bow from the waist, mindful of a master of ceremonies, and in a very solemn tone of voice, he suddenly asked them the most civil question imaginable. "Are you by any chance Argentines?"

The fat barbecue chef, foaming at the mustache now, his face only a few inches away from Pedro Camacho's (a confrontation that had forced him to bend way over), roared patriotically: "Yes, you bastard, we're Argentines—and proud of it!"

Once he had received this confirmation—really quite unnecessary since the moment they had spoken two words it was obvious from their accent that they were Argentines—I saw the Bolivian turn deathly pale, as though something had exploded inside him; his eyes blazed, he assumed a threatening expression, and whipping the air with his index finger, he apostrophized them thus: "I suspected as much. Well, then: clear out of here immediately and go sing tangos!"

The order was not meant humorously; his tone of voice was deadly serious. For a second the barbecue chefs just stood there, at a loss for words. It was plain to see that the scriptwriter wasn't joking: despite the fact that he was absolutely defenseless physically, the tiny little man was stubbornly holding his ground, his fierce eyes glaring at them scornfully.

"What was that you said?" the fat one finally blurted out, nonplussed and beside himself with rage. "Huh, huh? What was that again?"

"Go sing tangos and wash your ears!" Pedro Camacho said, enlarging on his order, in his impeccable accent. And then, after the briefest of pauses, with the audacity that was to be our downfall, he said slowly and distinctly, in a glacially calm voice: "If you don't want a beating."

This time I was even more surprised than the barbecue cooks. That this little man, scarcely taller than a dwarf and with the physique of a third-grade schoolchild, was threatening to thrash two Samsons weighing well over two hundred pounds apiece was not only mad but suicidal. But the fatter one was already going into action: he grabbed the Bolivian by the collar and, amid the laughter of the crowd that had gathered round, lifted him off his feet as though he were a feather, and shouted: "*You're* going to give *me* a beating? Well, we'll see about that, shorty . . ."

When I saw that the older brother was about to send Pedro Camacho flying with a straight right to the jaw, I was obliged to intervene. I grabbed the Samson's arm, trying at the same time to free the scriptwriter, who was suspended in midair, purple-faced and jerking his legs like a spider, and I managed to say something like: "Listen, don't be a bully, let him go," when suddenly, without warning, the younger brother gave me a punch that sent me sprawling on the ground. As I struggled to my feet in a daze and prepared to put into practice the philosophy taught me by my grandfather, a gentleman of the old school, who held that no Arequipan worthy of the name ever refuses an invitation to fight (and above all an invitation as clear as a sock in the jaw), I saw that the older brother was soundly boxing the artist's ears (he had mercifully chosen to cuff him rather than punch him, in view of his adversary's Lilliputian stature). Then, after that, as I traded rights and lefts with the younger barbecue cook (in defense of art, I thought to myself), I didn't see much else. The fight didn't last very long, but when people from Radio Central finally rescued us from the hands of the two hulking brutes, I had bumps and bruises all over and Pedro Camacho's face was so puffy and swollen that Genaro Sr. had to take him to the public emergency clinic. That afternoon, instead of thanking me for having risked my neck defending his exclusive star, Genaro Jr. bawled me out for a news item that Pascual, taking advantage of all the confusion, had managed to slip into two successive bulletins; the paragraph in question began (with a certain amount of exaggeration) as follows: "Thugs from the Río de la Plata today criminally attacked our news director, the celebrated journalist . . ."

When Javier turned up that afternoon in my shack at Radio Panamericana, he roared with laughter on hearing the story of the fight, and went with me to ask the scriptwriter how he felt. They'd put a pirate's patch over his right eye, and he was wearing two adhesive bandages, one on his neck and another under his nose. How did he feel? He gave a disdainful wave of his hand, dismissing the entire incident as of no importance, and made no attempt to thank me for having plunged into the fray out of solidarity with him.

His one and only comment delighted Javier. "It saved the lives of those two when people separated us. If it had gone on a few minutes more, the crowd would have recognized me and then they'd have lynched the poor things."

We went to the Bransa, where he told us that one day in Bolivia a soccer player "from *that* country" who'd heard his programs had turned up at the studio armed with a revolver, which luckily the guards had detected in time.

"You're going to have to be careful," Javier warned him. "Lima is full of Argentines now."

"It's a matter of little moment. Sooner or later, worms are going to eat all three of us," Pedro Camacho philosophized.

And he delivered us a lecture on the transmigration of souls, an article of faith with him. He told us a secret: if it were left to him to choose, he would like to be some calm, long-lived marine animal, such as a tortoise or a whale, in his next reincarnation. I took advantage of his good spirits to exercise my *ad honorem* role of intermediary between him and the Genaros that I had assumed some time ago and gave him Genaro Sr.'s message about the phone calls, the letters, the episodes in his serials that a number of people didn't understand. The old man begged him not to complicate his plots, to take into account the level of intelligence of the average listener, which was quite low. I tried to sugarcoat the pill by siding with him (as a matter of fact, I really was on his side, moreover): this urgent request was absurd, naturally, one should be free to write as one pleased, and I was merely repeating what they had asked me to tell him.

He heard me out in such silence and with such an impassive expression on his face that he made me feel very uncomfortable. And when I finished, he still didn't say a word. He swallowed the last sip of his verbena-and-mint tea, rose to his feet, muttered that he had to get back to his office, and left without even saying goodbye. Had he taken offense because I'd talked to him about the phone calls in front of someone he didn't know? Javier thought so, and advised me to offer him my apologies. I promised myself never to act as an intermediary for the Genaros again.

During that week I spent without seeing Aunt Julia, I went out at night several times with old friends from Miraflores whom I hadn't bothered to look up since the beginning of my secret romance. They were former schoolmates of mine or kids I'd known in the neighborhood, youngsters who were now studying engineering, like Blackie Salas, or medicine, like Pinky Molfino, or had gotten jobs, like Coco Lanas, pals with whom I'd shared wonderful things since I'd been knee-high to a grasshopper: pinball games and the Parque Salazar, going swimming at the Terrazas and the beaches of Miraflores, parties on Saturday nights, crushes on girls, movies. But on going out with them, after months of not seeing them, I realized that we were no longer the bosom buddies we'd once been; we were still great friends, but we no longer had as many things in common. On the nights we went out together during that week, we did the same daring things together that we'd done in the past: going to the old run-down Surco cemetery to prowl around in the moonlight amid the tombstones that had toppled over in some earthquake, trying to find a skull to make off with; skinny-dipping in the enormous Santa Rosa swimming pool near Ancón, still under construction; making the rounds of the gloomy, depressing brothels on the Avenida Grau. My pals were still the same as ever, cracking the same jokes, talking of the same girls, but I couldn't share with them the things that mattered most to me: literature and Aunt Julia. If I'd told them that I was writing stories and dreamed of being a writer, they would doubtless have thought, just as my cousin Nancy did, that I had a screw loose. And if I'd told them about my romance—as they told me about their conquests—with a divorcée, who was not my mistress but my sweetheart, my *enamorada* (in the most Miraflorine sense of that word), they would have taken me for (as a poetic, esoteric, very popular expression of those days went) a *cojudo a la vela*—an ass under full sail. I didn't feel the slightest scorn for them for not reading literature, nor did I consider myself superior because I was having a romance with a real, grownup woman who'd had lots of experience, but the truth of the matter was that on those nights, as we poked around graves under the eucalyptus and pepper trees of Surco, or splashed about beneath the stars of Santa Rosa, or drank beer and haggled over prices with the whores at Nanette's, I was bored, and found my thoughts dwelling more on my "Dangerous Games" (which had not appeared in *El Comercio* this week either) and on Aunt Julia than on what they were saying.

When I told Javier about my disappointing reunion with my old neighborhood gang of buddies, he stuck out his chest and replied: "It's because they're still just kids. But you and I are men now, Varguitas."

Twelve.

In the dusty downtown

section of the city, halfway down the Jirón Ica, is an old house, with balconies and jalousies, on whose walls ravaged by time and uncivilized passersby (sentimental hands that inscribe hearts and arrows and scribble names of women, perverted fingers that engrave sex organs and dirty words) one can still see, as from a great distance, faint traces of the original paint, that color used in colonial days to adorn aristocratic mansions: indigo blue. The building (once the residence of marquises?) is today a rickety, oft-repaired structure that has miraculously withstood not only earthquakes but the gentle winds of Lima, and even its fine mists. Riddled by termites from top to bottom, full of ratholes and shrews' nests, it has been divided and subdivided countless times, courtyards and rooms that need turns into hives, in order to house more and more tenants. A teeming multitude of modest means lives within (and risks being crushed to death beneath) its fragile walls and shaky ceilings. Occupying the second floor, in half a dozen rooms full of tumbledown furniture and bric-a-brac, perhaps not the most beautiful quarters imaginable, yet morally impeccable, is the Pensión Colonial.

It is owned and run by the Berguas, a family of three that came to Lima from the stony Andean city of innumerable churches, Ayacucho, over thirty years ago and that here (O Manes of life) has gradually declined physically, economically, socially, and even psychically, and will doubtless give up the ghost in this City of Kings and be reincarnated as fish, birds, or insects.

Today the Pensión Colonial is undergoing a painful decadence, and its boarders are humble, insolvent persons, in the best of cases little provincial parish priests come to the capital to deal with some archiepiscopal formality or other, and in the worst of cases little peasant women with purplish cheeks and vicuña eyes who keep their few coins knotted in pink handkerchiefs and recite the rosary in Quechua. There are no servants in the *pensión*, of course, and Señora Margarita Bergua and her daughter, a forty-year-old spinster who answers to the perfumed name of Rosa, are saddled with all the work of making the beds, cleaning, doing the shopping, preparing the meals. Señora Margarita Bergua (as the diminutive ending of her name might indicate) is a skinny little runt of a woman, with more wrinkles than a raisin, who, curiously enough, smells of cats (there are no cats in the *pensión*). She works without stopping from dawn to dark, and as she harriedly hurries through the house, through life, her movements are spectacular, for one of her legs is eight inches shorter than the other and hence she wears an elevator-type shoe, with a wooden platform resembling the box of boys who shine shoes on the street, built for her many years ago by a skillful sculptor of altarpieces back in Ayacucho, which makes the floorboards shake as she drags it along. She has always been thrifty, but over the years this virtue has degenerated into an obsession, and today there is no denying the fact that the harsh epithet "tightwad" fits her perfectly. She does not allow any boarder, for instance, to take a bath except on the first Friday of each month, and she has forced everyone staying at the *pensión* to adopt the Argentine habit—so widespread in the dwellings of that sister country—of flushing the toilet only once a day (she pulls the chain herself, just before going to bed), the hundred percent cause of that constant heavy, warm, fetid smell that pervades the Pensión Colonial and nauseates the boarders, especially in the beginning (with that typical female imagination that cooks up an answer for everything, she maintains that it makes them sleep better).

Señorita Rosa has (or rather had, since after the great nocturnal tragedy even this changed) the soul and the fingers of an artist. As a child, in Ayacucho, when the family was at its apogee (three stone houses and grazing land with sheep), she learned to play the piano and showed such talent that she even gave a recital in the municipal theater, attended by the mayor and the prefect, at which her parents, hearing the applause, wept with emotion. Encouraged by this glorious evening, at which Inca princesses also danced, the Berguas decided to sell everything they had and move to Lima so that their daughter could become a concert pianist. That was why they had purchased this huge old house (which they then rented out and sold off bit by bit), why they bought a piano, why they enrolled their gifted daughter at the National Conservatory. But the big lustful city soon shattered their provincial illusions. For the Berguas promptly discovered something that they would never have suspected: Lima was a den of a million sinners, and every one of them, without a single exception, was out to rape the inspired young girl from Ayacucho. At least that was what the adolescent with shining braided tresses recounted morning, noon, and night, her big round fear-filled eyes brimming with tears: her solfeggio teacher had leapt upon her, panting and snorting, and tried his best to consummate the sinful act using a pile of music scores as a mattress, the concierge of the conservatory had sidled up to her and asked her obscenely: "Would you like to be my hetaera?", two boys in her class had invited her to go to the lavatory with them to watch them pee, the policeman on the corner whom she had asked for directions had confused her with someone else and tried to fondle her breasts, and the bus driver had pinched her nipple as she had handed him her fare . . . Determined to defend the integrity of that hymen which, in accordance with moral precepts of the highlands, as inflexible as marble, the young pianist ought to sacrifice only to her future lord and master, her lawfully wedded spouse, the Berguas withdrew her from the conservatory, arranged for her to take lessons from a young lady who came to the house, dressed Rosa like a nun, and forbade her to go out on the street unless the two of them were with her. Twenty-five years had gone by since then, and as a matter of fact her hymen is still intact and in place, but at this point this is no longer of any great moment, inasmuch as outside of this attraction—for which, moreover, modern young men have nothing but scorn—the ex-pianist (after the tragedy the private lessons were stopped and the piano sold in order to pay the hospital and the doctors) has no others to offer. She is stouter and dumpier and all hunched over now, and since she is always bundled up in anti-aphrodisiac tunics and hooded cloaks that hide her hair and her forehead, she looks more like a bulky walking parcel than a woman. She insists that men paw her, frighten her with filthy propositions, and try to rape her, but at this juncture, even her parents wonder whether these ideas of hers were ever more than fantasies.

But the really moving, tutelary figure of the Pensión Colonial is Don Sebastián Bergua, an old man with a broad forehead, an aquiline nose, a penetrating gaze, the very soul of rectitude and goodness. An old-fashioned man, one might safely say, he has inherited from his distant ancestors, those Spanish conquistadors the brothers Bergua, natives of the mountain heights of Cuenca who came to Peru with Pizarro, not so much that tendency to indulge in excesses that led them to garrote hundreds of Incas (apiece) and to get a comparable number of vestals of El Cuzco pregnant, as their simon-pure Catholicism and their bold conviction that gentlemen of ancient lineage can live on their investments and on rapine, but not by the sweat of their brow. Since childhood, he had gone to Mass every day, taken Communion each Friday in homage to El Señor de Limpias, to whom he was fervently devoted, and he had flagellated himself or worn a hair shirt at least three days out of every month. His aversion to work, a base occupation fit only for Argentines, had always been so extreme that he even refused to make the rounds of his properties to collect the rents that were his means of livelihood, and once he had settled in Lima, he had never bothered to drop by the bank to collect the interest on the bonds in which he'd invested his money. Such duties, practical matters that females are capable of handling, had always devolved upon the diligent Margarita and, once the girl had grown up, on the ex-pianist as well.

Up until the tragedy that cruelly hastened the decline in the Berguas' fortunes, a curse visited upon a family whose very name will be forgotten, Don Sebastián's life in the capital had been that of a scrupulous Christian gentleman. He was in the habit of arising at a late hour of the morning, not out of laziness, but so as not to be obliged to eat his breakfast with the boarders—he did not hold humble folk in contempt yet he believed in the necessity of maintaining social and, above all, racial, distances—and eating a frugal repast, then going to Mass. Possessed of an inquiring mind permeable to history, he was in the habit of visiting different churches from one morning to the next—San Agustín, San Pedro, San Francisco, Santo Domingo—so that as he fulfilled his Christian duty to worship God he might at the same time delight his senses by contemplating the masterworks of colonial faith; moreover, these reminiscences of the past sculpted in stone transported his spirit to the days of the Conquest and the Colony—so much more colorful than the monotonous gray present—in which he would have preferred to live as a daring captain or a pious destroyer of idols. Steeped in his fantasies of the past, Don Sebastián would make his way back along the busy streets of the downtown area—rigid and reserved in his neat black suit, his shirt with gleaming, stiffly starched detachable collar and cuffs, and his turn-of-the-century patent-leather shoes—to the Pensión Colonial, where, comfortably settled in a rocking chair facing the balcony with its jalousies—so much in keeping with his nostalgia for the days of La Perrichola—he would spend the rest of the morning reading the newspapers half-aloud to himself (even the advertisements) so as to know what was going on in the world. Ever-faithful to the traditions of his forebears, after lunch—which he was obliged to share with the boarders, toward whom his manner was nonetheless unfailingly courteous—he observed the quintessentially Spanish rite of the siesta. On awakening, he once again donned his black suit, his starched shirt, his gray hat, and strolled down to the Tambo-Ayacucho Club, an institution on the Jirón Cailloma frequented by many friends and acquaintances from his lovely Andean homeland. Playing dominoes, stud poker, ombre, exchanging small talk about politics and sometimes—being as human as the next man—gossip about subjects not fit for the ears of young girls, he saw dusk descend and night fall. He then walked back at a leisurely pace to the Pensión Colonial, ate his soup and his pot-au-feu alone in his room, listened to one program or another on the radio, and went to sleep, at peace with his conscience and with God.

But all that was before. Today Don Sebastián never sets foot in the street, never changes his attire—which consists, day and night alike, of a brick-colored pair of pajamas, a blue bathrobe, wool socks, and alpaca slippers—and since the tragedy he has never again uttered a complete sentence. He no longer goes to Mass, no longer reads the newspapers. When he is feeling well, the longtime boarders (once they discovered that every man in the world was a satyr, the owners of the Pensión Colonial took in only females or decrepit males whose sexual appetites had—as was obvious at first glance—dwindled away due to illness or old age) see him wandering like a ghost through the dark, centuries-old rooms, his eyes blank, unshaven, his hair unkempt and full of dandruff, or see him swaying slowly back and forth in his rocking chair, mute and dazed, for hours on end. He no longer eats either breakfast or lunch with the boarders, for (fear of appearing ridiculous in the eyes of others that haunts aristocrats even in the poorhouse) Don Sebastián is unable to lift his spoon to his mouth and his wife and daughter must feed him. When he is feeling poorly, the boarders do not see him: the venerable old man stays in bed, with the door of his room locked. But they hear him: they hear his bellows, his sighs, his moans or screams that shake the windowpanes. Newcomers to the Pensión Colonial are surprised to discover that during these crises, as the descendant of conquistadors howls, Doña Margarita and Señorita Rosa go on sweeping, tidying up, cooking, serving at table, and conversing as though nothing were happening. These boarders think them heartless, cold as ice, indifferent to the suffering of a husband, a father. To those curious and impertinent recent arrivals who, pointing to the closed door, dare to ask: "Is Don Sebastián feeling ill?" Señora Margarita's answer is a grudging: "There's nothing wrong with him, he's remembering a bad scare he had, he'll be over it soon." And, in fact, two or three days later the crisis is over and Don Sebastián emerges from his room and is seen once again in the halls and rooms of the Pensión Bayer, pale and thin amid the spiderwebs, with a terrified look on his face.

What was this tragedy exactly? Where, when, how did it occur?

It all began with the arrival at the Pensión Colonial, twenty years before, of a young man with sad eyes dressed in the attire of a disciple of Our Lord of Miracles. He was a traveling salesman, born in Arequipa, suffering from chronic constipation, whose first name was that of a prophet and whose last name was that of a fish—Ezequiel Delfín (Dolphin)—and despite his youth he was taken in as a boarder because the physical signs of his spirituality (extreme emaciation, a deep pallor, delicate bones) and his evident religiosity—in addition to wearing a dark purple tie, breast-pocket handkerchief, and armband, he had a Bible hidden in his baggage, and a scapular peeked out of the folds of his garments—appeared to be a guarantee against any attempt on his part to sully the virtue of the pubescent girl.

And, in fact, in the beginning young Ezequiel Delfín brought nothing but satisfaction to the Bergua family. He had no appetite and nice manners, he paid his *pensión* bills promptly, and was given to such charming gestures as bringing Doña Margarita bunches of violets from time to time, offering Don Sebastián a carnation for his buttonhole, and giving Rosa musical scores and a metronome on her birthday. His shyness, which prevented him from ever speaking to a person without having first been spoken to, and in such a case, of always speaking in a soft voice and with lowered eyes, never looking directly at the person, and his refined behavior and vocabulary greatly pleased the Berguas, who soon became very fond of their boarder, and perhaps in their heart of hearts (a family won over for life to the philosophy of the lesser evil) they began to entertain the notion of eventually promoting him to the elevated status of son-in-law.

Don Sebastián in particular became very attached to him: did he perhaps see in this well-bred traveling salesman that son that his diligent crippled wife had been unable to bear him? One afternoon in December he took him to visit the Hermitage of Saint Rose of Lima, where he saw him toss a gold piece in the well and ask a secret favor, and on a certain torrid summer Sunday he invited him to have an orange sherbet in the arcades of the Plaza San Martín. Because he was so quiet and melancholy, the young man seemed elegant to Don Sebastián. Was he suffering from some mysterious malady of soul or body that was causing him to waste away, some love wound that could not be stanched? Ezequiel Delfín was as silent as the grave about himself, and when on occasion, with all due precaution, the Berguas had offered him a shoulder to cry on and asked him why he always kept so much to himself, being such a young man, why he never went to a party, a movie, why he never laughed, why he so often heaved a deep sigh, with his eyes staring into empty space, he merely blushed and, stammering an apology, ran to shut himself up in the bathroom, where he sometimes spent hours on end, maintaining that he was suffering from constipation. He came and went on his travels in connection with his job, like a veritable sphinx—the family never even managed to find out what sort of company he worked for, what products he sold—and here in Lima, when he wasn't out on the road, he spent his time shut up in his room (reading his Bible or absorbed in his devotions?). Because they were born matchmakers, and because they felt sorry for him, Doña Margarita and Don Sebastián urged him to come downstairs and hear Rosita practice "as a diversion," and he obediently did so: sitting motionless in a corner of the living room, he would listen attentively and applaud politely when she finished. He often accompanied Don Sebastián to morning Mass, and during Holy Week of that year he did the Stations of the Cross with the Berguas. He already seemed like a member of the family at that point.

Hence, the day that Ezequiel, who had just returned from a trip to the North, suddenly burst into sobs in the middle of lunch, startling the other boarders—a justice of the peace from Ancachs, a parish priest from Cajatambo, and two girls from Huanuco who were studying nursing—and spilled the meager portion of lentils that had just been served him onto the table, the Berguas were very concerned. The three of them took him up to his room, Don Sebastián lent him his handkerchief, Doña Margarita made him a cup of verbena-and-mint tea, and Rosa covered his feet with a blanket. Ezequiel Delfín calmed down after a few minutes, apologized for "his weakness," explained that he'd been very nervous lately, that he didn't know why but very often these days, at any hour of the day and no matter where he happened to be, he'd burst into tears all of a sudden. Covered with shame, in a voice that was almost a whisper, he revealed to them that he was often overcome by fits of terror: he would lie awake all night till dawn, all curled up in a ball and dripping with cold sweat, thinking of ghosts and filled with self-pity because he was so lonely. His confession brought tears to Rosa's eyes, and her little lame mother crossed herself. Don Sebastián offered to sleep there in the same bedroom with the terrified young man to comfort and reassure him. Ezequiel Delfín kissed Don Sebastián's hands in gratitude.

An extra bed was set up in the room and diligently made up by Doña Margarita and her daughter. Don Sebastián was then in the prime of life, his fifties, and was in the habit of doing fifty abdominals before getting into bed (he did his exercises before going to bed at night, instead of after getting up in the morning, so as to distinguish himself from the vulgar in this regard as well), but in order not to disturb Ezequiel, he skipped them that night. The nervous young man had retired early, after downing a lovingly prepared bowl of chicken-giblet broth and assuring them that the company of Don Sebastián had already put his mind at rest and that he was sure he'd sleep like a top.

The details of what happened that night were never to be erased from the memory of the gentleman from Ayacucho: they were to haunt him, awake or asleep, till the end of his days, and—who knows?—they were perhaps to continue to torment him in his next reincarnation. He had turned the light out at an early hour, had heard the regular breathing of the sensitive young man in the bed next to him, and, pleased and relieved, had thought to himself: He's dropped off to sleep. He felt himself getting sleepier and sleepier too, and had heard the bells of the cathedral and the uproarious laughter of a drunk somewhere off in the distance. Then he had fallen asleep and peacefully dreamed the most pleasant and reassuring of dreams: in a castle with a pointed tower, on whose walls were hung shields, titles of nobility, parchments with heraldic flowers and family trees tracing his ancestral lineage back to Adam, the Lord of Ayacucho (he himself!) was receiving abundant tribute and fervent homage from hordes of lice-ridden Indians who were thus simultaneously feeding his coffers and his vanity.

Suddenly—had fifteen minutes or three hours gone by?—something that could have been a noise, a presentiment, the faltering footfalls of a spirit, awakened him. In the darkness relieved only by a dim streak of light from the street filtering through the slit between the curtains, he managed to make out a silhouette rising from the bed next to his and silently floating toward the door. Still half asleep, he presumed that the constipated young man was going to the bathroom to try to move his bowels, or that he was feeling bad again, and asked in a low voice: "Ezequiel, are you all right?" Instead of an answer, he heard, very clearly, the bolt on the door being slid home (it was rusty and creaked). He did not understand, sat halfway up, and slightly alarmed, asked again: "Is anything the matter, Ezequiel? Can I help you?" He then was suddenly aware that the young man (cat-men so lightfooted they seem to be everywhere at once) had come back across the room and was now standing right next to his bed, blocking the little streak of light from the window. "Ezequiel, please answer me, what's the matter with you?" he murmured, fumbling about in the dark for the switch of the bedside lamp. At that instant he received the first knife thrust, the deepest jab of all, the one that sank into his chest as though it were butter and pierced a collarbone. He was certain he had screamed, cried for help, and as he tried to defend himself, to free himself of the sheets tangled round his feet, he was surprised that neither his wife nor his daughter nor any of the other boarders came running to his aid. But in fact no one heard anything at all. Later, as the police and the judge reconstructed the gruesome assault, they had all been amazed that Don Sebastián had not been able to disarm the criminal, since he was so robust and Ezequiel so frail. They had no way of knowing that in the bloody shadows the medical detail man had appeared to be possessed of a supernatural strength: Don Sebastián had managed to give only imaginary cries and try to guess the trajectory of the next knife thrust in order to ward it off with his hands.

He received fourteen or fifteen of them (the doctors were of the opinion that the gaping wound in his left buttock might have been—extraordinary coincidences that turn a man's hair white in a single night and make a person believe in God—the result of two blows in exactly the same place), evenly distributed all over his body, with the exception of his face, which—a miracle owed to El Señor de Limpias, as Doña Margarita thought, or to Saint Rose of Lima, as the latter's namesake claimed?—had not received so much as a scratch. The knife, as was learned later, belonged to the Berguas, a razor-sharp blade eight inches long that had mysteriously disappeared from the kitchen a week before and that left the body of the man from Ayacucho with more holes and gashes than that of a hired ruffian.

To what did he owe the fact that he didn't die? To chance, to God's mercy, and (above all) to an even greater quasi-tragedy. No one had heard anything; with fourteen—fifteen—knife wounds in his body, Don Sebastián had just lost consciousness and was slowly bleeding to death in the darkness; and the impulsive young man might have crept down to the street and disappeared forever.

But, like so many famous men in history, a strange caprice was his undoing. Once his victim had ceased to resist him, Ezequiel Delfín threw the knife down and instead of getting dressed got undressed. As naked as the day he was born, he opened the door, crossed the hall, entered Doña Margarita Bergua's room, and without further explanation flung himself on her bed with the unmistakable intention of fornicating with her. Why her? Why try to rape a lady of admittedly noble ancestry, but also in her fifties, with one leg shorter than the other, short and dumpy and, in a word, according to any known aesthetic criteria, undeniably and irredeemably ugly? Why not have attempted, rather, to pluck the forbidden fruit of the adolescent pianist, who, besides being a virgin, had vim, vigor, and vitality, raven hair, and alabaster skin? Why not try to steal into the secret seraglio of the nursing students from Huanuco, who were in their twenties and probably had firm, delectable flesh? It was these humiliating circumstances that led the Judiciary to accept the argument of the attorney for the defense that Ezequiel Delfín was mentally unbalanced and commit him to Larco Herrera instead of sending him to prison.

On receiving the unexpected amorous visit from the young man, Señora Margarita Bergua realized that something very serious was happening. She was a realistic woman and had no illusions as to her charms. "Even in my dreams, nobody tried to rape me, so I knew immediately that that stark-naked man was either utterly mad or a criminal," she declared. And so she defended herself like an enraged lioness: in her testimony she swore by the Virgin Mary that the impetuous intruder had been incapable of inflicting so much as a kiss upon her—and in addition to keeping her honor from being outraged, she had saved her husband's life. For as she fought off the pervert with tooth and nail, elbow and knee, she let out screams and shouts (real ones, in her case) that awoke her daughter and the other boarders. Rosa, the judge from Ancachs, the parish priest from Cajatambo, and the student nurses from Huanuco managed between them to overpower the exhibitionist and tie him up, and then all of them ran to look for Don Sebastián: was he still alive?

It took them nearly an hour to get an ambulance to take him to Arzobispo Loayza Hospital, and it was nearly three hours before the police arrived to rescue Lucho Abril Marroquín from the clutches of the young pianist, who, beside herself with fury (because of the wounds inflicted upon her father? because of the offense to her mother's honor? because perhaps—a human soul with turbid flesh and poisonous secret recesses—of the affront to herself?), was trying to scratch his eyes out and drink his blood. At the police station, the young medical detail man, recovering his usual gentle manner and soft-spoken voice, blushing out of sheer timidity as he spoke, roundly denied the evidence. The Berguas and the boarders were slandering him: he had never attacked anyone, he had never attempted to rape any woman, certainly not a cripple like Margarita Bergua, a lady who, because of her many kindnesses and thoughtful attentions, was—after, naturally, his own wife, that young woman with Italian eyes and musical knees and elbows who came from the country of love and song—the person whom he loved and respected more than anyone else in this world. His serenity, his courtesy, his meekness, the splendid character references given him by his superiors and co-workers at the Bayer Laboratories, the lily-whiteness of his police record, made the guardians of law and order hesitate. Could it be that (fathomless magic spell of deceptive appearances) all this was a plot cooked up by the wife and daughter of the victim and the other boarders against this sensitive young man? The fourth power of the state looked upon this hypothesis with favor and ordered the record to so show.

To further complicate matters and contribute to keeping the city in suspense, the object of the crime, Don Sebastián Bergua, was in no condition to settle the question, for he was lingering between life and death in the public clinic on the Avenue Alfonso Ugarte. He was given copious blood transfusions, which brought many of his compatriots from the Tambo-Ayacucho Club to the very brink of tuberculosis, for the moment they heard about the tragedy they had rushed to the clinic to donate their blood, and these transfusions, plus serums, sutures, disinfections, bandages, nurses on duty at his bedside round the clock, surgeons who reset his bones, rebuilt his organs, and calmed his nerves, exhausted in the space of just a few weeks the last of the family's financial resources (already vastly reduced by inflation and the galloping cost of living). The Berguas were therefore obliged to sell off their bonds at a ridiculously low price, to divide their property and rent it out in bits and pieces and hole up on the second floor, where they were now vegetating.

Don Sebastián managed to escape death, but in the beginning his recovery was apparently not complete enough to lay the suspicions of the police to rest. As a result of the knife wounds, the terror that he had undergone, or the moral sullying of his wife's honor, he was left a mute (and, it was rumored, an idiot as well). He could not utter a single word, he looked at everything and everybody with the lethargic inexpressiveness of a tortoise, and his fingers, too, would not obey him, since he could not (would not?) answer in writing the questions put to him when the insane man's case was tried.

The trial assumed major proportions and the City of Kings held its breath in suspense during the hearings. Lima, Peru—all of mestizo America?—followed the courtroom battle with passionate interest, the forensic disputes, the testimony and counter-testimony of the experts, the arguments of the public prosecutor and the attorney for the defense, a famous jurist who had come especially from Rome, the city of marble, to defend Lucho Abril Marroquín, because the latter was the husband of a little Italian girl who, besides being the legal expert's compatriot, was also his daughter.

The country was divided into two opposing factions. Those convinced of the innocence of the medical detail man—all the newspapers—maintained that Don Sebastián had been the victim of a murder attempt on the part of his wife and offspring, in collusion with the judge from Ancachs, the little parish priest from Cajatambo, and the nursing students from Huanuco, their motives doubtless having been the inheritance and monetary gain. The Roman jurist imperially defended this view, affirming that, having become aware of the gentle madness of Lucho Abril Marroquín, the family and the boarders had hatched a plot to foist the blame for the crime on him (or perhaps to induce him to commit it?). And he continued to adduce arguments in support of this thesis, which the organs of the press then enlarged upon, applauded, and claimed were proven fact: could anyone in his right mind possibly believe that a man would receive fourteen, and perhaps fifteen, knife thrusts in respectful silence? And if, as was only logical to presume, Don Sebastián Bergua had howled in pain, could anyone in his right mind possibly believe that neither the wife, nor the daughter, nor the judge, nor the priest, nor the nurses had heard those cries, given the fact that the walls of the Pensión Colonial were made of canestalks and mud, mere flimsy partitions through which one could hear a mosquito buzzing or a scorpion running about? And how was it possible, given the fact that the young boarders from Huanuco were nursing students with good grades, that they had not managed to give the wounded man first aid and had merely waited, nothing daunted, for the ambulance to arrive while the gentleman lay bleeding to death? And how was it possible that not one of the six adults, seeing that the ambulance was delayed, had had the idea, which should have been obvious even to an oligophrenic, of going to get a taxi, since there was a taxi stand right down the street from the Pensión Colonial on the nearest corner? Wasn't all this odd, devious, revealing?

After having been detained in Lima for three months, the little parish priest from Cajatambo—who had come to the capital intending to stay only four days to arrange to procure a new Christ for the church in his village because rowdy urchins had decapitated with their slingshots the one that had been there before—terrified at the prospect of being found guilty of attempted murder and spending the rest of his days in prison, had a heart attack and died. His death electrified public opinion and had disastrous consequences for the defense; the newspapers now turned their backs on the imported jurist, accused him of being a casuist, a practitioner of bel canto, a colonialist, a strange migratory bird from other shores, and of having caused the death of a good shepherd with his sibylline, anti-Christian insinuations, and the judges (docility of reeds bending with journalistic winds) disqualified him on the grounds that he was a foreigner, deprived him of the right to plead before the country's tribunals, and, in a decision that the newspapers hailed with nationalist ruffles and flourishes, ordered him deported to Italy as an undesirable alien.

The death of the little priest from Cajatambo saved the mother and the daughter and the boarders from probable prison sentences for attempted murder and criminal conspiracy. As the press and public opinion shifted radically, the public prosecutor also began to sympathize with the Berguas, and accepted, as he had at the beginning, the mother's and daughter's version of events. Lucho Abril Marroquín's new attorney, a native-born jurist, adopted an entirely different strategy: he conceded that his client had committed the crimes, but argued that he could in no way be held responsible for his acts, since he was suffering from paropsis and rachitis brought on by anemia, along with schizophrenia and other tendencies pertaining to the domain of mental pathology, as eminent psychiatrists corroborated in amiable depositions. As definite proof that the defendant was mentally deranged, they pointed to the fact that, among the four women in the Pensión Colonial, he had chosen the oldest one and the only one who was crippled. During the final summation by the public prosecutor (dramatic climax that deifies actors and makes spectators shiver with excitement), Don Sebastián, who up to that point had sat silent and bleary-eyed in his wheelchair, as though the trial had nothing to do with him, slowly raised one hand and with eyes suddenly red from the effort, anger, or humiliation, pointed fixedly, for an entire minute as timed by a chronometer (*dixit* a journalist), at Lucho Abril Marroquín. The gesture was judged to be as extraordinary as though the equestrian statue of Simón Bolívar had broken into a gallop . . . The court accepted all the arguments of the public prosecutor, and Lucho Abril Marroquín was shut up in the insane asylum.

The Bergua family never got back on its feet again. Its moral and material downfall dated from this period. Ruined by grasping medical and legal practitioners, they were forced to give up the private piano lessons (and as a consequence the ambition to make Rosa a world-famous concert artist) and reduce their standard of living to extremes that bordered on such pernicious habits as fasting and closing their eyes to filth. The enormous old house grew even older, and little by little dust accumulated everywhere, spiders invaded it, and termites devoured it; its clients became fewer and fewer, and it became a lower- and lower-class *pensión*, finally reaching the point of taking in maids and street porters. It touched bottom the day a beggar came knocking at the door, asking the shocking question: "Is this the Colonial *Flophouse*?"

And so, as the days, the months, followed one upon the other, thirty years went by.

The Bergua family appeared to have become habituated to its mediocrity, when suddenly something happened (an atomic bomb that early one morning totally destroys Japanese cities) that caused a flurry of excitement in the *pensión*. It had been years since the radio had worked, and years since the tight family budget had permitted the purchase of a daily newspaper. News of the outside world thus reached the Berguas' ears only rarely and indirectly, by way of the comments and the gossip of their uncultured guests.

But that afternoon (what an odd twist of fate) a truck driver from Castrovirreina let out a burst of vulgar laughter, accompanied by a greenish gob of spit, muttered: "That nut is really the limit!" and flung down on the badly scratched little table in the parlor the copy of *Ultima Hora* that he had just been reading. The ex-pianist picked it up and leafed through it. Suddenly (cheeks as deathly pale as a woman who has just been the victim of a vampire's kiss) she ran to her room, shouting for her mother to come at once. The two of them read and reread the crumpled news item together, and then, taking turns, they read it again, at the top of their voices, to Don Sebastián, who beyond the shadow of a doubt understood, for he immediately underwent one of those dramatic crises of his that caused him to hiccup violently, break into a sweat, burst into loud sobs, and writhe like a man possessed.

What was this piece of news that so alarmed this crepuscular family?

At dawn the day before, in a crowded ward of the Víctor Larco Herrero Psychiatric Hospital, in Magdalena del Mar, a ward of the state who had spent so many long years behind those walls that he should have been pensioned off by now had slit the throat of a male nurse with a scalpel, strung up a catatonic old man who slept in the bed next to his, thus causing him to strangle to death, and escaped to the city by athletically leaping over the wall of La Costanera. His behavior was most surprising, since he had always been remarkably peaceable and had never shown the least sign of being in an ugly mood and never been heard even to raise his voice. His one and only noteworthy occupation, in thirty years, had been to officiate at imaginary Masses in honor of El Señor de Limpias and to distribute invisible hosts to nonexistent communicants. Before making his escape from the hospital, Lucho Abril Marroquín—who had just reached the most distinguished age given a man to enjoy on this earth: his fiftieth birthday—had penned a most polite farewell letter: "I am very sorry, but I find myself obliged to flee these precincts. A fire awaits me in an old house in

Lima, where a crippled woman whose passion blazes like a torch and her family mortally offend God. I have been assigned the mission of extinguishing the flames."

Would he do so? Would he extinguish these flames? Would this man, come to life once again from the depths of the years, appear for the second time to plunge the Berguas in horror as he had now plunged them into terror? What fate lay in store for this panic-stricken family from Ayacucho?

Thirteen.

The memorable week began

with a picturesque episode (without the violence that had marked the encounter with the Argentine barbecue chefs), of which I was a witness and more or less a protagonist. Genaro Jr. spent all his time thinking up innovations for the programs, and one day he decided that we should include interviews in the newscasts to liven them up a little. He set Pascual and me to work, and from then on we began to broadcast a daily interview dealing with some current event on the Panamericana evening news report. This meant more work for the News Department (with no raise in salary), but I didn't regret it, because it was fun. As I put questions to cabaret entertainers and members of parliament, soccer players and child prodigies, in the studio on the Calle Belén or in front of a tape recorder, I learned that everyone, without exception, could be turned into a subject of a short story.

Before the picturesque episode occurred, the most curious person I interviewed was a Venezuelan bullfighter. He had been a tremendous success that season in the Plaza de Acho. Following his first corrida, he had been awarded several ears, and at his second, after a miraculous *faena,* he was awarded a hoof and the crowd bore him on their shoulders in triumph from the Rímac to his hotel on the Plaza San Martín. But at his third and last corrida—he had scalped his own tickets for it for astronomical prices—he didn't even get close enough to the bulls to see them, since he was seized with a deerlike panic and ran from them all afternoon; he didn't make even one decent pass at them and went in for the kill so clumsily that on his second bull of the day he was given four warnings. There had been a major riot in the stands: the indignant spectators had tried to burn down the Plaza de Acho and lynch the Venezuelan, who, amid deafening jeers and boos and a hail of cushions, had had to be escorted to his hotel by the Guardia Civil. The next morning, a few hours before he was to take the plane, I interviewed him in a little reception room in the Hotel Bolívar. I was dumfounded when I realized that he was less intelligent than the bulls he fought and almost as incapable as they were of expressing himself in words. He was unable to put a coherent sentence together, his verb tenses were all wrong, his manner of coordinating his ideas made one think of tumors, aphasia, monkey men. And the form in which they were uttered was no less extraordinary than the content: his speech habits were most unfortunate, an intonation full of diminutives and apocopes and shading off, during his frequent mental vacuums, into zoological grunts.

The Mexican I was assigned to interview on the Monday of this memorable week was, on the contrary, a lucid thinker and an eloquent speaker. He was the editor and publisher of a review, he had written books on the Mexican revolution, he was visiting Peru as the head of a delegation of economists and was staying at the Bolívar. He agreed to come to the radio station and I went to get him myself. He was a tall, erect, well-dressed gentleman with white hair who must have been close to his sixties. He was accompanied by his wife, a slight woman with bright eyes who was wearing a little hat with flowers. We blocked out the interview on our way from the hotel to the station and it was recorded in fifteen minutes. Genaro Jr. was terribly upset because, in answer to one question, the economist and historian violently attacked military dictatorships (we were suffering from one in Peru at the time, headed by a certain Odría).

The unexpected happened as I was escorting the couple back to the Bolívar. It was noon and the Calle Belén and the Plaza San Martín were jammed with people. We were walking along the street, with the husband in the center, his wife on his right, and me on his left on the curb side.

We had just passed by Radio Central, and simply to make conversation I was telling the important man once again that the interview had turned out magnificently, when all of a sudden I was definitely interrupted by the tiny voice of the Mexican lady. "Jesus, Mary, I'm about to faint . . ."

I looked at her: she was haggard, and blinking her eyes and moving her mouth in a most peculiar way. But what was really surprising was the economist-historian's reaction. On hearing his wife's warning, he glanced swiftly at her, and then at me, with a bewildered expression on his face, whereupon he immediately looked straight ahead of him again and, instead of stopping, quickened his pace. The Mexican lady was now beside me, grimacing. I managed to grab her by the arm just as she was about to collapse to the sidewalk. As she was such a frail little thing, I was able fortunately to hold her up and help her along, as the important man took off in great long strides, leaving me with the delicate task of dragging his wife along the street. People moved aside to let us by, stopped to stare at us, and at one point—we had gotten as far as the Cine Colón and, in addition to making faces, the little Mexican lady was now leaking spittle, mucus, and tears—I heard a cigarette vendor say: "What's more, she's pissing all over herself." It was true: the wife of the economist-historian (who had crossed La Colmena and disappeared amid the crowd milling about outside the doors of the Bolívar bar) was leaving a yellow trail behind her. When we reached the corner, I had no choice but to pick her up and, a gallant, spectacular cynosure of all eyes, carry her the remaining fifty yards, amid drivers honking, policemen whistling, and people pointing at us. The little Mexican lady writhed violently in my arms without letting up for a second and went on making faces, and my hands and nose told me that she was probably now doing something worse than urinating. From her throat there came an atrophied, intermittent sound. On entering the Bolívar, I heard someone curtly order me: "Room 301." It was the important man, half hidden behind some drapes. The moment he'd given me that order, he made off again, heading nimbly for the elevator, and as we went upstairs he did not deign to look at me or his consort even once, as though he did not wish to appear to be intruding. The elevator operator helped me carry the lady to the room. But the minute we'd put her down on the bed, the important man literally shoved us to the door and slammed it in our faces, without saying either thanks or goodbye: there was a sour look on his face at that moment.

"He's not a bad husband," Pedro Camacho was to explain to me later. "He's simply a very sensitive person with a great fear of looking ridiculous."

That afternoon I was to read a story that I'd just finished, "Aunt Eliana," to Aunt Julia and Javier. *El Comercio* never did publish the story about the levitating kids and I had consoled myself by writing another one, based on something that had happened in my family. Eliana was one of the many aunts who appeared at our house when I was little, and she was my favorite because she brought me chocolates and sometimes took me to tea at the Cream Rica. Everyone used to make fun of her fondness for sweets, and at our tribal gatherings there was much tongue-wagging about how she spent all her salary as a secretary on gooey pies, crusty croissants, fluffy sponge cakes, and thick chocolate at the Tiendecita Blanca. She was a plump, affectionate, jolly, talkative girl, and I used to come to her defense when people in the family would remark to each other behind her back that she was going to be an old maid if she didn't watch out. One day Aunt Eliana mysteriously stopped coming to visit us and the family never mentioned her name again. I must have been six or seven years old at the time, and I remember being suspicious of the answers I got from my parents when I asked about her: she'd gone off on a trip, she was sick, she'd be dropping by any day now. Some five years later the entire family suddenly appeared in mourning dress, and that night, at my grandparents' house, I learned that they had been to the funeral of Aunt Eliana, who had just died of cancer. I then learned what the mystery had been all about. Just as it appeared that Aunt Eliana was doomed to be a spinster for the rest of her life, she had unexpectedly married a Chinese, the owner of a grocery store in Jesús María, and the whole clan, beginning with her own parents, had been so horrified by this scandal—I had the impression at the time that what was so scandalous was the fact that the husband was Chinese, but I have now deduced that his principal taint was that he was a grocer—that they had decided to pretend she no longer existed and had never visited or received her from that day on. But when she died they forgave her—at heart, we were a sentimental family—attended her wake and her funeral, and shed many a tear for her.

My story was the monologue of a little boy lying in bed trying to unravel the mystery of his aunt's disappearance, and, as an epilogue, her wake. It was a "social" story, full of anger against the parents and their prejudices. I had written it in a couple of weeks and talked about it so much to Aunt Julia and Javier that they finally capitulated and asked me to read it to them. But before doing so that Monday afternoon, I told them what had happened that morning with the little Mexican lady and the important man. It was an error for which I paid dearly, since they found this tale much more amusing than my story.

Aunt Julia was now in the habit of coming down to join me for the evening at Panamericana. We had discovered that this was the safest place, since Pascual and Big Pablito were in on our secret and we could count on their complicity. She would appear after five, the hour when things began to quiet down around the place: the Genaros had gone home, and almost no one came prowling about the shack. My co-workers, by tacit agreement, would ask permission to "go have a cup of coffee," so that Aunt Julia and I could hug and kiss each other and talk alone. Sometimes I would get to work writing and she would sit reading a magazine or chatting with Javier, who invariably came up to join us around seven. We had come to form an inseparable group, and in this little room with its thin plasterboard walls my romance with Aunt Julia had come to have a marvelous naturalness. We could hold hands or kiss and nobody paid any attention. That made us happy. Shutting ourselves up inside the shack was to be free, to be ourselves, we could love each other, talk about what mattered most to us, and feel surrounded by an aura of understanding. To go outside beyond these narrow limits was to enter a hostile domain, where we were forced to lie and to hide.

"Is it all right to call this our love nest?" Aunt Julia asked me. "Or is that *huachafo* too?"

"Of course it's *huachafo*, and it's simply not permissible to call it that," I answered. "But we could name it Montmartre."

We played teacher and pupil and I explained to her what things were *huachafo*, what things it was not permissible to say or do, and I subjected her reading matter to an inquisitorial censorship, placing all her favorite authors on the forbidden list, beginning with Frank Yerby and ending with Corín Tellado. We had a great time and laughed like fools over this *huachafo* game, and every once in a while Javier would join in, with fervent dialectical flourishes.

Pascual and Big Pablito were also present during my reading of "Aunt Eliana," because they happened to be there at the time and I didn't have the nerve to chase them out, a fortunate turn of events for me as it turned out, since they were the only ones who praised my story, even though their enthusiasm was slightly suspect, inasmuch as they were my subordinates. Javier maintained that it lacked verisimilitude, that nobody would believe that a family would ostracize a girl merely because she married a Chinese, and assured me that if her husband was a black or an Indian the story could be salvaged. Aunt Julia dealt me a mortal blow by telling me that it struck her as melodramatic and that certain words, such as "tremulous" and "sobbing," sounded *huachafo* to her. I was just launching into a defense of "Aunt Eliana" when I spied my cousin Nancy in the doorway of the shack. One look sufficed to tell me what had brought her there.

"The family's discovered what's going on, and they're up in arms," she blurted out.

Smelling a bit of juicy gossip, Pascual and Big Pablito were all ears. I kept my cousin from going on with her story, asked Pascual to get the nine o'clock news bulletin ready, and the four of us, Nancy and Javier, Aunt Julia and I, went out for coffee. As we sat at a table in the Bransa, she went into more details. She had been in the bathroom shampooing her hair and had overheard a telephone conversation between her mother and Aunt Jesús. A cold chill had run down her spine on hearing the words "the pair of them" and discovering that they were talking about Aunt Julia and me. It wasn't very clear what the conversation was all about, except that they'd known about us for some time, because at one point Aunt Laura had said: "Can you imagine: even Camunchita saw them shamelessly holding hands on Olivar de San Isidro" (that was quite true, we'd done exactly that, just one afternoon, many months ago). When she came out of the bathroom ("trembling all over," as she put it), Nancy had found herself face to face with her mother and had tried to pretend she had no idea what was up, her ears were ringing from the noise of the hair drier, she couldn't hear one word, but Aunt Laura shut her up, gave her a dressing-down, and called her "a go-between for that fallen woman."

"By a 'fallen woman' she meant me?" Aunt Julia asked, more curious than angry.

"Yes, she meant you," my cousin answered, blushing. "They think you're the one who's responsible for starting the whole thing."

"That's true, I'm a minor, I was peacefully studying for my law degree, and then . . ." I said, but nobody laughed at my joke.

"If they find out I've told you, they'll kill me," Nancy said. "Swear to me you won't say a word."

Her parents had solemnly given her notice that if she committed the slightest indiscretion they wouldn't let her out of the house for a year, not even to attend Mass. They had given her such a stern lecture that she'd even hesitated whether she should tell us what had happened. The family had known everything since the very beginning and hadn't said a word, thinking that it was simply an inconsequential flirtation on the part of a flighty woman who wanted to add an exotic prize, an adolescent, to the list of amorous game she had bagged. But since Aunt Julia had not scrupled to parade about the streets and public squares hand in hand with the lad, and more and more friends and relatives had learned of the romance—even the grandparents knew what was going on, thanks to a bit of gossip passed on to them by Aunt Celia—the whole thing had become a scandal and something that was bound to harm the youngster (that is to say, me), who doubtless had lost all interest in studying ever since the divorcée had turned his head, and hence the family had decided to intervene.

"And what are they going to do to save me?" I asked, still not too panic-stricken at this point.

"Write to your folks," Nancy said. "Your two oldest uncles—Uncle Jorge and Uncle Lucho—already have."

My parents were living in the U.S., and my father was a stern man I'd always been very afraid of. I'd been brought up far away from him, with my mother and her family, and when my parents were reconciled and I went to live with him, we had never gotten along well together. He was conservative and authoritarian, given to cold rages, and if it was true that they'd written to him, the news would set him off like a bombshell exploding.

Aunt Julia grabbed my hand under the table. "You've turned deathly pale, Varguitas. This time you've got a really good subject for a short story."

"What you need to do is to keep your head screwed on straight and not go off the deep end," Javier said, trying to help me recover from the shock. "Don't panic, and let's plan the best possible strategy for facing the avalanche."

"They're furious with you, too," Nancy warned him. "They're calling you something terrible too, a, a—"

"A pander?" Aunt Julia smiled. And then, turning to me, she said with a sad look in her eyes: "What matters most to me is that they're going to separate us and I won't ever be able to see you again."

"That's *huachafo,* and can't be said like that," I told her.

"How well they've hidden their real feelings," Aunt Julia said. "Neither my sister, nor my brother-in-law, nor any of your relatives has even led me to suspect that they knew and that they hated me. The hypocrites: they've always been so affectionate with me."

"For the time being, the two of you have to stop seeing each other," Javier said. "Julia should go out with other men, and you should ask other girls out on dates. Let the family think you've had a fight."

Discouraged, Aunt Julia and I agreed that that was the only solution. But when Nancy left—we swore to her that we'd never betray her—followed by Javier, and Aunt Julia walked back with me to Panamericana, as we went down the Calle Belén, wet with misty rain, hand in hand, with our heads drooping dispiritedly, we both knew, without any need to say so, that such a strategy risked turning what was a lie into the truth. If we didn't see each other, if we each went out with other people, sooner or later it would all be over between us. But we agreed to phone each other every day, at precise hours that we set, and gave each other a long, lingering kiss on the mouth as we said goodbye.

As I went up to my shack in the rickety elevator, I felt, as I had at other times, an inexplicable desire to tell my troubles to Pedro Camacho. It was like a premonition, because the principal collaborators of the Bolivian scriptwriter—Luciano Pando, Josefina Sánchez, and Puddler—were waiting for me in the office, absorbed in an animated conversation with Big Pablito as Pascual padded out the news bulletin with all sorts of catastrophes (he had never obeyed my orders forbidding him to include items about dead people, naturally). They waited patiently while I gave Pascual a hand with the last-minute news, and when he and Big Pablito had said good night to us and left the four of us alone in the shack, they looked at each other in embarrassment before saying anything. It was quite plain that what they wanted to talk to me about was the artist.

"You're his best friend and that's why we've come to you," Luciano Pando murmured. He was a walleyed little man in his sixties, all bent over, who wore a greasy muffler day and night, winter and summer. He had on the only suit I'd ever seen him in, a brown one with little blue pinstripes, in tatters from being cleaned and pressed countless times. His right shoe had a tear across the instep through which you could see his sock. "It has to do with a very delicate matter. You've doubtless already guessed . . ."

"Not really, Don Luciano," I said to him. "Are you referring to Pedro Camacho? Yes, we're friends, it's true, although as you already know, he's a person one never really gets to know. Is there something wrong?"

He nodded, but then just stood there staring at his shoes and not saying a word, as though overwhelmed by the thought of what he was about to say. I looked questioningly at Josefina and Puddler, who were also standing there motionless, with grave expressions on their faces.

"We're doing this out of affection and gratitude," Josefina Sánchez trilled in her lovely velvet voice. "Because no one can possibly know, young man, how much we who work in this miserably paid profession owe to Pedro Camacho."

"We've always been made to feel we were fifth wheels, nobody thought our talents were worth two cents, we had such an inferiority complex we took ourselves to be worthless trash," Puddler said in a voice so filled with emotion that the thought crossed my mind all of a sudden that Pedro Camacho had met with some sort of accident. "Thanks to him, we discovered that ours was an artistic profession."

"But you're talking about him as though he were dead," I said.

"Because what would people do without us?" Josefina Sánchez said, citing the words of her idol without having heard what I'd just said. "Who else gives them the illusions and emotions that help them to go on living?"

She was a woman who had been given that beautiful voice of hers more or less to make up for the collection of awkward mistakes her body represented. It was impossible to guess exactly how old she was, though she had no doubt passed the half-century mark. Her hair was naturally dark, but she bleached it with peroxide and it peeked out, like yellow straw, from beneath a pomegranate-colored turban and hung down over her ears, without, unfortunately, hiding them altogether, for they were enormous, protruding from her head like dish antennas avidly picking up all the world's sounds. But her most striking feature was her double chin, a sac of loose folds of skin that drooped down over her multicolored blouses. She had a thick fuzz on her upper lip that might well have been described as a mustache, and she had fallen into the dreadful habit of fingering it as she spoke. Her legs were swathed in elastic support hose like that worn by soccer players, because she suffered from varicose veins. At any other time, her visit would have filled me with curiosity. But that night I was altogether preoccupied with my own problems.

"I know very well what all of you owe Pedro Camacho," I said impatiently. "There are good reasons why his serials are the most popular ones all over the country."

I saw them exchange looks and screw up their courage. "That's precisely the point," Luciano Pando finally said, anxious and upset. "In the beginning, we didn't pay any attention. We thought they were just careless slips, the sort of absentminded mistakes that everybody makes. And especially somebody who works from sunup to sundown every single day."

"But what is it exactly that's happening to Pedro Camacho?" I interrupted him. "I don't have any idea what you're talking about, Don Luciano."

"The serials, young man," Josefina Sánchez murmured, as

though committing a sacrilege. "They're becoming more and more bizarre."

"We actors and technicians are taking turns answering the telephone at Radio Central to fend off protests from the listeners," Puddler chimed in. His hair looked like shiny porcupine bristles, as though he'd applied great quantities of brilliantine to them; as usual, he was wearing a pair of stevedore's overalls, and shoes without laces, and he appeared to be on the point of bursting into tears. "So that the Genaros don't boot him out, sir."

"You know very well that he doesn't have a cent to his name and lives from hand to mouth like the rest of us," Luciano Pando added. "What would happen to him if they kick him out? He'd die of hunger!"

"And what about us?" Josefina Sánchez said proudly. "What would become of us without him?"

They all began to talk at once, telling me everything with a wealth of details. The inconsistencies (the "bloopers," as Luciano Pando put it) had begun about two months before, but at the beginning they were so trivial that probably only the actors noticed them. They hadn't said a word to Pedro Camacho because, knowing what he was like, nobody had dared to, and furthermore, for quite a long time they wondered whether he might not be playing deliberate tricks. But in the last three weeks things had become much more serious.

"It's all turned into a hopeless mess, I assure you, young man," Josefina Sánchez said disconsolately. "The serials have all gotten mixed up with each other, to the point that even we can't untangle one from the other."

"Hipólito Lituma has always been a sergeant in the Guardia Civil, the terror of the malefactors of El Callao, in the ten o'clock serial," Luciano Pando put in, all upset. "But in the last three days that's turned out to be the name of the judge in the four o'clock serial. His name used to be Pedro Barreda. Just to give you one example."

"And now Don Pedro Barreda's talking about exterminating rats, because they devoured his little girl," Josefina Sánchez said, her eyes brimming with tears. "When, before, it was Don Federico Téllez Unzátegui's baby daughter."

"You can imagine what a terrible time we have of it at recording sessions," Puddler stammered. "Saying and doing things that don't make any sense at all."

"And there's just no way of straightening out the whole mess," Josefina Sánchez murmured. "Because you've seen with your own eyes how Señor Camacho rules over the programs with an iron hand. He doesn't allow us to change even a comma. Otherwise, he falls into terrible fits of rage."

"He's exhausted—that's the explanation," Luciano Pando said, shaking his head sadly. "Nobody can work twenty hours a day and still think straight. He needs a vacation to get back to his old self."

"You get along well with the Genaros," Josefina Sánchez said to me. "Couldn't you have a talk with them? Just simply tell them he's exhausted and ask them to give him a few weeks' rest?"

"The hardest part will be convincing him to take them," Luciano Pando said. "But things can't go on like this. If they do, the Genaros will end up firing him."

"People keep calling the station all the time," Batán said. "It takes real genius to think up ways of evading their questions. And the other day there was even something about the whole business in *La Crónica*."

I didn't tell them that Genaro Sr. already knew and had asked me to have a talk with Pedro Camacho. We agreed that I should sound out Genaro Jr., and then, depending on his reaction, we would decide whether it was advisable for them to come see him themselves to speak up in the scriptwriter's defense in the name of all his co-workers. I thanked them for their confidence and tried to bolster their morale a little: Genaro Jr. had a more modern outlook than Genaro Sr. and was more understanding, and surely he could be persuaded to give Pedro Camacho a vacation. We went on talking as I turned out the lights and locked the shack. We shook hands and said goodbye on the Calle Belén. I saw the scriptwriter's three homely, generous-hearted co-workers disappear down the empty street in the misty rain.

I didn't sleep a wink that night. As usual, I found my dinner all ready and being kept warm for me in the oven at my grandparents', but I couldn't get a single mouthful down (and in order not to worry my granny, I threw the breaded steak and rice out of sight in the garbage can). The little old couple were in bed but still awake, and when I went into their room to give them a good-night kiss, I eyed them as closely as a police detective, trying to discover the slightest fleeting expression on their faces that would betray the fact that they were upset by my scandalous romance. Nothing, not a sign: they were affectionate and solicitous; my grandfather asked me about one of the words in his crossword puzzle. But they told me the good news: my mama had written that she and my papa would be coming down to Lima for a vacation very soon, and would send word as to the exact date of their arrival. They couldn't show me the letter because one of the aunts had taken it home with her. There was no question about it: this was the result of the traitorous letters the family had sent them about my romance. My father had doubtless said: "We're going down to Peru and straighten things out." And my mother: "How could Julia have possibly done a thing like that!" (She and Aunt Julia had been friends when my family lived in Bolivia and I hadn't yet reached the age of reason.)

I slept in a tiny little room, jam-packed with books, valises, and trunks in which my grandparents kept their memorabilia, a great many photographs of their long-ago splendor, when they had a large cotton plantation in Camaná, when grandfather played at being a pioneer farmer-settler in Santa Cruz de la Sierra, when he was consul in Cochabamba or prefect in Piura. Lying on my back in bed in the darkness, I thought a long time about Aunt Julia; sooner or later, in one way or another, they'd manage to separate us. It made me very angry and the whole thing seemed terribly stupid and shabby, and then all of a sudden the image of Pedro Camacho came to my mind. I thought of all the telephone calls back and forth between aunts and uncles and cousins about Aunt Julia and me, and I also began hearing in my imagination all the calls from radio listeners all upset and confused by those characters who'd suddenly changed names and leapt from the three o'clock serial to the five o'clock one, and by those episodes that were becoming as hopelessly tangled as jungle vines, and I tried my best to guess what could be going on in the scriptwriter's labyrinthine brain, but I didn't think it was the least bit funny; on the contrary, I was touched to think of the actors at Radio Central conspiring with the sound engineers, the secretaries, the doormen, to intercept the calls in order to keep the artist from being fired. I was touched that Luciano Pando, Josefina Sánchez, and Puddler had thought that I, a real fifth wheel, could influence the Genaros. How little they must think of themselves, what miserable salaries they must earn, if I seemed to them to be an important person by comparison! And every so often I was overcome with an irresistible desire to see, touch, kiss Aunt Julia at that very moment. Then finally I saw day break and heard the dogs barking at dawn.

I was at my desk in the shack at Panamericana earlier than usual that morning, and when Pascual and Big Pablito arrived at eight, I had already written the bulletins, read all the newspapers, and annotated and marked in red all the news items to be plagiarized. As I did all these things, I kept watching the clock. Aunt Julia called me at exactly the hour we'd agreed on.

"I didn't close my eyes all night long," she murmured in a faint voice I could barely hear. "I love you very much, Varguitas."

"I love you too, with all my heart," I whispered, feeling indignant on seeing Pascual and Big Pablito move closer so as to be able to hear better. "I didn't sleep at all either, thinking about you."

"You can't imagine how nice my sister and my brother-in-law were to me," Aunt Julia said. "We stayed up late playing cards. It's hard to believe that they know, that they're plotting against us."

"They are, though," I told her. "My parents have sent word that they're coming to Lima. And that's the only possible reason—they never travel at this time of year."

She didn't answer, and in my mind's eye I could see her on the other end, looking sad, furious, disappointed. I told her again that I loved her.

"I'll phone you again at four, as we agreed," she finally said. "I'm at the Chinese grocery store on the corner and there's a line waiting. Ciao."

I went down to Genaro Jr.'s office, but he wasn't there. I left a message for him that there was an urgent matter I needed to discuss with him immediately, and just to be doing something, to fill up in some way or other the emptiness I felt, I went to the university. It was the day of my class in penal law, taught by a professor who had always struck me as a character straight out of a short story. A perfect combination of satyriasis and coprolalia, he looked at his girl students as though he were undressing them and used anything and everything as an excuse for double entendres and obscene remarks. When one girl, who was very flat-chested, answered a question well, he congratulated her, savoring the word: "You're very *synthetic*, señorita," and on commenting on one article in the Code, he launched into a peroration on venereal diseases.

When I went back to the radio station, Genaro Jr. was waiting for me in his office. "I trust you're not here to ask me for a raise," he warned me the moment I entered the door. "We're on the edge of bankruptcy."

"I want to talk to you about Pedro Camacho," I said, to set his mind at ease on that score.

"Did you know he's started to do all sorts of outrageous things?" he said to me, as though laughing at a good joke. "He's been shifting his characters around from one serial to another, changing their names, mixing up all the plots, and gradually turning all the stories into one. A stroke of genius, don't you agree?"

"Well, I *have* heard what he's up to," I said, disconcerted by his enthusiasm. "As a matter of fact, I talked with the actors just last night. They're worried about him. He works much too hard, and they think he's in danger of collapsing from exhaustion. You might very well lose the goose that laid the golden eggs. Why not give him a little vacation so he can rest up a bit?"

"Give Camacho a vacation?" the impresario said in a shocked tone of voice. "Was he the one who suggested such a thing?"

No, I told him, it was the scriptwriter's co-workers who had suggested it.

"They're tired of working as hard as he wants them to and want to get rid of him for a few days," he said. "It would be insane to give him a vacation right now." He picked up a handful of papers from the desk and waved them triumphantly in the air. "We've beaten the record for the number of listeners again this month. In other words, his idea of tying the stories together works. My father's worried about these existentialist innovations, but they produce results—the surveys are right here to prove it." He laughed again. "So, as long as the listeners like what he's doing, we'll just have to put up with his eccentricities."

I didn't press the point, so as not to say the wrong thing. And after all, wasn't it quite possible that Genaro Jr. was right? Couldn't it very well be that the Bolivian scriptwriter had carefully planned every last one of these inconsistencies? I didn't feel like going home and decided to go on a spending spree. I persuaded the cashier at

Radio Panamericana to give me an advance on my salary, then went straight from the station to Pedro Camacho's cubicle to invite him to lunch. He was typing away like a madman, naturally. He accepted my invitation without enthusiasm, warning me that he didn't have much time.

We went to a typically Peruvian restaurant, behind the Colegio de la Immaculada on the Jirón Chancay, where the specialty of the house was traditional dishes of Arequipa that, I told him, might perhaps remind him of *picantes*, the famous Bolivian stews with fiery hot peppers. But the artist, faithful to his usual spartan diet, ordered only a bowl of consommé with egg and a purée of red beans that he barely tasted. He skipped dessert altogether, and with a flood of grandiloquent words that left the waiters dumfounded protested vehemently when they didn't properly prepare his verbena-and-mint tea.

"I'm having a bad time of it these days," I said to him after we had ordered. "My family's discovered my romance with your compatriot, and since she's older than I am and a divorcée, they're furious. They're going to take steps to separate us and I'm feeling very bitter about it."

"My compatriot?" the scriptwriter said in a surprised tone of voice. "Are you having an affair of the heart with an Argentine—pardon me—a Bolivian woman?"

I reminded him that he knew Aunt Julia, that we'd visited him in his room at La Tapada and shared his evening meal with him there, that I'd already told him about my love problems and that he'd prescribed prunes eaten on an empty stomach and anonymous letters as the cure. I did so deliberately, going into details, and observing him closely.

He listened to me very attentively, with a grave expression on his face, not blinking an eye. "It's not a bad thing if one is confronted with such contretemps," he said, sipping his first spoonful of consommé. "Suffering is a good teacher."

Whereupon he changed the subject, holding forth at length on the art of cooking and the necessity of being moderate in one's eating habits in order to maintain one's spiritual health. He assured me that consuming too much fat, starch, and sugar numbed people's moral sensibilities and inclined them toward crime and vice.

"Conduct a statistical survey of the people you know," he advised me. "You'll find that it's fat people above all who turn out to be perverts. On the other hand, you'll see that there's no such thing as a thin person with evil proclivities."

Though he was doing his best to hide the fact, he was ill at ease. He was not holding forth with his usual sincerity and heartfelt conviction, but, quite obviously, simply rattling on, his mind preoccupied by troubles he was trying to hide. A look of anxiety, fear, shame lurked in his tiny bulging eyes, and every once in a while he bit his lips. His long hair was full of dandruff, and as his neck danced back and forth in his shirt collar, I discovered that he was wearing a little medal around it that he kept fingering from time to time. "A most miraculous man: Nuestro Señor de Limpias," he explained, showing it to me. His black suit coat drooped from his shoulders and he looked pale. I had decided I wouldn't mention the serials, but all of a sudden, when I saw that he didn't even remember Aunt Julia or any of the conversations we'd had about her, I was seized with a morbid curiosity. We had finished the consommé with egg, and were drinking dark *chicha* as we waited for the main dish.

"I was talking with Genaro Jr. about you just this morning," I said in as casual a tone of voice as possible. "Good news: according to the ad-agency surveys, the number of people tuned in to your serials has gone up again this month. Even the stones are listening to them."

I noted that he stiffened, turned his eyes away, and began rapidly rolling up his napkin and unrolling it, blinking continuously. I hesitated as to whether I should pursue the subject further, but my curiosity got the better of me. "Genaro Jr. thinks that the increase in the number of listeners is due to your idea of mixing up the characters of different serials, of linking up the various plots," I told him, whereupon he dropped the napkin, his eyes searched mine, and he turned white as a sheet. "He thinks it's brilliant," I hastened to add.

As the artist just sat there staring at me, not saying a word, I went on talking, hearing my voice stammering. I spoke of the avant-garde, of experimentation. I cited or invented authors who, I assured him, had caused a sensation in Europe by introducing innovations very much like his: changing their characters' identity in the middle of the story, deliberately creating glaring inconsistencies to keep the reader in suspense. They had brought the bean puree and I began to eat, happy to be able to stop talking and lower my eyes so as not to have to watch the Bolivian scriptwriter getting more and more upset. We sat there in silence for some time as I ate and he stirred the bean puree and the grains of rice round and round on his plate with his fork.

"Something embarrassing is happening to me these days," I finally heard him say in a very low voice, as though talking to himself. "I'm losing track of where I am in my scripts, I'm not sure of what I'm doing, and confusions creep in." He looked at me in anguish. "I know that you're a loyal young man, a friend who can be trusted. Not a word of any of this to the merchants!"

I feigned surprise, overwhelmed him with assurances of my affection for him. He was not at all his usual self, but rather, a man in torment, insecure, vulnerable, his face a sickly green, with beads of sweat gleaming on his forehead.

He raised his fingers to his temples. "My head is a boiling volcano of ideas, of course," he declared. "It's my memory that's treacherous. That business about the names, I mean. I'm telling you this in all confidence, my friend. I'm not the one who's mixing them up; they're getting mixed up all by themselves. And when I realize what's going on, it's too late. I have to perform a juggling act to get them back in their proper places, to invent all sorts of clever reasons to account for all the shifting around. A compass that can't tell the north from the south can lead to grave, grave consequences."

I told him that he was exhausted, that nobody could work at the pace he did without destroying himself, that he simply had to take a vacation.

"A vacation? Not till I'm in my grave," he bristled, as though I'd insulted him.

But a moment later he humbly confessed that when he'd become aware of what he referred to as his "lapses of memory," he'd tried to set up a system of index cards. But that turned out to be impossible, he didn't even have the time to look back over the programs that had already been broadcast: every hour of his working day was taken up producing new scripts. "If I stop, it would be the end of the world," he murmured. And why couldn't his co-workers help him? Why couldn't he go to them when such doubts overcame him?

"I could never do that," he answered. "They'd lose all respect for me. They're simply raw material, my soldiers, and if I make a terrible mistake, it's their duty to follow my lead and make the same mistake."

He abruptly interrupted our dialogue to lecture the waiters about his verbena-and-mint tea, which he maintained was insipid, and then we had to rush back to the station, practically at a run, because it was time for the three o'clock serial. As we said goodbye, I told him I'd do anything I possibly could to help him.

"The one thing I ask of you is not to say one word to anyone," he said. And then, with his icy little smile, he added: "Don't worry: grave troubles are cured by grave remedies."

Back in my office up in the shack, I looked through the afternoon papers, circled the news items to crib for the bulletins, arranged for a six o'clock interview with a neurosurgeon doing historical research who had performed a cranial trepanation with Inca instruments lent him by the Museum of Anthropology. At three-thirty, I began eyeing the clock and the telephone, alternately. Aunt Julia called at four o'clock on the dot. Pascual and Big Pablito hadn't come back to the office yet.

"My sister talked to me at lunchtime," she said in a gloomy voice. "She told me the scandal's too serious for the family to ignore, that your parents are coming down to scratch my eyes out. She asked me to go back to Bolivia. What can I do? I have to go away, Varguitas."

"Will you marry me?" I asked her.

She gave a hollow little laugh.

"I'm serious," I insisted.

"Are you really asking me to marry you?" Aunt Julia laughed again, more amused this time.

"Is it yes or no?" I asked. "Hurry up and decide—Pascual and Big Pablito are just coming in."

"Are you asking me to marry you to show your family you're grown up now?" Aunt Julia asked me affectionately.

"There's that, too," I granted.

Fourteen.
The story of the Reverend

Father Don Seferino Huanca Leyva, that parish priest of the dung heap adjacent to the soccer-mad district of La Victoria known as Mendocita, began half a century ago, one night during the carnival season, when a young man of good family, who enjoyed mingling with the rabble, raped a carefree laundress, Black Teresita—in a Chirimoyo alleyway.

When the latter discovered that she was pregnant, seeing as how she already had eight children and no husband and knew it was unlikely that any man would lead her to the altar, what with all those kids, she immediately called upon the services of Doña Angélica, a wise old woman who lived on the Plaza de la Inquisición and acted as midwife, but was even better known as a supplier of house guests for limbo (in plain words: an abortionist). However, despite the poisonous concoctions (her own urine, in which mice had been marinated) that Doña Angélica had Teresita drink, the fetus that was the consequence of the rape, with a stubbornness that was a portent of what his character would be, refused to detach itself from the maternal placenta and remained there, curled up like a sciew thread, getting bigger and bigger and taking on a more and more definite form, until nine months after the fornicatory carnival, the laundress was necessarily obliged to give birth to him.

He was given the Christian name Seferino to please his godfather, a concierge at the Congressional Building who was named that, and his mother's two surnames. During his childhood, there was nothing that would have led one to guess he would one day become a priest, because what he liked most was not pious religious practices but spinning tops and flying kites. But from the very first, even before he knew how to talk, he gave every sign of having real character. The laundress followed a philosophy of education instinctively inspired by Sparta or Darwin that consisted of informing her offspring that if they wished to continue to exist in this jungle, they had to learn to bite and to be bitten, and that having milk to drink and food to eat was entirely their own concern once they'd reached the age of three, since by doing other people's washing ten hours a day and delivering it from one end of Lima to the other for another eight hours, she made just enough to feed herself and those of her children who had not yet arrived at the minimum age to fly on their own wings.

The rape-child gave proof of the same stubborn will to survive that had caused him to persist in living when in his mother's womb: he was able to feed himself by downing all the revolting refuse he collected from garbage cans, fighting with beggars and dogs over these filthy scraps. While his half brothers and half sisters died like flies of tuberculosis or food poisoning, or managed to live to adulthood though afflicted with rickets and psychic defects, thus only half passing the test, Seferino Huanca Leyva grew up in good health, physically robust and relatively sound mentally. When the laundress (a victim of hydrophobia?) was no longer able to work, it was Seferino who supported her, and later paid for a first-class funeral for her, conducted by the Guimet Undertaking Parlor, that El Chirimoyo regarded as the very best in the history of the neighborhood (by then he was the parish priest of Mendocita).

He was a precocious child who did all sorts of things to make himself a few pennies. As he learned to talk, he also learned to beg for alms from passersby on the Avenida Abancay, assuming the expression of a little gutter angel that melted the hearts of highborn ladies and loosened their purse strings. Later on, he was a shoeshine boy, a kid who guarded parked cars, a street peddler hawking newspapers, emollients, nougat, an usher at the soccer stadium, a secondhand clothes peddler. Who would ever have predicted that this child with dirty fingernails, filthy bare feet, a head of hair full of nits, his clothes covered with mends and patches, and his torso squeezed into an old sweater much too small for him and full of holes would one day become the most controversial parish priest in all of Peru?

How he learned to read was a mystery, since he had never set foot in a school. People in El Chirimoyo said that his godfather, the concierge who worked in the Congressional Building, had taught him the alphabet and showed him how to spell out syllables, and that the rest came to him (children of the gutter who by sheer tenacity become Nobel Prize winners) by dint of a pure effort of will. Seferino Huanca Leyva was twelve years old, making the rounds of the city's great mansions asking for worn-out clothes and old shoes (which he then sold in tenement districts and slums), when he met the person who was to provide him with the material means that enabled him to become a saint: an owner of vast landed estates, Mayte Unzátegui, of Basque origin, of whom it was impossible to say which was greater—her fortune or her faith, the size of her holdings or her devotion to Nuestro Señor de Limpias. She was coming out of her Moorish-style mansion on the Avenida San Felipe, in Orrantia, and her chauffeur was holding the door of her Cadillac open for her, when the lady spied the product of the rape, standing in the middle of the street next to his pushcart full of old clothes that he had collected that morning. His abject poverty, his intelligent eyes, his features of a headstrong young wolf pleased her. She told him she would come visit him at dusk that evening.

There was laughter in El Chirimoyo when Seferino Huanca Leyva announced that a lady in a big luxury car driven by a chauffeur in a blue uniform would be coming to see him after sunset. But when, at six o'clock, the Cadillac braked to a stop at the entrance to the alleyway and Doña Mayte Unzátegui, as elegant as a duchess, entered it and asked for Teresita, everyone was convinced (and dumfounded). Doña Mayte (one of those businesswomen who carefully calculate every moment of their time, including that required for menstruation) immediately made the laundress a proposal that caused her to shout for joy. Doña Mayte offered to pay for Seferino Huanca Leyva's education and give his mother a sum of ten thousand *soles* provided the boy became a priest.

It was thus that the rape-child came to be a student at Santo

Toribio de Mogrovejo seminary in Magdalena del Mar. Unlike others, who first feel a sense of vocation and then act, Seferino Huanca Leyva discovered that he had been born to be a priest, after he had become a seminarian. He proved to be a pious and diligent student, a favorite of his teachers, and the pride and joy of Black Teresita and his benefactress. But while his grades in Latin, theology, and patristics attained lofty heights, and his religiosity was irreproachably manifested in the form of Masses said, prayers recited, and self-flagellations administered, from his adolescence onward he began to show symptoms of what, in the future, at the time of the heated debates that his daring acts gave rise to, his defenders were to call impetuousness motived by religious zeal and his detractors evidences of the delinquent and criminal influence of El Chirimoyo. Thus, for instance, before being ordained he began to propound to his fellow seminarians the thesis that it was necessary to revive the Crusades, to do battle with Satan once more, not only with the feminine weapons of prayer and sacrifice, but also with the virile (and, he assured them, far more effective) ones of punches, butting with the head, and, if circumstances so required, knives and guns.

His superiors, alarmed, hastened to combat these wild ideas. But Doña Mayte Unzátegui, on the other hand, warmly applauded them, and inasmuch as the latifundian philanthropist was helping to support a third of the seminarians, the reverend fathers (bitter pill that is swallowed for budgetary reasons) were obliged to overlook what was going on and close their ears to Seferino Huanca Leyva's theories. And they were not merely theories: they were confirmed by practice. On the days when the seminarians were allowed out to visit their homes, the boy from El Chirimoyo invariably returned at nightfall with some example of what he called armed preaching. Thus, one day, on seeing a drunken husband beating his wife on one of the tumultuous streets of his neighborhood, he had intervened and broken the bully's shinbones with a couple of good swift kicks, followed by a lecture on the proper behavior of the good Christian husband. Another day, having surprised a greenhorn pickpocket trying to rob an old woman in the Cinco Esquinas bus, he had knocked him out by clouting him over the head (and then personally taking him to the public emergency clinic to get his face sewed up). Finally, one day, having surprised a couple taking their pleasure together like animals in the tall grass of the Bosque de Matamula, he had whipped the two of them till the blood came, and made them swear on their knees, if they didn't want another whipping, that they'd go get married forthwith. But Seferino Huanca Leyva's real red-letter day (so to speak), insofar as his axiom "Purity, like the alphabet, is best beaten into people's heads" was concerned, was the day on which he gave his tutor and Thomist-philosophy teacher, the gentle Father Alberto de Quinteros, a punch in the jaw, in the seminary chapel no less, because the latter, in a gesture of fraternity or an access of warm fellow feeling, had tried to kiss him on the mouth. A guileless, not at all spiteful man (he had come to the priesthood late in life, after earning fame and fortune as a psychologist who had first made a name for himself in a famous case in which he had cured a young doctor who had run over and killed his own daughter on the outskirts of Pisco), the Reverend Father Quinteros, on returning to the seminary from the hospital where they had stitched up the gash in his mouth and replaced with false ones the three teeth that had been knocked out, opposed the expulsion of Seferino Huanca Leyva, and he himself (with that generosity of great souls who turn the other cheek so often that they find their posthumous place on church altars) acted as sponsor of the rape-child at the Mass receiving him into the priesthood.

But during the time that Seferino Huanca Leyva was a seminarian, it was not only his conviction that the Church ought to combat evil pugilistically that upset his superiors, but to an even greater degree his (disinterested?) belief that masturbation, in any way, shape, or form, should definitely not be included in the vast repertory of mortal sins. Despite repeated reprimands from his mentors, who, citing the Bible and countless papal bulls, fulminated against the sin of Onan, endeavored to show him the error of his ways, the son of Doña Angélica the abortionist, stubborn by nature even before the day he was born, roused his comrades to rebellion by night by assuring them that the manual act had been conceived by God to compensate ecclesiastics for their vow of chastity, or in any event to make it bearable. Sin, he argued, resides in the pleasure offered by a woman's flesh, or (more perversely) the flesh of *another*, but why should there be any sin in the humble, solitary, unproductive relief offered by the conjoined efforts of one's own imagination and one's own fingers? In a composition read aloud in the class of the venerable Father Leoncio Zacarías, Seferino Huanca Leyva went so far as to suggest, through his interpretation of ambiguous episodes in the New Testament, that there were reasons for not rejecting as a mere wild hypothesis the possibility that Christ in person—perhaps after meeting Mary Magdalene?—might have fought against the temptation to commit an act of impurity by masturbatory means. Father Zacarías suffered a fainting spell and the protégé of the Basque pianist was very nearly expelled from the seminary for blasphemy.

He repented, apologized, did the acts of penance imposed upon him, and ceased for a time to propagate those outlandish ideas of his that incensed his mentors and inflamed his fellow seminarians. Nonetheless, he did not cease to put them into practice as far as he himself was concerned, for very soon his confessors again heard him say, the moment he knelt before the creaking grilles of their confessionals: "This week I have been in love with the Queen of Sheba, Delilah, and the wife of Holofernes." It was these infatuations that kept him from a journey abroad that would have enriched his mind. He had just been ordained, and since, despite his heterodox deliriums, Seferino Huanca Leyva had been an exceptionally hardworking student and no one ever doubted his intellectual brilliance, the Hierarchy decided to send him to the Gregorian University in Rome to study for a doctorate. The brand-new priest immediately announced his intention to do research (scholars who ruin their eyesight consulting the dusty manuscripts in the Vatican Library) on a thesis to be entitled: "On the solitary vice as the citadel of ecclesiastic chastity." When his project was angrily rejected, he gave up the trip to Rome and went off to bury himself in the inferno of Mendocita, from which he was never to emerge.

It was he himself who chose that district when he found out that all the priests in Lima feared it like the plague, not so much because of the concentration of microbes which had made its hieroglyphic topography of sandy footpaths and shacks of heterogeneous materials—cardboard, corrugated tin, straw matting, planks, rags, and newspapers—a laboratory of the most refined forms of infection and parasitosis, as because of the social violence that reigned in Mendocita. In those days, in fact, that section of the city was a University of Crime, particularly its most proletarian specialties:

breaking and entering, prostitution, knife fights, con games of every variety, drug pushing, and pimping.

In the space of a few days Father Seferino Huanca Leyva built with his own hands an adobe shack, leaving it with no door, furnished it with a broken-down secondhand bed and a straw mattress bought at La Parada, and announced that he would hold an open-air Mass at seven o'clock. He also let it be known that he would hear confessions from Monday to Saturday, women from two to six and men from seven to midnight, to prevent crowding. And he also announced that he intended to organize a class, from eight in the morning until two in the afternoon, in which the children of the neighborhood would be taught the alphabet, arithmetic, and the catechism. But his enthusiasm was shattered to smithereens when it met with hard reality. The turnout for his morning Masses consisted of a handful of rheumy-eyed old men and women with moribund physical reflexes who sometimes inadvertently engaged in that impious practice typical of the people of a certain country (famous for its beef cattle and its tangos?) of letting farts and relieving their bladders and bowels with all their clothes on during the Office. As for confession in the afternoon and the school for children in the morning, not one soul turned up, even out of curiosity.

What was the matter? The neighborhood faith healer, Jaime Concha, a robust former sergeant in the Guardia Civil who had turned in his uniform when headquarters had given him orders to execute a poor yellow man who had arrived in El Callao from some port in the Orient as a stowaway, and had since taken up the practice of folk medicine with such success that he had won the heart of all of Mendocita, had viewed the arrival of a possible competitor with such misgivings that he had organized a boycott in the parish.

Apprised of this by an informer (the ex-sorceress of Mendocita, Doña Mayte Unzátegui, a Basque with indigo-blue blood in her veins who had come down in the world and been dethroned as queen and sovereign of the neighborhood by Jaime Concha), Father Seferino Huanca Leyva realized (joys that blur men's eyes and inflame their hearts) that the right moment had come at last to put his theory of armed preaching into practice. He went up and down the streets swarming with flies, shouting at the top of his lungs like a circus barker to announce that at eleven o'clock on Sunday morning, in the vacant lot where neighborhood soccer matches were held, he and the faith healer would prove with their fists which of the two of them was the better man. When the muscular Jaime Concha appeared at Father Seferino's adobe hut to ask the priest whether this meant he was being challenged to a punching match, the only answer of the man from El Chirimoyo was to ask the sergeant in an icy voice whether he would prefer a knife fight to one with their bare fists. The ex-sergeant went away holding his sides with laughter and explaining to the neighbors that in the days when he'd been a Guardia Civil he used to kill vicious dogs he encountered on the street with one rap on their heads with his bare knuckles.

The fight between the priest and the healer caused extraordinary excitement, and not only all of Mendocita, but also La Victoria, El Porvenir, El Cerro San Cosme, and El Agustino came to watch it. Father Seferino turned up wearing trousers and a sports shirt and crossed himself before the fight, which was short but spectacular. The man from El Chirimoyo was physically less powerful than the ex-Guardia Civil, but trickier. The moment the fight started, he threw a handful of hot pepper powder in his opponent's eyes ("Where I come from, anything goes in a fight," he was later to explain to his fans), and when the giant (Goliath done in by one clever shot from David's sling) began to stagger about, unable to see, he weakened him with a series of kicks in the privates till he doubled over. Without giving him a chance to catch his breath, he then launched into a frontal attack aimed at his face, a hail of both rights and lefts, changing his style only after he'd knocked him to the ground. He finished off the massacre as he lay there, by stamping on his ribs and his belly. Howling with pain and shame, Jaime Concha admitted defeat. Amid the applause, Father Seferino Huanca Leyva fell to his knees and prayed devoutly, his face turned heavenward and his hands crossed on his breast.

This episode—which even got into the newspapers and which upset the archbishop—began to win Father Seferino the sympathies of his still-potential parishioners. From that time on, the morning Masses were better attended and a number of sinners, especially female ones, asked to make their confession, though naturally these rare cases were not enough to fill up even a tenth of the vast schedule that the optimistic parish priest—making a rough estimate of the capacity for sin of the inhabitants of Mendocita—had set up. Another thing that was well received in the neighborhood and won him new clients was his behavior toward Jaime Concha after the latter's humiliating defeat. Father Seferino himself helped the neighbor women put Mercurochrome and arnica on him, and informed him that he would not boot him out of Mendocita, that on the contrary (generosity of Napoleons who offer champagne and their daughter in marriage to the general whose army they have just wiped out) he was prepared to keep him on in the parish by appointing him sacristan. The healer was authorized to continue to provide philters for friendship and enmity, the evil eye and love, but at moderate prices that the priest himself would set, and the one thing he was forbidden to do was concern himself with questions having to do with the soul. He was also permitted to continue his practice as a bonesetter and treat those who dislocated a member or had pains in their joints, on condition that he not try to care for people suffering from other ailments, who were to be referred to the public clinic.

The way in which Father Seferino Huanca Leyva succeeded in attracting the youngsters of Mendocita (flies that smell honey, pelicans that spy fish) to his once-scorned school was highly unorthodox and brought him his first grave warning from the ecclesiastical authorities. He let it be known that, for every week they attended his classes, the children would receive a little colored picture as a reward. This bait would not have been sufficient to lure the eager crowd of ragamuffins that it did had the euphemistic "little colored pictures" offered by the son of El Chirimoyo not been in reality pictures of naked women whom it was difficult to mistake for virgins. To those mothers of his little pupils who expressed their surprise at his pedagogical methods, the priest solemnly explained that, however incredible it might seem, the "little pictures" would keep their offspring from being tempted by impure flesh and make them less obstreperous, more docile, and drowsier.

To win over the girls of the neighborhood, he took advantage of the inclinations that made woman the first Biblical sinner and enlisted the services of Mayte Unzátegui, who was also placed on the parish staff and given the title of assistant. Mayte Unzátegui (wisdom that only twenty years as madam in the brothels of Tingo María can bring) succeeded in winning the hearts of the little girls by giving them courses that they found great fun: how to paint their lips and cheeks and eyelids without having to buy makeup in stores, how to pad out their breasts and hips and bottoms with cotton, pillows, and even newspapers, how to do the dances that were the latest rage: the rumba, the huaracha, the porro, the mambo. When the Visitor from the Hierarchy came to inspect the parish and saw the whole bunch of impudent brats in the girls' section of the school taking turns wearing the only pair of spike-heeled shoes in the neighborhood and waggling their behinds provocatively under the magisterial supervision of the former bawdyhouse mistress, he rubbed his eyes in utter disbelief. Finally, on recovering his powers of speech, he asked Father Seferino if he had founded an Academy for Prostitutes.

"The answer is yes," Black Teresita's son, a man who had no fear of words, replied. "Since they'll be forced to take up that profession one day in any case, they can at least be talented at it."

(It was this episode that led to his receiving the second grave warning from the ecclesiastical authorities.)

But it is not true, as rumors spread by his detractors had it, that Father Seferino was the number-one pimp of Mendocita. He was merely a realistic man, who knew life like the palm of his hand. He did not encourage prostitution, but, rather, tried to make it more decent and fought valiant battles to keep the women who earned their living by selling their bodies (all the women in Mendocita between the ages of twelve and sixty) from contracting gonorrhea and being exploited by their procurers. The eradication of the twenty-some pimps of the district (and, in certain cases, their rehabilitation) was a heroic labor in the field of public health and social welfare that earned Father Seferino a number of knife wounds and the congratulations of the mayor of La Victoria. To achieve this end, he applied his philosophy of armed preaching. Using Jaime Concha as a town crier, he spread the word that the law and religion forbade men to live like parasites off inferior beings, and that consequently any male in the district who exploited females would be forced to confront his fists. He was thus obliged to break Greaseball Pacheco's jaw, leave the Stud blind in one eye, Strong-Arm Pedrito impotent, He-Man Sampedri a slavering idiot, and Muscleman Huambachano black and blue all over. During this campaign worthy of Don Quixote, he was ambushed one night and cut to ribbons with knives; his assailants, believing they'd done him in, left him lying in the mud for starving dogs to devour. But the life force of the Darwinian young man was stronger than the rusty knife blades that stabbed him, and he survived, though he bore for the rest of his life, it is true—marks of steel on the body and face of a man that lustful women find exciting—the half-dozen scars that, after the trial, were responsible for the commitment to a psychiatric institution, as an incurable madman, of the ringleader of his attackers, that native of Arequipa with the Biblical first name and the maritime surname, Ezequiel Delfín.

The priest's sacrifices and efforts bore the fruits he had hoped for, and Mendocita, to everyone's amazement, was freed of every last one of its pimps. Father Seferino was the idol of the women in the neighborhood; from that time on, they came in throngs to Mass and went to confession every week. To make the profession that earned them their daily bread less hard on them, Father Seferino invited a doctor from Acción Católica to come to the district to give them advice on sexual prophylaxis and instruct them in practical ways of detecting the presence of the gonococcus, in their client or in themselves, before it was too late. In cases in which the birth-control techniques that Mayte Unzátegui taught them proved ineffective, Father Seferino brought a disciple of Doña Angélica's in from El Chirimoyo to Mendocita to dispatch to limbo the tadpoles of love for sale. The grave warning that he received from the ecclesiastical authorities when they discovered that the priest was recommending the use of condoms and diaphragms and was in favor of abortions was his thirteenth.

The fourteenth came as a result of the so-called trade school that he had the audacity to set up. In it, experts of the district, in delightful informal talks (an anecdote here, an anecdote there, beneath the overcast skies or the occasional stars of the Lima night), taught novices with virgin police records various ways of making a living. They could learn, for instance, the exercises that turn fingers into intelligent, extremely discreet intruders capable of slipping into the innermost recesses of any purse, pocket, wallet, or briefcase and recognizing, amid all the heterogeneous objects inside, the booty they covet. They could discover how, with the patience of a good craftsman, any wire can take the place of the most baroque key to open a door, and how the ignition of different makes of cars can be started if, perchance, one does not happen to be the owner of the vehicle. Lessons were given on how to snatch jewelry on the streets, on foot or on a bicycle, how to scale walls and break windows of houses without making a sound, how to do plastic surgery on any object that suddenly changed owner, and how to get out of various Lima jails without the authorization of the chief of police. Even such arts and crafts as the manufacture of knives and—rumors born of envy?—the distilling of cocaine from coca paste were taught in this school, which finally earned Father Seferino the friendship and fellowship of the men of Mendocita, as well as his first run-in with the police of La Victoria, who took him down to headquarters one night and threatened to bring him to trial and get him put behind bars as a Gray Eminence of crime. He was rescued from that fate, naturally, by his influential benefactress.

Even this early on, Father Seferino had become a popular figure, receiving a great deal of publicity in newspapers and magazines and on the radio. His innovations were the object of heated discussion. There were those who regarded him as a protosaint, a forerunner of the new batch of priests who were to revolutionize the Church, and there were those who were convinced that he was a fifth columnist of Satan whose mission was to undermine the House of Peter from within. Mendocita (thanks to him or through his fault?) became a tourist attraction: the curious, the devout, reporters, snobs ventured into the former paradise of the underworld to see, touch, interview, or ask Father Seferino for his autograph. This publicity divided the Church: one faction considered it beneficial to the cause, and the other, harmful.

When Father Seferino Huanca Leyva triumphantly announced, on the occasion of a procession in honor of El Señor de Limpias—whose cult he had introduced in Mendocita, where it had caught on like wildfire—that there was not a single living child in the parish, including those born in the last ten hours, who had not been baptized, the faithful were filled with pride and the Hierarchy, after its many admonitions, for once sent him its congratulations.

On the other hand, however, he provoked a scandal when, on the occasion of the feast of the patron saint of Lima, St. Rosa, he announced in an open-air sermon he delivered in the vacant-lot soccer field of Mendocita that within the boundaries of his dusty parish there was not a single couple whose union had not been sanctified before God and the altar of his adobe shack. In stupefaction, since they knew very well that in the ex-Empire of the Incas the most solid and most respected institution—outside of the Church and the army—was concubinage, the prelates of the Peruvian Church came (dragging their feet?) to confirm the truth of this extraordinary claim with their own eyes. What they found as they nosed about the promiscuous households of Mendocita left them appalled and with an aftertaste of cheapened sacraments in their mouths. They found Father Seferino's explanations abstruse and full of incomprehensible slang (the son of El Chirimoyo had forgotten the pure Castilian of his seminary days after his many years in the slums and adopted all the barbarisms and solecisms of the underworld argot of Mendocita), and it was the ex-faith healer and ex-Guardia Civil, Lituma, who explained to them the system used to abolish concubinage. It was sacrilegiously simple. It consisted of Christianizing, before the Gospels, all couples who had taken up with each other or were about to do so. After having taken their pleasure together for the first time, they hastened to their beloved priest to have him marry them in due and proper form, and Father Seferino, without bothering them with impertinent questions, conferred the sacrament upon them. And since this system resulted in people in the neighborhood getting married several times without having been left a widower between spouses (aeronautical speed with which the couples of the district broke up, exchanged partners, and formed new couples), Father Seferino repaired the damages thus caused, insofar as sin was concerned, through the purifying sacrament of confession. (He had explained this by citing a proverbial phrase that, in addition to being heretical, was vulgar: "One love bite hides another.") Forbidden such practices, admonished, very nearly slapped in the face by the archbishop, Father Seferino Huanca Leyva also celebrated a sort of anniversary thanks to this entire episode: grave warning number 100.

Thus, amid bold innovations and much-publicized reprimands, the object of heated controversy, loved by some and reviled by others, Father Seferino Huanca Leyva reached the prime of life: his fifties. He was a man with a broad forehead, an aquiline nose, a penetrating gaze, the very soul of rectitude and goodness, whose conviction, since his auroral days as a young seminarian, that imaginary love was not a sin but on the contrary a powerful bodyguard for chastity, had in fact been sufficient to keep him pure, when there arrived in Mendocita (serpent in Paradise that takes on the voluptuous, luxuriant, lustfully resplendent forms of the female) a pervert named Mayte Unzátegui who claimed to be a social worker (in reality she was—a woman after all?—a prostitute).

She maintained that she had worked with selfless devotion in the wilds of Tingo María, ridding the bellies of the natives of parasites, and had fled from there, very annoyed and upset, because a pack of carnivorous rats had devoured her son. She was of Basque, and hence aristocratic, descent. Despite the fact that her turgescent horizons and gelatinous jiggling when she walked ought to have alerted him to the danger, Father Seferino Huanca Leyva committed (attraction of the abyss that has seen monolithic virtues succumb) the insane error of taking her on as an assistant, believing that, as she claimed, her aim was to save souls and kill parasites. In reality, she wanted to lead him into sin. She put her program for so doing into practice, coming to live in the adobe hovel, sleeping on a makeshift bed separated from him by a ridiculous little curtain which, moreover, was transparent. At night, by candlelight, on the pretext that they made her sleep better and kept her in good physical health, the temptress did exercises. But was Swedish gymnastics the proper term for that Thousand and One Nights harem dance that the Basque woman performed, standing in one spot waggling her hips, shaking her shoulders, wriggling her legs, and coiling her arms, a spectacle that the panting ecclesiastic witnessed through the little curtain lighted by the flickering candle as though watching a disturbing Chinese shadow play? And later, as everyone in Mendocita lay silently sleeping, Mayte Unzátegui, on hearing the creaking of the bed on the other side of the curtain, had the audacity to ask, in a mellifluous voice: "Are you having trouble getting to sleep, Father dear?"

It is quite true that, in order to conceal her evil designs, the beautiful corruptress worked twelve hours a day, giving vaccinations and treating scabies, disinfecting hovels and taking oldsters out for airings. But she did so dressed in shorts, with her legs and shoulders and arms and midriff exposed, maintaining that she'd fallen into the habit of going about that way in the jungle. Father Seferino continued to exercise his creative ministry, but he grew noticeably thinner, had dark circles under his eyes, kept constantly looking about to see where Mayte Unzátegui was, and on spying her passing by, his mouth fell open and a little stream of venial saliva wet his lips. It was at this time that he took to going about with his hands in his pockets night and day, and his sacristan, the ex-abortionist Doña Angélica, prophesied that at any moment now he would begin spitting up the blood of galloping consumption.

Would the pastor succumb to the evil spell of the social worker, or would his debilitating antidotes enable him to ward it off? Would his counterremedies lead him to the insane asylum, to the grave? In a sporting spirit, the parishioners of Mendocita followed this contest and began making wagers, with fixed time limits and a wide range of allergic outcomes on which the bettor could place his money: the Basque woman would be made pregnant by priest-seed, the man from El Chirimoyo would kill her to kill temptation, or he would defrock himself and marry her. But life itself, naturally, beat everyone at the game by using a marked card.

Arguing that the Church must return to its earliest days, to the pure and simple Church of the Gospels, when all believers lived together and shared their earthly possessions, Father Seferino initiated an energetic campaign to restore true communal life in Mendocita—a veritable laboratory of Christian experimentation. Couples were to become part of communities of fifteen to twenty members who would share the work, the maintenance, and the domestic tasks of the collectivity between them, and would live together in dwellings remodeled to house these new nuclei of social life that would replace the traditional couple. Father Seferino set the example, enlarging his adobe hut and installing in it, in addition to the social worker, his two sacristans: Lituma the ex-sergeant and Doña Angélica the ex-abortionist. This micro-commune was the first one to be set up in Mendocita, and was to serve as a model for those to follow.

Father Seferino stipulated that within each catholic community the members of each sex were to enjoy the most democratic equality. The males were to address each other in the familiar form, and the females likewise, but in order to ensure that the differences in musculature, intelligence, and common sense established by God would not be forgotten, he advised the females to use the formal term of address when speaking to the males and as a sign of respect try not to look them straight in the eye. The tasks of cooking, sweeping, fetching water from the public fountain, killing cockroaches and rats, washing clothes, and other domestic chores were to be rotated and the money earned—through honest labor or in any other manner—by each member was to be turned over to the community down to the last penny, whereupon it would be redistributed in equal shares after communal expenses had been taken care of. The living quarters were not to have any inside partitions, so as to do away with the sinful habit of secrecy, and all the activities of everyday life, from evacuation of the bowels to sexual embrace, were to be carried out in full view of the others.

Even before the police and the army invaded Mendocita, with a cinematographic display of rifles, gas masks, and bazookas, and made the raid that kept men and women from the district shut up in police barracks for many days, not because of what they really were or had been (thieves, thugs, whores), but because they were subversives and dissidents, and Father Seferino was brought before a military tribunal and charged with establishing, under cover of his priestly functions, a bridgehead for Communism (he was acquitted, thanks to the influence exerted by his benefactress, the millionaire heiress Mayte Unzátegui), the experiment in archaic Christian communal living was already doomed.

Doomed, naturally, by the ecclesiastical authorities, who officially condemned it (grave warning number 233) on the grounds that it was highly suspect as a theory and insane as a practice (the facts, alas, proved that they were right), but doomed above all by the nature of the men and women of Mendocita, clearly allergic to collectivism. The number-one problem was the traffic in sex. In the stimulating promiscuity of the collective dormitories, under cover of the darkness, the most ardent fondlings, seminal rubbings, frictions took place from mattress to mattress, or outright rapes, acts of sodomy, impregnations, and as a consequence crimes of passion multiplied. Problem number two was theft: instead of doing away with the appetite for property, communal living exacerbated it to the point of madness. The members stole from each other even the fetid air they breathed. Rather than fraternally uniting the people of Mendocita, cohabitation made them mortal enemies. It was in this period of chaos and disorder that the social worker (Mayte Unzátegui?) announced that she was pregnant and ex-sergeant Lituma admitted that he was the father. With tears in his eyes, Father Seferino gave his Christian blessing to this union brought about by his socio-Catholic innovations. (People say that since then he sobs all night long and chants elegies to the moon.)

But almost immediately thereafter he was obliged to face an even worse catastrophe than that of having lost this Basque woman whom he had never managed to possess: the arrival in Mendocita of a formidable rival, the evangelical minister Don Sebastián Bergua. The latter was a man still in the flower of youth, athletic-looking, with strong biceps, who the moment he arrived announced that he proposed to win over to the true religion—the reformed church—all of Mendocita, including the Catholic priest and his three acolytes, within a period of six months. Don Sebastián (who before he became a minister had been—a gynecologist worth millions?) had the financial means to impress the people of the district: he had a brick house built for himself, paying the men in the neighborhood royally for the work they did on it, and began giving what he called "religious breakfasts," to which he invited, free of charge, those who attended his Bible talks and learned certain hymns by heart. Seduced by his eloquence and his baritone voice, or by the coffee with milk and bread with cracklings that went with them, the people of Mendocita began to desert Catholic adobe for Evangelical brick.

Father Seferino naturally resorted at this point to armed preaching. He challenged Don Sebastián Bergua to fisticuffs to prove which of the two of them was the true servant of God. Weakened by his excessive practice of the Exercise of Onan that had enabled him to resist the temptations of the Devil, the man from El Chirimoyo was k.o.'d by Don Sebastián Bergua's second punch; for twenty years the latter had done calisthenics and boxed for an hour a day (in the Remigius Gymnasium in San Isidro?). It was not his having lost two incisors and been left with his nose permanently flattened that plunged Father Seferino into despair, but rather, the humiliation of being beaten at his own game and noting that with each passing day he was losing more parishioners to his adversary.

But (bold men who grow even bolder in the face of danger, and firm believers in the old saying, "For a terrible ill, a worse remedy") one day the man from El Chirimoyo mysteriously brought to his adobe hut several jerry cans full of a liquid which he hid from the gaze of the curious (but which any sensitive nose would have immediately recognized as kerosene). That night, when everyone in Mendocita was fast asleep, accompanied by his faithful Lituma, he boarded up the doors and windows of the brick house from the outside, using thick planks and big stout nails. Don Sebastián Bergua was sleeping the sleep of the just, dreaming of an incestuous nephew who, repenting having raped his sister, ended up a papist priest in a Lima slum: Mendocita? He was unable to hear Lituma's hammer blows which transformed the Evangelical temple into a rat trap because Doña Angélica, the ex-midwife, on orders from Father Seferino, had given him a thick anesthetic potion. Once the Mission was hermetically sealed, the man from El Chirimoyo personally sprinkled it with kerosene. Then he crossed himself, lit a match, and was on the point of throwing it. But something caused him to hesitate. Ex-sergeant Lituma, the social worker, the ex-abortionist, the dogs of Mendocita saw him standing there, tall and gaunt, beneath the stars, with a look of torment in his eyes, holding the lighted match between his fingers, pondering whether he should roast his enemy to death.

Would he do so? Would he toss the match? Would Father Seferino Huanca Leyva turn the Mendocita night into a raging inferno? Would he thus ruin an entire life devoted to religion and the common good? Or would he blow out the little flame that was burning his fingertips, open the doors of the brick house, and fall to his knees to beg the Evangelical minister's forgiveness? How would this parable of the slums end?

Fifteen.

The first person I talked

to about my having proposed to Aunt Julia was not Javier but Nancy. After my telephone conversation with Aunt Julia, I called my cousin and suggested that we go to the movies together. But we ended up instead at El Patio, a bar-and-grill in Miraflores on the Calle San Martín and a favorite hangout of wrestlers that Max Aguirre, the Luna Park promoter, brought to Lima. The establishment—located in a small two-story building designed to house middle-class tenants that thoroughly detested being turned into a bar—was empty when we arrived, and we were able to have a quiet conversation as I consumed my tenth cup of coffee of the day and Nancy had a Coca-Cola.

The minute we sat down, I began to think up various ways of breaking the news to her gently. But she was the one who started the conversation, bursting with news she couldn't wait to tell me. The night before, there had been a family meeting at Aunt Hortensia's, attended by a dozen relatives, to discuss "the affair." At this gathering, it had been decided that Uncle Lucho and Aunt Olga would ask Aunt Julia to go back to Bolivia.

"They did so for your sake," Nancy explained. "It seems that your father is beside himself with rage and wrote a really scary letter."

Uncle Jorge and Uncle Lucho, who loved me dearly, were very worried now as to what punishment he might decide to inflict on me. It was their thought that if Aunt Julia had already left when he arrived in Lima, he would be placated and deal less harshly with me.

"As a matter of fact, all that is of no importance now," I assured her smugly. "Because I've asked Aunt Julia to marry me."

Her reaction was spectacular and caricatural, like a double take in a film. She choked on her Coca-Cola, was overcome by a frankly overdone coughing fit, and her eyes filled with tears.

"Stop clowning, you idiot," I said angrily. "I need your help."

"It wasn't your news that made me do that—I just swallowed the wrong way," my cousin stammered, drying her eyes and trying to clear her throat. And a few seconds later, lowering her voice, she added: "But you're still just a kid. Do you have the money to get married? And what about your father? He'll kill you!"

But the very next moment, piqued by her terrible curiosity, she bombarded me with questions about things I hadn't had time to think about: Had Julita said yes? Were we going to elope? Who were our witnesses going to be? We wouldn't be able to be married in church because she was divorced, right? Where were we going to live?

"But, Marito," she said again after she finished firing off all these questions one after the other, completely taken aback once again, "don't you realize that you're only eighteen years old?"

She burst out laughing then, and I did too. I told her that she might very well have reason on her side, but that what I needed now was her help in carrying out my plan. We'd grown up together and seen each other through lots of things, we loved each other dearly, and I knew she'd be on my side no matter what happened.

"Of course I'm going to help you if you ask me to, even if what you're trying to do is utter madness, even if they kill me as well as you," she finally said. "And, by the way, have you thought of what the whole family's going to say if you really get married?"

We had a great time for a while imagining just what various aunts and uncles and cousins would say and do when confronted with the news. Aunt Hortensia would burst into tears, Aunt Jesús would rush off to church, Uncle Javier would utter his classic all-purpose exclamation ("What shamelessness!"), and our youngest cousin, Jaimito, who was three years old and lisped, would ask: "What doeth getting married mean, Mama?" The game ended when we burst into hysterical laughter, bringing the waiters running to see what was so funny. When we calmed down, Nancy agreed to be our spy, to report to us all the family's maneuvers and intrigues. I had no idea how many days it would take me to get everything ready and I needed to know what the relatives were up to in the meantime. She also agreed to act as Aunt Julia's messenger, and to take her out of the house with her every so often so that I could see her.

"Okay, okay, I'll be your fairy godmother. But if someday I need one, I hope the two of you will do as much for me."

As I was walking her home, my cousin suddenly smote her forehead with the palm of her hand. "What luck—I just remembered something! I can get you exactly what you need. An apartment in a villa on the Calle Porta. A one-room studio, with a little kitchen and a bath, really tiny but just darling. And only five hundred a month."

It had been vacated just a few days before and a friend of hers had it up for rent; Nancy could speak to her. I was amazed at my cousin's practicality; while I wandered about in the romantic stratosphere of the problems before me, she was capable of turning her mind to the down-to-earth problem of where the two of us would live. Moreover, five hundred *soles* a month for an apartment was within my reach. All I needed now was to earn a little more money "for the extras" (as my grandfather put it). Without thinking about it twice, I asked Nancy to tell her friend that she had a renter.

After leaving Nancy, I hurried to Javier's *pensión* on the Avenida 28 de Julio, but there were no lights on in the house and I didn't dare wake up the owner, a woman with a terrible temper. I felt very frustrated, because I needed to tell my best friend about my great plan and get his advice. I didn't sleep well and had nightmares all that night. I had breakfast at dawn with my grandfather, who always got up at daybreak, and hurried to Javier's *pensión* again. I met him just as he was leaving, and we walked to the Avenida Larco to take the jitney to Lima. The night before, for the first time in his life, he'd listened to an entire chapter of one of Pedro Camacho's serials, along with the owner of his *pensión* and the other boarders, and he was impressed.

"Your pal Camacho is capable of anything, I must say. Do you know what happened in the one last night—the one about an old boardinghouse in Lima run by a poor family that's come down from the sierra? Everyone was sitting around the lunch table talking and all of a sudden an earthquake hit. It was all so realistic—the doors and windows shaking, the screams—that we all leapt to our feet and Señora Gracia ran out into the garden . . ."

I imagined Puddler, that genius, snoring to imitate the earth's deep rumble, reproducing the dance of Lima's houses and buildings by shaking baby's rattles or rubbing glass marbles together in front of the microphone, and cracking nuts with his feet or knocking stones together to produce the sounds of roofs and walls cracking and stairways coming crashing down, as Josefina, Luciano, and the other actors panicked, prayed, screamed with pain, and begged for help under Pedro Camacho's watchful eye.

"But the earthquake isn't the half of it," Javier interrupted me as I was telling him of Puddler's extraordinary feats. "To top everything off, the entire boardinghouse fell in and everyone inside was crushed to death. Not a single one got out alive—can you believe it? A guy who's capable of killing off every last one of his characters in a story by having them die in an earthquake is worthy of respect."

We'd arrived at the jitney stop and I couldn't keep my secret a minute longer. I summed up in a few words what had happened the evening before and the great decision I'd come to.

He pretended not to be at all taken aback by my news. "Well, well, you, too, are capable of anything," he said, shaking his head pityingly. And then, a moment later: "Are you sure you want to get married?"

"I've never been this sure of anything in my life," I swore to him.

And by then that was quite true. The evening before, when I'd asked Aunt Julia to marry me, it had seemed like something I hadn't really thought about, a mere phrase, almost a joke, but now, after talking with Nancy, I felt very sure of myself. It seemed to me that I was telling him of an irrevocable decision that I had long pondered.

"The one thing I'm sure of is that all these mad things you're up to are going to land me in jail," Javier commented resignedly, once we were in the jitney. And then, a few blocks later, as we reached the Avenida Javier Prado: "You don't have much time. If your aunt and uncle have asked Julita to leave, she can't stay with them very much longer. And you'll have to pull the whole thing off before the bogeyman gets here, because with your father on the scene, you're going to have a hard time of it."

We sat there for a while not saying anything as the jitney went down the Avenida Arequipa, stopping on the corners to let passengers out and pick up others. As we were passing the Colegio Raimondi, Javier spoke up again, his mind totally occupied with the problem now: "You're going to need money. How are you going to manage that?"

"I'll ask for an advance at the radio station. Sell all the old things I have—clothes, books. And pawn my typewriter, my watch, anything else I can put in hock for cash. And start looking like crazy for extra work."

"I've got some things I can pawn, too—my radio, my pens, my good watch," Javier said. Half closing his eyes and adding up sums on his fingers, he calculated: "I think I can lend you around a thousand *soles*."

We separated at the Plaza San Martín and agreed we'd meet at noon up in my cubbyhole in the Panamericana shack. Talking with him had done me good and I arrived at the office in a good mood, feeling very optimistic. I read the newspapers, selected the news items to be put on the air, and for the second day in a row, Pascual and Big Pablito found the first bulletins all finished when they came in. Unfortunately, both of them were in the office when Aunt Julia called, and ruined the conversation. I didn't dare tell her in front of them that I'd talked with Nancy and Javier.

"I have to see you this very day, even if it's only for a few minutes," I begged her. "Everything's coming along nicely."

"I'm really down in the dumps all of a sudden," Aunt Julia said. "I've always been able to keep my spirits up no matter what, but right now I feel lower than a snake's belly."

She had a good excuse to come downtown without arousing suspicion: making reservations for her flight back to La Paz at the Lloyd Aéreo Boliviano office. She'd come by the station around three that afternoon. Neither she nor I mentioned the subject of marriage, but it upset me to hear her talk about planes. The minute I hung up, I went down to the Lima city hall to find out what documents were necessary for a civil marriage. I had a friend who worked there and he was the one who tracked down all the information for me, thinking it was for a relative of mine who wanted to marry a foreigner who was a divorcée. The requirements turned out to involve all sorts of very worrisome stumbling blocks. Aunt Julia had to present her birth certificate and a copy of her divorce decree validated by the Ministry of Foreign Relations of both Bolivia and Peru. I, too, had to present my birth certificate. But since I was a minor, I also needed a duly notarized authorization from my parents to marry, or else be "emancipated" (declared to have attained my legal majority) by them, before the judge of the juvenile court. Both things were out of the question.

I left the city hall making calculations; just getting Aunt Julia's papers validated, provided, of course, that she had them here with her in Lima, could take weeks. If she didn't have them with her, and had to ask for them to be sent from Bolivia by the proper authorities, the municipal registrar and the clerk of the divorce court respectively, it might take months. And then there was my birth certificate. I'd been born in Arequipa, and writing to a relative there to get me a copy would also take time (besides being risky). I envisioned one difficulty after another, like a series of challenges presenting themselves, but instead of dissuading me, they merely made me all the more determined (even as a youngster, I'd always been very stubborn). Halfway back to the radio station, as I was walking by the offices of *La Prensa,* I had a sudden inspiration and headed, almost at a run, for the university campus. Dripping with sweat by the time I got there, I made my way to the administrative office of the Faculty of Law, where the secretary, Señora Riofrío, who was in charge of giving out course grades, greeted me with her usual maternal smile and kindly listened to the complicated story I told her, involving urgent legal formalities, a unique opportunity to get a job that would help me pay for my studies.

"It's against the rules," she complained, benignly rising from her rickety old desk and walking over to the files, with me right beside her. "You students are all alike—you know I'm good-hearted and you take advantage of me. Doing all of you favors like this is going to cost me my job someday, and nobody's going to lift a finger for me."

As she searched around among the students' records, raising

little clouds of dust that made us both sneeze, I told her that if such a thing ever happened, everybody in the law school would go out on strike. She finally found my folder, with a copy of my birth certificate in it, just as I'd remembered, which she handed to me with the warning that she could only let me have it for half an hour. It took me no more than fifteen minutes to have two photocopies of it made in a bookstore on the Calle Azángaro and return one of them to Señora Riofrío. I went back to the radio station flushed with triumph, feeling capable of pulverizing any and every dragon I might encounter.

I was sitting at my desk, after writing up two more news bulletins and taping an interview for Panamericano with Gaucho Guerrero (an Argentine long-distance runner who had become a naturalized Peruvian citizen and whose entire life was devoted to beating his own record; he would run round and round a public square, for entire days and nights at a stretch, and was capable of eating, shaving, writing, and sleeping as he ran), deciphering, amid the bureaucratic prose of the certificate, some of the details surrounding my birth—I had been born on the Bulevard Parra; my grandfather and my Uncle Alejandro had been the ones who went to the city hall to announce my entry into this world—when Pascual and Big Pablito came in and distracted me. They were talking about a fire, laughing fit to kill as they went on about the victims' agonized shrieks as they roasted to death. I tried to go on reading my abstruse birth certificate, but the comments of my two editors about the Guardias Civiles of the commissariat of El Callao that had been sprinkled with gasoline and set on fire by a demented pyromaniac, every last one of whom had been burned to cinders, from the chief on down to the humblest flatfoot, and even the dog that was the commissariat's mascot, distracted me again.

"I've seen all the papers and I missed that one—where did you read about it?" I asked them. And to Pascual: "I warn you: you're not to use up all the time on today's bulletins talking about the fire." And to the two of them: "You're hopeless sadists, both of you."

"It's not a news item—it's the eleven o'clock serial," Big Pablito explained. "The one about Sergeant Lituma, the terror of the underworld of El Callao."

"He got fried to death, too," Pascual chimed in. "He could have gotten out alive, he was just leaving to make his rounds, but he went back in to rescue his captain. His good heart was the death of him."

"It was the dog, Choclito, he went back in to rescue, not the captain," Big Pablito corrected him.

"That wasn't ever really clear," Pascual said. "One of the jail doors fell on him. I wish you could have seen Don Pedro Camacho while he was burning to death. What a great actor!"

"And how about Puddler?" Big Pablito put in enthusiastically, eager to give credit where credit was due. "If anybody had told me you could create a roaring inferno with just two fingers, I wouldn't have believed it. But I saw him do it with my own two eyes, Don Mario!"

Javier's arrival interrupted the conversation. The two of us went off to have our usual cup of coffee together at the Bransa, and once we'd sat down I gave him a quick rundown of what I'd found out about the necessary papers and triumphantly showed him the copy of my birth certificate.

"I've been doing some thinking and I have to tell you that you're making a stupid mistake getting married," he said the minute I'd finished, a bit ill at ease at being so outspoken. "Not only because you're still just a kid, but above all on account of the question of money. You're going to have to work your ass off at all sorts of dumb jobs just to have enough to eat."

"In other words, you're telling me exactly what my father and mother are going to tell me," I said mockingly. "Aren't you going to mention that if I get married that'll be the end of my studying law? That I'll never become a great jurist?"

"That if you get married you won't even have time to read. That if you get married you'll never become a writer," Javier answered.

"We're going to have a fight if you go on this way," I warned him.

"Okay then, I'll hold my tongue." He laughed. "I've done as my conscience dictated by predicting the future I see in store for you. And I must admit that if Nancy were willing, I'd get married myself, this very day. Where do we begin, then?"

"Since there's no chance of getting my parents to give their consent or to emancipate me, and since it's also possible that Julia doesn't have all the necessary papers, the only solution is to find a kindhearted mayor."

"What you really mean is one who can be bribed," he corrected me. He examined me as though I were a beetle. "But who are you in any position to bribe, you penniless wretch?"

"A mayor with his head in the clouds who won't notice details. One who'll fall for most any kind of sob story."

"Okay, let's start looking for this extraordinary creature, a kindhearted idiot who'll perform the ceremony even though it's against every law in the books." He laughed again. "Too bad Julita's divorced. Otherwise, you could get married in church. That'd be easy—there are any number of priests who are kindhearted idiots."

Javier always cheered me up, and we ended up joking about my honeymoon, about the fees he was going to charge me for his services (helping him abduct Nancy, of course), and regretting not being in Piura, where it was such a common thing for couples to elope that there would have been no problem finding the kindhearted idiot required. By the time we said goodbye to each other, he'd promised to start looking for a mayor that very afternoon and to pawn all his possessions that weren't indispensable in order to help out with the wedding expenses.

Aunt Julia had said she'd come by the office at three, and when she hadn't shown up by three-thirty, I began to worry. At four, my fingers were getting in each other's way as I typed, and I was chain-smoking. At four-thirty, Big Pablito, seeing how pale I was, asked me if I wasn't feeling well. At five, I had Pascual phone Uncle Lucho's house and ask to speak to her. She hadn't come back there. She still hadn't come back half an hour later, or at six or at seven. After the last evening newscast, instead of getting off the jitney at my grandparents' street, I went on as far as the Avenida Armendáriz and hung around my aunt's and uncle's house, without daring to knock at the door. I spied Aunt Olga through the windows, changing the water in a vase of flowers, and a few minutes later I saw Uncle Lucho turn out the lights in the dining room. I walked around the block several times, overcome by contrary emotions: anxiety, anger, sadness, a desire to slap Aunt Julia's face, and a desire to kiss her. I was just completing one of these agitated turns around the block when I saw her get out of a big expensive car with diplomatic plates. I strode over to the car, my legs trembling with fury and jealousy, and determined to punch my rival in the nose, whoever he might be. He turned out to be a gentleman with white hair, and moreover, there was a lady sitting inside the car. Aunt Julia introduced me, explaining that I was a nephew of her brother-in-law's, and I discovered that I was meeting the ambassador of Bolivia and his wife. I felt ridiculous, and at the same time as though I'd had a great load taken off my chest. When the car drove off, I grabbed Aunt Julia by the arm and almost dragged her bodily across the avenue and down toward the Malecón.

"Good heavens, what a temper," I heard her say as we came within sight of the sea. "You looked as though you were about to strangle poor Dr. Gumucio."

"You're the one I'm going to strangle," I said to her. "I've been waiting for you since three o'clock this afternoon and it's now eleven at night. Did you forget that we had a date?"

"I didn't forget. I stood you up on purpose," she said firmly.

We'd reached the little park in front of the Jesuit seminary. It was deserted, and though it wasn't raining, the grass, the laurel trees, the geraniums were glistening from the dampness. The mist was forming ghostly little umbrellas around the yellow cones of light from the lampposts.

"Well, let's postpone this fight to another day," I said to her, sitting her down on the edge of the jetty, with the deep-pitched, synchronous sound of the breaking waves mounting from below. "There's very little time now and a great many problems. Do you have a copy of your birth certificate and your divorce decree here?"

"What I have here is my ticket back to La Paz," she said, patting her purse. "I'm leaving at 10 a.m. on Sunday. And I'm happy. I've had it up to here with Peru and Peruvians."

"I'm sorry to have to tell you, but for the moment it just isn't possible for us to go live in another country," I said, sitting down next to her and putting my arm around her. "But I promise you that someday we'll go live in a garret in Paris."

Up till then, despite the hostile things she'd said, she'd been calm, half joking, very sure of herself. But suddenly a bitter look came over her face and she said in a harsh tone of voice, without looking at me: "Don't make things more difficult for me, Varguitas. It's your parents' fault that I'm going back to Bolivia, but I'm also going back because what's happening between us is stupid. You know very well we can't get married."

"Yes, we can," I said, kissing her on the cheek, on the neck, holding her tight, avidly touching her breasts, searching for her mouth with mine. "We need to find a kindhearted idiot of a judge, that's all. Javier's helping me. And Nancy's already found us a little apartment in Miraflores. There's no reason for us to be pessimistic."

She let me kiss and caress her, but she remained distant, very sedate. I told her about my conversation with Nancy, with Javier, my inquiries at the city hall, the way I'd managed to get a copy of my birth certificate, and told her that I loved her with all my heart, that we were going to get married even though I had to kill a whole bunch of people. When I tried to force her teeth apart with my tongue, she resisted, but then she opened her mouth and I was able to enter it and taste her palate, her gums, her saliva. I felt Aunt Julia's free arm creep around my neck, felt her huddle up close to me and begin to cry with sobs that shook her bosom. I consoled her in a voice that was an incoherent murmur, kissing her the while.

"You're still just a little kid," I heard her say softly, half laughing and half crying, as I told her, without pausing for breath, that I needed her, that I loved her, that I'd never let her go back to Bolivia, that I'd kill myself if she went away. Finally, she began to talk again, in a very soft voice, trying to make a joke: "Anyone who sleeps with little kids always wakes up soaking wet in the morning. Have you ever heard that old saw?"

"That's *huachafo* and an impermissible proverb," I answered, drying her eyes with my lips and my fingertips. "Do you have those papers here with you in Lima? Could your friend the ambassador certify them?"

She was calmer now. She'd stopped crying and was looking at me with tender affection. "How long would it last, Varguitas?" she asked me in a voice tinged with sadness. "How long before you'd get tired of me? A year, two years, three? Do you think it's fair that in two or three years you'll leave me and I'll have to start all over again?"

"Can the ambassador certify them?" I persisted. "If he certifies that they're valid in Bolivia, it'll be easy to get them certified as valid in Peru. I'll find some friend in the Ministry to help us."

She sat there looking at me, feeling sorry about all the trouble I was going to and at the same time deeply moved. A smile slowly appeared on her face. "If you'll swear to put up with me for five years, without losing your heart to anyone else, loving only me, okay," she said. "For five years of happiness I'll do this utterly mad thing."

"Do you have the papers?" I asked her, smoothing her hair, kissing it. "Will the ambassador certify them?"

She did have the papers and we did manage to get the Bolivian embassy to certify them with any number of multicolored seals and signatures. The entire business took barely half an hour, since the ambassador diplomatically swallowed Julia's story: she needed the papers certified that very morning, in order to comply with a formality that would allow her to take out of Bolivia the property she'd received as part of the divorce settlement. Nor was it difficult to get the Peruvian Minister of Foreign Relations to certify the Bolivian documents in turn. I got a helping hand from a professor at the university, an adviser of the Chancellery, for whom I had to invent another involved radio serial: a woman dying of cancer, who had to marry the man she'd been living with for years, just as soon as possible, so as to die at peace with God.

There in the Palacio de Torre Tagle, in a room with old colonial wood paneling centuries old and impeccably dressed young men, as I waited for the bureaucrat, apprised of the emergency situation by a telephone call from my professor, to put more seals on Aunt Julia's birth certificate and collect the necessary signatures that went with them, I heard about yet another catastrophe. An Italian boat, anchored at a dock in El Callao, loaded with departing passengers and visitors bidding them bon voyage, had all of a sudden, contrary to all known laws of physics and reason, begun turning round and round in circles, then listed to port and sank rapidly in the Pacific, with everyone on board lost—either fatally injured, drowned, or, incredibly, devoured by sharks. I learned this from the conversation of two ladies sitting next to me, also waiting while some formality was being taken care of. They were not joking; to them this shipwreck was a tragedy.

"It happened on one of Pedro Camacho's radio serials, am I correct?" I butted in.

"Yes, on the one at four o'clock," the older of the two ladies replied, a bony, energetic woman with a heavy Slavic accent. "The one about Alberto de Quinteros, the cardiologist."

"The doctor who was a gynecologist last month," a young girl sitting at a desk typing chimed in, smiling and putting her finger to her temple to indicate that somebody had obviously lost his mind.

"Didn't you hear yesterday's broadcast?" the lady in glasses who was with the foreign woman said in her unmistakable Lima accent. "Dr. Quinteros was on his way to Chile for a vacation, with his wife and Charo, his little girl. And all three of them drowned!" she said, in a voice filled with grief.

"They all drowned," the foreign woman put in. "The doctor's nephew Richard, and Elianita and her husband, Red Antúnez, that stupid idiot, and even the little baby born of the incestuous relation, Rubencito. They'd come down to the boat to see them off."

"But what's really funny is that Lieutenant Jaime Concha, who's from another serial, also drowned, especially since he'd already died in the El Callao fire three days before," the girl at the desk, who'd stopped typing, butted in again, dying with laughter. "Those serials have all turned into a tremendous joke, don't you think?"

One of the impeccably dressed young men, who had all the earmarks of an intellectual (specialty: Our Country's Borders), smiled at her indulgently and said to the rest of us in a tone of voice that Pedro Camacho would have had every right to describe as argentine: "Didn't I tell you that that device of carrying characters over from one story to another was invented by Balzac?" But he then drew a conclusion that gave him away: "If he discovers that Camacho's plagiarizing him, he'll get him sent to jail."

"What's so funny isn't that he carries them over from one serial to another but that he brings them back to life," the girl argued in her own defense. "Lieutenant Concha burned to death as he was reading a Donald Duck, so how is it possible for him to drown to death now?"

"Maybe he's just unlucky," the impeccably dressed young man who was bringing me my papers suggested.

I left with my papers now anointed and blessed, leaving the

two ladies, the secretary, and the young diplomats engaged in an animated discussion of the Bolivian scribe. Aunt Julia was waiting for me in a café and laughed when I recounted the whole episode to her; it had been some time since she'd listened to her compatriot's broadcasts.

Except for getting the papers certified, which had turned out to be so simple, all the other formalities, during this week of endless red tape and inquiries and running around, by myself or with Javier, to the mayor's office of every district in Lima, were frustrating and exhausting. I didn't set foot in the radio station except for the Panamericana news broadcast, and turned the job of preparing all the hourly bulletins over to Pascual, who was thus able to offer the radio listeners a veritable festival of accidents, crimes, acts of mayhem, and kidnappings that caused as much blood to be shed via Radio Panamericana as was being shed on the airwaves at Radio Central by my friend Camacho in his systematic genocide of his characters.

I began my rounds very early in the morning. The first mayor's offices I visited were those of the run-down municipalities farthest from downtown Lima: El Rímac, El Porvenir, Vitarte, Chorrillos. I explained the problem a hundred and one times (blushing furiously the first few times, and after that with the greatest aplomb) to mayors, deputy mayors, municipal councilors, secretaries, janitors, messenger boys, and each time the answer was a categorical no. I ran into the same stumbling block each time: unless I could produce notarized proof of my parents' consent, or of my having been emancipated by them before the judge of the juvenile court, I could not get married. I then tried my luck in the mayor's offices of the districts in the center of town (except for Miraflores and San Isidro, since there might be someone around who knew my family), with precisely the same result. After looking over my papers, the functionaries would inevitably crack jokes at my expense that were like so many kicks in the belly: "So you want to marry your mama, do you?" or "Don't be a fool, my boy, why get married? Just shack up with her and that'll be that." The only place where there was a ray of hope was in the mayor's office in Surco, where a plump, beetle-browed male secretary told us that the matter could be arranged for ten thousand *soles*, "because lots of people will have to be paid to keep their mouths shut." I tried to bargain with him, and had gotten him down to five thousand *soles*, a sum I'd have great difficulty scraping together, but at that point, as though suddenly frightened by his own audacity, he backed down and ended up kicking us out of the office.

I talked on the phone with Aunt Julia twice a day and lied to her, telling her that things were going along without a hitch, that she should have a small suitcase all packed containing the things of hers she considered indispensable, that at any moment now I'd be calling to say, "Everything's all set." But I was feeling more and more demoralized. On Friday evening, when I returned to my grandparents' house, I found a telegram from my parents: "Arriving Monday, Panagra, flight 516."

That night, after tossing and turning in bed for a long time as I thought things over, I finally turned on the lamp on the nightstand, fished out the notebook in which I kept a list of subjects for stories, and wrote down, by order of preference, the options that lay before me. The first was to marry Aunt Julia and confront the family with a legal fait accompli that they would be obliged to accept, like it or not. But inasmuch as there were only a few days left now and the municipal authorities all over Lima were proving so refractory, this first option was turning out to be more and more utopian. The second was to flee abroad with Aunt Julia. But not to Bolivia; the idea of living in a world where she had lived without me, where she had so many friends and acquaintances, not to mention an ex-husband, bothered me. The best country for us would be Chile. She could go off to La Paz, to fool the family, and I would light out for Tacna, in an intercity bus or a jitney. I'd manage in one way or another to cross the border illegally to Arica, and from there I'd proceed overland to Santiago, where Aunt Julia would come to join me or be waiting for me. The possibility of traveling and living without a passport (getting one would also require written permission from my parents) didn't strike me as an insuperable obstacle, and in fact it rather pleased me: it sounded like something straight out of a romantic novel. If the family, as they were certain to do, tracked me down and forced the authorities to return me to Peru, I would run away again, as many times as necessary, and that was how I'd live my life till

I reached that longed-for, liberating twenty-first birthday. The third option was to kill myself, leaving an eloquent, well-written suicide note, that would plunge my parents in remorse.

The next day, at a very early hour, I rushed over to Javier's *pensión*. We'd fallen into the habit of going over the events of the day before each morning as he shaved and showered and drawing up a plan of action for the day just beginning. Sitting on the toilet seat watching him lather his face, I read him my list of options as I had outlined them in my notebook, with comments in the margin.

As he rinsed the lather off, he argued insistently that I should change the order of my preferences and put suicide at the head of my list. "If you kill yourself, the junk you've written will automatically attract attention, people with a morbid turn of mind will want to read your stories, and it'll be easy to bring them out as a book," he said persuasively as he dried his face. "You'll be a famous writer—posthumously, I grant you."

"You're going to make me miss the first news bulletin," I said, to hurry him up. "You can stop the Cantinflas act—I don't find your jokes the least bit funny."

"If you did yourself in, I wouldn't have to miss so many days at work or so many of my classes at the university," Javier went on as he got dressed. "The best possible thing would be for you to go through with it today, right away, this very morning. That way, I wouldn't have to pawn my things, which naturally I'm never going to be able to redeem before they auction them off, because, is there any chance you'll be able to pay me back someday?"

And as we were trotting down the street to the jitney stop, still convinced that he was a first-rate comedian, he went on: "And one last thing: if you kill yourself, you'll be the talk of the town, and reporters will flock to interview your best friend, your confidant, the witness of the tragedy, and his picture will be in all the papers. Don't you think there's a good chance that your cousin Nancy would be swayed by all that publicity I'd get?"

In the (horribly named) Bureau of Pignoration on the Plaza de Armas, we pawned my typewriter and his radio, my watch and his pens, and I finally persuaded him that he should also pawn his watch. Despite bargaining furiously, all we managed to get was two thousand *soles*. Earlier on, without my grandparents' noticing, I had little by little sold my suits, shoes, shirts, ties, sweaters to secondhand clothes dealers on the Calle La Paz, till I had practically nothing left but the clothes on my back. But the immolation of my wardrobe brought me barely four hundred *soles*. I had better luck, however, with Genaro Jr, whom I finally persuaded, after a dramatic half hour, to give me four months' salary in advance and deduct the amount advanced me from my paychecks over a year's time. The conversation had an unexpected ending. I had sworn that I needed the money urgently to pay for a hernia operation my granny had to have, a plea that had left him unmoved. But then suddenly he said: "All right, I'll give you the advance," and then added, with a friendly smile: "But admit that it's to pay for your girlfriend's abortion." I lowered my eyes and begged him not to give my secret away.

On seeing how depressed I was at having gotten so little money for the things we'd pawned, Javier went back to the radio station with me, since we'd decided that we'd both ask for the afternoon off from our respective jobs so as to go to Huacho together. Perhaps the municipal authorities in the provinces would turn out to be more sentimental. I arrived in my office up in the shack just as the phone was ringing. It was Aunt Julia, beside herself with rage. The night before, Aunt Hortensia and Uncle Alejandro had dropped by Uncle Lucho's for a visit, and had refused to even say hello to her.

"They looked at me like something the cat dragged in, and I wouldn't have been at all surprised if they'd called me a whore to my face," she said indignantly. "I had to bite my tongue to keep myself from telling them to go you know where. I held my temper for my sister's sake, and for ours too, so as not to make things worse than they are already. How's everything going, Varguitas?"

"Monday, first thing," I assured her. "You should say you're postponing your flight to La Paz for a day. I've got everything almost ready."

"Don't worry too much about finding that obliging mayor," Aunt Julia said. "I'm so furious now I don't give a damn. Even if you don't find one, we'll run away together anyway."

"Why don't the two of you get married in Chincha, Don Mario?" I heard Pascual say the minute I hung up. Seeing how dumfounded I was, he turned beet-red: "It's not that I'm a busybody who's trying to stick my nose in your affairs. We couldn't help overhearing the two of you, that's all, and naturally we tumbled to what was going on. I'm just trying to help. The mayor of Chincha's my cousin and he'll marry you on the spot, with or without papers, whether you're of age or not."

Everything was miraculously resolved that very day. Javier and Pascual went to Chincha by bus that afternoon, with all the papers and instructions to get everything all set for Monday. As they were off doing that, I went with my cousin Nancy to rent the one-room studio apartment in Miraflores, asked for three days off from work (I got them after a Homeric discussion with Genaro Sr., boldly threatening to quit if he refused to let me have the time off), and organized my escape from Lima. On Saturday night Javier returned with good news. The mayor was a congenial young guy, and when Javier and Pascual had told him the whole story, he'd laughed and applauded our plans to elope. "How romantic!" he'd commented. He'd kept the papers and assured them, "just between us," that there would be a way of getting around posting the banns as well.

On Sunday I phoned Aunt Julia to inform her that I'd found our kindhearted idiot of a mayor, that we'd elope the following day at eight o'clock in the morning, and that at noon we'd be husband and wife.

Sixteen.

Joaquín Hinostroza Bellmont,

who was destined to bring stadium crowds to their feet, not by making goals or blocking penalty kicks but by making memorable decisions as a referee at soccer matches, and whose thirst for alcohol was to leave traces and debts in many a Lima bar, was born in one of those residences that mandarins had built for them thirty years ago, in La Perla, with the aim of turning that vast empty tract of land into the Copacabana of Lima (an aim that miscarried due to the dampness, which—punishment of the camel that stubbornly insists on passing through the eye of the needle—ravaged the throats and bronchia of the Peruvian aristocracy).

Joaquín was the only son of a family that, in addition to being wealthy, had ties (dense forest of trees whose intertwining branches are titles and coats of arms) with the blue bloods of Spain and France. But the father of the future referee and drunkard had put patents of nobility aside and devoted his life to the modern ideal of multiplying his fortune many times over, in business enterprises that ranged from the manufacture of fine woolen textiles to the introduction of the cultivation of hot peppers as a cash crop in the Amazon region. The mother, a lymphatic madonna, a self-abnegating spouse, had spent her life paying out the money her husband made to doctors and healers (for she suffered from a number of diseases common to the upper class of society). The two of them had had Joaquín rather late in life, after having long prayed to God to give them an heir. His birth brought indescribable happiness to his parents, who, from his cradle days, dreamed of a future for him as a prince of industry, a king of agriculture, a magus of diplomacy, or a Lucifer of politics.

Was it out of rebellion, a stubborn refusal to accept this radiant social and chrematistic glory to which he was destined, that the child became a soccer referee, or was it due to some psychological shortcoming? No, it was the result of a genuine vocation. From his last baby bottle to the first fuzz on his upper lip he had, naturally, any number of governesses, imported from foreign countries: France, England. And teachers at the best private schools in Lima were recruited to teach him numbers and his ABC's. One after the other, all of them ended up giving up their fat salary, demoralized and hysterical in the face of the little boy's ontological indifference toward any sort of knowledge. At the age of eight he hadn't yet learned to add, and, as for the alphabet, was still learning, with the greatest of difficulty, to recite the vowels. He spoke only in monosyllables, was a quiet child who never misbehaved, and wandered from one room to the other of the mansion in La Perla, amid the countless toys imported from every corner of the globe to amuse him—German Meccano sets, Japanese trains, Chinese puzzles, Austrian tin soldiers, North American tricycles—looking as though he were bored to death. The one thing that seemed to bring him out of his Brahmanic torpor from time to time were the little cards with pictures of soccer players that came with boxes of Mar del Sur chocolates; he would paste them in fancy albums and spend hours on end looking at them with great interest.

Terrified at the idea that they had brought into this world an offspring who was the product of too rigid inbreeding, a hemophiliac and mentally defective, doomed to become a public laughingstock, the parents sought the aid of science. A series of illustrious disciples of Aesculapius were summoned to La Perla.

It was the city's number-one pediatrician, Dr. Alberto de Quinteros, the star of his profession, who shed the dazzling light of his knowledge on the boy's case and opened his tormented parents' eyes. "He is suffering from what I call the hothouse malady," he explained. "Plants that don't grow outside in a garden, amid flowers and insects, become sickly and produce blossoms whose scent is nauseating. This child's gilded cage is making an imbecile of him. All his governesses and tutors should be dismissed and he should be enrolled in a school where he can associate with boys his own age. He'll be normal the day one of his schoolmates punches him in the nose!"

Prepared to make any and every sacrifice to decretinize him, the haughty couple agreed to allow Joaquincito to plunge into the plebeian outside world. The school they chose for him was, naturally, the most expensive one in Lima, that of the Padres de Santa María, and in order not to destroy all hierarchical distinctions, they had a school uniform made for him in the regulation colors, but in velvet.

The famous doctor's prescription produced noticeable results. Admittedly, Joaquín received unusually low grades, and (the lust for lucre that brought Luther) in order for him to pass his exams, his parents were obliged to make donations (stained-glass windows for the school chapel, wool surplices for the acolytes, sturdy desks for the little school for poor children, et cetera), but nonetheless the fact is that the boy became sociable and from that time on he occasionally appeared to be happy. And it was during this period that the first sign of his genius (his uncomprehending father called it a vice) manifested itself: an interest in soccer. When they were told that young Joaquín, their apathetic, monosyllabic offspring, was transformed into an energetic, garrulous creature the moment he put on soccer shoes, his parents were delighted. They immediately purchased a vacant lot adjoining their mansion in La Perla to turn it into a soccer field, of appreciable size, where Joaquincito could play to his heart's content.

From then on, every afternoon when classes let out, twenty-two pupils—the faces changed, but the number was always the same—could be seen getting off the Santa María bus on the foggy Avenida de las Palmeras to play soccer on the Hinostroza Bellmonts' field. After the game was over, the family always invited the players in for tea with chocolates, gelatine desserts, meringues, and ice cream. The wealthy parents rejoiced to see their little Joaquín panting happily each afternoon.

After a few weeks, however, Peru's pioneer hot-pepper grower noticed something odd. He had twice, three times, ten times found Joaquincito refereeing the game. With a whistle in his mouth and a little cap with a sun visor perched on his head, he would run after the players, call fouls, impose penalties. Although the boy seemed to have no complexes about fulfilling the role of referee rather than playing, the millionaire was incensed. He invited these boys to his house, stuffed them with sweets, allowed them to hobnob with his son as though they were equals, and then they had the nerve to foist the humble role of referee off on Joaquín? He very nearly opened his Dobermans' cages to give those insolent boys a good scare. But in the end he merely reprimanded them severely. To his surprise, the boys protested that they were not to blame and swore that Joaquín was the referee because he wanted to be, and the supposed injured party solemnly confirmed, taking God as his witness, that what they said was true. A few months later, consulting his memorandum book and the reports of his groundskeepers, the father found himself confronted with these statistics: of the 132 games played on his field, Joaquín Hinostroza Bellmont had not played in a single one and had refereed 132. Exchanging glances, the father and mother said to themselves subliminally that something wasn't right: how could this possibly be considered normal behavior? And again they called upon science for help.

It was the most renowned astrologer in the city, a man who read souls in the stars and mended the minds of his clients (he preferred to call them his "friends") by means of the signs of the zodiac, Professor Lucio Assmule, who, after casting many horoscopes, interrogating the heavenly bodies, and absorbing himself in lunar meditation, pronounced his verdict, which, if perhaps not the most accurate one, was in any event the one most flattering to the parents.

"The child knows at the cellular level that he is an aristocrat, and faithful to his origins, he cannot tolerate the idea of being equal to the others," he explained to them, removing his glasses—to ensure that the bright gleam of intelligence that appeared in his eyes on announcing a prediction would be all the more visible? "He would rather be a referee than a player because the person who referees a match is the one in command. Did you think that Joaquincito was engaging in a sport out there on that green rectangle? You're wrong, altogether wrong. He is indulging an ancestral appetite for domination, singularity, and hierarchical distinction which undoubtedly is in his very blood."

Sobbing for joy, the father smothered his son with kisses, declared himself a man blessed by heaven, and added a zero to the check in payment of the fee, already a princely sum, set by Professor Assmule. Convinced that this mania for refereeing his schoolmates' soccer matches stemmed from a driving will to power and a superiority complex that would one day make his son the master of the world (or, in the very worst of cases, of Peru), the industrialist frequently abandoned his multiple office of an afternoon in order (sentimental weakness of the lion whose eyes brim with tears on seeing its cub tear apart its first lamb) to come to his private stadium in La Perla to paternally rejoice at the sight of Joaquín, dressed in the splendid uniform he'd given him as a present, blowing the whistle on that bastard horde (the players?).

Ten years later, the disconcerted parents couldn't help wondering whether the astral prophecies might not have been too optimistic. Joaquín Hinostroza Bellmont was now eighteen years old and had reached the last grade in his high school several years after the boys who'd been his classmates at the beginning, and it was only thanks to his family's philanthropy that he had managed to get that far. There were no signs anywhere of the genes of a conqueror of the world that, according to Lucio Assmule, were camouflaged beneath the innocent whim to referee soccer games, whereas, on the other hand, it was becoming terribly obvious that this son of aristocrats was a hopeless disaster when it came to anything but awarding free kicks. Judging by the things he said, he had an intelligence that placed him, Darwinianly speaking, somewhere between the oligophrenic and the monkey, and his lack of wit, of ambition, of interest in anything save his frantic activities as a referee, made him a profoundly dull person.

It is true, however, that insofar as his first vice was concerned (the second was alcohol), the boy displayed something that deserved to be called talent. His teratological impartiality (in the *sacred* space of the soccer field and the *magic* time of competition?) earned him a reputation as a referee among the students and teachers at Santa María, as did (hawk that from the clouds spies beneath the carob tree the rat that will be its lunch) his vision that permitted him to detect, infallibly, at any distance and from any angle, the sly kick in the shins given the center forward by the defensive half, or the vicious elbow blow dealt the goalie by the wing who jumped with him. His omniscient knowledge of the rules and the happy intuition that enabled him to fill in the gaps in the rule book with lightning decisions were also extraordinary. His fame soon spread beyond the walls of Santa María and the aristocrat of La Perla began to referee interscholastic games, district championships, and one day the news got around that—at the stadium in El Potao?—he had substituted for a referee in a second-division match.

Once he finished high school at Santa María, Joaquín's bewildered parents were faced with a problem: his future. The idea of sending him to the university was painfully rejected, to spare the boy pointless humiliations and inferiority complexes and avoid further drains on the family fortune in the form of donations. An attempt to get him to learn foreign languages ended in a resounding failure. After a year in the United States and another in France, he had not picked up a single word of English or of French, and in the meantime his already rachitic Spanish became positively tubercular. When Joaquín returned to Lima, the manufacturer of woolen textiles finally resigned himself to the fact that his son would never have a degree after his name, and thoroughly disillusioned, put him to work in the tangled thickets of the many interlocking family enterprises. As might have been predicted, the results were catastrophic. Within two years, his acts or omissions had driven two spinning mills into bankruptcy, and put the most flourishing firm of the conglomerate—a road-construction company—deeply into debt, and the hot-pepper plantations in the jungle had had their entire crop eaten by insects, flattened by avalanches, engulfed by floods (thus proving that Joaquincito was a jinx). Stunned by his son's immeasurable incompetence, his pride wounded, the father lost all his energy, became nihilistic, and neglected his various businesses so badly that in a short time they were bled white by greedy lieutenants, and he developed a laughable tic: sticking out his tongue and trying (inanely?) to lick his ear. Following in his wife's footsteps, his nervousness and bouts of insomnia delivered him into the hands of psychiatrists and psychoanalysts (Alberto de Quinteros? Lucio Assmule?), who soon relieved him of whatever good sense and money he had left.

His progenitors' financial ruin and mental collapse did not drive Joaquín Hinostroza Bellmont to the brink of suicide. He went on living in La Perla, in a ghostly mansion that little by little had faded, grown moldy, lost its gardens and soccer field (sold to pay off debts), been abandoned and invaded by filth and spiders. The young man spent his days refereeing the street games gotten up by the homeless ragamuffins of the district, in the vacant lots separating La Perla from Bellavista. It was at one of these matches fought by rowdy urchins, right in the middle of a street, with a couple of stones serving as goals and lampposts as boundary markers, which Joaquín (*arbiter elegantiarum*, dressed in evening clothes, to dine in the middle of the jungle) refereed as though they were championship finals, that the son of aristocrats met the person who was to make him a star and a victim of cirrhosis of the liver: Sarita Huanca Salaverría?

He had seen her play several times in these street matches and had even penalized her repeatedly for her aggressive manner of charging her adversary. They called her Virago, but Joaquín had never suspected that this adolescent with the sallow complexion, dressed in blue jeans and a ragged sweater, and wearing a pair of old house slippers, was a female. He discovered this fact erotically. One day, after he had given her a penalty for what was unquestionably foul play (she'd scored a point by kicking the ball and the goalie at the same time), she'd responded by uttering a crude insult having to do with his mother.

"What was that you said?" the son of aristocrats shot back indignantly—thinking that at that very moment his mother was doubtless swallowing a pill, sipping a sedative potion, receiving a painful injection? "If you're a man, I dare you to repeat it."

"I'm not one, but I'll repeat it," Virago replied. And (honor of a Spartan woman capable of allowing herself to be burned alive rather than take back what she has said) she repeated the rude insult, embroidering it with gutter adjectives.

Joaquín tried to throw a punch at her, but it landed in thin air, and the next moment he found himself lying on the ground, knocked down by a roundhouse from Virago, who then fell on him, hitting him with her fists, feet, knees, elbows. And there on the ground (violent gymnastics on the canvas that end up resembling passionate embraces) he discovered—stupefied, erogenized, ejaculating—that his adversary was a woman. The emotion aroused in him by this wrestling match, along with its attendant unexpected turgescences, was so intense that it changed his life. After making his peace with her after the fight and learning that her name was Sarita Huanca Salaverría, he invited her then and there to go to the movies with him to see a Tarzan film, and a week later he proposed to her. Sarita's refusal to become his wife, or even allow him to kiss her, drove Joaquín classically to drink and to cheap bars. Within a short time, he went from being a romantic drowning his troubles in whiskey to being a hopeless alcoholic capable of trying to quench his African thirst with kerosene.

What was it that awakened in Joaquín this passion for Sarita Huanca Salaverría? She was young, with the svelte physique of a banty rooster, a complexion tanned by exposure to the elements, hair cut in bangs like a *jeune premier* ballet dancer, and as a soccer player she wasn't bad. All in all, her manner of dress, the things she did, the company she kept seemed very odd for a woman. Was it precisely this perhaps—a penchant for originality bordering on vice, a frantic tendency toward bizarre behavior—that made her so attractive to the aristocrat? The first time he took Virago to the run-down mansion in La Perla, his parents looked at each other in disgust once the two of them had left. The former millionaire summed up all his bitterness in a single phrase: "We've engendered not only an imbecile but a sexual pervert as well."

Nonetheless, while Sarita Huanca Salaverría was responsible for Joaquín's becoming an alcoholic, she served at the same time as the trampoline that catapulted him from his status as a referee of street games played with a ball made of rags to championship matches in the National Stadium.

Virago was not content merely to refuse the aristocrat's passionate advances; she took great pleasure in making him suffer. She accepted his invitations to the movies, to soccer matches, to bullfights, to restaurants, she allowed him to shower her with expensive presents (on which her love-smitten suitor spent the last dregs of the family fortune?), but she did not permit Joaquín to speak to her of love. The moment he tried to tell her how much he loved her (timidity of a stripling who blushes and gets all choked up on paying compliments to a flower), Sarita Huanca Salaverría would rise to her feet in fury, insult him with a vulgarity worthy of Bajo el Puente, and demand to be taken home.

It was then that Joaquín began to drink, going from one cheap bar to another, and mixing his drinks in order to obtain rapid and explosive effects. It was a common sight for his parents to see him coming home at the hour when night owls go to roost, stumbling through the rooms of the La Perla mansion, leaving behind him a trail of vomit. Just as he seemed about to dissolve in alcohol, a telephone call from Sarita would bring him back to life. He would get his hopes up once more and the infernal cycle would begin all over again. Consumed with bitterness, the man with the tic and his hypochondriac spouse died almost at the same time and were buried in a mausoleum in the Presbítero Maestro Cemetery. The tumbledown mansion in La Perla, what was left of the surrounding property, and all the other meager assets that still remained were handed over to creditors or confiscated by the state. Joaquín Hinostroza Bellmont was obliged to work for a living.

Considering the sort of person he was (his past deafeningly proclaimed that he would either die of consumption or end up begging on the streets), he did more than well for himself. What profession did he choose? Soccer referee! Goaded on by hunger and the desire to go on spoiling the disdainful Sarita, he began asking for a few *soles* from the urchins who asked him to referee their games, and on seeing that they managed to pay him by prorating the sum among themselves, two plus two are four and four and two are six, gradually raised his fees and began watching where his money went. As his skills on the soccer field became well known, he secured contracts for himself at junior competitions, and one day he boldly presented himself at the Association for Soccer Referees and Coaches and applied for membership. He passed the examinations with a brilliance that dizzied those who from that moment on he was able to refer to (conceitedly?) as his colleagues.

The appearance of Joaquín Hinostroza Bellmont—black uniform with white pinstripes, little green sun visor on his forehead, silver-plated whistle in his mouth—in the José Díaz National Stadium marked a red-letter day in the history of Peruvian soccer. A veteran sports reporter was to write: "With him, unbending justice and artistic inspiration entered our stadiums." His rectitude, his impartiality, his quick and unerring eye for fouls and his adroitness at meting out exactly the right penalty, his authority (the players always lowered their eyes when they spoke to him, and addressed him as Don), and his physical fitness that enabled him to run for the entire ninety minutes of a match and never be more than ten meters from the ball, soon made him popular. As someone once put it in a speech, he was the only referee who was never disobeyed by the players or attacked by the spectators, and the only one who received an ovation from the grandstands after every match.

Were these talents and efforts due only to an exceptional professional conscience? This was a partial explanation, to be sure. But the most profound reason behind them was that Joaquín Hinostroza Bellmont wanted most of all (the secret of a young man who triumphs in Europe but whose days are nonetheless filled with bitterness, because what he really wanted was the applause of his little village in the Andes) to impress Virago with his magic skills as a referee. They were still seeing each other, nearly every day, and scabrous popular gossip had it that they were lovers. In reality, despite his amorous stubbornness, which had remained undiminished throughout the years, the referee had not managed to overcome Sarita's resistance.

One day, after picking him up off the floor of a cheap bar in El Callao, taking him to the *pensión* in the center of town where he lived, wiping away the spittle and sawdust he was covered with, and putting him to bed, Sarita Huanca Salaverría revealed to him the secret of her life. Joaquín Hinostroza Bellmont thus learned (pallor of a man who has received the vampire's kiss) that in her early youth there had been an accursed love and a conjugal catastrophe. In fact, between Sarita and her brother (Richard?) a tragic love affair had taken place that (cataracts of fire, a rain of poison on humanity) had led to her becoming pregnant. She had cleverly entered into matrimony with a suitor whom she had previously disdained (Red Antúnez? Luis Marroquín?), so that the child born of incest would not have a blot upon his name, but the happy young husband (the Devil sticking his tail in the pot and curdling the sauce) had discovered her trickery in time and repudiated the treacherous wife who had tried to pass off another man's child as his. Forced to have an abortion, Sarita abandoned her family of noble lineage, her elegant residential district, her impressive name, and becoming a tramp, had acquired the personality and nickname of Virago in the vacant lots of Bellavista and La Perla. From that time on, she had sworn never again to give herself to a man and to live the rest of her life, for all practical purposes (except, alas, that of the production of spermatozoa?), as a male.

Learning of the tragedy, seasoned with sacrilege, the transgression of taboos, the trampling underfoot of civic morality and religious commandments, of Sarita Huanca Salaverría did not destroy Joaquín Hinostroza Bellmont's passionate love; on the contrary, it made it all the more intense. The man from La Perla even conceived the idea of curing Virago of her traumas and reconciling her with society and men; he wanted to make of her, once again, a very feminine young woman of Lima, a charming, flirtatious, piquant little rascal—like La Perricholi?

As his fame spread, he was asked to referee international matches in Lima and abroad, and received offers to work in Mexico, Brazil, Colombia, Venezuela, which (patriotism of the scientist who turns down the computers of New York in order to go on experimenting with his tubercular guinea pigs in the laboratories of the Peruvian School of Medicine) he always refused; at the same time, his siege of the incestuous Sarita's heart became more stubborn than ever.

And it seemed to him that he glimpsed certain signs (Apache smoke signals on the hills, tom-toms in the African rain forest) that Sarita Huanca Salaverría might yield. One afternoon, after coffee with croissants at the Haití, on the Plaza de Armas, he managed to hold the girl's right hand between his for more than a minute (precisely: the chronometer in his referee's head timed it). Shortly thereafter, there was an international match in which the team that had won the Peruvian championship confronted a band of assassins from a country of little renown (Argentina, or something like that?), who showed up on the playing field in cleated shoes, knee guards, and elbow patches which were really weapons to injure their adversary. Paying no attention to their arguments (as a matter of fact, they were telling the truth) that in their country that was how soccer was played (topping it off with torture and crime?), Joaquín Hinostroza Bellmont ordered them off the field, with the result that the Peruvian team won a technical victory for lack of an opposing team. The referee, naturally, was carried out of the stadium in triumph on the shoulders of the crowd, and Sarita Huanca Salaverría, once they were alone (a burst of patriotic enthusiasm? sportive sentimentality?) threw her arms around his neck and kissed him. Once, when he was taken ill (cirrhosis was insidiously, fatally mineralizing the liver of the Man of the Stadiums and beginning to cause him to suffer periodic crises), she took care of him, never once leaving his bedside, during the entire week that he remained in the Hospital Carrión, and one night Joaquín saw her shed tears (for him?). All this encouraged him, and continually thinking up new arguments, he proposed to her every day. But it was to no avail. Sarita Huanca Salaverría attended all the matches that he interpreted (the sportswriters were now comparing his refereeing to conducting a symphony), she accompanied him when he went abroad, and she had even moved to the Pensión Colonial, where Joaquín lived with his sister the pianist and his aged parents. She refused, however, to allow this fraternity to cease to be chaste and turn into joyous lovemaking. The uncertainty (daisy with an infinite number of petals to be torn off) continued little by little to aggravate Joaquín Hinostroza Bellmont's alcoholism, to the point where eventually he was more often drunk than sober.

Alcohol was the Achilles' heel of his professional life, the millstone around his neck that, according to those in the know, kept him from being invited to Europe to referee. How to explain, on the other hand, how a man who drank as much as he did was able to practice a profession demanding such taxing physical effort? The fact is that (enigmas paving the path of history) he pursued both vocations at the same time, and from his thirtieth year on, they overlapped: Joaquín Hinostroza Bellmont began refereeing matches drunk as a skunk and continued to referee them in his mind afterwards in bars.

Alcohol did not dull his talents: it neither blurred his vision nor lessened his authority nor set back his career. It is quite true that every so often he was overcome by an attack of the hiccups in the middle of a match, and that (calumnies that poison the air and stab genuine merit in the back) there were those who swore that once, overcome by Saharan thirst, he grabbed a bottle of liniment out of the hands of a medical attendant hurrying out onto the field to aid a player and gulped it down as though it were cold water.

But such episodes—a collection of picturesque anecdotes, the mythology that surrounds genius—in no way hindered his triumphant march to fame and glory.

And so, amid the thundering applause of the crowd in the stadium and the penitential drinking bouts whereby he endeavored to drown his remorse (inquisitor's pincers that dig about in living flesh, the rack that breaks bones) in his soul of a missionary of the true faith (Jehovah's Witnesses?) for having impulsively raped, on a mad night in his youth, a minor from La Victoria (Sarita Huanca Salaverría?), Joaquín Hinostroza Bellmont reached the prime of life: his fifties. He was a man with a broad forehead, an aquiline nose, a penetrating gaze, the very soul of rectitude and goodness, who had climbed to the heights of his profession.

It was at this juncture that Lima became the site of the most important soccer event of the half century, the final match of the South American Championship series, between two teams who in the semifinals had each overwhelmingly defeated their opponents: Bolivia and Peru. Although tradition recommended that a referee from a neutral country be chosen to preside over this match, the two teams, and (chivalry of the Altiplano, Andean nobility, Aymara point of honor) the foreigners in particular, insisted that the famous Joaquín Hinostroza Marroquín referee the match. And since players, substitutes, and coaches threatened to strike if this demand was not granted, the Federation finally agreed and the Jehovah's Witness was given the mission of presiding over this match that everyone prophesied would be a memorable one.

The stubborn gray clouds of Lima lifted that Sunday, permitting the sun's warm rays to shine down upon the contest. Many people had spent the night in line in the open air, hoping to be able to buy tickets (even though everyone knew they had been sold out for a month). From dawn on, all around the National Stadium, swarms of people milled about looking for scalpers and prepared to commit every imaginable crime in order to get in. Two hours before the match, the stadium was so jam-packed there wasn't room for a fly. Several hundred citizens of the great country to the south (Bolivia?), come to Lima from their limpid mountain heights by plane, by car, and on foot, had banded together in the eastern grandstand. The wild cheers and locomotives of visitors and natives had raised the excitement in the stadium to fever pitch as the crowd waited for the teams to appear on the field.

In view of the magnitude of this concentration of the populace, the authorities had taken precautions. The most famous brigade of the Guardia Civil, the one which, in the space of a few months (heroism and self-sacrifice, boldness and urbanity) had cleared every last lawbreaker and malefactor out of El Callao, was brought to Lima to ensure security and civil behavior in the stands and on the playing field. Its chief, the celebrated Captain Lituma, the terror of crime, walked feverishly about the stadium and made the rounds of the gates and the adjacent streets, checking to make sure that the patrol squads were at their proper stations and issuing inspired orders to his doughty adjutant, Sergeant Jaime Concha.

Amid the roaring crowd in the western grandstand when the starting whistle blew, battered and bruised and almost unable to breathe, were, in addition to Sarita Huanca Salaverría, who (masochism of the victim fallen head over heels in love with the man who has raped her) never missed one of the matches that Joaquín refereed, the venerable Don Sebastián Bergua, risen only recently from the bed of pain on which he lay as a result of the knife wounds he had received at the hands of the medical detail man Luis Marroquín Bellmont (who was in the northern grandstand of the stadium, by very special permission of the Board of Prisons?), his wife Margarita, and his daughter Rosa, now completely recovered from the bites inflicted upon her—O accursed Amazon dawn—by a pack of rats.

There was nothing to foreshadow the impending tragedy when Joaquín Hinostroza (Tello? Delfín)—who, as usual, had been obliged to make the tour of the stadium to acknowledge the applause—alert and agile, blew the starting whistle. On the contrary, the match proceeded in an enthusiastic, courteous atmosphere: the players' passes, the fans' applause acclaiming the forwards' shots for the net and the goalkeepers' blocks. From the very first moment, it was evident that the oracles would be fulfilled: the teams were evenly matched and the play fair but hard. More creative than ever, Joaquín Hinostroza (Abril?) glided across the turf as though on roller skates, never getting in the players' way and invariably placing himself at the very best angle, and his decisions, stern but just, prevented (heat of battle that turns a contest into a brawl) the match from degenerating into violence. But (limits of the human condition) not even a saintly Jehovah's Witness could prevent the fulfillment of what destiny (impassivity of the fakir, British phlegm) had plotted.

The irreversible infernal mechanism began to function in the second half, when the score was tied 1–1 and the spectators found themselves with no voice left and their palms burning. Captain Lituma and Sergeant Concha said to each other, naïvely, that everything was going very well: not a single incident—a robbery, a fight, a lost child—had occurred to spoil the afternoon.

But at precisely 4:13 p.m., the fifty thousand spectators saw the totally unexpected happen, before their very eyes. From the most crowded section of the southern grandstand, an apparition suddenly emerged—black, thin, very tall, one enormous tooth—nimbly scaled the fence, and rushed out onto the playing field uttering incomprehensible cries. The people in the stands were less surprised to see that the man was nearly naked—all he had on was a tiny loincloth—than they were to see that his body was covered, from head to foot, with scars. A collective gasp shook the stands; everyone realized that the tattooed man intended to kill the referee. There could be no doubt of it: the shrieking giant was running straight toward the idol of the world of soccer (Gumercindo Hinostroza Delfín?), who, totally absorbed in his art, had not seen him and was going on modeling the match.

Who was the imminent assailant? Was it perhaps that stowaway who had mysteriously arrived in El Callao and been caught by the night patrol? The same unfortunate wretch whom the authorities had euthanasiacally decided to shoot to death and whose life the sergeant (Concha?) had spared on a dark night? Neither Captain Lituma nor Sergeant Concha had time to check. Realizing that if they did not act at once, a national glory might be the victim of an attack on his life, the captain—superior and subordinate had a method of communicating with each other by blinking—ordered the sergeant to go into action. Without rising to his feet, Jaime Concha drew his revolver and fired the twelve bullets in it, every one of which lodged in different parts of the nudist's body (at a distance of fifty yards). In this way the sergeant had finally complied (better late than never, as the old saying goes) with the orders he had been given, for, in fact, it was the stowaway of El Callao!

Seeing its idol's potential murderer, whom an instant before it had hated, riddled with bullets was enough to cause the crowd (capricious whims of a fickle flirt, coquettishness of a changeable female) to side immediately with him, to transform him into a martyr, and to turn against the Guardia Civil. A collective hissing, booing, whistling that deafened the birds in the sky rose from the stands as the crowd voiced its protest at the sight of the black lying on the field bleeding to death from the twelve bullet holes. The sound of gunfire had disconcerted the players, but the Great Hinostroza (Téllez Unzátegui?), true to himself, had not allowed the match to be stopped, and went on with his brilliant refereeing, nimbly sidestepping the interloper's corpse, deaf to the whistling from the stands, to which jeers, taunts, insults were now added. The first multicolored cushions were already sailing through the air, soon to become a veritable deluge raining down on Captain Lituma's police detachment. The latter smelled a hurricane in the offing and decided to act quickly. He ordered his men to prepare to launch tear-gas bombs, his intention being to prevent at all costs a terrible bloodbath. And a few moments later, when the barriers around the ring had been breached at many points and here and there impassioned taurophiles bent on mayhem were rushing into the arena, he ordered his men to hurl a few grenades on the edges of the bullring. A few tears and coughing fits, he thought, would calm the enraged protestors down and peace would reign once again in the Plaza de Acho as soon as the wind had dispersed the chemical effluvia. He also ordered a group of four Guardias to surround Sergeant Jaime Concha, who had become the principal target of the hotheads: they were obviously determined to lynch him, even if they were obliged to confront the bull to do so.

But Captain Lituma was forgetting one essential fact: in order to keep out the spectators without tickets who were milling about outside the bullfight stadium and threatening to force their way in, he had ordered the gates and metal grilles blocking access to the stands to be lowered. When the Guardias Civiles, complying immediately with his orders, let fly with their tear-gas grenades and here and there, within a few seconds, pestilential fumes spread in the stands, the spectators' reaction was to clear out instantly. Leaping to their feet in a panic, shoving, pushing as they covered their mouths with their handkerchiefs and tears began streaming from their eyes, they ran toward the exits. The human tide then realized that the way out was blocked by the metal gates and grilles hemming them in. Blocked? Only for a few seconds, until the front ranks of each column, transformed into ramrods by the pressure of those behind them, stove them in, knocked them down, ripped them apart, and tore them from their hinges. And thus the inhabitants of El Rímac who chanced to be strolling by the Plaza de Toros at four-thirty that Sunday afternoon witnessed a barbarous and most unusual spectacle: suddenly, amid deathly crackling flames, the doors of the Plaza de Acho burst asunder and began to spit out mangled corpses which (troubles never come singly) were also being trampled underfoot by the panicked crowd escaping through the blood-soaked breaches.

Among the first victims of the Bajo el Puente holocaust were the introducers of the Jehovah's Witnesses sect in Peru: the man from Moquegua, Don Sebastián Bergua, his wife Margarita, and his daughter Rosa, the eminent flutist. The religious family lost their lives through what ought to have saved them: prudence. For the moment that the cannibal climbed the barrier, rushed out into the ring, and was about to be mangled to death by the bull, Don Sebastián Bergua, with furrowed brow and a dictatorial finger, had given his tribe the order: "Retreat." It was motivated not by fear, a word unknown to the evangelist, but by good sense, the thought that neither he nor members of his family ought to appear to be involved in any sort of scandal and thus give his enemies a pretext for trampling the good name of his faith in the mud. And so the Berguas hurriedly abandoned their seats on the sunny side of the ring and were making their way down the grandstand steps to the exit when the tear-gas grenades went off. The three of them were standing, beatifically, in front of metal grille number 6, waiting for it to be raised, when they caught sight of the lachrymose crowd descending upon them from behind with a great roar. They had no time to repent of sins they had never committed before they were literally mashed to bits (turned into a puree, a human soup?) against the metal grille by the terrified multitude. A second before passing on to that other life that he denied existed, Don

Sebastián managed to cry out, a stubborn, heterodox believer still: "Christ died on a tree, not on a cross!"

The death of the mentally unbalanced assailant who had attacked Don Sebastián Bergua with a knife and raped Doña Margarita and the concert artist was (would the expression be appropriate?) less unfair. For, once the tragedy had begun, young Marroquín Delfín thought he spied his opportunity: amid the confusion, he would escape from the guard whom the Board of Prisons had ordered to accompany him in order that he might attend the historic bullfight, and flee from Lima, from Peru; once abroad, under another name, he would begin a new life of crime and madness. Illusions that turned to dust moments later when, at the gate of exit number 5 (Lucho? Ezequiel?) Marroquín Delfín and the prison guard Chumpitaz, who was holding him by the hand, had the dubious honor of forming part of the first row of taurophiles crushed to death by the crowd. (The intertwined fingers of the police officer and the medical detail man, though those of corpses, set tongues to wagging.)

The demise of Sarita Huanca Salaverría had at least the elegance of being less promiscuous. It was a case of a tremendous misunderstanding, of an erroneous evaluation of acts and intentions on the part of the authorities. When the incidents occurred, when she saw the cannibal gored to death, the smoke of the grenades, and heard the screams of the crowd as their bones shattered, the girl from Tingo María decided that (love-passion that takes all fear of death away) she should be at the side of the man she loved. Unlike the crowd, therefore, she descended into the bullring, and was thus saved from being trampled to death. This did not save her, however, from the eagle eye of Captain Lituma, who caught sight, amid the spreading clouds of tear gas, of an unidentified figure leaping over the barrier and rushing toward the torero (who, despite everything, went on inciting the bull to charge and making passes on his knees). Convinced that his obligation, so long as he had a single breath of life left in him, was to prevent the matador from being attacked, Captain Lituma drew his revolver and with three rapid shots in succession cut short the career and life of the woman possessed by love: Sarita fell dead at the very feet of Gumercindo Bellmont.

The man from La Perla was the only one, amid all the victims of that Greek afternoon, to die a natural death—if it is possible to describe as natural the phenomenon, unheard of in these prosaic times, of a man dying of heart failure on seeing his beloved lying dead at his feet. He fell to the ground alongside Sarita, and the two of them, with their last breath, managed to embrace and thus enter, clasped in each other's arms, the dark night of hapless lovers (such as a certain Romeo and Juliet?) . . .

And then the peace officer with the immaculate service record, sadly contemplating the fact that, despite his experience and sagacity, not only had the peace been disturbed but the Plaza de Acho and environs had been turned into a cemetery of unburied corpses, used his last remaining bullet to (old sea dog who goes down with his ship to the bottom of the ocean) blow his brains out and bring his biography to a (manly but not brilliant) end. The moment they saw their chief take his life, the morale of the Guardias fell apart; forgetting discipline, esprit de corps, love for the institution, they thought only of shedding their uniforms, hiding in the civilian clothes they tore off the corpses, and escaping. A number of them succeeded in doing so. But not Jaime Concha, whom the survivors first castrated, then hanged with his own leather chest belt from the crosspiece of the bull-pen door. And there the decent chap who read Uncle Donalds, the diligent centurion remained, dangling back and forth beneath the sky of Lima, which (as if wishing to be in keeping with what had happened?) had become filled with roiling clouds and begun to rain down its usual winter drizzle . . .

Would this story end thus, in Dantesque slaughter? Or, like the Phoenix (the Hen?), would it be reborn from its ashes in the form of new episodes and recalcitrant characters? What would the outcome of this taurine tragedy be?

Seventeen.

We left Lima at nine

o'clock in the morning, taking a jitney at the university campus. Aunt Julia had left my aunt's and uncle's house on the pretext of doing some last-minute shopping before her trip, and I my grandparents' house as though I were going to work as usual at the radio station. She was carrying a paper sack with a nightgown and a change of underwear; I had put my toothbrush, a comb, and a razor (which, to tell the truth, I didn't often need as yet) in my pockets.

Pascual and Javier were waiting for us at the university campus and had already bought the jitney tickets. Luckily, no other passengers turned up. Pascual and Javier very discreetly sat down in the front seat with the driver, leaving the back seat for Aunt Julia and me. It was a typical winter morning, with an overcast sky and a continual drizzle that escorted us a good part of the way across the desert. During very nearly the entire trip, Aunt Julia and I kissed passionately and held hands without exchanging a word, as we listened to the murmur of conversation between Pascual and Javier, mingled with the sound of the engine, and from time to time a comment from the driver. We arrived in Chincha at eleven-thirty; there was splendid sun now and it was delightfully warm. The clear sky, the luminous air, the noisy hustle and bustle on the streets filled with people all seemed favorable omens. Aunt Julia smiled happily.

As Pascual and Javier headed for the city hall to see if everything was ready, Aunt Julia and I went to get a room at the Hotel Sudamericano. It was an old single-story wood-and-adobe brick building, with a covered patio that served as a dining room, and a dozen tiny rooms along either side of a narrow hall with a tiled floor, like a bordello. The man at the desk asked us for identification papers; my journalist's card was enough to satisfy him, and when I added "and wife" next to my name in the guest register he merely gave Aunt Julia a mocking look. The little room that we were given had a cracked tile floor with bare earth showing through, a sagging double bed with a quilt in a green diamond pattern, a little chair with a straw seat, and a couple of stout nails on the wall to hang our clothes on. The minute we stepped inside, we embraced passionately and stood there kissing and caressing till Aunt Julia pushed me away, laughing. "Stop right there, Varguitas, we have to get married first."

She was all excited, her eyes shining with joy. I felt that I loved her very much and was happy to be marrying her, and as I waited for her to wash her hands and comb her hair in the common bathroom down the hall, I vowed to myself that we wouldn't be like all the married couples I knew, one more disaster, but would live happily ever after, and that getting married wouldn't stop me from becoming a writer someday. Aunt Julia finally came out and we walked hand in hand to the city hall.

We found Pascual and Javier standing in the doorway of a café, having a cold drink. The mayor had gone off to preside over an inaugural ceremony of some sort, but would be back soon. I asked them if they were absolutely certain they'd definitely arranged for Pascual's relative to marry us at noon, and they made fun of me. Javier cracked jokes about the impatient bridegroom and made a terrible pun: "Better wait than never." To pass the time, the four of us strolled around the Plaza de Armas beneath the tall eucalyptus and oak trees. There were some kids running around chasing each other and some old men having their shoes shined as they read the Lima papers. Half an hour later, we were back at the city hall. The secretary, a skinny little man with enormous glasses, passed on the bad news: the mayor had returned from the inauguration, but he'd gone to have lunch at El Sol de Chincha.

"Didn't you tell him we were waiting for him for the marriage ceremony?" Javier said reprovingly.

"He was with a group of people and it wasn't the right moment," the secretary replied with the air of an expert in matters of etiquette.

"We'll go find him at the restaurant and bring him back," Pascual said to me reassuringly. "Don't worry, Don Mario."

By asking around, we finally found El Sol de Chincha, near the Plaza. It was a typical provincial restaurant, with little tables without tablecloths, and a stove at the back, sputtering and smoking, with women bustling about it with copper pans and pots and platters full of wonderful-smelling dishes. There was a phonograph blaring out a Peruvian waltz at top volume, and the place was full of people. Just as Aunt Julia, standing in the doorway, was starting to say that it might be more prudent to wait till the mayor had finished his lunch, the latter recognized Pascual and called him over to his table in one corner. We saw the Panamericana editor being greeted with a big hug by a rather fair-haired young man who had gotten up from a table with half a dozen other people, all men, sitting around it, each with a bottle of beer in front of him. Pascual motioned to us to come over.

"Of course—the fiancés—I'd completely forgotten," the mayor said, shaking our hands and looking Aunt Julia over from head to foot with an expert eye. He turned to his companions, who contemplated him with servile expressions on their faces, and informed them, in a loud voice so as to make himself heard over the waltz: "These two have just eloped from Lima and I'm going to marry them."

There was laughter, applause, hands reaching out to shake ours, and the mayor insisted that we sit down with them and ordered more beer to drink a toast to our happiness.

"But you're not to sit next to each other—you've got all the rest of your life for that," he said euphorically, taking Aunt Julia by the arm and seating her next to him. "The right place for the bride-to-be is here beside me, since luckily my wife isn't here."

Everyone at the table applauded his little joke. All of them were older than the mayor, merchants or planters dressed in their best, and they all appeared to be as drunk as he was. Some of them knew Pascual and asked him how things were going for him in Lima and when he was going to come back home. Sitting next to Javier at one end of the table, I was trying my best to smile, drinking little sips of nearly lukewarm beer, and counting the minutes ticking by. The mayor and the others soon lost interest in us. The bottles kept coming, by themselves at first, then accompanied by raw fish marinated in lemon juice, smoked sole, almond pastries filled with custard, and then by themselves again. Nobody remembered the marriage ceremony, not even Pascual, who, with bloodshot eyes and a thick tongue, had joined in with the others and was singing sentimental songs with the mayor. Having flirted with Aunt Julia all through lunch, the latter was now trying to put his arm around her and leaning his bloated face toward hers. With little forced smiles, Aunt Julia was keeping her distance and casting anxious looks in our direction every so often.

"Cool it, old pal," Javier kept saying to me. "Don't think about anything but the marriage ceremony."

"It seems to me the whole thing's gone down the drain," I said when I heard the mayor, who was high as a kite now, talking about bringing in guitarists, closing El Sol de Chincha, having a private dancing party. "And I predict I'll end up in jail once I've punched that stupid bastard in the nose."

I was furious and determined to knock his block off if he got out of line. I got to my feet and told Aunt Julia that we were leaving. Vastly relieved, she stood up immediately and the mayor made no attempt to hold her back. He went on singing *marineras*, on key, and as we started for the door he gave us a little farewell smile that struck me as being sarcastic, but Javier, who was following along behind us, said that it was merely alcoholic. As we were walking back to the Hotel Sudamericano, I began saying nasty things about Pascual, whom I blamed—I don't know why—for the entire absurd lunch.

"Don't be a spoiled brat, and learn to keep a cool head," Javier said reprovingly. "That cousin of his is plastered to the gills and doesn't remember a thing. But don't worry, he'll marry you today. Wait in the hotel till I call you."

The moment Aunt Julia and I were alone in the room, we fell into each other's arms and began kissing with a sort of desperation. We didn't say a word, but our hands and mouths spoke volumes about all the intense and beautiful things we were feeling. We'd begun to embrace standing just inside the door, and little by little we drew closer to the bed, first sitting down on it and finally lying down on it, without ever having let go of each other. Half blind with happiness and desire, I fondled Aunt Julia's body with inexpert, eager hands, with all her clothes on at first, and then I unbuttoned her brick-colored blouse, badly wrinkled now, and was kissing her breasts when there was an inopportune knock at the door.

"Everything's all set, you concubines," we heard Javier's voice say. "In five minutes, in the mayor's office. The famous kindhearted idiot is waiting for us."

We leapt up from the bed, dazed and happy, and Aunt Julia, beet-red with embarrassment, straightened her clothes, as meantime, like a little boy, I closed my eyes and thought about abstract, respectable things—numbers, triangles, circles, my granny, my mama—to make my erection go away. Taking turns in the bathroom down the hall, we washed and combed our hair a little, then walked back to the city hall, so fast that we arrived all out of breath. The secretary immediately ushered us into the mayor's office, a big room with a Peruvian seal of state hanging on the wall, overlooking a desk with little flags and official registers and half a dozen benches, like a schoolroom. With his face washed and his hair still damp, calm and collected, the rubicund burgomaster bowed ceremoniously to us from behind the desk. He was an entirely different person: formal and solemn. Javier and Pascual, standing on either side of the desk, smiled at us roguishly.

"Well then, let's begin," the mayor said, his voice betraying him: thick and hesitant, as though his tongue were blocking it. "Where are the papers?"

"You have them, sir," Javier answered, with infinite politeness. "Pascual and I left them with you on Friday so as to expedite matters, remember?"

"You really must be sozzled if you've forgotten, cousin." Pascual laughed in an equally drunken voice. "Especially since you were the one who asked us to leave them with you."

"Well, the secretary must have them, then," the mayor muttered in embarrassment. Giving Pascual a dirty look, he called out: "Secretary!"

It took the skinny little man with enormous glasses several

minutes to find the birth certificates and Aunt Julia's divorce decree. We waited in silence as the mayor smoked a cigarette, yawned, and impatiently looked at his watch. The secretary finally brought them in, scrutinizing them with a disgusted look on his face. As he laid them down on the desk, he murmured in a slightly officious tone of voice: "Here they are, sir. There's a problem on account of the young man's age, as I've already told you."

"Did anybody ask you?" Pascual said, taking a step in his direction as though he were about to strangle him.

"I'm only doing my duty," the secretary said. And then, turning to the mayor, he insisted acidly, pointing to me: "He's only eighteen and he hasn't presented a document proving he has official court permission to marry."

"How come you've got such an imbecile for an assistant, cousin?" Pascual burst out. "What's keeping you from booting him out and bringing in somebody with a few more brains?"

"Be quiet. The alcohol you've consumed has gone to your head and you're getting nasty," the mayor said. He cleared his throat to give himself a little time, crossed his arms, and looked at Aunt Julia and me gravely. "I'm prepared to allow you to dispense with posting banns, in order to do you a favor. But this other is a more serious matter. I'm very sorry."

"What!" I said to him, completely taken aback. "Haven't you known since Friday that I'm a minor?"

"What's this whole stupid farce all about, anyway?" Javier chimed in. "You and I had an understanding that you'd marry them without any problem."

"Are you asking me to commit a crime?" the mayor huffed. He too was indignant now. And with an air of injured dignity he added: "Furthermore, don't raise your voice like that when you speak to me. People with manners settle misunderstandings by talking things over, not by shouting."

"But you've gone mad, cousin," Pascual said in a fury, pounding on the desk. "You agreed, you knew there was an age problem, you said it didn't matter. Don't pull this amnesiac bit on me or start splitting legal hairs. Marry them once and for all and stop screwing around!"

"Don't use dirty words in front of a lady, and don't drink any more, because you can't hold your liquor," the mayor replied serenely. He turned to the secretary and motioned for him to leave the room. Once we were alone, he lowered his voice and gave us a conspiratorial smile. "Can't you see that that guy is a spy for my enemies? Now that he's caught on, I can't marry you. I'd be up to my neck in trouble in no time."

There was nothing I could say to persuade him: I swore to him that my parents lived in the U.S. and that was the reason I hadn't presented a court dispensation, that nobody in my family was going to make trouble if he married us, that the minute Aunt Julia and I were man and wife we'd be going off to live abroad for the rest of our lives.

"We were all agreed. You can't play a dirty trick like this on us," Javier said.

"Don't be such a hard-ass, cousin," Pascual said, taking him by the arm. "Don't you realize we've come all the way from Lima?"

"Quiet down and stop ganging up on me. I think I've got an idea. Yes, that's the solution, all right. Your troubles are over," the mayor finally said, getting up from his desk and winking at us. "Tambo de Mora! Martín the fisherman! Go down there right now. Tell him I sent you. Martín the fisherman, a sambo, a really nice guy. He'd be delighted to marry you. It's better that way, a little village, no fuss. Martín, Martín the mayor. Just slip him a little tip and that'll be it. He can barely read or write—he won't even look at your papers."

I tried to persuade him to come with us, I joked with him, I buttered him up, I pleaded with him, but there was nothing doing: he had appointments, work to do, his family was waiting for him. He showed us to the door, assuring us that the whole thing could be taken care of in a couple of minutes in Tambo de Mora.

We found an old beat-up taxi right in front of the city hall and arranged with the driver to take us to Tambo de Mora. During the ride, as Javier and Pascual were talking about the mayor and Javier was saying that he was the worst cynic he'd ever met in his life and Pascual was trying to lay all the blame on the secretary, the taxi driver spoke up and put in his two cents' worth, calling the burgomaster of Chincha all sorts of nasty names and adding that all he cared about in life was shady business deals and graft. Aunt Julia and I sat holding hands, looking into each other's eyes, and every so often I would whisper in her ear that I loved her.

We arrived in Tambo de Mora at dusk, and from the beach we

saw a fiery disk sinking into the sea, in a cloudless sky with myriad stars just beginning to come out. We wandered about the two dozen shacks built of cane stalks daubed with mud that constituted the village, amid boats with hulls staved in and fishing nets full of holes stretched out between stakes to be mended. We could smell fresh fish and the sea. Half-naked little black kids surrounded us, eating us alive with questions: who were we, where did we come from, what did we want to buy? We finally found the mayor's shack. His wife, a black keeping a hot fire burning in a brazier with a straw fan, wiping the sweat from her forehead with her other hand, told us that her husband was still out fishing. Looking up at the sky, she added that he'd be back in any minute now. We went down to the little beach to wait for him, and for an hour, sitting on a dead tree trunk, we watched the boats come back in, the day's work over, the fishermen laboriously beach them on the sand, their wives chop the heads off the fish and gut them, right there on the beach, doing their best to hold off the hungry dogs. Martín was the last to come in. It was dark now and the moon had risen.

He was a black with gray hair and an enormous belly, a waggish, talkative sort who, despite the cool night air, was wearing nothing but an old pair of pants that clung to his skin. We greeted him as though he were a being descended from heaven, helped him beach his boat, and escorted him home. As we made our way through the village by the dim light of the cooking fires inside the villagers' shacks without doors, we explained the reason for our visit.

Baring his big horse-teeth, he burst out laughing. "No way, pals, you're going to have to hunt up some other dummy to fry you that kettle of fish," he said in his deep, melodious voice. "I helped pull off another little trick like that and nearly got a bullet through my head for my trouble."

He then told us how, a few weeks before, in order to do the mayor of Chincha a favor, he'd overlooked the fact that banns hadn't been posted and married a young couple. Four days later, who should show up, beside himself with rage, but the husband of the "fiancée" ("A girl born in the village of Cachiche, where all the women have brooms and fly on them at night," he said); she'd been married for two years, and her husband threatened to kill the pander who had dared to lawfully wed the adulterous pair.

"My colleague in Chincha knows all the tricks—he's such a

clever devil he'll be going straight to Heaven one of these days," he joked, slapping his big belly gleaming with little drops of sea water. "Every time something rotten comes his way, he sends it to Martín the fisherman as a present, and let the nigger get rid of the corpse. Take my word for it, he's a crafty one!"

There was no way of talking him into changing his mind. He refused even to have a look at our papers, and countered every argument that Javier, Pascual, and I could think of—Aunt Julia didn't say a word but couldn't help smiling now and again at the fisherman-mayor's sly humor—by cracking more jokes about his colleagues from Chincha or by telling us once again, with great peals of laughter, the story of the husband who'd been out to kill him for having wed the little witch from Cachiche to another man when he, her spouse, was neither dead and buried nor divorced from her. When we returned to his shack, we found an unexpected ally: his wife. He himself explained to her what we wanted as he dried his face, his arms, his broad chest, and sniffed hungrily at the pot boiling on the brazier.

"Marry them, you heartless sambo," the woman said to him, nodding her head pityingly in Aunt Julia's direction. "Just look at the poor thing, they've spirited her away and she can't get herself married, she must be suffering from all she's been through. Don't you even care—or has being mayor turned your head?"

Martín's big flat feet padded back and forth on the beaten-earth floor of the shack as he fetched glasses and cups, as meanwhile we mounted another attack and offered him everything we could think of: from our eternal gratitude to a fat fee that would bring him as much as he could earn by many a day's work fishing. But he was adamant, and finally told his wife in no uncertain terms not to stick her nose in affairs that were none of her business. But the next minute he was as affable as ever and shoved a glass or a cup in each of our hands and poured us all a little drink of pisco.

"Just so you won't have made the trip for nothing, my friends," he consoled us, without the least hint of sarcasm in his voice, raising his glass. His toast, in view of the circumstances, was one we could all drink to: "Here's wishing the bride and groom the best of luck."

As we bade him goodbye, he told us we'd made a mistake by

coming to Tambo de Mora, on account of the unfortunate precedent of the girl from Cachiche. But we should go to Chincha Baja, El Carmen, Sunampe, San Pedro, or any of the other little villages round about, where we could be married on the spot.

"The mayors of those villages are all loafers. They don't have a thing to do, and when they see a marriage ceremony coming their way, they're drunk with joy," he shouted after us.

We went back to where the taxi was waiting for us, not saying a word to each other. The driver informed us that we'd have to have another talk about the fee he'd be obliged to charge, since he'd had to wait for us for such a long time. During the trip back to Chincha we agreed that the next day, as soon as it was light, we would make the rounds of all the villages and hamlets in those parts, one by one, offering generous gratuities, till we found a damned mayor who'd marry Aunt Julia and me.

"It's nearly nine o'clock," Aunt Julia said all of a sudden. "Do you suppose my sister's received the message?"

I'd made Big Pablito memorize and repeat ten times what he was to say to my Uncle Lucho or my Aunt Olga, and to make certain that he got it right, I'd written it down on a piece of paper: "Mario and Julia have gotten married. Don't worry about them. They're fine, and will be coming back to Lima in just a few days." He was to call them at 9 p.m. from a public phone booth and hang up immediately after he'd given them the message. I lit a match and looked at my watch: yes, the family had already received it.

"They must be firing one question after another at Nancy," Aunt Julia said, trying her best to speak in an offhand tone of voice, as though commenting on something in which she was in no way involved. "They know she's an accomplice. They're going to give the poor thing a hard time."

The ancient taxi bounced up and down on the road full of potholes, threatening to turn over at any moment, and every last bolt and panel of its carcass creaked. The moon was shedding its dim light on the dunes, and from time to time we caught sight of silhouettes of palms, fig trees, and acacias. The sky was studded with stars.

"So they've doubtless already told your papa the news," Javier said. "The minute he got off the plane. What a reception!"

"I swear to heaven we'll find a mayor," Pascual said. "I'll refuse to admit I was born in the province of Chincha if we can't get you married somewhere in these parts tomorrow. My word of honor."

"Do they need a mayor to marry them?" the driver said, pricking up his ears. "Have you abducted the little lady? Why didn't you tell me before—don't you trust me? I'd have taken you to Grocio Prado. The mayor there is a pal of mine and he'd have married you on the spot."

I proposed that we go on to Grocio Prado then and there, but he dissuaded me. The mayor probably wasn't in the village at this hour, but out at his little farm, an hour's ride from town by burro. It was best to wait till the next day. We made arrangements with the driver to come by to pick us up at eight the following morning, and I offered him a fat tip if he'd put in a good word for us with his buddy.

"Of course I will," he said, reviving our spirits. "You'll be married in the village of the Blessed Melchorita—what more could you ask?"

The dining room at the Hotel Sudamericano was just about to close, but Javier persuaded the waiter to have them fix us something to eat. He brought us Cokes and plates of fried eggs with warmed-up rice that we barely touched. Suddenly, halfway through the meal, we realized that we were talking almost in whispers, like conspirators, and we burst into hysterical laughter. As we were leaving for our respective rooms—Pascual and Javier had planned to go back to Lima that same day after the wedding, but as things hadn't gone as expected, they were staying on and in order to save money were sharing a room—we saw half a dozen men, some of them in boots and riding pants, come into the dining room and shout for beers. Their drunken voices, their boisterous laughter, their clinking glasses, their stupid jokes, their vulgar toasts, and later on their belches and vomiting were the background music of our wedding night. Despite the bureaucratic frustration of the day, it was an intense and beautiful wedding night, during which, in that old bed that screeched like a cat as we embraced and was no doubt crawling with fleas, we made love several times, with a fire reborn again and again, and as our hands and lips taught us to know each other and give each other pleasure, we told each other that we loved each other, that we would never lie to, cheat on, or leave each other. When they knocked on our door—we'd asked them to wake us at seven—the drunks had just shut up and we were still lying there awake, naked and curled up together on the quilt with the green diamond pattern, dizzy and drowsy with pleasure, looking at each other gratefully.

Our morning toilette, in the common bathroom of the Hotel Sudamericano, was a heroic feat. The shower appeared not to have ever been used before, water spurted from the rusty shower head in all directions except that of the bather, and great quantities of a blackish liquid came out before the water ran clear. There were no bath towels, just a dirty rag for people's hands, so we had to dry ourselves with the bed sheets. But we were happy and excited and the inconveniences amused us. We found Javier and Pascual, already dressed, in the dining room, sallow-faced with sleep, looking disgustedly at the catastrophic state the place had been left in by the drunks of the night before: broken glasses, cigarette butts, pools of vomit and spit on which a hotel employee was throwing pails of sawdust, and a terrible smell. We went out to have our morning coffee down the street, in a little café from which we could see the tall leafy trees in the square. It was an odd sensation, coming from the gray fog of Lima, to see the day beginning with bright hot sunshine and a cloudless sky. When we got back to the hotel, the taxi driver was there waiting for us.

On the trip to Grocio Prado, along a dusty stretch of road that led past vineyards and cotton plantations and from which we could see the dark skyline of the Andes looming up in the distance on the other side of the desert, the driver, in a sudden fit of talkativeness that sharply contrasted with our total silence, rattled on and on about the Blessed Melchorita: she had given everything she had to the poor, cared for the old and the sick, comforted the suffering, and within her own lifetime had become so famous that the faithful came from all the villages in the province to pray in her presence. He told us about some of her miracles. She had saved people dying of incurable diseases, spoken with saints who had appeared to her, seen God, and made a perpetually blooming rose flower on a rock.

"She's more popular than the Little Blessed One of Humay and El Señor de Luren—as can easily be seen from the number of people who come to her hermitage and her procession," he said. "There's no reason why she shouldn't be declared a saint. You people who are from Lima, be active in her behalf and support her cause. It's a just one, believe me."

When we finally arrived, covered with dust from head to foot, in the broad treeless main square of Grocio Prado, we found out for ourselves how popular Melchorita was. Hordes of children and women surrounded the taxi and with much shouting and gesticulating offered to take us to see her hermitage, the house where she'd been born, the place where she'd mortified herself, where she'd worked her miracles, where she'd been buried, and tried to sell us pious images, prayers, scapulars, and medals with the Blessed One's effigy. The driver had to convince them that we weren't pilgrims or tourists before they would leave us in peace.

The municipal building, a tiny, wretched adobe hut with a tin roof, lay drowsing in the sun on one side of the square. It was closed.

"My pal will be along soon," the driver said. "Let's wait for him in the shade."

We sat down on the sidewalk beneath the overhanging roof of the municipal building, and from there we could see that at the end of the straight dirt streets, lined with rickety little shacks and cane-stalk shanties and leading less than fifty yards in any direction, the farms and the desert began. Aunt Julia was sitting next to me, with her head leaning on my shoulder and her eyes closed. We'd been sitting there for half an hour, watching the pack drivers going past, on foot or on the backs of their burros, and the women going to fetch water from a little stream flowing by one corner, when an old man on horseback rode by.

"You waiting for Don Jacinto?" he asked, removing his big straw hat. "He's gone to Ica to talk to the prefect and try to get his boy out of the military barracks. The soldiers came and took him away to do his service in the army. Don Jacinto won't be back before nightfall."

The driver proposed that we wait in Grocio Prado and spend the day visiting the Melchorita pilgrimage sites, but I insisted on trying our luck in other villages. After bargaining for some time, he finally agreed to stay with us till noon.

It was only nine in the morning when we began the rounds that took us through practically the entire province of Chincha, jouncing along mule paths, getting stuck on desert trails half buried in sand, approaching the sea at times and at others the foothills of the Andes. Just as we were entering El Carmen we had a blowout, and since the driver didn't have a jack, the four of us had to hold the car up while he put the spare tire on. After midmorning, the sun, which had grown hotter and hotter and was now downright torture, heated the taxi up like a tin box and we were all dripping with sweat as though in a Turkish bath. The radiator began to steam and we had to fill a can with water to take with us so as to cool it off every so often.

We talked with three or four mayors of districts and as many deputy mayors of hamlets that at times consisted of no more than twenty shacks. They were simple rural types whom we had to hunt up at their little farms where they were at work in the fields, or in their little village shops where they were selling cooking oil and cigarettes to their constituents; we found one of them, the mayor of Sunampe, lying in a ditch sleeping off a hangover and had to shake him awake. Once we'd located the municipal authority in question, I would get out of the taxi, accompanied sometimes by Pascual, sometimes by the driver, sometimes by Javier—we eventually learned by experience that the more of us there were, the more intimidated the mayor tended to be—to explain the situation. No matter what arguments I put forward, I would invariably see a look of mistrust come over the face, a gleam of alarm appear in the eye of the farmer, fisherman, or shopkeeper (the mayor of Chincha Baja introduced himself as a "healer"). Only two of them turned us down flat: the mayor of Alto Larán, an old man who went on loading his pack mules with bales of alfalfa as I talked with him, and informed us that he never married anyone who wasn't from the village; and the mayor of San Juan de Yanac, a mestizo farmer who was terrified when he saw us, thinking we were the police coming to question him about some misdeed. When he found out what we wanted, he was furious. "No, not a chance, there's something fishy going on if a white couple come to get married in this godforsaken village." The others all gave us more or less the same excuses. The most common: the civil register had been lost or was filled up, and until they sent a new one from Chincha there was no way of registering deaths or births or marrying anybody at the town hall. It was the mayor of Chavín who came up with the most imaginative reply: he couldn't marry us because he was too pressed for time; he had to go out right then and shoot a fox that had been killing two or three hens a night in the district. The one place we very nearly succeeded was Pueblo Nuevo. The mayor listened to us attentively, agreed, and said that exempting us from posting banns was going to cost us five hundred *soles*. He didn't make any fuss about my age and apparently believed us when we assured him that the law had been changed and one now reached one's majority at eighteen, not twenty-one. We had already taken our places in front of the plank laid across two barrels that served him as a desk (the municipal building in this hamlet was an adobe hut with a roof full of holes, through which we could see the sky), when the mayor began laboriously reading our papers, one word at a time. When he realized that Aunt Julia was Bolivian, it scared him off. We explained to him that this was no obstacle, that foreigners had the right to marry too, and offered him more money, but it was no use. "I don't want to get into any trouble," he said. "The fact that this young woman is Bolivian could be a very serious matter."

We went back to Chincha around three in the afternoon, half dead from the heat, covered with dust, and depressed. On the outskirts of town, Aunt Julia began to cry. I hugged her, whispered in her ear that she mustn't get upset, that I loved her, that we'd get married even if we had to visit every single village in Peru.

"I'm not crying because we can't get married," she said, trying to smile through her tears. "I'm crying because this whole thing is getting so ridiculous."

None of the four of us was very hungry, so our lunch consisted of a cheese sandwich and a Coke that we downed standing up at a counter. Then we went off to take a rest. Despite our night without sleep and the frustrations of that morning, we still had the heart to make love, passionately, on the diamond-patterned quilt, in the murky light. From the bed we could see the faint feeble beams of sunlight that had managed to filter through a skylight with glass panes covered with grime. Immediately afterward, instead of getting up to join our accomplices in the dining room, we fell asleep. It was a fitful, anxious sleep, with intense rushes of desire that caused us to grope about for each other and caress each other instinctively, followed by bad dreams; we told each other about them when we woke up and learned that both of us had seen the faces of relatives in them, and Aunt Julia laughed when I told her that at one moment in my dreams I'd found myself living through one of Pedro Camacho's recent catastrophes.

I was awakened by someone knocking on the door. It was dark in the room, and streaks of electric light were visible through the cracks in the blinds over the window. I called out that I'd be there in a minute, and shaking my head to rouse myself from my torpor, I struck a match and looked at my watch. It was 7 p.m. I felt the whole world come crashing down on me: another day wasted, and what was worse, I now had almost no money left to go on searching for mayors. I groped my way over to the door in the dark, opened it, and was about to be sharp with Javier for not having awakened me sooner, when I saw that he was grinning from ear to ear.

"Everything's all set, Varguitas," he said, proud as a peacock. "The mayor of Grocio Prado is making the entry in the register and filling out your marriage certificate this very minute. Stop sinning and get a move on, you two. We'll wait for you in the taxi."

He closed the door and I heard him laugh as he walked down the hall. Aunt Julia had sat up in bed, rubbing her eyes, and in the semi-darkness I managed to catch just a glimpse of the surprised, slightly incredulous look on her face.

"The very first book I write, I'm going to dedicate to that taxi driver," I said as we were getting dressed.

"Don't chant a victory hymn just yet." Aunt Julia smiled. "I'm not going to believe it even when I see the marriage certificate."

We rushed out of the hotel, and as we passed the dining room, where a whole bunch of men were already drinking beer, somebody made such a clever flattering remark about Aunt Julia that many of them laughed. Pascual and Javier were waiting in the taxi, but it wasn't the same one that had taken us around that morning, nor was it the same driver.

"The other one tried to get cute and take advantage of the situation by charging double," Pascual explained to us. "So we told him he could go to hell and hired this gentleman here, a really honest, upright man."

I was suddenly panic-stricken, thinking that the change of drivers was going to mean another wild-goose chase. But Javier reassured us. It wasn't the other driver who'd gone with the two of them to Grocio Prado that afternoon, but this one. They told us, as though they were a couple of kids who'd pulled a fast one on us, how they'd decided to "let us get some rest" and spare Aunt Julia the painful experience of yet another refusal and gone to Grocio Prado by themselves to see what they could do. They'd had a long conversation with the mayor.

"A cultivated, enlightened mestizo, one of those superior men that are a unique product of the province of Chincha," Pascual said. "You're going to have to give thanks to Melchorita by coming to her procession."

The mayor of Grocio Prado had calmly listened to Javier's explanations, carefully scrutinized all the papers word for word, thought the matter over for some time, and then laid down his conditions: a thousand *soles*, but only if a 6 on my birth certificate were changed to a 3, thus making it appear that I'd come into the world three years earlier.

"The intelligence of the proletariat," Javier said. "We're a decadent class, believe me. It never crossed our minds that that was the solution, and this man of the people, with his brilliant common sense, saw it in a flash. It's a fait accompli: you're of age."

Right there in the town hall, the mayor and Javier between them had changed the 6 to a 3, by hand, and the man had said: "What difference does it make if the ink isn't the same? What matters is what the paper says."

We arrived in Grocio Prado about eight in the evening. It was a clear night, with stars in the sky; and pleasantly warm. Little flames flickered in all the shacks and shanties in the village. We saw another dwelling all lighted up, with a great many candles gleaming through the cane-stalk walls, and Pascual, crossing himself, told us it was the hermitage where the Blessed Melchorita had lived.

In the town hall, the mayor was just finishing recording the marriage in a big register with a black cover. The dirt floor of the one-room building had been wetted down only a little while before and wisps of vapor rose from it. On the table were three lighted candles, and we could make out by their dim glow a Peruvian flag pinned up with thumbtacks and a framed photograph of the President of the Republic on the whitewashed walls. The mayor was a stout, impassive man of about fifty; he was laboriously writing the entry in the register with an old-fashioned nib pen that he dipped into a wide-mouthed inkwell after each sentence. He greeted Aunt Julia and me with a bow. I calculated that, at the rate at which he was writing, it had no doubt taken him more than an hour to make the entry. When he finished, he said without budging from his chair: "There have to be two witnesses."

Javier and Pascual stepped forward, but only the latter was accepted by the mayor, since Javier was a minor. I went out to have a word with the driver, who had stayed behind in the taxi; he agreed to be our witness if I would pay him a hundred *soles*. He was a skinny mestizo, with a gold tooth; on the trip to Grocio Prado he'd smoked one cigarette after another and hadn't spoken a single word.

When the mayor showed him where he was to sign his name, he shook his head sadly. "What a shame," he said, in a regretful tone. "Who ever heard of a wedding without even one miserable bottle to drink to the health of the bride and groom? I can't be a party to a thing like that." He gave us a pitying look and added as he went out the door: "Wait a second for me."

Folding his arms, the mayor closed his eyes and appeared to be falling asleep. Aunt Julia, Pascual, Javier, and I looked at each other, not knowing what to do. I finally made up my mind to go out onto the street and hunt up another witness.

"That's not necessary. He'll be back," Pascual said, keeping me from leaving. "What's more, he was quite right to say what he did. We should have thought of the wedding toast. That sambo's shown us all up."

"All this takes steady nerves," Aunt Julia whispered, grabbing my hand. "Don't you feel as if you were holding up a bank and the police were going to come bursting in any minute?"

The taxi driver was gone for a good ten minutes that seemed like ten years, but finally he came back clutching two bottles of wine. The ceremony could now continue. Once the witnesses signed, the mayor had Julia and me sign, opened a copy of the Civil Code, and bringing it closer to one of the candles, read us, as slowly as he had written the entry in the register, the articles appertaining to conjugal obligations and duties. He then handed us a certificate and announced that we were man and wife. We kissed each other and then the witnesses and the mayor embraced us. The driver uncorked the bottles of wine with his teeth. There were no glasses, so we drank straight out of the bottle, passing it from hand to hand after each swallow. On the ride back to Chincha—all of us were both happy and relieved—Javier made a disastrous attempt to whistle the Wedding March.

After paying the taxi driver, we walked over to the Plaza de Armas so that Javier and Pascual could catch a jitney back to Lima. There was one that would be leaving in an hour, so we had time to eat dinner at El Sol de Chincha. During the meal, we decided on a plan. As soon as Javier got back to Miraflores, he would go to my Aunt Olga's and Uncle Lucho's to take the family's temperature and then would telephone us. Aunt Julia and I would go back to Lima the following morning. Pascual would have to invent a good excuse to justify his not having shown up for more than two days at the radio station.

We left the two of them at the jitney stop and went back to the Hotel Sudamericano, chattering away like an old married couple. Aunt Julia was feeling a little queasy and thought it was the wine we'd drunk in Grocio Prado. I told her that it had tasted like a superb vintage to me, but I didn't tell her that it was the first time in my life that I'd ever drunk wine.

Eighteen.

The bard of Lima, Crisanto

Maravillas, was born in the old city, in a little alleyway off the Plaza de Santa Ana from the rooftops of whose dwellings the most graceful kites in Peru were flown, beautiful objects made of tissue paper that the good nuns cloistered in the convent of Las Descalzas ran to look at through their skylights when they soared elegantly into the air over Los Barrios Altos. In fact, the birth of the child who in years to come would raise the Peruvian waltz, the *marinera*, the polka to heights worthy of a kite, coincided with the baptism of one, a fiesta that brought the best guitarists, drummers, and singers of the neighborhood together in the Callejón de Santa Ana. On opening the little window of room H, where the birth took place, to announce that the population count of that corner of the city had increased, the midwife predicted: "If he survives, he'll be a popular singer."

But it appeared doubtful that he would survive: he weighed less than a kilo and his little legs were so shrunken that he would probably never walk. The father, Valentín Maravillas, who had spent his life trying to acclimatize devotion to El Señor de Limpias in the district (he had founded the Brotherhood in his own room and—rash act, or clever trick to ensure himself a long old age—had sworn that before his death it would have more members than that of Our Lord of Miracles), proclaimed that his patron saint would carry off the extraordinary feat: he would save his son's life and enable him to walk like a normal Christian. The mother, María Portal, a cook with magic fingers who had never had so much as a cold in her life, was so upset on seeing that the child she had so long dreamed of and prayed to God for was this creature (the larva of a hominid? a miserable fetus?) that she threw her husband out, claiming that he was responsible and accusing him in front of all the neighbors of being only half a man because of his sanctimonious piety.

In any event, Crisanto Maravillas survived, and managed to learn to walk despite his ridiculous little legs. Without elegance, naturally, but, rather, like a puppet that jerks ahead step by step by making three separate motions—lifting the foot, bending the knee, lowering the foot—and so slowly that to those walking along with him it seemed as though they were following a religious procession making its way through congested narrow streets at a snail's pace. But at least Crisanto could get around without crutches and by himself, his parents (now reconciled) said. Kneeling in the Church of Santa Ana, his eyes brimming with tears, Don Valentín thanked El Señor de Limpias, but María Portal said that the one and only worker of this miracle was the most famous Aesculapius of the city, whose specialty was cripples and who had turned countless paralytics into sprinters: Dr. Alberto de Quinteros. María had prepared memorable Peruvian banquets in his house and the savant had taught her the massages, exercises, and treatments required in order that Crisanto's legs, despite being so spindly and rachitic, would be able to support him and get him about in this world.

It cannot be said that Crisanto Maravillas had a childhood like that of other children of the traditional quarter in which he had chanced to be born. Fortunately or unfortunately for him, his weak constitution did not allow him to share in any of those activities that strengthened the bodies and minds of the boys in the neighborhood: he did not play soccer with a ball made of rags, he was never able to box in a ring or have a fistfight on a street corner, he never participated in those pitched battles fought with slingshots, stones, or kicks that in the streets of old Lima brought urchins from the Plaza de Santa Ana face to face with gangs from El Chirimoyo, Cocharcas, Cinco Esquinas, El Cercado. He was not able to go with his pals from the little public school on the Plazuela de Santa Clara (where he learned to read) to steal fruit from the orchards of Cantogrande and Ñaña, or swim naked in the Rímac or ride burros bareback in the pasture lots of El Santoyo. So short that he was practically a dwarf, as skinny as a broom, with his father's chocolate-colored skin and his mother's straight hair, Crisanto watched his pals from a distance, with intelligent eyes, as they amused themselves, sweated, grew, and toughened themselves in those adventures that were forbidden him, and on his face there would appear an expression of—melancholy resignation? quiet sadness?

It seemed at one point that he would become as religious as his father (who, in addition to his worship of El Señor de Limpias, had spent his life carrying various Christs and Virgins in processions and wearing the habit of a number of different orders), since for years he was a faithful acolyte in the churches round about the Plaza de Santa Ana. As he was diligent, had all the responses down pat, and appeared to be the soul of innocence, the priests in the neighborhood closed their eyes to the fact that his movements were so slow and clumsy and frequently summoned him to serve Mass, ring the little bell during Holy Week reenactments of the Via Crucis, or bear the censer in processions. Seeing him enveloped in his acolyte's surplice, which was always too big for him, and hearing him recite the responses with devotion, in good Latin, at the altars of Las Trinitarias, San Andrés, El Carmen, La Buena Muerte, and the little church of Cocharcas (for he was summoned even by the priests of that distant quarter), María Portal, who would have wished her son a tempestuous career as a soldier, an adventurer, an irresistible Don Juan instead, repressed a sigh. But the king of the Brotherhood of Lima, Valentín Maravillas, felt his heart swell with pride at the thought that this child of his own flesh and blood seemed destined to become a priest.

But they were all mistaken: the boy did not have a religious vocation. He was possessed of an intense inner life and had found no answer as to where, how, by what means he might nourish his sensibility. His precocious thirst for poetry, his hunger for spirituality were assuaged by the atmosphere of sputtering candles, burning incense and prayers, statues covered with ex-votos, responses and rites, crosses and genuflexions.

María Portal gave the Discalced Carmelite nuns a helping hand with their domestic labors and their pastrymaking and hence was one of the rare persons allowed inside the strictly cloistered convent. The famous cook took Crisanto with her, and as the boy grew (in age, not in stature), the nuns became so accustomed to seeing him (a mere object, a tattered rag, a little half-being, a human trinket) that they allowed him to wander about the cloister as María Portal and the good sisters prepared the celestial pastries, the quivering custards, the snow-white meringues, the floating-island puddings, and the marzipan that they then sold to earn money for the missions in Africa. And that was how Crisanto Maravillas, at the age of ten, learned what love was . . .

The young girl who instantly attracted him was named Fátima; she was his own age and in the feminine universe of the Discalced Carmelites she fulfilled the humble duties of a domestic servant. When Crisanto Maravillas saw her for the first time, she was just finishing washing down the flagstone walkways of the cloister and was about to water the lilies and roses in the garden. She was a slip of a girl who, despite the fact that she was bundled up in a shapeless burlap garment full of holes and had all her hair tucked up under a bit of coarse cotton cloth like a coif, was unable to conceal her origins: an ivory complexion, dark blue circles under her eyes, an arrogant chin, slender ankles. She was (aristocratic tragedies envied by the vulgar) a foundling. She had been abandoned one winter night, wrapped in a sky-blue blanket, in the convent turnbox on the Calle Junín, along with a message in elegant handwriting blurred by teardrops: "I am the offspring of an accursed love, the despair of an honorable family, and I could not live within society without being a continual guilty reminder of the sin of the parents who brought me into this world. Since they have the same father and the same mother, they are prevented from loving each other, from keeping me, and from recognizing me. You, blessed Discalced Carmelites, are the only persons who can raise me without being ashamed of me or making me feel ashamed of myself. My tormented procreators will generously reward the Congregation for this act of charity that will open the gates of Heaven unto you."

Alongside the offspring of incest, the nuns found a sack full of money. This (pagan cannibals who must be evangelized, clothed, and fed) was what finally made them decide to take the child in: she would be raised as their servant, and later, if she proved to have a vocation, they would make of her another slave of Our Lord in a white habit. They would christen her Fátima, since she had been found in the turn-box on the anniversary of the day that the Virgin had appeared to the little shepherd children of Portugal. And so the little girl grew up, withdrawn from the world, amid the virginal walls of the Carmelite convent, in an unpolluted environment, without seeing a single man (before Crisanto) save for the old gout-ridden Don Sebastián (Bergua?), the chaplain who came once a week to absolve the good sisters of their (always merely venial) sins. She was sweet-natured, gentle, docile, and the most discerning nuns said that (purity of the soul that sharpens the vision and beatifies the breath) they noted in her behavior unmistakable signs of sanctity.

In a superhuman effort to overcome the timidity that made him tongue-tied, Cristano Maravillas approached the girl and asked if he could help her water the flower garden. She consented, and from that day forward, each time that María Portal went to the convent, while she was in the kitchen cooking with the nuns, Fátima and Crisanto swept the cells together or scrubbed the patios together or changed the flowers on the altar together or washed the windows together or waxed the floors together or dusted the missals together. Between the ugly young boy and the pretty young girl there arose (first love that is always remembered as the best) a bond that—only death would break?

It was when the young half-cripple was nearing the age of twelve that Valentín Maravillas and María Portal noticed the first signs of that inclination which in a short time was to make of Crisanto a miraculously inspired poet and a famous composer.

It all happened during the celebrations that, at least once a week, brought the people who lived round about the Plaza de Santa Ana together. When a baby was born or there was a wake (celebrating a happy event or healing a wound?)—pretexts were never lacking—revels were organized, in the garage of Chumpitaz the tailor, in the little back courtyard of the Lamas' hardware store, in the alleyway where the Valentíns lived, that went on till dawn, accompanied by the strumming of guitars, the booming of *cajones*, the rhythmic clapping of hands, the voices of the tenors. As the couples, in fine fettle (fiery brandy and the aromatic viands of María Portal!), struck sparks on the tiles as they danced, Crisanto Maravillas watched the guitarists, the singers, the drummers, as if their words and sounds were something supernatural. And when the musicians took a break to have a smoke or a drink, the youngster reverently approached the guitars, stroked them very gently so as not to frighten them, strummed the six strings, and arpeggios were heard . . .

It was soon evident that the cripple had an aptitude, a remarkable gift. Possessed of an unusually good ear, he could listen to any rhythm and repeat it immediately, and although his tiny hands were weak he could expertly accompany any sort of Peruvian music on the *cajón*. Whenever the musicians took time out to eat or drink, he learned the secrets of their guitars by himself and became their intimate friend. People in the neighborhood soon grew accustomed to seeing him play along with the other musicians at fiestas.

His legs had grown no longer, and though he was now fourteen, he looked like an eight-year-old. He was very thin, for (a convincing sign of an artistic nature, a slenderness characteristic of those who are inspired) he suffered from a chronic lack of appetite, and if María Portal, with her military determination, had not been around to stuff him full of food, the young bard would have wasted away to nothing. Yet this frail creature did not know the meaning of the word "fatigue" when it came to music. The guitarists of the neighborhood would collapse on the floor, exhausted, after playing and singing for hours and hours, get cramps in their fingers, and become so hoarse they might have been mistaken for mutes, but the cripple would remain seated on a little chair with a straw bottom (little Japanese feet never quite touching the floor, tiny tireless fingers), drawing exquisite harmonies from the strings and singing as though the fiesta had just begun. He did not have a powerful voice; he would have been unable to emulate the prodigious feat of the celebrated Ezequiel Delfín, who, on singing certain waltzes in the key of G, shattered the windowpanes opposite him. But the lack of strength of his voice was compensated by his faultless intonation, his maniacal perfectionism, his richness of shading that never slighted or botched a note.

Nonetheless, it was his talents as a composer rather than as an interpreter that were to make him famous. The fact that the young cripple of Los Barrios Altos knew how to compose Peruvian music as well as play it and sing it came to light one Saturday night during a tumultuous fiesta that filled the Callejón de Santa Ana with colored streamers, noisemakers, and confetti as the whole neighborhood celebrated the cook's saint's day. At midnight the musicians surprised the revelers by playing a polka that no one had ever heard before, with words in the form of a clever dialogue:

¿Cómo?
Con amor, con amor, con amor
¿Qué haces?
Llevo una flor, una flor, una flor
¿Donde?
En el ojal, en el ojal, en el ojal
¿A quién?
A María Portal, María Portal, María Portal . . .*

The catchy rhythm made all those present feel an irresistible urge to dance, hop, skip, and the words amused and touched them. Everyone was consumed with curiosity: who had composed the polka? The musicians turned their heads and indicated that it was Crisanto Maravillas, who (modesty of the truly great) lowered his eyes. María Portal smothered him with kisses, Brother Valentín wiped away a tear, and the entire neighborhood rewarded the new composer with an ovation. In the city of La Perricholi, a creative artist had been born.

Crisanto Maravillas's career (if this pedestrian athletic term is the proper one to describe a mission bearing the stamp of—the divine afflatus?) was meteoric. Within the space of a few months, his songs were known all over Lima, and within a few years they had entered the memory and the heart of all Peru. He was not yet twenty when Abels and Cains alike conceded that he was the most beloved composer in the country. His waltzes enlivened the fiestas of the rich, were danced at the feasts of the middle class, and were the staple fare of the poor. The orchestras of the capital vied with

* *How?*
With love, with love, with love
Doing what?
Wearing a flower, a flower, a flower
Where?
In my lapel, my lapel, my lapel
For whom?
For María Portal, María Portal, María Portal . . .

each other as intrepreters of his music, and there was not a man or woman who, on deciding to embark upon the arduous career of a professional singer, did not include in his or her repertory the marvels of Maravillas. His compositions came out on records and circulated in song sheets, and in view of his vast following, radio programs and magazines were obliged to feature him regularly. In the popular imagination, in the gossip that made the rounds, the crippled composer of Los Barrios Altos became a legendary figure.

Fame and popularity did not turn the head of the unpretentious youngster, who greeted this adulation with a swanlike indifference. He left high school a year before graduating, in order to devote himself to his art. With the gratuities pressed on him for playing at fiestas, giving serenades, or composing acrostics, he was able to buy himself a guitar. The day it became his he was happy: he had found a confidant for his troubles, a companion for his loneliness, and a voice for his inspiration.

He did not know how to read or write music, and never learned. He worked by ear, and by intuition. Once he had learned the melody, he sang it to the mestizo Blas Sanjinés, a teacher in the neighborhood, who set it down in notes on music paper. He never had the slightest desire to make a paying business of his talent: he never copyrighted his compositions or charged royalties for the use of them, and when friends came to him with the news that mediocrities from the lower depths of the artistic world were plagiarizing his melodies and his lyrics, he merely yawned in boredom. Despite this disinterest, he found himself earning a certain amount of money, sent to him by record companies or radio stations, or forced upon him by people who had asked him to play at a party. Crisanto gave all this income to his parents, and when they died (he was thirty years old at the time), he spent it with his friends. He never wanted to leave Los Barrios Altos, nor room H on the little alleyway where he had been born. Was this out of fidelity and affection toward his humble origins, out of love for the gutter? These feelings no doubt played a certain role. But above all it was because in this narrow back street he was only a stone's throw from the offspring of consanguineous parents, whose name was Fátima, whom he had first met when she was a servant girl and who had now taken the veil and pronounced her vows of obedience, poverty, and (alas!) chastity as the bride of Christ.

This had been, and still was, the secret of his life, the reason for that sadness that everyone (blindness of the multitude to the soul's wounds) attributed to his withered legs and his dwarflike, asymmetrical physique. Moreover, thanks to this difformity that made him appear years younger, Crisanto had continued to accompany his mother to the religious citadel of the Discalced Carmelites, and he had been able to see the girl of his dreams at least once a week. Did Sister Fátima love the cripple as he loved her? There is no way of knowing. A hothouse flower, ignorant of the lubricious mysteries of the pollen of the fields, Fátima had acquired a conscience, feelings, grown from childhood to adolescence to adulthood in the aseptic world of the convent, surrounded by old women. Everything that had reached her ears, her eyes, her imagination had been rigorously filtered through the moral sifting-screen of the Order (the strictest of the strict). How could this creature who was virtue incarnate have guessed that what she believed belonged to God (love?) could also be a human interchange?

But (water that flows down the mountainside to the sea, little calf that before opening its eyes seeks the teat to suck the white milk) perhaps she did love him. In any event, he was her friend, the only person her own age she knew, the only playmate she had ever had, if "play" is the proper word for the work they shared—sweeping floors, cleaning windowpanes, watering plants, lighting candles—as María Portal, the illustrious seamstress, taught the nuns the secret of her embroideries.

But it is also true that the two of them, from childhood on, talked a great deal together during these years. Naive dialogues—she was innocent; he was shy—in which (delicacy of lilies and spirituality of doves) they spoke to each other of love without the word ever crossing their lips, by way of interposed subjects, such as the pretty colors of Sister Fátima's collection of pious images and the explanations that Crisanto gave her of what streetcars, automobiles, movies were. All this was recounted, for those who had ears to hear, in Maravillas's songs dedicated to that mysterious woman whose name was never mentioned, save in the very famous waltz whose title so intrigued his admirers: "Fátima is the Virgin of Fátima."

Though he knew that he would never be able to take her out of the convent and make her his, Crisanto Maravillas was happy just seeing his muse a few hours each week. These brief encounters left him all the more profoundly inspired, and were thus responsible for the birth of his many *mozamalas, yaravíes, festejos,* and *resbalosas.* The second tragedy of his life (after his being born physically disabled) occurred the day when, by chance, the Mother Superior of Las Descalzas came upon him as he was emptying his bladder. Madre Lituma's cheeks changed color several times and she was seized with an attack of the hiccups. She ran to ask María Portal how old her son was, and the seamstress confessed that, despite the fact that his height and build were those of a child of ten, he was past eighteen. Crossing herself, Mother Lituma forbade him ever to enter the convent again.

It was very nearly a mortal blow for the bard of the Plaza de Santa Ana, who was immediately taken ill with a romantic malady defying diagnosis. He remained bedridden for many days—extremely high fevers, melodious fits of delirium—as doctors and faith healers tried unguents and spells to bring him out of his coma. When he finally rose from his sickbed, he was a specter and could barely stand up. But (could it have been otherwise?) being cruelly separated from his beloved proved beneficial to his art: his music became so tenderly sentimental that it brought tears to the eye, and his lyrics became dramatically virile. Crisanto Maravillas's great love songs date from these years. Each time his friends, singing along with his sweet melodies, listened to those heartbreaking words that spoke of an imprisoned young girl, a little goldfinch in a cage, a little wild dove caught in a trap, a plucked flower hidden from sight in the Temple of the Lord, and of a grief-stricken man loving from a distance, without hope, they asked themselves: "Who is she?" And (curiosity that was Eve's undoing) they tried to guess which of the women who besieged the bard was the heroine in question.

For, despite his dwarflike stature and his ugliness, the women of Lima were as though bewitched by the magic spell of Crisanto Maravillas's charms. White women with fortunes in the bank, little mestizo demimondaines, mulatresses from the slums, young girls who were just learning to live or older women who were straying yet again from the path of virtue showed up at modest room H, on the pretext of seeking his autograph. They made eyes at him, gave him little presents, flattered him, wheedled, suggested places where they might meet, or made out-and-out advances on the spot. Was it because these women, like those of a certain country that displays its pretentiousness in the very name of its capital (favorable winds, good weather, healthy air?), habitually sought out deformed men, due to a stupid prejudice whereby they are deemed to be better, matrimonially speaking, than normal men? No, in this case it was because the splendor of his art surrounded the homunculus of the Plaza de Santa Ana with a spiritual aura that either blinded them to his wretched physical appearance or made him seem all the more desirable because of it.

Crisanto Maravillas (gentleness of the invalid recovering from tuberculosis) politely discouraged these advances and subtly hinted to the women soliciting his favors that they were wasting their time. On such occasions he would utter an esoteric phrase that unleashed an indescribable whirlwind of gossip round about him: "I believe in fidelity and am a little Portuguese shepherd boy."

The life he led in those days was the bohemian one of gypsies of the spirit. He arose around noon and usually had breakfast with the parish priest of the Church of Santa Ana, a former examining magistrate in whose chambers a Quaker (Don Pedro Barreda y Zaldívar?) had mutilated himself to prove that he was innocent of a crime of which he had been accused (having killed a black stowaway who had arrived in the country in the hold of a passenger liner from Brazil?). Profoundly moved by this incident, Dr. Don Gumercindo Tello had thereupon exchanged his judge's robes for a priest's cassock. The story of the mutilation was immortalized by Crisanto Maravillas in a *festejo* for guitar, *quijada,* and *cajón,* entitled "Blood Absolves Me."

The bard and Father Gumercindo were in the habit of walking together through these streets of Lima where Crisanto (artist whose talents were nourished by life itself?) found characters and subjects for his songs. His music—tradition, history, folklore, gossip—immortalized in melody the types and customs of the city. In the pits just off the Plaza del Cercado and in Santo Cristo, Maravillas and Father Gumercindo watched fighting cocks being trained for championship matches in the Coliseo de Sandia, and thus was born the *marinera* "Watch Out for the Cock the Color of Red Pepper, Mama"; or they took the sun in the little square of Carmen Alto, where, seeing the puppeteer Monleón amusing everyone in the neighborhood with his little rag marionettes, Crisanto found the subject of the waltz "The Young Miss from Carmen Alto" (it begins: "Alas, my love, you have little fingers made of wire and a heart of straw"). It was also, doubtless, during these strolls through the old town that Crisanto came across the little old ladies in black shawls who appear in his waltz "Devout Little Lady, You Too Were a Woman Once," and watched the adolescent street fights mentioned in the polka "The Urchins."

Around six in the evening, the two friends would separate: the priest would return to his parish church to pray for the soul of the cannibal murdered in El Callao, and the bard would go to the garage of Chumpitaz the tailor. There, with the group of his intimates—Sifuentes the *cajón* drummer, Tiburcio the *quijada* player, Lucía Acémila the singer? Felipe and Juan Portocarrero the guitarists—he would rehearse new songs, work up arrangements, and as dusk was falling, somebody would bring out the fraternal bottle of pisco. And so, between musicmaking and conversation, rehearsing and a bit of alcohol, the hours went by. When it got dark, the group would go off to eat at one restaurant or another of the city, where the artist was always an honored guest. On other days, fiestas awaited them—birthdays, engagements, weddings—or dates at some club. They would make their way home at dawn and the bard's friends would bid him goodbye at the door of the building where he lived. But once they had left and were home in their hovels sleeping, a misshapen little figure with a clumsy gait would emerge from the alleyway. A ghostly silhouette in the dawn fog and drizzle, he would make his way through the damp shadows and sit down in the deserted Plaza de Santa Ana on the stone bench opposite the convent of Las Descalzas. The cats of early morning would then hear the most deeply felt arpeggios ever to pour forth from an earthly guitar, the most ardent songs of love born of human inspiration. Those devout old ladies already abroad at that hour who sometimes spied him there, singing softly and weeping in front of the convent, spread the vicious rumor that, drunk with vanity, he had fallen in love with the Virgin herself, and serenaded her at daybreak.

Weeks, months, years went by. Crisanto Maravillas's fame (destiny of a balloon that expands and rises, following the sun) spread, as did his music. No one, however, not even his intimate friend the parish priest Gumercindo Lituma, a former Guardia Civil brutally beaten by his wife and children (for raising rats?) who, as he convalesced, had heard the call of the Lord, guessed the story of Crisanto Maravillas's inordinate passion for the cloistered Sister Fátima, who during all these years had been trotting from one chore to another on her way to sainthood. The chaste couple had not been able to exchange a single word since the day the Mother Superior (Sister Lucía Acémila?) discovered that the bard was a creature endowed with virility (despite what had occurred on that fateful morning in the chambers of the examining magistrate?). But down through the years they had had the happiness of seeing each other, though only with difficulty and at a distance. Once she became a nun, Sor Fátima, like her sisters in the convent, took her turn at prayer in the chapel, where the Carmelites kept a perpetual vigil, by twos, twenty-four hours a day. The nuns keeping vigil were separated from the public by a little wooden grille, and though its openings were very small, people on both sides were able to see each other through it. This explained in large part the stubborn religiosity of the bard of Lima that had often made him the victim of the mocking jokes of those in his neighborhood, taunts which he answered by composing the pious *tondero* "Yes, I Am a Believer."

Crisanto, it is true, spent a great deal of his time in the Carmelite chapel. He would enter several times a day, cross himself, and cast a glance at the grille. If—with beating heart, racing pulse, shivers up and down his spine—he recognized Sister Fátima through the little square openings in the wooden grille, kneeling at one of the prie-dieus perpetually occupied by silhouettes in white habits, he would immediately fall to his knees on the colonial tiles. He placed himself in an oblique position (his physique was a help in this respect, for it was not easy to tell whether one was seeing him full-face or in profile), which allowed him to give the impression that he was looking at the altar, when in reality his eyes were fixed on the long veils, the snowy starched folds enveloping the body of his beloved. From time to time Sister Fátima (breaths that the athlete takes to redouble his efforts) interrupted her prayers, raised her eyes toward the altar (ruled off in squares?), and thereupon recognized Crisanto's shadowy interposed silhouette. An imperceptible smile would then appear on the little nun's niveous face and a tender sentiment would be revived in her delicate heart on catching sight of her childhood friend. Their eyes would meet and in those few seconds (Sister Fátima would feel obliged to lower hers) they told each other—things that would have made even the angels in Heaven blush? Because, yes, it was quite true—this young girl who had been miraculously saved from being crushed to death by the wheels of the car driven by the medical detail man Lucho Abril Marroquín, which had knocked her down one sunny morning on the outskirts of Pisco when she was not yet five years old, and who had become a nun in thanks to the Virgin of Fátima, had with the passage of time come, within her solitary cell, to love the bard of Los Barrios Altos with a sincere heart.

Crisanto Maravillas had resigned himself to not marrying his beloved carnally, to merely communicating with her in this subliminal fashion in the chapel. But he never resigned himself to the thought—cruel for a man whose only beauty was his art—that Sister Fátima was not able to hear his music, those songs that she unwittingly inspired. He suspected (a certainty for anyone who cast one glance at the thick fortified walls of the convent) that the serenades which, risking pneumonia, he had been offering her each morning at dawn for twenty years never reached the ears of his beloved. One day Crisanto Maravillas began to incorporate religious and mystical themes in his repertory: the miracles of Saint Rose of Lima, the (zoological?) feats of Saint Martin of Porres, stories of the martyrs, and maledictions of Pontius Pilate followed songs celebrating humble folkways. His success among the masses was in no way diminished thereby, and at the same time he attracted a new legion of fanatical admirers: priests and monks, nuns, Acción Católica. Peruvian music, ennobled, perfumed with incense, enriched by sacred themes, began to leap over the walls that had imprisoned it in drawing rooms and clubs and be heard in places where it would previously have been inconceivable: churches, processions, retreat houses, seminaries.

This clever plan took him ten years to carry out, but in the end it was successful. The convent of Las Descalzas could not refuse the offer it received one day: the bard beloved by all the parish, the poet of church gatherings, the musician of the Stations of the Cross offered to give in its chapel and cloisters a song recital to raise money for African missionaries. The archbishop of Lima (wisdom clad in purple, and ear of a connoisseur) sent word that he authorized the performance and that, for a few hours, he would suspend the rules governing the order in order to enable the strictly cloistered Carmelites to enjoy the music. He himself planned to attend the recital with his retinue of dignitaries.

The event, a red-letter day in the history of the City of the Viceroys, took place on the day that Crisanto reached the prime of life: his fiftieth birthday? He was a man with a penetrating forehead, a broad nose, an aquiline gaze, the very soul of rectitude and goodness, and possessed of a graceful physical bearing that mirrored the beauty of his spirit.

Even though (precautions on the part of the individual whom society tramples to bits) personal invitations had been sent out and fair warning had been given that no one without one would be admitted to the recital, reality weighed more heavily in the balance: the police lines, under the command of the celebrated Sergeant Lituma and his right-hand man Corporal Jaime Concha, gave way like tissue paper before the multitudes. They had been gathered there since the evening before, and now they (reverently) invaded the cloisters, the galleries, the stairways, the vestibules. The invited guests were obliged to enter through a secret door leading directly to the balconies above, where, crowded together behind ancient railings, they settled down to enjoy the performance.

When, at 6 p.m., the bard (conquistador's smile, navy-blue suit, lithe step of a gymnast, flowing golden locks) entered, escorted by his orchestra and chorus, an ovation that echoed from the rafters resounded in the chapel of Las Descalzas. As Gumercindo Maravillas knelt there, reciting an Our Father and an Ave Maria in his baritone voice, his eyes (as melting as honey?) identified, among the heads, a host of friends.

Sitting in the first row was a celebrated astrologer, Professor (Ezequiel?) Delfín Acémila, who, scrutinizing the heavens, measuring the tides, and making Cabalistic passes, had foretold the fate of the city's millionairesses, and (simplicity of heart of the savant who plays games of marbles) had a weakness for Peruvian music. Also present, dressed to the nines, with a red carnation in his buttonhole and a brand-new straw hat, was the most popular black in Lima, the one who, having crossed the ocean as a stowaway in the hold of—an airplane?—had made a new life for himself here (devoted to the civic pastime of killing rodents through the use of poisons typical of his tribe, thereby earning a fortune?). And (coincidences that are the work of the Devil or sheer chance) among those present, attracted by their common admiration for the musician, were the Jehovah's Witness Lucho Abril Marroquín, who by virtue of the epic deed he had performed (guillotining the index finger of his right hand with a keen-edged paper knife?) had earned himself the nickname of Maimie, and Sarita Huanca Salaverría, the charming, capricious Victorian belle who had demanded such a great sacrifice of him as a token of his love. And how could the bard of Lima have failed to see, deathly pale and anemic amid the multitude of devotees of Peruvian music, Richard Quinteros, the young man from Miraflores? Taking advantage of the fact that, for the one and only time in his life, the doors of the convent of the Carmelites had been opened, he had slipped into the cloister in the midst of the crowd to see, if only from a distance, that sister of his (Sister Fátima? Sister Lituma? Sister Lucía?), sequestered within its walls by her parents in order to rid her of her incestuous love. And even the Berguas, deaf-mutes who never left the Pensión Colonial where they lived, devoting their lives to the altruistic occupation of teaching poor deaf-and-dumb children to communicate with each other by means of gestures and grimaces, had come, infected by the universal curiosity, to see (since they were unable to hear) the idol of Lima.

The apocalypse that was to plunge the city into mourning was unleashed after Father Gumercindo Tello had begun his recital. As the hundreds of people gathered in the doorways and the patios, on the stairways, the rooftop terraces listened, hypnotized, the singer, accompanied by the organ, was interpreting the last notes of the exquisite apostrophe: "My Religion Is Not for Sale." The first wave of applause that greeted Father Gumercindo (good and evil that mingle like coffee and milk) was the undoing of the audience. For, too absorbed in the song, too eager to join in the plaudits, the bravos, the cheers, they confused the first symptoms of the cataclysm with the tumultuous emotion aroused in them by the Canary of the Lord. They did not react in the few seconds during which it was still possible to run, to leave the building, to seek safety. When (volcanic roar that shatters the eardrums) they discovered that it was not themselves but the earth that was trembling, it was too late. For the only three doorways of the convent of the Carmelites (happenstance, will of God, blunder of the architect?) had been blocked by the first cave-ins, and the great stone angel now obstructing the main portal had crushed beneath it Sergeant Crisanto Maravillas, who, aided by Corporal Jaime Concha and Private Lituma, had been trying to evacuate the convent as the first tremors were felt. The valiant citizen and his two aides were the first victims of the subterranean conflagration. There, thus, met their end (cockroaches squashed by a shoe sole), buried beneath an impassive granite statue, in the holy portals of the convent of the Carmelites (to await the Last Judgment?), the three musketeers of the Peruvian Corps of Firemen.

Meanwhile, inside the convent, the faithful brought together there by music and religion died like flies. The applause had been followed by a chorus of lamentations, screams, shrieks of terror. The noble stones, the ancient bricks were unable to withstand the —convulsive, interminable—quaking of the depths. One by one the walls cracked apart and collapsed, crushing to death those who were trying to scale them to reach the street. Several celebrated exterminators of mice and rats thus met their death: the Berguas? Seconds later (din of Hell, dust clouds of a tornado) the second-floor galleries caved in, sending those who had sought places higher up to better hear Mother Gumercinda hurtling down (living projectiles, human meteors) on the multitude crowded together in the courtyard below. There, thus, met his death, his skull smashed in on the flagstones, the Lima psychologist Lucho Abril Marroquín, who had rid half the citizens of that capital of their neuroses thanks to a treatment he had invented (consisting of playing a noisy game of ninepins?). But it was the collapse of the roof of the Carmelite convent that produced the greatest number of fatalities in the shortest time. There, thus, met her death, among others, Mother Lucía Acémila, who had gained such world renown after deserting her former sect, the Jehovah's Witnesses, by writing a book praised by the Pope: "Deriding the Tree Trunk in the Name of the Cross."

The death of Sister Fátima and Richard (irresistible rush of passion that neither blood nor the veil can stay) was even more tragic. During the centuries that the fire lasted, the two of them remained unharmed, locked in each other's arms, while round about them people were perishing, asphyxiated, trampled to death, burned to cinders. The fire was now over, and amid ashes and thick clouds of smoke, the two lovers still embraced, surrounded by corpses. The time to make their way out into the street had come. Grasping Mother Fátima by the waist, Richard had dragged her over to one of the breaches opened in the walls by the raging fire. But the lovers had taken only a few steps when (infamy of the carnivorous earth? the justice of Heaven?) the earth yawned open beneath their feet. The fire had consumed the trap door concealing the colonial crypt in which the Carmelite sisters preserved the bones of their dead; it was through this opening that the (Luciferian?) brother and sister fell, their bodies shattering to bits against the ossuary below.

Was it the Devil who carried them off? Was Hell the epilogue of their love? Or was it God, taking pity on their terrible suffering, who bore them up to Heaven? Had this story of blood, song, mysticism, and fire ended, or would it have an extra-terrestrial sequel?

Nineteen.

Javier phoned us from Lima

at seven o'clock in the morning. It was a very bad connection, but even all the crackling and buzzing on the line could not conceal the alarm in his voice.

"Bad news," he told me straight out. "Lots of bad news."

About fifty kilometers outside Lima, the jitney in which he and Pascual had been returning to the city the night before had gone off the road and rolled over in the sand. Neither of them had been hurt, but the driver and another passenger had suffered serious contusions; it had been a nightmare trying to get a car to stop in the middle of the night and lend them a hand. Javier was dead tired by the time he got back to his *pensión*. And on his arrival there he'd had an even worse scare. My father had been waiting for him at the door. Livid with rage, he had approached Javier, brandishing a revolver and threatening to shoot him if he didn't reveal instantly where Aunt Julia and I were. Utterly panic-stricken ("Till that moment, the only time I'd ever seen revolvers was in the movies, old pal"), Javier had sworn to him, taking his mother and all the saints as his witnesses, that he had no idea, that he hadn't seen me for a week. My father had finally calmed down a little and left Javier a letter that he was to deliver to me personally. In a daze after what had just happened, Javier ("I had quite a night of it, Varguitas, believe me") had decided, once my father had left, to go have a word with my Uncle Lucho straightway to find out whether my mother's side of the family had also worked itself up into such an insane rage. My uncle had received him in his bathrobe. They had talked for nearly an hour. Uncle Lucho, it turned out, wasn't furious, just sad, worried, troubled. Javier confirmed the fact that Aunt Julia and I had complied with all the formalities and were legally married, and also assured my uncle that he, too, had done his best to dissuade me, to no avail. Uncle Lucho suggested that Aunt Julia and I return to Lima at once to take the bull by the horns and try to settle things.

"The big problem is your father," Javier said, winding up his report. "The rest of the family will eventually accept the situation. But your dad's foaming at the mouth. You can't imagine what he says in that letter he left for you!"

I scolded him for reading other people's letters, and told him that we were coming back to Lima immediately, that I would come by to see him at the office where he worked or would phone him. As she was getting dressed, I told Aunt Julia everything he'd said, not hiding anything from her, but at the same time trying to make everything that had happened sound less violent.

"What I don't like at all is the business with the revolver," she commented. "I presume that the person he really wants to put a bullet through is me, right? Listen, Varguitas, I do hope my father-in-law won't shoot me right in the middle of my honeymoon. And isn't it awful about that jitney accident? Poor Javier! Poor Pascual! Our madness has really gotten them into a heap of trouble."

She wasn't the least bit frightened or upset by the prospects that lay in store for us; she seemed very happy and determined to face up to any and every disaster that might await us. And that was how I felt, too. We paid the hotel bill, walked over to the Plaza de Armas to have our morning coffee, and half an hour later were on our way back to Lima, in an ancient jitney. During almost the entire trip we kept kissing on the mouth, on the cheeks, on the hands, whispering into each other's ear that we loved each other, and paying no attention to the uneasy looks of the other passengers and the driver, who kept sneaking glances at us in the rearview mirror.

We arrived in Lima around 10 a.m. It was a gray day, the fog turned all the people and all the buildings into ghostly apparitions, and the air was so damp we felt as though we were breathing water. The jitney dropped us off at Aunt Olga's and Uncle Lucho's. Before knocking on the door, we squeezed each other's hand hard to screw up our courage. Aunt Julia had turned very serious all of a sudden and I could feel my heart pounding.

It was Uncle Lucho himself who came to the door to let us in. He gave us a smile that seemed terribly forced, kissed Aunt Julia on the cheek, and kissed me, too.

"Your sister's still in bed, but she's awake," he said to Aunt Julia, pointing toward the bedroom. "Go on in."

He and I went and sat down in the living room, from which one could see the Jesuit seminary, the breakwater, and the sea when there was no fog. The only things visible at that moment were the blurred outlines of the wall and the red-brick rooftop terrace of the seminary.

"I'm not going to pull your ears, because you're too big for that now," Uncle Lucho murmured. He looked really dejected, and his face showed that he'd spent a sleepless night. "Do you have any idea, though, what a mess you've gotten yourself into?"

"It was the only way to keep them from separating us," I said, a reply I'd already rehearsed in my mind. "Julia and I love each other," I went on. "We haven't done anything on the spur of the moment. We've thought everything through and we know what we're doing. I promise you we're going to make out all right."

"You're still just a kid, you don't have a profession or even a roof over your head, you'll have to give up your studies and work like a slave to support your wife," Uncle Lucho muttered, lighting a cigarette and shaking his head. "You've cooked your own goose. Nobody's happy about the situation, because everybody in the family was hoping you'd amount to something. We're heartsick at seeing you dive headfirst into mediocrity because of a mere passing fancy."

"I'm not going to give up my studies, I'm going to get my degree, I'm going to do exactly what I would have done if I hadn't gotten married," I assured him heatedly. "You have to believe me and make the family believe me. Julia's going to help me, I'll study now, I'll feel more like working."

"For the moment, the first order of business is to pacify your father, who's fit to be tied," Uncle Lucho said, in a less stern tone of voice all of a sudden. He'd done his duty and pulled my ears, and now he seemed ready to help me. "He won't listen to reason, and is threatening to turn Julia in to the police and I don't know what-all."

I said I'd talk to him and try to get him to accept the facts. Uncle Lucho looked me up and down: it was shameful for a brand-new bridegroom to be going around in a dirty shirt. I should go back to my grandparents' house, take a bath, change my clothes, and then reassure them, because they were very worried about me. We talked a while more, and even had coffee together, but Julia still hadn't come out of Aunt Olga's bedroom. I strained my ears trying to make out whether they were weeping, shouting, arguing with each other inside. But not a sound came through the closed door. Aunt Julia finally came out, by herself. Her face was bright red, as though she'd been out in the sun too long, but she was smiling.

"Well, you're alive at least and all in one piece," Uncle Lucho said to her. "I thought your sister was going to snatch you bald-headed."

"She very nearly slapped my face when she first saw me," Aunt Julia confessed, sitting down beside me. "She said awful things to me, naturally. But I take it that, despite everything, I can stay here with you till things blow over."

I rose to my feet and said I had to go to Panamericana: it would be tragic if I lost my job at this point. Uncle Lucho saw me to the door, told me to come back for lunch, and when I kissed Aunt Julia goodbye as I left, I saw him smile.

I rushed to the corner grocery store to call my cousin Nancy, and luckily for me she was the one who answered the phone. When she recognized my voice, she was struck speechless for a moment. We agreed to meet in ten minutes in the Parque Salazar. When I arrived at the park, she was already there, dying of curiosity. Before she'd tell me anything, I had to recount the whole Chincha adventure and answer the endless questions she asked me about the most unexpected details: what dress, for instance, Aunt Julia had worn for the wedding ceremony. What delighted her and made her burst into peals of laughter (though she didn't believe me) was my slightly distorted version of events wherein the mayor who had married us was a black, half-naked, barefoot fisherman. After that, I finally got her to tell me how the family had greeted the news. It had all been quite predictable: goings and comings from one house to another, animated family councils, innumerable telephone calls back and forth, copious tears, and apparently my mother had been extended everyone's sympathies, visited, and kept company as though she'd lost her only son. As for Nancy, convinced that she was our ally, they had besieged her with questions and threats, trying to get her to tell them where we were. But she had held her ground, vehemently denying everything, and had even shed a few great crocodile tears that allayed their suspicions somewhat.

Nancy, too, was worried about my father's reaction. "Don't even consider going to see him till he gets over his terrible fit of temper," she warned me. "He's so furious he might very well kill you."

I asked her about the little apartment she'd rented for us, and once again her sense of practicality amazed me. She'd spoken with the owner that very morning. There were things that had to be fixed in the bathroom, a door had to be replaced and painted, and therefore it was going to be at least ten days before we could move in. My heart sank when I heard this. As I was walking back to my grandparents', I wondered where in the world we'd be able to find a roof over our heads for those two weeks.

I arrived at my grandparents' house without having solved the problem, and found my mother waiting there for me in the living room. When she caught sight of me, she burst into a spectacular flood of tears. She gave me a tremendous hug, and as she stroked my eyes, my cheeks, and ran her fingers through my hair, half choking with sobs, she kept repeating with infinite pity in her voice: "My baby, my little darling, my treasure, what have they done to you, what has that woman done to you?" I hadn't seen her for nearly a year, and though her face was swollen with weeping, I found her prettier and younger-looking than ever. I did my very best to calm her, assuring her that they hadn't done anything to me, that I was the one who had decided, entirely on my own, that I wanted to get married. Every time the name of her brand-new daughter-in-law came up in the conversation, she burst into tears all over again; she fell into fits of rage in which she referred to Julia as "that old lady," "that brazen hussy," "that divorcée." All at once, in the middle of this scene, I realized something that had never crossed my mind before: it wasn't so much what people would say but religion that was making her feel so heartbroken.

She was a fervent Catholic and it wasn't the fact that Aunt Julia was older than I was that was upsetting her so much as the fact that she was divorced—in other words, forbidden to remarry within the Church.

With the help of my grandparents, I finally managed to quiet her down. The two oldsters were a model of tact, kindness, and discretion. Grandfather merely said to me, as he gave me his usual brusque kiss on the forehead: "Well, poet, you've finally turned up again, have you? You had us worried." And my granny, after hugging and kissing me repeatedly, said in my ear in a half whisper so my mother wouldn't hear, with a sort of mischievous complicity: "And what about Julita—is she all right?"

After taking a long shower and changing my clothes—I felt liberated on getting rid of the ones I'd had on for four days—I was able to have a talk with my mother. She'd stopped crying and was having a cup of tea made for her by my granny, who was sitting on the arm of my mother's chair, caressing her as though she were a little girl. I tried to get a smile out of my mother with a joke that didn't sit well with her at all ("But, Mama, you should be happy, I've married a great friend of yours"), but then I struck more sensitive chords by swearing to her that I wouldn't give up my studies, that I'd go on and get my law degree, that I might even change my mind about the Peruvian diplomatic service ("the ones that aren't idiots are pederasts, Mama") and become a foreign officer, the dream of her life. She gradually softened up, and though she still looked grief-stricken, she asked me about the university, my grades, my work at the radio station, and scolded me for being such an ungrateful son that I hardly ever wrote to her. She told me that my marriage had come as a terrible blow to my father: he, too, had great ambitions for me, and that was why he was bent on keeping "that woman" from ruining my life. He'd consulted lawyers, the marriage wasn't valid, he'd have it annulled, and might bring charges against Aunt Julia for corrupting the morals of a minor. My father was so enraged that for the moment he didn't want to see me, to prevent "something terrible" from happening, and was demanding that Aunt Julia leave the country immediately or suffer the consequences.

I replied that Aunt Julia and I had been married precisely in order not to be separated and that it was going to be very difficult to force my wife to leave the country two days after the wedding. But my mother didn't want to discuss the subject. "You know your papa, you know what a terrible temper he has, you'll have to do what he wants, because if you don't . . ." and a terror-stricken look came into her eyes. I finally told her that I was going to be late for work, that we'd talk some more later, and before I left, I tried again to set her mind at ease about my future, assuring her that I'd go on and get my law degree.

As I headed back downtown in a jitney, I had a gloomy presentiment: what if I found somebody sitting at my desk when I got to the office? I'd been gone for three days, and in the last few weeks, because of all the frustrating running around I'd had to do trying to arrange for us to be married, I hadn't once looked over the news bulletins before they went on the air, and Pascual and Big Pablito must have done all sorts of horrendous things in them. I thought soberly of what would happen if, on top of all the personal complications of the moment, I were to lose my job as well, and began to think up arguments that would arouse the sympathies of Genaro Jr. and Genaro Sr. But on entering the Panamericana building, with my heart in my shoes, to my tremendous surprise the dynamic impresario, whom I happened to meet in the elevator, greeted me as though we'd seen each other only ten minutes before. He had a serious look on his face.

"There's no doubt about it: we're in the midst of a catastrophe," he said to me, shaking his head sadly; it was as though we'd been discussing the subject just a moment before. "What are we going to do now, can you tell me that? They have to put him away."

He got off the elevator on the third floor, and to compound the confusion, I'd assumed a doleful expression and murmured, as though I knew exactly what he was talking about: "Good heavens, what a pity." I felt happy that something so serious had happened that my absence had gone unnoticed. Up in the shack, Pascual and Big Pablito were listening to Nelly, Genaro Jr.'s secretary, with faces a mile long. They barely said hello to me and nobody cracked a single joke about my having gotten married. They looked at me in despair.

"They've taken Pedro Camacho off to the insane asylum," Big Pablito stammered, his voice breaking. "What a sad thing, Don Mario!"

Then, between them, with Nelly doing most of the talking, since she had followed what was going on from the Genaros' office, they told me all the details. Everything had started during those very days when I was all wrapped up in my prematrimonial troubles. The catastrophes, the fires, earthquakes, auto accidents, shipwrecks, train derailments were the beginning of the end, for they had wreaked havoc with the radio serials by killing off dozens of characters in the space of a few minutes. This time, the actors and technicians of Radio Central, in a panic, had stopped trying to serve as a bulwark protecting the scriptwriter, or had been unable to prevent the radio listeners' expressions of utter bewilderment and their protests from reaching the Genaros' ears. But the latter had already been alerted by the daily papers, whose radio columnists had been making derisive remarks about Pedro Camacho's cataclysms for days. The Genaros had called him into their office and questioned him, taking every possible precaution so as not to hurt his feelings or exasperate him. But in the middle of the conversation he'd had a nervous collapse: the catastrophes were stratagems to enable him to begin the stories all over again from scratch, since his memory was failing him, and he could no longer remember what had happened in the plots in previous episodes, nor which character was which, nor which serial they belonged to, and—"weeping hysterically and tearing his hair," Nelly assured me—he confessed to them that in the last few weeks his work, his life, his nights had been torture. The Genaros had called in a famous Lima physician, Dr. Honorio Delgado, who had immediately announced that the scriptwriter was in no condition to work; his "exhausted" brain had to have a rest.

We were all ears listening to Nelly's tale when the phone rang. It was Genaro Jr.; he needed to see me immediately. I went down to his office, convinced that the moment had come when I'd receive, at the very least, a severe warning. But he greeted me as he had in the elevator, presuming that I knew all about the problems confronting him. He had just talked with Havana on the phone, and was foaming at the mouth because CMQ, taking advantage of his situation, of the emergency, had quadrupled the price it was asking for its serials.

"It's a tragedy, an incredible stroke of bad luck, Camacho's programs were the ones with the best listener ratings, advertisers were fighting for air time on them," he said, shuffling papers on his desk. "What a disaster to have to fall back on those sharks at CMQ again!"

I asked him how Pedro Camacho was, if he'd seen him, how long it would be before he'd be able to come back to work.

"There's no hope for him," he growled, with a sort of fury, but finally went on in a more compassionate tone of voice. "Dr. Delgado says that his psyche is undergoing a process of deliquescence. Deliquescence. Do you understand what he means by that? That his mind is falling to pieces, I suppose, that his brain is rotting, or something like that—right? When my father asked Dr. Delgado if his recovery might possibly take months, his reply was: 'Years, perhaps.' Can you imagine!"

He bowed his head, his spirits crushed, and with the certainty of a soothsayer predicted what was going to happen: when sponsors found out that the scripts from now on were going to be from CMQ, they'd cancel their contracts or demand a fifty percent reduction in advertising rates. And to top everything off, it was going to be three weeks to a month before the new serials arrived, because Cuba was in a mess, what with the terrorism and the guerrillas, CMQ had been turned topsy-turvy, with people arrested and all kinds of troubles. But leaving Radio Central listeners without any serials at all for a month was unthinkable, the station would lose its audience, Radio la Crónica or Radio Colonial would lure them all away, they'd already begun to be tough competition because they were broadcasting cheap, vulgar Argentine soap operas.

"By the way, that's why I asked you to come down here," he added, looking at me as though he'd just noticed that I was there. "You've got to give us a hand. You're more or less of an intellectual, and it'll be an easy job for you."

The job he was speaking of was to search around in the storeroom of Radio Central, where all the old serials, the ones from before Pedro Camacho's arrival, were kept, look through them, and find the ones that could be used right away while waiting for the new ones from CMQ to arrive.

"We'll pay you extra, naturally," he informed me. "We don't exploit anybody around here."

I felt enormous gratitude toward Genaro Jr. and great sympathy for his problems. Even if he gave me only a hundred *soles* extra, they'd be a boon to me at this point.

As I was leaving his office, his voice stopped me at the door. "Hey, I hear you've gotten married." I turned around; he was gesturing affectionately in my direction. "Who's the victim? A woman, I trust? Well, congratulations. We'll have to have a drink together to celebrate."

I called Aunt Julia from my office. She told me that Aunt Olga had calmed down a little, but every so often was overcome with amazement all over again and kept saying: "You're out of your mind." Aunt Julia wasn't terribly upset that the apartment wasn't quite ready to move into ("Well, Varguitas, all I can say is that we've slept apart for such a long time that we can go on that way for two weeks more"), and she told me that after taking a nice long bath and changing her clothes she felt very optimistic. I told her I wouldn't be able to come by for lunch because I had to go through a huge stack of serials, but that we'd see each other that night. I got the Panamericana newscast and two bulletins out and then went digging in the storeroom of Radio Central. It was a cellar with no light and full of cobwebs, and as I went inside I heard mice scampering around in the dark. There were papers everywhere: in piles, scattered about loose, tied together in bundles. The dust and the dampness made me start sneezing immediately. It was impossible to work down there, so I began carting armfuls of paper upstairs to Pedro Camacho's cubbyhole and sat down at what had been his desk. There was not a trace of him left: neither the dictionary of quotations, nor the map of Lima, nor his sociologico-psychologico-racial index cards. The filthy mess that the old serials from CMQ were in was unbelievable: the dampness had blurred the texts, mice and cockroaches had nibbled the pages and left droppings all over them, and the scripts had gotten as hopelessly mixed up with each other as Pedro Camacho's plots. There wasn't much choosing to be done; the most I could hope to do was try to find a few legible texts.

I'd been having a fit of allergic sneezing for three hours as I dove into syrupy horrors, trying to put together a few serials as though they were jigsaw puzzles, when the door of the cubbyhole opened and Javier walked in.

"It's incredible that at a time like this, with all the problems you've got, you're letting yourself get carried away again by that Pedro Camacho mania of yours," he said angrily. "I've just come from your grandparents'. The least you could do is find out what's happening and start trembling in your boots."

He flung two envelopes down on the desk strewn with tear-jerkers. One was the letter my father had left with him the night before. It read:

"Mario: I'm giving that woman forty-eight hours to leave the country. If she does not do so, I shall use my influence and personally see to it that she pays dearly for her effrontery. As for you, I should like to inform you that I am armed and will not allow you to make a fool of me. If you do not obey to the letter and this woman does not leave the country within the time limit that I have indicated above, I shall put five bullets through you and kill you like a dog, right in the middle of the street."

He had signed it with his two family names and added a postscript: "You can go ask for police protection if you wish. And to remove all possible doubts as to my intentions, I herewith affix my signature once again to my decision to kill you, wherever I find you, like a dog." And he had indeed signed his name a second time, in an ever bolder hand than the first time.

The other envelope had been handed to Javier by my granny half an hour before, so that he could bring it to me at the office. It had been delivered to the house by a Guardia Civil; it was a summons to appear at the Miraflores commissariat at nine o'clock the following morning.

"The worst thing isn't the letter, but the fact that, given the state I saw your father in last night, he may very well carry out his threat," Javier said consolingly, sitting himself on the windowsill. "What are we going to do, old pal?"

"For the moment, go see a lawyer," was the one thing that occurred to me. "About my marriage and this other business. Do you know anybody who'd be willing to give us legal advice free, or let us pay later?"

We went to see a young attorney, a relative of Javier's, with whom we'd gone surfing a couple of times at the Miraflores beach. He was very friendly, laughed good-humoredly at all our adventures in Chincha, and teased me a bit; and as Javier had thought, he refused to accept any money from me. He explained that the marriage was not null and void but could be declared so because the date on my birth certificate had been altered. But such an annulment would require a court proceeding. If suit was not brought within two years, the marriage would automatically be valid and could no longer be annulled. As for Aunt Julia, it was indeed possible to denounce her as a "corrupter of the morals of a minor," to swear out a complaint against her at the commissariat and have her arrested, at least temporarily. There would then be a trial, but he was certain that, in view of the circumstances—that is to say, given the fact that I was eighteen and not twelve—it was inconceivable that the prosecution would win the case: any court would acquit her.

"But even so, if he wants to, your dad can give Julita a very hard time of it for a while," Javier concluded as we were walking back to the radio station along the Jirón de la Unión. "Is it true that he's got pull in government circles?"

I didn't know; maybe he was the friend of some general, the bosom buddy of some minister. All of a sudden, I decided that I wasn't going to wait till the next day to find out what they wanted of me at the commissariat. I asked Javier to help me rescue a few serials from the magma of papers at Radio Central so I could lay my doubts to rest that very day. He agreed to help, and also offered to come visit me if they threw me in jail—and bring me cigarettes each time.

At six that evening I gave Genaro Jr. two serials that I'd more or less patched together and promised him that I'd have three more the following day; I took a quick look at the 6 and 8 p.m. bulletins, promised Pascual that I'd be back for the Panamericana newscast, and half an hour later Javier and I were at the commissariat on the Malecón 28 de Julio, in Miraflores. We waited a good while, and finally the commissioner—a major in uniform—and the chief of the police detectives received us. My father had come that morning to ask them to take an official deposition from me as to what had gone on. They had a handwritten list of questions, but the chief of detectives took my answers down on a typewriter, and this took a long time because he was a terrible typist. I admitted that I'd gotten married (and pointed out emphatically that I had done so "of my own free will") but I refused to say where or before what official. I also refused to reveal who the witnesses had been.

The questions were such that they appeared to have been drawn up by a shyster lawyer with dirty work in mind: my date of birth and immediately thereafter (as though the answer were not implicit in the preceding question) whether I was a minor or not, where I lived and with whom, and of course, how old Aunt Julia was (they kept referring to her as Doña Julia), a question that I also refused to answer, saying it was not the gentlemanly thing to reveal a woman's age. This aroused a childish curiosity on the part of the two police officials, who, after I had signed the deposition, assumed a paternal air and asked me, "merely out of curiosity," how many years older than I the "lady" was. When we left the commissariat, I suddenly felt very depressed, with the uncomfortable sensation that I was a thief or a murderer.

Javier thought I'd put my foot in it; my having refused to reveal the place where the marriage ceremony had been performed was an act of defiance that would make my father even more furious, and completely useless, since he'd be able to find out in just a few days.

I couldn't bring myself to go back to the radio station that night in the mood I was in, so I went to Uncle Lucho's. It was Aunt Olga who came to the door; she greeted me with a grave face and a murderous look, but didn't let a peep out and even offered me her cheek to kiss. She went into the living room with me, where Aunt Julia and Uncle Lucho were sitting. One look at them sufficed to tell me that things were going from bad to worse. I asked them what was up.

"Events have taken a terrible turn," Aunt Julia said to me, interlocking her fingers with mine, and I could see how much this upset Aunt Olga. "My father-in-law is trying to have me thrown out of the country as an undesirable alien."

Uncle Jorge, Uncle Juan, and Uncle Pedro had gone to talk to my father that afternoon, and had come back badly frightened by the state they'd found him in. A cold fury, a fixed stare, a way of speaking that made it unmistakable that nothing could possibly get him to change his mind. He was categorical: Aunt Julia had to leave Peru within forty-eight hours or suffer the consequences. It so happened that he was an intimate friend—a former schoolmate, perhaps—of the Minister of Labor in the dictator's cabinet, a general named Villacorta, he'd already talked to him, and if Aunt

Julia refused to leave the country voluntarily, she would be put aboard the plane by soldiers. As for me, if I didn't obey him, I would pay dearly for it. And, as he'd done with Javier, he showed the revolver to my uncles. I completed the picture by showing them my father's letter and telling them about the police interrogation. The letter had one virtue at least: it won my aunt and uncle over a hundred percent to our cause. Uncle Lucho poured us all whiskies and as we sat there drinking them Aunt Olga suddenly began to cry and ask how all this could possibly be, her sister treated like a common criminal, threatened by the police, when the two of them belonged to one of the best families in Bolivia.

"There's no other solution except for me to leave, Varguitas," Aunt Julia said. I saw her exchange glances with my aunt and uncle and realized that they'd already talked the matter over. "Don't look at me that way, it's not a plot against you, it's not forever. Just till your father gets over his tantrum. To avoid more scandal."

They had discussed the situation and among the three of them they'd come up with a plan. They'd decided that Bolivia was out of the question and that Aunt Julia ought to go to Chile, to Valparaíso, where her grandmother lived. She would stay there just long enough for people's tempers to calm down, and would come back the moment I gave her the word. I objected furiously; Aunt Julia was my wife, I'd gotten married so that we could be together, the two of us would leave the country together. They reminded me that I was a minor: I couldn't apply for a passport or leave Peru without my parents' permission. I said I'd sneak over the border illegally. They asked me how much money I had to go abroad to live. (I was hard put even to buy cigarettes on some days: after paying the wedding expenses and the rent on the little apartment, there wasn't a *sol* left of the advance from Radio Panamericana or of the money I'd gotten from selling my clothes and putting my things in hock.)

"We're married now and they can't take that away from us," Aunt Julia said, running her fingers through my hair and kissing me as tears welled in her eyes. "It's only for a few weeks, a few months at most. I don't want you to get a bullet through you on account of me."

During supper, Aunt Olga and Uncle Lucho presented their

arguments to try to persuade me. I had to be reasonable, I'd done as I pleased and gotten married, and now I had to make a temporary concession to keep something irreparable from happening. I had to understand their position; as Aunt Julia's sister and brother-in-law, they were in a very delicate situation vis-à-vis my father and the rest of the family: they couldn't be either for or against her. They would help us, they were doing so at that very moment, and I had to do my part, too. While Aunt Julia was in Valparaíso, I would have to look for more work, because if not, how the devil were we going to live, who was going to support us? My father would eventually calm down and accept the facts.

Around midnight—my aunt and uncle had gone discreetly off to bed and Aunt Julia and I were making love in the worst possible circumstances, half dressed, filled with anxiety, our ears alert for the least little sound—I finally gave in. There was no other way out. The following morning we would try to exchange her plane ticket to La Paz for one to Chile. Half an hour later, as I was walking down the streets of Miraflores, heading for my little bachelor's room at my grandparents', I felt bitter and powerless, and I cursed myself for not having even enough money to buy myself a revolver, too.

Aunt Julia went to Chile two days later, on a plane that left at dawn. The airline had had no objection to exchanging the ticket, but there was a difference in price, which we were able to meet thanks to a loan of fifteen hundred *soles* made us by none other than Pascual. (He left me openmouthed with amazement when he told me that he had five thousand *soles* in a savings account, a sum that, considering the salary he earned, was a really heroic feat.) So as to be able to give Aunt Julia some money to take with her, I went to the bookseller on the Calle La Paz and sold all the books I still had left, including my copies of the Civil Codes and my law textbooks, and then bought fifty U.S. dollars for her.

Aunt Olga and Uncle Lucho went to the airport with us. I had stayed over at their house the night before. Aunt Julia and I didn't sleep, and we didn't make love. After supper my aunt and uncle went off to their bedroom and I sat on the end of Aunt Julia's bed, watching her carefully pack her suitcase. Then we went and sat in the living room in the dark. We stayed there for three or four hours, holding hands, cuddled up in the armchair together, talking in low voices so as not to wake up the relatives. We embraced every so often, turning our faces toward each other and kissing, but we spent most of the time smoking and talking. We talked about what we'd do once we were back together again, how she'd help me with my work, and how, in one way or another, sooner or later, we'd go to Paris to live in that garret where I would become a writer at last. I told her the story of her compatriot Pedro Camacho, who was now in a private mental hospital, surrounded by madmen and in all likelihood going mad himself, and we made plans to write each other every day, long letters in which we'd tell each other absolutely everything we did, thought, and felt. I promised her that by the time she came back I'd have everything all arranged and would be earning enough money to make ends meet. When the alarm clock went off at five, it was still pitch-dark outside, and when we arrived at Limatambo airport an hour later, it was just barely beginning to get light. Aunt Julia was wearing the blue tailored suit that I liked so much and that looked so pretty on her. She seemed very calm when we said goodbye, but I could feel her trembling in my arms; I, on the other hand, seeing her enter the plane as I watched from the visitors' terrace, felt a lump in my throat and tears in my eyes.

Her Chilean exile lasted one month and fourteen days. For me, these were six decisive weeks, during which (thanks to my importuning of friends, acquaintances, fellow students, professors, whom I sought out, earnestly beseeched, pestered, drove mad with my pleas to lend me a helping hand) I managed to land myself seven jobs, including, naturally, the one I was already holding down at Panamericana. The first one I nailed down was at the library of the Club Nacional, next door to the radio station; it consisted of spending two hours a day there, between morning news bulletins at the station, making a list of the new books and magazines that arrived and cataloguing everything already in the library. A history professor at San Marcos, in whose course I had had outstanding grades, took me on as an assistant; every day from three to five I went to his home in Miraflores, where I noted down on filing cards various subjects that had been dealt with by chroniclers, for a projected History of Peru for which he would be writing the volumes on the Conquest and Emancipation. The most picturesque of these new jobs was a contract from the Lima Bureau of Public

Welfare. In the Presbítero Maestro Cemetery were a series of grave plots, dating from the colonial era, for which all records had been lost. My task was to decipher the inscriptions on the gravestones and compile lists of all the names and dates. It was a job I could do whenever I found the time, and I was paid at piecework rates for it: one *sol* per dead person. I worked at this in the late afternoons and early evenings, between the 6 p.m. news bulletin and the Panamericana newscast, and Javier, who was free at those hours, would go with me. As it was winter and it got dark early, the director of the cemetery, a fat man who claimed that he had witnessed in person the inauguration of eight presidents of Peru before Congress, lent us flashlights and a little ladder so that we could read the inscriptions way up high in the tombs. At times, pretending to each other that we heard voices, moans, chains clanking and spied ghostly silhouettes flitting about amid the tombs, we ended up giving ourselves a real scare. Besides going to the cemetery two or three times during the week, I devoted every Sunday morning to this task. The remaining jobs were more or less (rather less than more) of a literary nature. In a column entitled "The Man and His Work," I interviewed a poet, novelist, or essayist each week for the Sunday supplement of *El Comercio*; I wrote a monthly article in the magazine *Cultura Peruana* for a section that I had invented, called "Men, Books, and Ideas": and, finally, another professor who was a friend of mine entrusted me with the job of writing a text on Civic Education for candidates for enrollment at the Universidad Católica (despite the fact that I was a student at the rival university, San Marcos); every Monday I had to come up with an essay for him on one or another of the many subjects dealt with in this pre-enrollment course, ranging from symbols of the Motherland to the polemics between the Indigenists and the Hispanicists, and passing by way of native flora and fauna.

Thanks to all these jobs (which made me feel something like a rival of Pedro Camacho's), I contrived to triple my income and earn enough with the seven of them for two people to live on. I asked for advances on each job and was able to redeem my typewriter, indispensable for the newspaper and magazine assignments (although I wrote many of the articles at Panamericana), and also give Nancy money to buy things to furnish and decorate the rented apartment, which the owner had ready for occupancy within the two weeks promised. The morning she turned this little studio apartment and the minuscule bathroom over to me was one of great joy. I continued to sleep at my grandparents', however, because I decided I'd celebrate definitely moving into the apartment on the day that Aunt Julia arrived, but I went there almost every night to write articles and draw up my lists of the dead. Even though all my time was taken up at one or another of my jobs all day long, and continually running back and forth between them, I didn't feel tired or depressed; on the contrary, I was full of energy and, as I remember, I even read as much as I always had (though I did so only in the innumerable buses and jitneys I had to take every day).

Faithful to the promise we'd made each other, Aunt Julia wrote me every day, and my granny would hand me the letters with a mischievous twinkle in her eye, murmuring: "Well now, I wonder who this little letter could be from, do you have any idea?" I, too, wrote regularly (it was the last thing I did every night, so sleepy at times that I felt tipsy), telling her all the many things I'd done that day. In the days following her departure I kept running into my countless relatives, at my grandparents', at Uncle Lucho's and Aunt Olga's, in the street, and discovering the reactions of each. They varied a good deal and some of them were quite unexpected. Uncle Pedro's was the most severe: he left me standing there with my outstretched hand and turned his back after giving me an icy look. Aunt Jesús shed great floods of tears and embraced me, whispering dramatically: "You poor child!" Other aunts and uncles chose to act as though nothing had happened; they were affectionate with me, but didn't mention Aunt Julia and pretended not to know we'd been married.

I hadn't seen my father, but I knew that once his demand that Aunt Julia leave the country had been met, he'd cooled off a bit. My parents were staying with paternal aunts and uncles, whom I never visited, but my mother came to my grandparents' house every day and we saw each other there. She adopted an ambivalent, affectionate, maternal attitude toward me, but every time the taboo subject came up, directly or indirectly, she turned pale, tears came to her eyes, and she assured me: "I'll never accept it." When I suggested she come see the little apartment, she was as offended as though I'd insulted her, and she always spoke of my having sold my books and my clothes as though it were a Greek tragedy. I cut her short by saying: "Mama dearest, don't begin another of your radio serials." She never spoke of my father either, and I didn't ask about him, but I learned through other relatives who saw him that his wrath had given way to despair as to the future that awaited me, and that he was in the habit of saying: "He'll have to obey me till he's twenty-one; after that, he can ruin his life if he wants to."

Despite my multiple jobs, I wrote another story during these weeks. It was called "The Blessed One and Father Nicolás." It took place in Grocio Prado, of course, and was anticlerical: the story of a sly little priest who, noting the fervent devotion of the people to Melchorita, decided to industrialize it for her benefit, and with the cold ambition of a good businessman set up a multiple operation: manufacturing and selling pious images, scapulars, good-luck charms, and all sorts of relics of the Blessed One, charging admission to the places where she had lived, taking up collections and organizing raffles to build her a chapel and pay the expenses of delegations sent off to Rome to hurry her canonization along. I wrote two different epilogues, in the form of newspaper items: in one of them, the inhabitants of Grocio Prado discovered all the business dealings that Father Nicolás was involved in and lynched him, and in the other the little priest eventually became the archbishop of Lima. (I decided I would wait until I read the story to Aunt Julia to choose which of the two endings I would use.) I wrote it in the library of the Club Nacional, where my job as cataloguer of acquisitions was more or less symbolic.

The soap operas I rescued from the storeroom of Radio Central (a task that brought me two hundred *soles* extra salary) were condensed to make a month's worth of broadcasts—the time it would take for the scripts from CMQ to arrive. But neither the old serials nor the new ones, as the dynamic impresario had correctly predicted, were able to keep the gigantic audience that Pedro Camacho had won for the station. The surveys showed that the number of listeners had fallen off, and the ad rates had to be lowered so as not to lose sponsors. But this was not a terrible disaster for the Genaros; as inventive and go-getting as ever, they soon found a new gold mine in the form of a program called "The

Sixty-Four-Thousand *Soles* Question." It was broadcast from Le Paris, a movie theater, and on it contestants who were experts on various subjects (cars, Sophocles, soccer, the Incas) answered questions for sums that could reach that figure. Through Genaro Jr., with whom I sometimes had coffee at the Bransa on La Colmena (though only on rare occasions now), I kept track of Pedro Camacho's whereabouts. He'd spent almost a month in Dr. Delgado's private clinic, but as it was very expensive, the Genaros managed to have him transferred to Larco Herrera, the public asylum, where, apparently, he was being treated with kindness and respect. One Sunday, after cataloguing tombs in the Presbítero Maestro Cemetery, I took a bus to the entrance of Larco Herrera, intending to pay him a visit. I was bringing him as a present some little bags of verbena and mint so he could have his herb tea. But just as I was about to pass through the main gate of that prisonlike place, along with other visitors, I changed my mind. The idea of seeing the scriptwriter shut up inside that crowded institution—during my first-year psychology class at the university, we'd been sent to work on the wards as student assistants—just one more madman among hordes of other madmen, was so distressing I couldn't make myself go inside. I turned around and went back to Miraflores.

That Monday I told my mama that I wanted to have a talk with my father. She counseled me to be careful, not to say anything that might make him angry, not to get myself into a situation where he might do me harm, and gave me the phone number of the house where he was staying. My father informed me that he would receive me the following morning, at eleven, in what had been his office before he left for the United States. It was on the Jirón Carabaya, at the end of a tiled corridor on both sides of which there were apartments and offices. At the Import/Export Company —I recognized several employees I'd met before when he was working there—I was shown into the managing director's office. My father was alone, sitting at his former desk. He was wearing a cream-colored suit and a green tie with white polka dots; he looked to me as though he'd lost weight since the year before and seemed a bit pale.

"Hello, Papa," I said as I stood in the doorway, trying my best to speak in a firm voice.

"Tell me what it is you've come to tell me," he said, in a tone of voice more neutral than wrathful, pointing to a chair.

I sat down on the edge of it and took a deep breath, like an athlete about to perform. "I've come to tell you what I'm doing, what I'm going to do," I stammered.

He sat there without saying a word, waiting for me to go on. Then, speaking very slowly so as to appear calm and collected, and carefully watching his every reaction, I gave him a detailed account of all the jobs I'd found, how much I earned from each, how I had divided my time so as to fit them all in and do my homework and prepare for my exams at the university besides. I didn't tell any lies, but I presented everything in the most favorable light possible: I'd organized my life in an intelligent, responsible way and was anxious to get my degree. After I finished, my father remained silent, waiting for me to sum up what I'd had to say.

Swallowing hard, I did so. "So you see that I can earn my living, support myself, and go on with my studies." And then, hearing my voice trailing off till it was barely audible: "I've come to ask your permission to send for Julia. We're married and she can't go on living by herself."

He blinked, turned paler still, and for a moment I thought he was going to have one of those fits of rage that had been the nightmare of my childhood. But all he said to me, curtly and coldly, was: "As you know, this marriage isn't legal. Being a minor, you can't get married without your parents' permission. So if you've married, you've been able to do so only by presenting a fake document authorizing you to do so or by tampering with your birth certificate. In either case, the marriage can easily be annulled."

He explained that the falsification of a legal document was a serious offense, punishable by law. If anyone had to pay the penalty for the mischief done, it wouldn't be me, a minor, for the judges would presume me to be the innocent accomplice, but the person who was of legal age, who would logically be considered the real perpetrator. After this legal explanation, proffered in an icy tone of voice, he went on talking for a long time, little by little allowing his emotion to show through. I thought that he hated me, when the truth was that he had always acted only for my own good; if he had sometimes been severe with me, his one aim had been to correct my faults and prepare me for the future. My rebellion and my defiance would be the ruin of me. By getting married, I had put the noose around my own neck. He had been opposed to it because he was thinking of my own good and not, as I believed, because he wished to do me harm, for what sort of a father was it who didn't love his son? Furthermore, he realized that I'd fallen in love, there was nothing wrong with that; after all, it proved I was a man. It would have been far worse, for example, if I'd turned out to be a fairy. But getting married at the age of eighteen, when I was still a kid, a student, to a mature woman and a divorcée to boot, was utter madness, the real consequences of which I would realize only later on in my life, when, because of this marriage, I'd become a wretched, embittered man who'd gotten nowhere in life. That wasn't what he wanted for me at all, his one wish for me was the best and most illustrious life possible. In a word, I should try at the very least not to give up my studies, because I'd always regret it. He stood up and I too rose to my feet. An uncomfortable silence ensued, punctuated by the clattering of the typewriters in the other room. Stammering, I promised to get my university degree, and he nodded approvingly. As we said goodbye, after a second's hesitation we put our arms around each other.

I went from his office to the central post office and sent a telegram: "Amnesty granted you by Papa. Will send return ticket soonest. Love." I spent that afternoon at the historian's, at the rooftop shack at Panamericana, at the cemetery, racking my brains as to how I could rake up enough money for the ticket. That night I made a list of people I could ask for a loan, and how much I could ask each of them for. But the next day a telegraphed reply was delivered to me at my grandparents': "Arriving tomorrow LAN flight. Love." I learned later that Aunt Julia had gotten the money to pay for her ticket by selling her rings, her brooches, her bracelets, her earrings, and nearly all of her clothes. So when I went to meet her at Limatambo airport on Thursday night, she was a woman without a cent to her name.

I took her directly to the little apartment, which had been personally waxed and polished by Cousin Nancy, who had also decorated it with a red rose, accompanied by a note that said "Welcome." Aunt Julia looked the entire apartment over as though it were a new toy. She was amused to see the index cards for the cemetery all neatly filed, my notes for the *Cultura Peruana* article, the list of writers to be interviewed for *El Comercio*, and the work schedule and the budget I'd drawn up, theoretically proving that we would have enough money to live on. I told her that after making love to her I'd read her a story entitled "The Blessed One and Father Nicolás" so she could help me decide on the right ending.

"Well, Varguitas," she said, laughing, as she hastily undressed. "You're growing up. And now, so that everything will be perfect and you'll get rid of that baby face of yours, promise me you'll let your mustache grow."

Twenty.

The marriage to Aunt Julia

was really a success and it lasted a good bit longer than all the parents and even she herself had feared, wished, or predicted: eight years. In that time, thanks to my persistence and her help and enthusiasm, plus a fair amount of good luck, other predictions (dreams, desires) had come true. We had managed to go to Paris and live in the famous garret, and for better or for worse I had become a writer and published several books. I never completed my law studies, but in order to make it up to my family in some way and earn a living more easily, I got myself a university degree, in an academic perversion as boring as law: Romance philology.

When Aunt Julia and I were divorced, copious tears were shed in my vast family, because everyone (beginning, naturally, with my mother and father) adored her. And when, a year later, I married again, a cousin of mine this time (the daughter of Aunt Olga and Uncle Lucho, by some odd coincidence), it created less of an uproar within the family than the first time (it consisted for the most part of a great flurry of gossip), This time, however, there was a perfectly planned conspiracy to force me to marry in the Church, in which even the archbishop of Lima was involved (he was, it goes without saying, a relative of ours), who hastened to sign the dispensations authorizing the union. But by that time the family was already panic-proof and could predict (which is tantamount to saying forgave beforehand) my blackest misdeeds.

I had lived with Aunt Julia in Spain for a year and in France for five, and later I went on living with my cousin Patricia in Europe, in London first and then in Barcelona. In those days I had an arrangement with a magazine in Lima: I sent it articles and in return received a plane ticket that allowed me to come back to Peru every year for a few weeks. These trips, thanks to which I saw my family and friends, were very important to me. I was planning to go on living in Europe indefinitely, for a great many reasons, but above all because I had always been able to find work there—as a journalist, translator, lecturer, or professor—that left me free time. When we arrived in Madrid the first time, I'd said to Aunt Julia: "I'm going to try to be a writer; I'm not going to accept anything but jobs that won't take me too far afield from literature." "Shall I cut a slit in my skirt, put on a turban, and go hustle clients on the Gran Vía starting today?" she said. But I was really very lucky. Teaching Spanish at the Berlitz School in Paris, writing news bulletins at France-Presse, translating for UNESCO, dubbing films in the studios at Gennevilliers, or preparing programs for the French national radio-television network, I had always found jobs that brought in enough to live on yet allowed me to devote at least half of each day exclusively to my writing. The problem was that everything I wrote had to do with life in Peru. As time and distance began to blur my perspective, I felt more and more insecure about my writing (at the time I was obsessed with the idea that fiction should be "realistic"). But I found the very thought of living in Lima inconceivable. When I remembered the seven simultaneous jobs I'd held there, which together had earned me barely enough to feed us, left me scarcely any time to read, and given me no opportunity to write except on the sly in the few slack moments during my work day or at night when I was already dead tired, my hair stood on end and I vowed to myself I'd never live that way again, even if it meant dying of starvation. Moreover, Peru had always seemed to me a country of sad people.

Hence the agreement I had, first with the daily *Expreso* and then with the magazine *Caretas*, to write articles in exchange for two plane tickets a year, was a real stroke of luck. That month that Patricia and I spent in Peru each year, usually in winter (July or August), enabled me to steep myself in the atmosphere, the landscapes, the lives of the people that I had been trying to write about in the previous eleven months. It was tremendously useful to me (I don't know if this was true in purely material terms, but certainly it was true psychologically), a kind of "energy injection," to hear Peruvian spoken again, to hear all round me those turns of phrase, expressions, intonations that put me back in the midst of a milieu I felt viscerally close to but had nonetheless moved far away from, thus missing out each year on the innovations, losing overtones, resonances, keys.

My visits to Lima were, thus, vacations during which I literally didn't rest for a second and from which I returned to Europe exhausted. Just between the countless relatives of my vast forest of a family and my numerous friends, we had invitations to lunch and dinner every single day, and the remainder of my time was occupied doing background research for my writing. One year, for instance, I'd taken a trip to the Alto Marañón area to see, hear, and smell from close up a world that was the scene of the novel I was writing, and another year, accompanied by diligent friends, I had systematically explored the nocturnal haunts—cabarets, bars, brothels—that were the locales of the dissipated life led by the protagonist of another story. Mixing work and pleasure—since I never considered this "research" a duty but, rather, a task that always enriched my life and was a most enjoyable diversion in itself, above and beyond the literary benefits that I might gain from it—I did things on these trips that in earlier days, when I lived in Lima, I had never done, and that now that I've returned to Peru to live I never do either: going to little popular clubs and to theaters to see indigenous folk dances, wandering about the tenements of slum districts, strolling through sections of town that I was not very familiar with or didn't know at all, such as El Callao, Bajo el Puente, and Los Barrios Altos, betting at the racetrack, nosing about in the catacombs of colonial churches and the (supposed) house of La Perricholi.

That year, however, I devoted my time to more bookish research. I was writing a novel that took place in the era of General Manuel Apolinario Odría (1948–56), and during my month's vacation in Lima I went to the periodicals section of the Biblioteca Nacional a couple of mornings each week, to leaf through newspapers and magazines from those years and even read, somewhat masochistically, some of the speeches the dictator's advisors (all lawyers, to judge from the forensic rhetoric) wrote for him. On leaving the Biblioteca Nacional around noon I would walk down the Avenida Abancay, which was beginning to turn into an enormous market of itinerant peddlers. On the sidewalks a dense crowd of men and women, many of them dressed in ponchos and peasant skirts, sold the most heterogeneous collection of wares imaginable, everything from needles and hairpins to dresses and suits, laid out on blankets or newspapers spread out on the ground or at stands knocked together out of wooden crates, oil drums, and canvas awnings, plus all sorts of things to eat, of course, prepared right there on the spot in little braziers. This Avenida Abancay was one of the thoroughfares in Lima that had changed the most. Jam-packed now and possessed of a distinct Andean flavor, a street on which it was not rare to hear Quechua spoken amid the strong odor of fried food and pungent seasonings, it in no way resembled the broad, austere avenue frequented by white-collar workers and an occasional beggar down which, ten years before, when I was a first-year student at the university, I used to walk on my way to that same Biblioteca Nacional. There in those blocks, one could see, and touch, in a nutshell, the problem of the migration from the countryside to the capital, which in that decade had doubled the population of Lima and caused to spring up like mushrooms, on the hillsides, the dunes, the garbage dumps, that ring of slums where thousands and thousands of people ended up, rural folk who had left the provinces because of the drought, the back-breaking working conditions, the lack of prospects for a better future, hunger.

Getting to know this new face of the city, I walked down the Avenida Abancay toward the Parque Universitario and what had previously been San Marcos (the various faculties had been moved to the outskirts of Lima and the building where I had studied humanities and law was now occupied by a museum and offices). I was visiting the place not just out of curiosity and a certain nostalgia but also for literary reasons, since, in the novel I was working on, a number of episodes took place in the Parque Universitario, in the main classroom building of San Marcos, and in the secondhand bookstores, the billiard parlors, and the filthy café-bars of the neighboring streets. As a matter of fact, I was standing in front of the pretty Chapel of Illustrious National Heroes that morning, gawking like a tourist at the peddlers in the vicinity

—bootblacks, vendors hawking pastries, ice cream, sandwiches—when I felt a hand on my shoulder. It was—twelve years older, but the same as ever—Big Pablito.

We gave each other a big bear hug. He really hadn't changed at all: he was the same sturdily built, smiling mestizo with the asthmatic wheeze, who barely lifted his feet off the ground as he walked and thus seemed to skate through life. He didn't have a single gray hair, despite the fact that he must have been close to sixty by then, and his straight hair was carefully slicked down with quantities of brilliantine, like an Argentine of the 1940's. But he was much better dressed than when he was (theoretically) a newsman at Radio Panamericana: a green plaid suit, a loud tie (it was the first time I'd ever seen him wearing one), and brightly polished shoes. And on his index finger was a gold ring with an Inca design. I was so pleased to see him that I suggested we go have a cup of coffee together. He agreed and we ended up at a table in the Palermo, a little combination bar-and-grill also linked in my memory to my years at the university. I told him I wouldn't ask him how life had treated him since one look at him sufficed to show that it had treated him very well.

Glancing down at the gold ring on his finger, he smiled complacently. "I can't complain," he admitted. "After all the hard times I went through, my luck changed in my old age. But first, let me buy you a glass of beer, just because I'm so glad to see you." He called the waiter over, ordered us Pilseners, good and cold, and gave a hearty laugh, which brought on one of his traditional fits of asthmatic wheezing and gasping. "They say that once a man gets married he's a goner. Well, it was exactly the opposite with me."

As we drank our beer, Big Pablito, with pauses forced on him by his bronchia, told me that when television arrived in Peru, the Genaros had made him a doorman, with a maroon uniform and a kepi, at the studios they had built on the Avenida Arequipa for Channel 5.

"From a newsman to a doorman—it sounds like I was demoted," he said with a shrug. "And I'll admit it was a demotion, as far as titles are concerned. But I ask you, can you eat a title? They raised my salary—that's what really counts."

Being a doorman wasn't killing work: announcing visitors, tell ing them where the various departments were located, making the spectators waiting to attend broadcasts form orderly lines. The rest of his time he spent discussing soccer with the policeman stationed on the corner. But then, in addition—and he clacked his tongue, savoring a pleasant memory—after a few months, one of his duties was to go every noon to buy those pasties filled with meat and cheese that they make at the Berisso, a place on Arenales, a block away from Channel 5. The Genaros were crazy about them, and so were the office clerks, the actors, the announcers, the producers, to whom Big Pablito also brought back *empanadas*, and earned good tips for doing so. It was on these trips back and forth between the television station and the Berisso (his uniform had earned him the nickname of the Fireman among the kids of the neighborhood) that Big Pablito had struck up an acquaintance with his future wife. She was the woman who made these delicious, crusty delicacies: the cook at the Berisso.

"She was impressed by my uniform and my general's kepi. She took one look at me and fell at my feet." Big Pablito laughed, choked, drank a sip of his beer, choked and wheezed some more, and went on. "A gorgeous brunette. Twenty years younger than yours truly. A pair of tits so firm a bullet wouldn't pierce them. Like I'm telling you, Don Mario, a real eyeful."

He'd begun by striking up a conversation with her and dishing out compliments, she'd laughed, and they'd started going out together, just like that. They'd fallen in love and had a romance straight out of a movie. The brunette had energy to spare, was filled with ambition, and had her head chockful of plans. She was the one who'd decided they should open a restaurant. And when Big Pablito asked "What'll we use for money?" she had said: what they'd both have coming when they left their jobs. And though it seemed utter madness to him to trade certainty for uncertainty, she'd had her way. The severance pay the two of them received was enough to buy a tiny little place on the Jirón Paruro, and they had had to ask everybody they knew to lend them money to buy tables and kitchen equipment, and Big Pablito himself had painted the walls and the name of the place over the door: The Royal Peacock. The first year they'd barely made enough to live on and had worked like slaves. They'd get up at the crack of dawn to go to La Parada, the wholesale market, to buy the best ingredients and pay the lowest prices, and they did everything themselves: she cooked and he waited on table and acted as cashier, and the two of them swept and cleaned up. They slept on mattresses they laid out each night between the tables after they closed up. But from the second year on, they drew more and more customers. So many that they'd had to take on a boy to help in the kitchen and another to wait on table, and after a while they were even obliged to turn clients away because there was no more room. And then the brunette had had the idea of renting the place next door, which was three times as big. They'd done so and hadn't regretted it. They'd even put tables on the second floor now, and had a little place of their own to live in across the street from The Royal Peacock. Seeing as how they got along so well together, they got married.

I congratulated him, and asked him if he'd learned to cook.

"I've got an idea," Big Pablito suddenly said. "Let's go hunt up Pascual and we'll have lunch at the restaurant. I'd like the two of you to be my guests, Don Mario."

I accepted, because I've never discovered how to refuse invitations, and also because I was curious to see Pascual. Big Pablito had told me he was now the editor of a weekly scandal sheet, that he too had come up in the world. They saw each other regularly—Pascual was a steady customer at The Royal Peacock.

The office of the weekly *Extra* was a fair distance away, on a street off the Avenida Arica, in Breña. We took a bus there that didn't exist in my day. We had to wander around the neighborhood for some time, because Big Pablito didn't remember the exact address. We finally found it, in a narrow little alleyway behind the Cine Fantasía. From the outside it was evident that *Extra* hadn't exactly struck it rich: a sign bearing the name of the weekly was hanging precariously from one nail between two garage doors.

Once inside, one could see that the two garages had been converted into one office by simply making an opening in the wall between them, without even squaring it up or roughing off the edges, as though the mason had abandoned the job before he was half done. The opening was partitioned off by a cardboard screen, scribbled all over, as in the toilets of public buildings, with dirty words and obscene drawings. On the walls of the garage we'd first come into, amid damp spots and dirt stains, were photos, posters, and front pages of *Extra*: one recognized certain well-known faces of soccer players and singers, and those, apparently, of criminals and victims. Each front page was full of screaming headlines, and I managed to make out phrases such as "Kills Mother So As To Marry Daughter," and "Police Raid Masked Ball: All Men!" This garage appeared to be used as the copy room, the darkroom, and the "morgue" of the weekly. The place was so cluttered that it was hard to thread our way through it: little tables with typewriters, on which two guys were hurriedly typing, piles of unsold returned copies of the paper that a kid was doing up into bundles and tying up with string; in one corner was an open standing wardrobe full of negatives, photos, plates; and behind a table, one of whose legs had been replaced by three bricks, a girl in a red sweater was noting down moneys received in an account book. The things and the people in the place seemed to be in sad straits. Nobody stopped us or questioned us or answered us when we said hello.

On the other side of the screen, in front of walls also covered with sensational front pages, there were three desks, each with a little square of cardboard on which the function of its occupant was written, by hand, in ink: editor-in-chief, chief copy editor, managing editor. When they saw us enter the room, two persons bending over, looking at galleys, raised their heads. The one standing was Pascual.

He gave each of us a friendly hug. Unlike Big Pablito, he'd changed quite a lot: he'd gotten fat and had a paunch and a double chin, and somehow there was a look about him that made him seem almost an old man. He'd grown himself a very odd, almost Hitlerian mustache, which was turning gray. He greeted me with what were clearly signs of great affection, and when he smiled, I saw that he had lost some of his teeth. He then introduced me to his colleague, a swarthy, dark-haired man in a mustard-colored shirt, who remained sitting at his desk.

"The editor of *Extra*," Pascual said. "Dr. Rebagliati."

"I almost put my foot in my mouth," I told Pascual as I shook hands with Dr. Rebagliati. "Big Pablito told me that you were the editor."

"We've gone downhill, but not that far," Dr. Rebagliati said. "Have a seat, have a seat."

"I'm chief copy editor," Pascual explained to me. "This is my desk."

Big Pablito told him we'd come to take him off to The Royal Peacock to celebrate the good old days at Panamericana. Pascual was all for it, but he hoped we wouldn't mind, we'd have to wait for him a few minutes, he had to take the galleys there on his desk round to the printer's on the corner, it was urgent because they were just putting the edition to bed. He went off and left me sitting face to face with Dr. Rebagliati. When the latter learned that I lived in Europe, he devoured me with questions. Was it true that Frenchwomen were pushovers, as he'd always heard? Were they as expert and as shameless in bed as they were reputed to be? Was it true that females in every country had their very own special tricks? He'd personally heard, for instance, extremely interesting things (Big Pablito's eyes rolled in delectation as he listened to him) from people who'd traveled a lot. Was it true that Italian women were crazy about sucking cock? That Parisian women weren't ever satisfied unless one bombarded them from behind? That Scandinavian women made out with their own fathers? I answered Dr. Rebagliati's verborrhea as best I could as he contaminated the atmosphere of the little room with his lustful, seminal intensity, and regretted more and more having allowed myself to be trapped into accepting an invitation to this repast that would no doubt end up at some ungodly hour. Amazed and all worked up by the editor's sociologico-erotic revelations, Big Pablito laughed and laughed. When Dr. Rebagliati's curiosity eventually wore me out, I asked if I could use his phone.

A sarcastic look came over his face. "It's been cut off for a week now, because we haven't been able to pay the bill," he said with brutal frankness. "Because, as you can very well see, this rag is going under and all of us imbeciles who work here are going under with it."

And he immediately went on to tell me, with masochistic pleasure, that *Extra* had been born in the Odría era, under very favorable auspices: the regime placed ads in it and slipped it money under the table to attack certain individuals and defend others.

Moreover, it was one of the few publications that were allowed to appear, and it had sold like hotcakes. But once Odría had been ousted, cutthroat competitors had appeared on the scene and *Extra* had gone broke. And it was at that point that he had taken it over, when it was already on its last legs. And he had gotten it back on its feet, by changing its policy, by turning it into a scandal sheet. Everything had gone smoothly for a while, despite the debts hanging round its neck like a millstone. But in the last year, with the price of paper going up and up, the mounting expenses at the printer's, the campaign waged against it by its enemies, and the loss of advertising revenue, things had gone sour. Moreover, they had lost several court suits brought by riffraff accusing them of libel. And now the panic-stricken owners had offered all the stock to the editors so that the creditors wouldn't get everything when the rag went into bankruptcy. Which was about to happen any day now, since in the last few weeks the situation had become tragic: there was no money for the payroll, employees were making off with typewriters, selling the desks, stealing everything that was of any value, getting what they could before everything caved in.

"It won't last another month, my friend," he repeated, snorting with a sort of pleased disgust. "We're already corpses—can't you smell the rot?"

I was about to tell him that indeed I could, when the conversation was interrupted by a skeletonlike little figure, so thin that he entered the room through the narrow opening without any need to push the screen aside. He had a rather ridiculous German-style haircut and was dressed like a tramp, in worn blue overalls and an old patched shirt under a grayish sweater that was much too tight for him. The most unusual thing about his attire was his footgear: faded red tennis shoes, so old that one of them had a length of string tied around the end of it as though the sole were loose or about to fall off. The minute he laid eyes on him, Dr. Rebagliati began to read him the riot act.

"If you think you can go on making a fool of me, you're wrong," he said, approaching him with such a threatening air that the skeleton gave a little leap backward. "Weren't you to bring the stuff on the arrival of the Monster of Ayacucho last night?"

"I brought it, sir. I was here with all the pertinent details half an hour after the patrolmen brought the decedent into the Prefecture," the little man declaimed.

I was so dumfounded that I must have looked as though I were in a daze. The perfect diction, the warm timbre of the voice, the words "pertinent" and "decedent" could only have come from him. But how, with that physique and getup, could this scarecrow that Dr. Rebagliati was eating alive possibly be the Bolivian scriptwriter?

"Don't lie; have the courage at least to own up to your faults. You didn't bring the material and Gumball couldn't finish his article and the facts are going to be all wrong. And I don't like articles with factual errors, because that's bad journalism!"

"I brought it, sir," Pedro Camacho answered, in a terrified but polite tone of voice. "I found the office here closed. It was eleven-fifteen on the dot. I asked a passerby the exact time, sir. And then, because I knew how important this material was, I went to Gumball's house. And I waited for him out on the sidewalk till two in the morning, but he didn't come back home to sleep. It isn't my fault, sir. The patrolmen who were bringing the Monster in got caught in a rock slide that blocked the highway and didn't arrive till eleven instead of nine. Don't accuse me of dereliction of duty. For me, *Extra* comes first, even before my health, sir."

Little by little, not without an effort, I related, I compared what I remembered of Pedro Camacho with what was before me. The bulging eyes were the same, though they had lost their fanaticism, their obsessive gleam. The light in them now was dim, opaque, fleeting, panicked. And his facial expressions and gestures, his manner of gesticulating as he spoke, that unnatural movement of his arm and hand that made him look like a circus barker, were the same as before, as was his incomparable, measured voice, as spellbinding as ever.

"What happens is that you're too tightfisted ever to take a bus or a jitney, you always arrive everywhere too late, that's the pure and simple truth of the matter," Dr. Rebagliati fumed hysterically. "Don't be so stingy, damn it, spend the four pennies it costs to take a bus and get where you're supposed to be on time!"

But the differences were greater than the resemblances. The principal change in his appearance was due to the haircut. Having the locks that had come down to his shoulders shorn and what was left cropped so close to his skull that his head appeared to be shaved had made his face look more angular, smaller; it had lost character and authority. Moreover, he was a very great deal thinner; he looked like a fakir, a specter almost. But what really kept me from recognizing him at first was his attire. I had never seen him dressed in anything but black, the funereal, shiny suit and the little bow tie that were inseparable from his person. Now, with this pair of stevedore's overalls, this much-mended shirt, these tennis shoes with string tied round them, he looked like a caricature of the caricature he had been twelve years before.

"I assure you that things don't turn out the way you think, sir," he said, standing his ground. "I've demonstrated to you that I arrive at any assigned destination faster on foot than in those pestilential public vehicles. It's not out of niggardliness that I walk places, but in order to fulfill my duties more diligently. And frequently, sir, I run."

In this respect, too, he was the same as before: his total lack of a sense of humor. He spoke without the slightest spark of wit, or even of emotion, in an automatic, depersonalized way, though the things he was saying would have been unthinkable coming from him in the old days.

"That's enough of your nonsense and your manias. I'm too old to bamboozle." Dr. Rebagliati turned to us, taking us as witnesses. "Have you ever heard anything so ridiculous? That a person can make the rounds of the commissariats of Lima faster on foot than by bus? And this gentleman wants me to swallow shit like that." He turned once again to the Bolivian scriptwriter, who hadn't taken his eyes off him or given the rest of us so much as a sidelong glance. "I don't have to remind you, because I imagine that you remember it every time you sit down with a plate of food in front of you, that we're doing you a big favor around here by giving you work when we're in such terrible straits that we have to let reporters go, not to mention messengers. You could at least be grateful and do your job properly."

At this point Pascual came back in, announcing from the screen: "Everything's all set, the edition's gone to press," and apologizing for having made us wait.

I walked over to Pedro Camacho as he was about to leave. "How are you, Pedro?" I said, holding out my hand. "Don't you remember me?"

He looked me up and down, squinting his eyes and bringing his face closer, looking surprised, as though this were the first time in his life that he'd ever seen me. Finally, he extended his hand, shook mine briefly and ceremoniously, made his characteristic bow, and said: "Pleased to meet you. My name is Pedro Camacho."

"But this can't be," I said, feeling quite distraught. "Have I gotten as old as all that?"

"Stop pretending you've had one of your attacks of amnesia," Pascual said, clapping him on the back so hard he staggered. "Don't you remember how you spent all your time cadging coffees at the Bransa off him, either?"

"No, it was verbena-and-mint tea," I joked, scrutinizing Pedro Camacho's face, at once politely attentive and indifferent, for some sign of recognition.

He nodded (I saw his nearly bare skull) and gave me a very brief, courteous smile that exposed his teeth to the air for a second or so. "Highly recommended for the stomach, an excellent digestive, and moreover it burns up fat," he said. And then rapidly, as though making a concession in order to be free of us: "Yes, it's possible, I don't deny the fact. We might indeed have met before." And he added: "It's been my pleasure."

Big Pablito had also walked over to him. He put an arm around his shoulder, in a paternal, mocking gesture. As he rocked him back and forth, half affectionately and half derisively, he turned to me and said: "The thing is, Pedrito doesn't want to remember when he was somebody, now that he's a fifth wheel around this place." Pascual laughed, Big Pablito laughed, I pretended to laugh, and even Pedro Camacho gave a little forced smile. "He even tries to make out that he doesn't remember either Pascual or me." He patted him on his nearly bare pate, as though he were a little dog. "We're going to have lunch together to celebrate those days when you were king. You're in luck, Pedrito, you'll have a good hot meal today. I want you to come along as my guest!"

"I'm most grateful, colleagues," he answered immediately, making his ritual bow. "But it's not possible for me to come with you. My wife is waiting for me. She'd worry if I didn't come home for lunch."

"She's got you tied to her apron strings, you're her slave, aren't you ashamed of yourself?" Big Pablito said, rocking him back and forth again.

"Have you gotten married?" I asked, dumfounded, unable to imagine Pedro Camacho with a home, a wife, children. "Well, congratulations, I always thought you were a confirmed bachelor."

"We've celebrated our silver wedding anniversary," he replied in his usual precise, aseptic tone of voice. "A wonderful wife, sir. Self-sacrificing and unbelievably good-hearted. We were separated, due to circumstances that life brings in its train, but when I needed help, she came back to lend me every possible aid. A wonderful wife, as I said. She's an artiste, a foreign artiste." I saw Big Pablito, Pascual, and Dr. Rebagliati exchange a mocking look, but Pedro Camacho appeared not to notice. After a pause, he went on: "Well, have a good time, colleagues, I shall be with you in thought."

"Watch out that you don't let me down again, because it'll be the last time," Dr. Rebagliati warned him, as the scriptwriter was disappearing behind the screen.

Pedro Camacho's footfalls had not yet died away—he must have been heading for the street door—when Pascual, Big Pablito, and Dr. Rebagliati burst into peals of laughter, winking at each other, exchanging sly looks, and pointing to the opening he had just left by.

"He's not as dumb as he pretends to be, he comes on as the devoted spouse to hide the fact that his wife makes him wear horns," Dr. Rebagliati crowed. "Every time he talks about his wife I feel a terrible urge to say to him: 'Stop using the word "artiste" for what in good Peruvian we call a cheap stripteaser.'"

"You can't imagine what a monster she is," Pascual said to me, with the look of a kid who's just seen a bogeyman. "An Argentine years past middle age, fat as a sow, with bleached hair and makeup an inch thick. She sings tangos half-naked, at the Mezzanine, that nightclub for penniless wretches on the skids."

"Shut your traps, don't be ungrateful, you've both screwed her," Dr. Rebagliati said. "And I have too, for that matter."

"Singer or not, she's a whore," Big Pablito exclaimed, his eyes blazing. "I know what I'm talking about. I went to see her at the Mezzanine and after the show she made a pass at me and offered to give me a blow job for twenty *libras*. I said no, old girl, you haven't got any teeth left and what I go for is nice little nips on the cock. So not even if you do it for free, not even if you pay me. Because I swear, Don Mario, she doesn't have a tooth in her head."

"They'd been married before," Pascual told me as he rolled down his shirtsleeves and put his suitcoat and tie back on. "In Bolivia, before Pedrito came to Lima. It seems she left him to go off whoring around somewhere back there. They got together again when he was put in the mental asylum. That's why he goes around saying that she's such a self-sacrificing woman. Because she went back to him when he was crazy."

"He's as grateful to her as a dog, because it's thanks to her that they have food on the table," Dr. Rebagliati corrected him. "You don't think they can live on what Camacho earns gathering information for us at police stations, do you? They eat on what she brings in from whoring around, otherwise he'd have gotten t.b. long ago."

"To tell the truth, Pedrito doesn't need much to eat on," Pascual said. And he explained. "They live in a back alley in Santo Cristo. He's really come down in the world, hasn't he? My colleague, Dr. Rebagliati here, doesn't believe me that he was somebody in the days when he wrote soap operas, when they mobbed him for autographs."

We left the room. In the garage next door the young girl working on the account books, the reporters, and the kid bundling up return copies had all gone home. They had turned out the light and the jumble of office furniture and the disorder now had a certain eerie air about it. As we went out into the street, Dr. Rebagliati closed the door and locked it. Walking abreast, the four of us headed toward the Avenida Arica in search of a taxi. To make conversation, I asked why Pedro Camacho was just a messenger and not a reporter.

"Because he doesn't know how to write," Dr. Rebagliati answered predictably. "He's pretentious, he uses words that nobody understands, the negation of journalism. That's why I keep him on to make the rounds of the police stations. I don't need him, but he entertains me, he's my buffoon, and what's more, he costs less than an office boy." He laughed obscenely and asked: "Well now, to put it bluntly, am I or am I not invited to that lunch of yours?"

"Of course you are, that goes without saying," Big Pablito answered. "You and Don Mario are the guests of honor."

"Pedro Camacho's a guy with all sorts of weird ideas," Pascual said, returning to the subject as we were heading for the Jirón Paruro in the taxi. "He refuses to take a bus, for instance. He goes everywhere on foot; he says it's quicker. The very thought of how far he walks every day makes me tired; just making the rounds of the police stations in the middle of town takes him a good many miles. You saw the state his shoes were in, didn't you?"

"He's a fucking skinflint, that's what," Dr. Rebagliati said disgustedly.

"I don't think he's a tightwad," Big Pablito defended him. "He's just a wee bit touched in the head, and on top of it, a guy whose luck has run out."

The lunch went on and on for hours, a succession of Peruvian dishes, multicolored and burning hot, washed down with cold beer, and there was a little of everything at it, risqué stories, anecdotes from bygone days, all sorts of gossip about one person or another, a pinch of politics, and I was obliged to try to satisfy, once again, the editor's tireless curiosity regarding the women of Europe. There was even the threat of a fistfight at one point when Dr. Remagliati, drunk now, began to go too far with Big Pablito's wife, a brunette of around forty who was still very attractive. But by straining my ingenuity, I contrived to keep the three of them from saying another word about Pedro Camacho all during that endless afternoon.

By the time I arrived at Aunt Olga's and Uncle Lucho's (who had gone from being my wife's sister and brother-in-law to being my parents-in-law), night was falling. My head ached and I felt depressed. Cousin Patricia received me with a distinctly unfriendly look on her face. She told me that with all my alibis about gathering documentation for my novels I might well have been able to pull all kinds of fast ones on Aunt Julia and make her play dumb, not daring to say a word to me so people wouldn't think she was committing a crime of *lèse-culture*. But as far as she, Patricia, was concerned, she couldn't care less whether she committed crimes of *lèse-culture*, and therefore the next time I left the house at eight in the morning on the pretext that I was going to the Biblioteca Nacional to read the speeches of General Manuel Apolinario Odría and came back at eight in the evening with bloodshot eyes and reeking of beer, and no doubt with lipstick stains on my handkerchief, she'd scratch my eyes out or break a plate over my head. My cousin Patricia is a girl with lots of spirit, quite capable of doing precisely what she's promised.